Praise for
L. A. BANKS
&
THE VAMPIRE HUNTRESS LEGEND SERIES

THE FORSAKEN

"Readers already enthralled with this sizzling series can look forward to major plot payoffs." —*Publishers Weekly*

THE DAMNED

"All hell breaks loose—literally—in the complex sixth installment . . . stunning." —*Publishers Weekly*

"In [*The Damned*], relationships are defined, while a dark energy threatens to destroy the entire squad. Banks' method of bringing Damali and Carlos back together is done with utmost sincerity and integrity. They have a love that can weather any storm, even when dire circumstances seem utterly overwhelming. Fans of this series will love *The Damned* and, no doubt, will eagerly await the next book." —*Romantic Times BOOKreviews*

"Banks again takes readers into a cliff-hanging, nail-biting battle of cogent versus pernicious. I do caution you to stabilize your mental faculties and guard your jugular, someone has to be sacrificed. *The Damned* is intense, climactic, unbelievable, and scorching hot! Kudos to Banks for keeping this series fresh, heterogeneous, erotic, and still tasting of spiritualism."

—RAWSISTAZ

THE FORBIDDEN

"Passion, mythology, war and love that lasts till the grave—and beyond . . . Fans should relish this new chapter in a promising series." —*Publishers Weekly*

"Superior vampire fiction." —*Booklist*

"Gripping." —*Kirkus Reviews*

"In this third adventure, Banks fleshes out the rich world Damali and her friends and enemies inhabit, making it an even more exciting place to visit. Another thrilling tale." —*Booklist*

"Hip, fresh, and fantastic." —Sherrilyn Kenyon, *New York Times* bestselling author of *Dark Side of the Moon*

THE AWAKENING

"An intriguing portrait of vampiric society, reminiscent of Anne Rice and Laurell K. Hamilton." —*Library Journal*

"L. A. Banks has taken her Huntress series to another level; the action, adventure and romance have readers tingling with anticipation . . . I find myself addicted to this series." —Book-Remarks.com

"With *The Awakening*, Banks solidifies her intriguing, dark series as a project worth watching." —*Booklist*

"Again, Banks brilliantly combines spirituality, vampires, and demons (and hip-hop music) into a fast-paced tale that is sure to leave fans of her first novel, *Minion*, panting for more."

—*The Columbus Dispatch*

MINION

"Banks's mastery of character creation shines through in the strong-willed Damali . . . a sure-fire hit . . . pretty dramatic fiction." —*The Philadelphia Daily News*

"[*Minion*] literally rocks the reader into the action-packed underworld power struggle between vampire rivals with a little demon juice thrown in." —*The Philadelphia Sunday Sun*

"Banks [is] wildly creative and invents a totally new and refreshing milieu." —*Fangoria*

"[A] tough, sexy new vampire huntress challenges the dominance of Anita Blake and Buffy . . . Damali is an appealing heroine, the concept is intriguing, and the series promising."

—Amazon.com

The CURSED

A Vampire Huntress Legend

L. A. BANKS

St. Martin's Paperbacks

THE CURSED

Copyright © 2007 by Leslie Esdaile Banks.
Excerpts from *The Shadows* and *Bite the Bullet* copyright © 2008 by Leslie Esdaile Banks.

Library of Congress Catalog Number: 2007010153

ISBN: 0-312-94772-0
EAN: 978-0-312-94772-9

Printed in the United States of America

St. Martin's Griffin trade paperback edition / July 2007
St. Martin's Paperbacks edition / June 2008

St. Martin's Paperbacks are published by St. Martin's Press, 175 Fifth Avenue, New York, NY 10010.

10 9 8 7 6 5 4 3 2 1

As always, my thanks go to the Creator, as well as to the fantastic readers of this series, because you were the ones who made this story take shape and come alive, who gave it wings, and allowed it to take flight. I cannot begin to tell you how deeply I appreciate your wonderfully positive energy, your upbeat e-mails, and the way you have embraced what has come from my imagination. You all have made my dreams come true—the dream to be able to write an epic legend with dragons and angels and all sorts of wild creatures, yet with a serious moral to the story. *Thank you* for that. So I say to you, keep your dreams alive, just as hope spurs so many positive gifts. There is nothing you cannot achieve or do if you just believe! Ashe!

ACKNOWLEDGMENTS

My daughter for her patience and constant love (Helena), my agent (Manie) and my editor (Monique), guys, you are "the dream team." ☺ Then what would the VHL be without The Street Team? (Holla!) Plus we have the entire St. Martin's team, from fabulous cover art (Michael) to sales (Gina, you go, girl—smile!), support staff (Miss Kia), publicity (Colleen), events coordination (the inimitable Harriet), and every person who functions behind the scenes to make this happen. (Matthew: big hug for allowing us to go this far, man!) Then let's not forget the Yahoo! Groups, the forum, and MySpace moderators, along with the new fan club president: Alicia, Gudrun, Chantay, and LaShonda, respectively. They keep the info flowing and the buzz buzzing each and every day. Whew, bless you! Plus, we've got folks kicking up dust like awesome Webmaster Walt Stone, *hot* publicist Iola Harper, plus Sheila Clover on new vids, and Sherine and Monique working behind the scenes. There's a whole hidden team that people don't see—much like the Guardians, but they are handlin' their bizness and making it look like it's easy when it's not. You *all* are deeply appreciated—much love!

PROLOGUE

Level Seven . . . Hell

Lilith stood before her husband, her breathing nonexistent, her body as still as stone. A curtain of darkness covered her along with a sheen of terror-produced sweat.

"So, where does this leave us?" the Unnamed One said in a very quiet tone, his voice releasing on a weary sigh. "Explain your position."

For a moment she couldn't force her vocal cords to respond as he circled her, the echoing sound of his hooves against the cavern floor a reminder of his vast destructive power.

"My son, Dante, is gone. Slain by a Neteru. My grandson exterminated by his own mother—Eve . . . a Neteru now undoubtedly elevated to finally reign with Aset for her selfless act. Tell me, dearest Lilith, where shall we begin our dance of pain?"

He'd breathed out his question with such eerie calm that she closed her eyes, no longer straining against the impenetrable darkness to see him. She didn't have to; she already knew the beast within him was beyond appeasement. She'd failed. Her time was nigh.

"We are where we wanted to be," she finally said, her tone resigned. "There is no more to say to you than that, beloved. Do what you will with me."

A slow, deep, rumbling chuckle filled his bedchamber. "We are where we wanted to be," he repeated in a flat, sarcastic tone. "I cannot fathom what I should do with you for this debacle. Come, come, now, my dear. You can do better than that."

Tears of remorse filled her eyes and she shook her head. "You warned me, and Cain is extinct. What else can I say? There is no way to hide the truth from you. That is where we are . . . where we ultimately wanted to be."

"How interesting. Where we wanted to be. *That* you will have to explain further, before I snuff out your very existence from my realms."

He walked away from her, and she noticed that she no longer heard hooves but just the soft pad of his bare feet against the stone floor.

"Amuse me with your bullshit, Lilith—give it a good attempt, just for the sport of it, at least. For you see, I am so bereft that even I wonder at the need to commence the Armageddon. I keep asking myself whether it would be more efficient simply to scorch the earth with my wrath and be done. Yet even I am beholden to a certain cosmic fate of timing. So make it good while I await the appointed hour of battle between the Light and the absolute Darkness. Tell me something that will give me pause."

He lifted the pitch blackness around her and returned her night vision so that she could fully see him. Oddly, rather than appearing as the hideous monster of unspent rage, he was standing before her, his arms folded over his massive chest with a wry, sexy smile on his handsome face. This was far from what she'd expected and a much more deadly version of his fury than he'd ever shown her. The terror his quiet composure produced made her breaths shallow. They stared at each other for a moment.

"Your heir lives in the realm you could never breach, as promised," she said carefully. "He is growing in Nod, being cultivated within a living, hybrid womb."

Her husband slowly unfurled his huge, black feathered wings, casting a shadow over her body, but she was glad that he was still calm enough that the more horrifying leather ones he owned hadn't presented. She watched his dark eyes, also noting that they hadn't begun to glow, and then allowed her eyes to study his mouth. No battle-length fangs. Yet the pain he could exact didn't require a transformation, just the blink of a thought.

Lilith sighed, choosing each word as though it might spare her meager existence within the very fragile seconds of amnesty he'd afforded her. "Right now, they are blind—the Guardians, the Covenant, and the Neterus, and probably both Neteru Councils as well. They think they've won, and are in celebration. This gives our heir a chance to develop and grow unmolested. Patience is the key. However, the loss of Cain was unavoidable . . . he allowed emotion and rage to rule him, and he prematurely rushed in—"

"And was therefore expendable," her husband said coolly, coming close enough to touch her cheek. "You did well," he added, delicately caressing her face with a smooth palm. "Cain had delusions of grandeur and thought he could replace even me. Very foolish. His extinction was only a matter of time . . . although I would have liked to have delivered that fate myself. I suppose I will have to be mollified with the eternal torture of his soul. You robbed me of that pleasure, yet again."

Lilith stiffened. "It was never my intent to rob you of any pleasure, my beloved. Sense me for a lie. I swear to you, my goal was honorable."

He smiled a dashing smile. "And the road to Hell is always paved with good intentions. We both know that. So, perhaps I should be thankful that you found your way home, hmmm?" He let his hand fall away from her cheek. "Given all those in my charge who have been recently released to the Light, I'm glad you haven't made a run for the border." His smile widened. "I'm also very pleased that you didn't side with Cain against me, or try to resurrect some old bond with Adam. That would have been very unfortunate—would have made me truly irrational."

Relief shot through her so quickly that it made her limbs tremble. "I would never allow Cain to attempt a coup against you, beloved," she whispered, staring at her husband's eyes to sense for any mercurial change that could happen. "And if I ever see Adam again, he's a dead man."

"You know the time is near?" Her husband tilted his head and assessed her from head to toe.

She nodded but couldn't speak as her husband's strangely melodic voice coated her insides with hot desire. But she staved off the sensation, knowing that he was at his most lethal when appearing most seductive.

"I take it that you are aware by now that I rode Cain's energy the night he descended to Dante's throne? What a rush . . . I had forgotten how amorous you could be."

She dared not speak, not sure of his strange mood. Her only option was to continue to watch the dangerous entity before her closely.

"You didn't know, did you?" He laughed and then sighed. "Therefore, what you saved, really, is *our* heir, Lilith . . . which is the only reason I didn't rip your lungs out for being so presumptuous about the fruit of my loins."

"I meant no disrespect," she whispered, and quickly averted her eyes to the barren rock floor.

"Look at me," he commanded, but there was a strange gentleness to his tone. He waited until she complied. A pleasant smile graced her husband's face as he arched an eyebrow and chuckled, shaking his head. "Yours, mine, and ours. I couldn't resist, not when you and Cain barreled down to my chambers and nearly blew through my doors. So erotically insane—I was moved."

"I'm glad you enjoyed it," she whispered, not taking her eyes off him, lest he turn instantly violent.

He smiled and slid his hand up her torso to tighten against her throat. "Oh, I definitely enjoyed it. You two were spectacular together." He chuckled again softly and loosened his grip. "Cain and I have bonded in seed to penetrate your ova . . . so, tell me, who is this host womb?"

"An angel hybrid," Lilith said just above a whisper, and then held her breath awaiting his reaction.

"An *angel* hybrid . . . in Nod?"

"Yes," she said, stiffening again to brace for a hard blow.

To her surprise, her husband's black wings enfolded her in a feathery blanket and he threw his head back and simply laughed. "Oh, Lilith . . . how you devised something so delightful steals my breath. Stay with me on Level Seven for a while, yes?"

Stunned, she simply stared at him. He was *asking* her, as though she had the option to refuse any command?

"As you desire, always," she said quietly.

"No . . ." he murmured, his voice low and seductive. "Only if *you* also desire to visit for a while."

The way he was speaking to her reminded her of how they first met; that first seduction when she ran from Adam's house to seek refuge in the Darkness and under the power of his raven-black wings. Gently stroking his square jaw she nodded, allowing her body to finally relax and yield into his embrace. She watched a slight flicker of blue-black flames rim his nostrils and a wave of wanton desire filled her as it oozed from his pores to cover her skin with inviting heat.

"I came to you when there was nowhere for me to go, and you alone gave me sanctuary." She ran the pad of her thumb over his mouth, sensing for safety the entire time. "When you speak to me like this . . . there is no other place I'd rather be."

"I remember those early days," he murmured, nuzzling her neck to find the side of her throat that he'd first marked eons ago. He kissed the overly sensitive spot, studying the surface of her skin and released a long, fatigued breath. "So many demons after me and not a mark worthy of my challenge, except Cain. I know you must be as disappointed as I with this outcome."

"I am," she murmured hesitantly. "Cain was the only one that could have given you a good run for your money." Censoring herself, she held back any mention of Carlos as her husband continued to stare at her throat, hoping he didn't decide to summarily rip it out to begin a siege of unending torture.

"What shall I do to amuse myself while we wait, now that he's gone and Carlos is beyond my immediate grasp? Devastating humanity is growing old . . . they are so easy to pollute and turn to my ways."

"I'll rebuild the Vampire Council for you," she said quickly, her voice an urgent plea as she stared up into her husband's still languid eyes, beseeching his continued calm. "I'm sure that I can find—"

"Leave the Vampire Council to Fallon Nuit to rule. . . . I'll repair that sonofabitch as best I can. But I have something better for you. I'm done playing with him—he bores me, and he couldn't take the torture half as well as you did. He screamed like a little girl the whole time. The sound of his voice was so tiring that even after I ripped out his throat that brought no satisfaction."

"I'll stay with you," she whispered, shivering under the sensual intensity of her husband's hold. "Until the end."

"With me there will be no end," he murmured against the now red glowing marks at her throat. "Never."

"This is why I said until the end—that will never come."

He nodded and kissed her neck until she moaned, suckling new blood to spill over the surface of her skin without even breaking the vein with his fangs.

"The others that are left are so weak. You are the only one in the universe worth a damn who truly understands me, Lilith," he whispered, his hands lazily stroking her back. "Remember our first negotiation?"

"It is branded into my consciousness," she said, melting against him.

"Mine, too. All the carnal pleasure of this world and that of the forthcoming future is what I gave you that night. You were so afraid, but also so desirous that I was taken." He hesitated and peered at her without blinking. "You made *my heir*, Lilith. You were the only one capable, and you stole it, secreted it away, and hid it in plain sight of the Light. Tonight, I need to be taken. No one *ever* takes me . . . it is so rare, and only you have done that to me, choosing me over Adam and the Light.

That absolutely took me by surprise, just as you've done so now. I never expected what you just told me about an heir to be delivered from your lips without fraud." His fingers trembled as they traced her cheek. "Take me."

A gasp cut off her statement as she tried to respond by touching the bite mark she'd left on his throat millennia ago. Seeing him so completely undone raised her courage and spiked her desire, and she allowed her fangs to slowly lower as his eyes slid shut. The moment he inhaled, she struck him with a cobra-quick bite, breaking the skin at his throat. Her unanticipated strike caused a violent shudder within him that passed through them both until his head dropped back.

"I am so pleased, *Lilith.* Surprise me." He'd breathed out her name with the fire in his lungs. "You deserve no less than all the pleasure of the ages tonight," he said in a garbled whisper while holding her tighter, "plus all that has ever been since the beginning . . . it has been a long time for us, yes?"

"Yes," she said in *Dananu* against his shoulder, trembling so hard she felt faint. "I've missed you so, this way."

"I agree," he replied in *Dananu,* his voice deep and ragged with passion. "Before, I visited you with a month of painful torture . . . but I have changed my mind. How about a month of pleasurable torture, fair exchange for your surprise gift, to supplant my earlier rage?"

"Yes!" she shrieked, clasping his subtly bulking shoulders until her nails dug into his flesh. She bit him again hard, raking his skin with her fangs while sending a black current of energy up his spine that made him groan. "I will take you until you go blind and drop from the agony of pure pleasure in total exhaustion—like old times," she hissed into his ear, black blood filling her eyes as she made the vow and swooned under his ardent caress. "I've learned so much over the years . . . let me show you until the next full moon. One whole month of stabbing your mind with Neteru images . . ."

"You still own those?" he whispered in a hot breath against her throat.

"Yes. Adam's, Cain's, Carlos's, and even Dante's. I will

hold nothing away from you—even Eve's and Damali's, through their males, I have as my surprise offering to you. Even the spark of conception of your heir is yours to have through me. Will that make us even . . . make up for the robbery you felt?"

"Yes . . ." he moaned, dropping to his knees while holding her tightly and instantly transforming the stone beneath them into burning desert sand. "Show me all."

"Let me do that while I desecrate every orifice on your body to remind you why you made me your wife above all other demons."

"You were my first and best, Lilith. Thrust my mind," he whispered between his teeth. "The only one to endure my all."

She seized his mind and gored it with every major catastrophe he'd visited upon the planet and infused it with the most erotically intense images she could wrest from her knowledge of the strong Neterus he hadn't bested.

"Like that . . . don't stop," he gasped, splaying his hands against her back. "Take me!"

She tore at his throat and gave him the fleeting image of Cain with Damali. "After all I've endured to make you happy, I want a month of pure pleasure with you *alone* . . . plus my return to favor as your second in command on Level Seven, not Six," she said, panting in *Dananu* through his thick black blood as it spilled down her chin. "I used to give you a hundred demon births a day and she took that from me. From us. Work with me, husband, to protect what we have left in Nod. That is multiple surprises for the loss of one."

He lifted his head and stared at her, nodding, his eyes glowing black as his fangs slowly lengthened. His vertebrae quickly elongated, his tail now twining with hers in a feral, serpentine dance. He winced with unconcealed pleasure as she climbed up his body and wrapped her legs around his waist to mount him.

"So be it," he whispered sensually. "Then, for now, we'll be even."

PART

I

Standing on the
Edge of Hell

CHAPTER ONE

Tahiti...

He was lacing up his Tims in the living room of their hotel suite by the time Damali opened her eyes, struggled to sit up, and half-stumbled through the doorway to argue. But there was nothing she could tell him. None of this was up for debate.

It was a knowing that slammed his core, sat him straight up in bed, killed his libido, and sent him over the edge of the mattress, ready for war. Never in his life had he been so sure about what he had to do. What hit him felt like a white lightning charge direct from the archon's table of old.

He'd mentally sent the call out to the brothers already. Twelve days of bliss and the honeymoon was over. The meeting was already scheduled—2100 hours, sharp. Nary a man in the joint objected. They all knew what time it was. It was about protecting theirs—if the world got saved as a fringe benefit, cool. They all had something serious to lose. A preemptive strike was in order. An unmistakable energy jolt, throne level, had run up Carlos's spine, just like it hit Shabazz's locks and fucked with Mike's hearing in a low, relentless buzz. Dan and J.L. felt it no differently than Rider and Jose smelled it. Pure sulfur was rising.

Carlos stared at Damali. She lifted her chin and folded her arms over her chest. He would not be moved. Fine as she was, standing there half-naked and draped in white silk, that was the primary reason he was gonna do what he had to do. Unlike all the times in the past where the team sat back, hid, waited for trouble to come to their door, this time his squad was going in to blow the roof off the mother—first.

"So, I guess there's nothing I can say to you?"

"Nope," Carlos muttered, pulling his foot down from the white wall and collecting a snub-nosed pump shotgun off the coffee table to stash in his long, black leather coat.

Damali stared at the huge boot print he'd left on the wall for a second and sighed hard. "Don't you think we should have a full team meeting about this?" She stepped away from the bedroom door, worry blotting out the fury in her eyes.

"Nope."

"Well, at least won't you tell me where y'all are going?"

"Nope," he said, hoisting up an Uzi to sling over his shoulder.

"Stop," she said, walking deeper into the suite, now talking with her hands. "Team protocol. One half of the team will not know where the other half is—not done, brother. And you all just can't up and leave Tahiti on a dime, no explanation, no nothing, Carlos!"

He stared at the door. "You'd better go put some clothes on before the brothers get here."

"Carlos Rivera, are you listening to me?"

His response was very simplistic and to the point as he went to the door. "Nope."

Big Mike was two steps from the door as Carlos swung it open. Carrying a shoulder launcher, Mike pounded Carlos's fist.

"Ride or die, brother," Mike said in a low, ready-for-war rumble, and then nodded toward Damali. "Evenin', D."

Consumed with frustration, she raced into the bedroom, grabbed a T-shirt and her jeans, and hurriedly threw them on. She looked at her ten-carat engagement ring and matching diamond-studded wedding band and sighed, then slipped them into her small front jeans pocket. Clearly, the honeymoon was over for everybody, and there was no sense in getting her rings fouled by nasty demon gook if she had to go to war. *Men!* They'd lost their minds. She came out of the bedroom like a bee had stung her, just in time to see Rider roll through the door with Shabazz, both giving Carlos a silent fist pound and her a brief nod as though she were a civilian.

Shabazz slammed a clip into Black Beauty, his eyes ablaze, locks lifted off his shoulders by two inches, blue arc crackling. Rider's forearms bulged as he carried something ridiculous that looked like a custom-made Gatling gun. Damali's eyes tore around the stone faces, hoping that the younger male members of the team would bring some sanity to whatever had set the senior brothers off. But as soon as Jose rolled through the door with a red bandana tied around his head, wearing a long leather coat, toting a crossbow with a snub-nosed welded to it, and J.L. stepped in behind him looking straight Samurai, her hopes considerably dimmed. By the time Bobby and Dan came in, she'd sat down heavily on the edge of the nearby dining room table.

Dan strolled in wearing a leather coat that swept the ground and clutching dual AK-47s. Bobby gripped handheld Ingram semis in both hands. Berkfield was with them, his seniority providing no rational balance whatsoever. He was strapped with grenades on a flak-jacket vest like he was going to 'Nam and carrying an M-16. There would definitely be no reasoning with them.

"I got black-box vamp on all scents coming off artillery. Everybody's ammo demon-readied, hallowed-earth shells and shit?" Carlos asked in a low rumble, gaining nods all around. "Then let's do this."

"Hold it, hold it, hold it," Marlene yelled, running down the hall, breasts bouncing, barefoot, wearing only a purple lace-and-satin robe. Her eyes wild, she circled on Shabazz, breathing hard and pointing at him. "Not after all we've been through, and *not* without saying good-bye—*ever.*"

Marjorie was on her heels, her eyes frantic, as she

clutched the front of her pink silk negligee closed. "Richard, have you lost your mind?"

For Damali, it was an out-of-body experience. She knew the delay might take a few minutes, but she wasn't even wasting her breath to argue. These men were already as good as gone. She knew her husband. There was that certain look that Carlos got in his eyes that she'd come to learn— that "no means no" stare. She sighed as Inez burst in behind Marlene and Marj, trying to make an impact against a stone wall. Before her girlfriend opened her mouth, she could tell by the look on her brother Mike's face that, audio-sensor or not, he wasn't trying to hear it.

"Baby, don't do this. . . . Listen, we can figure out a plan, a team strategy," Inez said, tears rising quickly as she whirled around in a white silk teddy, vastly overexposed. "I heard you all the way down the hall talking that ride-or-die mess." When he didn't move, she threw her arms around his waist.

"Suga, stay with 'Mali, hear?" was all Big Mike said as he peeled her away from his body, brushed her mouth with a kiss, and gave her a gentle bear shove toward Damali.

Stunned, Inez hugged herself and went to Damali, whispering thickly, "Say something to them, girl!"

For a moment, Damali didn't answer her. Mike had spoken like he always did, real low and quiet, almost subsonic when he's upset. How in the hell did Inez hear that all the way down the hall?

"Ain't nothing to say," Damali finally muttered, shaking her head. "This is a testosterone thing, and obviously we wouldn't understand."

Juanita's voice hit a decibel as she was coming down the hall that made Mike, Carlos, and Jose cringe. "Oh, Jesus, no, Jose," she shrieked, red silk robe billowing as she slid into the suite, tears streaming. "I just got married and I'm not trying to be no widow. No, don't you leave me, Jose Ciponte, or I'll never forgive you if you die." She stretched out her arms. "I'm *your wife, por favor*! You crazy? What am I gonna do without you, answer me that!"

"That's what I'm saying," Marlene hollered, her voice breaking. " 'Bazz, you of *all* people in here know my heart can't take a move like this."

Shabazz never got a chance to respond. Krissy had swung into the room barely covered in an ivory Victoria's Secret deep-plunge sheath, holding on to the edge of the door like she was about to bust a Jet Li move. Damali started toward her, to catch her in case she fell, because the poor girl was obviously rushing down the hall so fast that she almost missed the opening and then barreled into J.L.'s arms. Jasmine and Heather were right behind her with jewel-green and aqua silk flowing, and threatening to accidentally set off ammo as they threw themselves into Bobby's and Dan's arms. All the guys could do was raise the weapons toward the ceiling and kiss the tops of their heads, repeatedly muttering, "It'll be cool."

Tara strolled in shaking her head, eyes filled and glittering with unshed tears. There was resignation in her stride, a slow and deadly calm of a woman who'd seen way too much over many, many years. She tied the sash on her ice-blue robe and drew a deep breath, as though carefully measuring her words the way she carefully tied her sash.

"I could smell the hysteria, Jack Rider. The damned testosterone jumping off your skins with the adrenaline. If you die on me, I'll kill you. Thirty years . . . *thirty years,* and I only get to have you to myself again for twelve days before you start up hunting sulfur trails?" Tara sucked in a shuddering breath. "I do *not* believe you." She waltzed away. "I need a shot of Jack Daniel's, I swear."

"Now that the entire team is assembled . . ." Damali pushed off the table, walked over to the door, and slammed it hard. "I guess we can have a real meeting."

Madness was the only description her mind could scavenge. Damali allowed her hard gaze to rake the male Guardians. Every man was cloaked in a shotgun-concealing leather duster, black jeans or fatigues, black combat boots or Tims, and sporting a black wife-beater shirt or a vest. For a moment she wondered if they had previously discussed battle uniform, too. This didn't make no kinda sense!

"Okay. I give up. You're men," Damali said, throwing her hands up as she glared at Carlos and then the others. "You're grown. Can't nobody keep you from a ride-or-die." Her hands went to her hips when no one spoke to even begin negotiating. "Fine. Do as you please. I just have one question though. Why? Why now, why so crazy, why without a group plan? And what is this *bullshit* about only taking half the team—the men? Just answer me that and I'll stand down. No argument. We can lock on your coordinates and send in reinforcements if you get boxed in, whatever. I just wanna know, what detonated y'all tonight?"

Surly glances passed between the men and they answered in unison, "Lilith."

Silence strangled the room and raised blue arcs of static to crackle up from the rug. For once, the female squad members were at a temporary loss for words. Carlos's eyes met Damali's in a hard glare and then he glanced at his watch as though he were about to bounce any second.

Open a channel, Carlos, Damali mentally said, her voice more mellow. *Baby, what happened?*

I'll go into it later, D, but trust me when I say that after twelve days of being with their wives, every man in here is ready to die tonight. No telling whose wife is pregnant—and to get a strong Lilith-topside vamp vibe, they were all hitting my brain with SOS messages like you wouldn't believe. Every brother had the same question—"Yo, Rivera, you feel that?"

Then we all need to be involved, Damali's mind shouted back. *You need to get with that!*

No, D, what you all need to get with is the fact that ain't nobody on the team ready for their woman to be battling or even linked to them in a way she could possibly get hurt—not even psychically. Berkfield is going because Krissy could be carrying his grandkid, just like Shabazz ain't never trying to lose Marlene again in this lifetime. Same deal with Rider about Tara. Every brother done prayed on it, had his own

one-on-one with his Maker, and came to his own conclusion.
I'm not forcing anybody to do shit, D. Case closed.

"That's unrealistic!" Damali said out loud accidentally,
the information was freaking her out so badly.

"Is it?" Shabazz said, his gaze sweeping the group. "You
heard the man, D. We're all ready to go out shooting."

"Whoa, whoa, whoa," Marlene said, quickly stepping into
the center of the all-male circle and slowly walking around
Shabazz. "You're a tactical. How did you hear what two
telepaths were saying?"

Shabazz stared at Marlene for a moment and slowly lowered his weapon. "I don't know. I heard it as clear as day,
though."

"That's my department," Marlene said, pressing her hand
to her chest, "but I was never strong enough to pick up from
those two if they had a blocked, direct transmission going."

"Mar," Damali said quietly. "Your locks are lifting off
your shoulders."

Marlene quickly touched her hair and watched the strong
blue-white static current run over her hands. "Oh, shit! I'm
not a tactical."

"I've got it, too," Heather said, staring at her hands and
then at Dan.

Krissy nodded, staring at the bluish, flickering wash that
crept over her fingertips, and then glanced at J.L.

"I'm scared," Jasmine said. "I admit it! All right. I don't
want you to get killed so, Bobby, put down that damned gun
and talk to me!" His weapon left his hand in a hard midair
yank and hung suspended as Jasmine turned away and began
to cry.

"Oh . . . shit . . . that's a wizard move if ever I saw one,"
Bobby murmured.

Juanita covered her nose and dry heaved. "The static
discharge is messing with my sinuses. I need air."

Jose just stared at her for a moment. "Baby, just as a sensory
test, tell me what's in the fridge down the hall in Marlene's
room," he asked, stepping in close to Juanita.

"I don't know, and who cares?" Juanita said in a tone close to a wail. "Champagne, some mango, watermelon, avocado sushi—without fish, some—"

"Oh, my Father . . ." Marlene whispered. "The girl got a nose."

"Look, the club section is starting to fill up, people," Berkfield said, his eyelids fluttering. "We need to move."

"Sho' he right. About fifty big blood suckas at the bar. I got 'em," Mike rumbled and pounded Jose's fist.

"Yeah, I got them punk bitches by the gaming tables," Jose said.

"You saw something in your head, Richard?" Marjorie asked in awe.

"Wait!" Inez hollered, putting her hands up. "You can *see*, Mike?"

"Yeah, baby—"

"Since when?" Inez shrieked, now walking around in a tizzy.

"My point exactly," Juanita said, going up to Jose and stroking his cheek. "Baby, you couldn't ever see; don't you think something is way wrong up in this joint?"

"Okay, fellas, just hold up for a second, okay—you all can go, we couldn't stop you if we wanted to, but check it out . . . don't you find any of this a little strange?" Damali's voice was strident as her hands went to her hips.

"I need to do a divination," Marlene said.

"We ain't got time for all of that right now, baby," Shabazz said, his eyes hard.

"This club," Marjorie asked. "Where is it?"

Carlos looked around at the assembled male warriors, gave them a discreet nod, and they stepped in close to him. "Babylon," he muttered, then he quickly folded the group away into a silver splinter of light.

Pandemonium broke out in the suite.

"I cannot believe they did something like that!" Inez yelled, walking in a circle where the male team had been.

Both Marlene and Damali glanced at each other as though

to say, that was a Rivera move if ever they saw one. They let their breaths out hard at the same time and spoke in unison. "Puhlease . . . I can."

THEIR LANDING WAS silent right inside the main entrance—not a funnel cloud or a light burst, but rather a mere parting between the fabric of time-space density allowing them to never break stride. The message jettisoned from Carlos's mind to the brothers: *Let me ask for her and Nuit, then we leave a calling card.*

Silent nods with angry eyes were the response. Carlos glanced at Rider first, the message clear: *No matter what, Yonnie is still my boy. You won. Leave the man his dignity.*

Rider's response was one word as they began walking forward. "Done."

Leather coats dusted ankles, hair on backs of necks bristled, and heavy weapons caused sweat to slick palms—not from fear, but from fury grips. They stood at the edge of the high crevice and looked down; their entry had been so smooth that even the darkside's border guards didn't see them . . . then again, it could have had something to do with the heat waves of pure rage rising off each man that blinded them. Right now, the Guardian team fit right in with the population at Hell's gate.

The team stared down at the six-hundred-foot drop to the main floor. Designed for a spectacular entry, the only way in was to demon-scamper over the crags, tunnel up from a portal, or touch down vampire-style in a funnel cloud.

They'd entered ground zero through a small cave slit that opened out to a wider cavern. Glittering gold-laden bars serving blood and human flesh provided an endless demon feast before them. Writhing, naked bodies twisted in every imaginable carnal act littered the floors as well as the plush, crimson surfaces swathed in Bedouin silks and black drapes.

Persian rugs covered gleaming black marble floors as musclebound servers brought fresh golden goblets of blood to sate the enraptured. Massive gold leaf–covered fountains with depraved images spiraled in orgies spewed human blood for bathers reenacting the last days of Sodom and Gomorrah. Huge gaming tables with world territories and human lives at stake in the gold chips were heavily loaded with gamblers. Carlos motioned with his chin toward the pit bulls walking the perimeter at the top of the cavern with Harpies riding their backs.

Everybody got the layout? Carlos's steely gaze roved over the group. *Don't sleep on nothing down here.*

Stone-jawed nods were his answer. With that, he folded the team away, and opened them out onto the floor as though coming in for a vamp landing.

Seven battle-ready males wafting adrenaline and more approached the bar, drawing hisses of admiration from nearby female entities.

"Lilith send you boys to join the party?" a long, lithe, snakelike female asked Big Mike, beginning to coil around his legs. Her skin was made of glistening almond-hued scales like that of a yellow boa, and her eyes were an eerie shade of hazel that bordered on green-gray-gold. Each of her long platinum tresses seemed alive, as though they were tiny snakes, as she swayed invitingly before Mike. "And you're dinner, too . . . she thinks of everything."

The moment she pulled back to strike, Big Mike whipped out a snub-nosed pump shotgun and shoved it into her mouth as she lurched forward, fingering the trigger. "Baby, if you're gonna give me deep throat, do it like a pro—don't bite."

She gagged and eased off the weapon. "I like your style," she murmured, uncoiling from his leg and stroking his groin. "What you're packing under the belt is to die for, lover. My bad, on jumping the gun with a first strike—shoulda known a man like you would wanna be the aggressor. Let me make it up to you?"

"Later," Mike grumbled, keeping the barrel of his gun trained on her. "Get off me, bitch."

Carlos cut a glance at the bartender as the Amanthra

withdrew from Mike with sad eyes. A sexy female vampire had blown him a kiss, and he could tell she'd telepathically told the bartender to give him whatever he wanted. Although she remained on her barstool, she shot random erotic images his way, then licked two fingers and dragged them down her cleavage.

"Keep dreaming, baby," Carlos muttered as she slid her hand up her shirt and released a soft moan. He glanced at Bobby and Dan to be sure that the redhead with crystal green eyes and double-D cleavage hadn't messed up the younger brothers.

"She has to do way better than that," Bobby said, totally unfazed.

Dan pounded his fist, chuckling when she flipped them both the bird and strode away. "Good night to you, too—skank."

"I guess after being called by Lilith, everything else in here is a minor temptation?" the bartender crooned, his handsome caramel-hued face flawlessly boyish as he smiled at Carlos. He lowered his luminescent brown eyes, delicate black lashes shadowing them as Carlos gave him a hard grit. "No response, strong silent type?"

"Your problem, dude?" Rider said in a half-snarl, leaning closer to a second-gen vamp than was normally advisable. "You wanna ease up off my brother before my trigger finger gets itchy?"

The bartender flinched to attempt a quick snatch at Rider, and six barrels pointed at him with distinctive clicks. He eased back with a sheepish grin and held both hands up in front of his chest.

"Like I said," Rider muttered through his teeth. "Wanna fix the man his drink and fuck off?"

"My apologies," the bartender murmured sensuously. "But the testosterone and adrenaline trail you gentlemen have is captivating the whole bar . . . with well-fed human blood as the foundation carrier, too—whew . . . a damned delicacy that only the vixen herself could provide. Tell me, are you all off limits and only hers for dinner—is that why you're all so touchy—or did she send you as a gift for us? If she gave explicit orders, then no one would dare cross her . . . but if not . . ."

"Private label, neat," Carlos said in *Dananu,* ignoring the probing question.

"Yes, *sir,*" the bartender said with an awed gasp. "And she trained you in the mother tongue, too? Do you all speak it, or just the hunk that smells incredible?" He drifted away and came back with Carlos's order. "Oh, wait 'til I tell *the crew.*" His gaze perused the seven stone faces that were ignoring him and staring out on the floor, scanning the scene before them. "After she's done, you have to stay for a while and talk that nasty *Dananu* to me."

Carlos didn't respond, but made sure the horny vamp stayed in his peripheral vision until he moved away to serve other revelers. He kept his eyes roving for any signs of Yonnie. In his mind, as much as this was gonna end up as a drive-by, he wanted to let his boy know that he was still family and had a haven—if things hadn't changed. But Carlos quickly shook the futile thought. Any emotion considered soft and accidentally picked up on in here would get a man immediately smoked.

The team looked up in unison to see something they'd never seen before. A fine, brunette, female vamp still moving as mist had sidled up to Rider from behind. But before her hands slid across his shoulders, he'd vamp-snatched her and slammed her head against the bar, holding her by the throat.

"Never in the throat without my permission," Rider growled, a 9mm at her temple. "We clear?" He flung her away from him and eyed her with disdain. "Seconds. I hate 'em."

The team tried not to gape. Rider's speed was something they could talk about later, as well as how he'd seen her behind him at the bar without turning around, as though he had vamp three-sixty sight line. Regardless, their cover was holding; the old-heads had it on lock. Female were-demons were smiling a little too much at Shabazz and Big Mike for Carlos's liking, but he had to let it go. Old tracers, he told himself.

Carlos kept everybody in his peripheral vision. Lilith's lair was heavily fortified and the bouncers patrolling the upper rims were no joke. Standing seven feet tall with ten-inch fangs and barrel chests to rival WWE wrestlers, he knew they'd have to shoot those big bastards first, along with the Hell dogs they held by long chains.

But any minor bar fights, even mortal combat down in the main pit, was nothing more than a floor show—and the spectators would applaud the victor and eat the scraps when it was done. Therefore, for the moment, Carlos took a gamble that they could press for answers without causing a complete riot.

As soon as the bartender leaned over his drink and licked his lips at Carlos, offering him an Ecstasy-laced joint, Carlos snatched him over the bar hard and punched him in the face, breaking off a fang.

"You got something else to say after my boy told you to back the fuck up and stop sweatin' me?" Carlos had placed a 9mm at the bartender's temple so quickly that he couldn't mist out of his grasp.

The bartender put both hands up in front of his chest, his nervous, red glowing eyes darting between Carlos and eight menacing pairs of Guardian eyes. "Hey, hey, hey, you gentlemen never said she'd sent you just for her bed and her dinner—we didn't know."

"So, where is that slimy bitch, anyway?" Carlos said, his lips curling into a snarl as battle-length fangs began to lower.

"She went below to give her husband his due," the bartender said, swallowing hard as his eyes went to half-mast. "Damn, I see why she sent for you, though . . . are you sure you don't want anything, sir, until, she uh, returns?"

Fury tightened Carlos's grasp on the bartender's throat as he hurled him back against the glasses, breaking several bottles and shelves. "Get that motherfucker out of my face," he muttered and spun toward his team. "She ain't here. Damn!"

"Fallon ain't either," Jose said, glancing around at the appreciative vampire gazes as phantoms slipped between succubae and incubi, whispering. "So, brother?"

"Let's leave a calling card," Carlos said in a low, lethal voice. "Like right about now."

Weapons came from under coats, double-handed firing in an automatic spray. Hallowed-earth shells whizzed by like tracers, burning the very air as they met targets to incinerate. Guards from the upper levels hurled down to the floor as sulfur rose and screaming demons unprepared for the onslaught took cover, some dying in their mating frenzy only to look up at the last moment. Bat-winged Hell dogs swooped off the ledges bearing acid-dripping fangs, their twelve glowing eyes roving the floor with rage while their razor-sharp spaded tails lashed wildly in the air.

Mike dropped to one knee and pulled the compact shoulder launcher out of his coat, mounted it on his burly sinew, shoved in a shell from a hidden coat pocket, aimed, and fired. The splatter and cinders from one airborne pit bull ignited another that accidentally flew through its path. Rider had gotten four bouncers in a single shell shot right through their heads with his right hand while firing the Gatling gun with his left.

Dan mowed down anything moving behind the bar and then advanced on the gaming tables. Jose was his tandem street sweeper with a snub-nosed pumping dead-aim, serving chest blasts into high-roller demons and splattering the gaming tables' green felt. J.L. had run up the side of a cavern wall and balanced on a precipice in a Ninja move on the edges of his toes to draw a flock of Harpies to him. Blue-arc tactical charge held him in place as he lifted his weapons and took steady aim. As soon as they got within range J.L. released a hail of bullets from an assault rifle, dropping burning bodies, then pivoted off the cliff edge to land on his feet with Bobby covering him.

Berkfield had run into the teaming throng of an orgy, pulled the pins on two grenades with his teeth, hurled them, and dove for safety behind a bar. But a were-demon looked up at the same time he did. In two seconds, Berkfield had drawn and blown the back of the demon's skull off. Bobby was over the bar in a blink, and reached down to yank his father up. They stood back-to-back, firing at anything coming their way, blowing demon guts out and spattering gook everywhere.

Carlos flung his spent weapons to Big Mike and Rider, his goal now to run deep into the cavern, headed for Lilith's shrine—her bed. The outer area was like her foyer; he had to go in deep to make an impact in her house.

Hand-to-hand combat brought him surreal pleasure. All the shit they'd taken him through . . . Raw battle-frenzy rippled through Carlos's system as he heart-snatched stunned male sentries and neutered drone lovers on the way to Lilith's golden, demon-headed sanctuary. To defile that carnal place would definitely send her a message: her primary lair had been breached after all these centuries, the squad that did it went for broke, and she was vulnerable—thus weak, and her reinforcements weren't shit against the Guardian forces.

But the moment he neared the high monument that sat alone on a steep crag of black malachite almost a half-mile deep into her lair, a giant black cobra—her regular lover and familiar—uncoiled from under her bed in a jealous rage, green eyes glowing, black scales gleaming, fangs dripping as it hissed. He could feel the thing before him hesitate, clearly not sure if Lilith had sent him as a new playmate, but furious at the invasion. Carlos outstretched his arm and drew the blade of Ausar into his grip.

"You tell that bitch that Rivera was here!" Carlos shouted. "And the next time she fucks with *my family,* or brings that punk bastard, Fallon Nuit, with her to my door, it's her head and his nuts!"

The serpent swayed its huge, Hyundai-sized head and

snapped, its eyes narrowed on Carlos from its position above him. Then from beneath the bed, several more heads emerged, until the thick body came out to reveal that it was a hydra, not a serpent. The tricky question for Carlos now was which head was the main one? Plus the damned thing moved like greased lightning. He could still hear gunfire report behind him, which meant his team was holding its own. From his peripheral vision, he saw Shabazz and J.L. racing in to assist.

Not even waiting for the command, Shabazz was liquid motion and had stunned the beast with a tactical charge from his locks and right hand. The blue arc rippled right down Black Beauty's barrel and discharged the shell with it to blow away one head. J.L. flipped out of the way of a strike to dig one of Dan's spent AK-47s into the monster's eye, only landing to blow out the other, firing from 9mms with both hands.

Sword raised, Carlos took a running leap forward into the air with a Neteru battle cry, his coat billowing out from him, propelled by fury. His silver glare burned the creature like lasers had been trained on it, making it flop and screech to be out of his line of vision, and then he released the blade swing. A huge head crashed to the cavern floor as Carlos dropped onto Lilith's bed. Serpents hidden beneath her red silk sheets wriggled and scampered away at his intrusion, and he pulled a handheld Uzi out of his shoulder holster and began shooting the bed, making it bleed black and green blood.

The hydra went down slowly, the other heads whining and hissing as the mortally wounded creature nuzzled the gushing site of the main beheading. Fury still had a choke hold on Carlos, and he rammed his sword into the center of the bed, wishing Lilith had been there versus her sumptuous mattress, and then unceremoniously lopped off the golden heads of the four posts.

But he jumped back amazed as they bled red blood and the little gargoyle figures at the tops of each post grappled at their cut throats.

Down beside his teammates in seconds, Carlos nodded as they picked up the pace to rejoin the battle on the main floor. Gunshots had ceased, only occasional bursts. Each man's heart slammed into his chest as he ran, hoping for the best, trying to prepare for the worst—only to see the entire team standing in the middle of sulfur plumes rising in hot, yellow smoke from the floor.

A sea of decapitated and mutilated demon bodies stretched out before them on the ground, piles of ash and cinders covered the bars, littering the crevices and crags where they'd dropped. Golden furniture and gaming tables were shot to smithereens. Glass was everywhere from exploded bottles. Guardian eyes briefly studied the carnage knowing that if anything twitched, it could still get up and bite.

"Raze the place," Shabazz muttered.

Carlos lifted his blade, ready to send a blast of white light from it, when a cavern opened behind the far wall, sucking the whole bar and half the shelving behind it down into it. Instantly, Carlos spun. J.L. was up on the golden surface of another bar in two flips, fly-kicking Harpies back, and then balanced on the edge of a sliver of remaining shelving to flip off and send two Harpies right into Carlos's blade. Shabazz threw his head back, released a warrior's yell, and suddenly upper and lower canines ripped through his gums. His clothes had been left in a pool of fabric where he'd been standing. Liquid feline motion, Shabazz's body elongated into a huge, sleek jaguar, his claws ridding Harpies of appendages and entrails as he went to J.L.'s aid. The team froze for a moment, stupefied. Berkfield flung a hallowed-earth grenade down into the cavern that had opened, and the team jumped back from the explosion that sealed the hole.

Bobby was blowing away miscellaneous Harpies that had escaped out of the air with Dan standing at his flank and Jose on the other side. A swarm of Harpies came at Big Mike, and the gunners couldn't get a shot off without hitting Mike. He reared back, hauled off, and threw a cinder-block punch into the eye of the small whirl, causing Harpies to fall out of formation and bounce to the ground, stunned. Bobby, Dan, and Jose picked them off like they were shooting pigeons. The moment the team fell back into formation, all in a line near Carlos, he lowered the blade of Ausar, raised the disc of Heru as a shield, and released a cannon jolt of white light from the tip of the blade to flash-burn everything demonic in their wake.

"Move out," Carlos said, slowly lowering the shield and watching Lilith's main lair burn with great satisfaction.

Shabazz swept up his clothes, and team members shared incredulous glances but remained mute as he hurriedly robed.

Suddenly a deafening clap of thunder knocked them to the ground and scattered them like bowling pins. The sonic boom made boulders begin to fall in on the cavern, pelting the team with dangerous projectiles. He had to get his team out of there—had to get them all into a centralized group so he could burn through the universe's fabric without leaving any of his men behind. Carlos gathered his Guardian brothers with effort, straining to shield them with a stretched Heru discus and helping them up quickly with his energy so they could run toward him.

Dangerous energy fatigue was setting in as he tried to focus. In the midst of the chaos, a massive, blinding, white-winged stallion snorting blue-white flames, eyes glowing silver, its silver hooves razor-deadly, dropped down. The riding warrior owned a familiar face. His dark arm was outstretched to the team, the other held a huge crossbow with a silver stake that glinted off his gold, Kemetian crown.

"I told you we had your back, brother," Adam said, as several more Neteru kings dropped down to collect Guardian soldiers. "We'll seal your home in black-box safety—go to your queens. Rest. This battle is won. Tomorrow, however, is another day."

"OKAY, WE HAVE already established that they're crazy," Damali said, losing patience with the group's insistent questions, mainly because she couldn't answer them. "I want a prayer-line grappling hook on each man in there. White light, pure everything you've got, to bring 'em home. You ladies got that?"

"Yeah," Juanita said, "but what's going on, maybe it's from the darkside—like how do we know about them being able to do things they hadn't before—"

"It's got to be the marriage merger," Marlene said, her voice quiet and reverent and her gaze distant. "Of one flesh . . . seven joining seven, strengthened by the bond that joins mind, body, and spirit as one under the auspices of white light." She brought her gaze to the team. "They got us in them, and they're in us. I'm calling Father Pat. It's time to get the Covenant back involved anyway, if they went after Lilith buck-wild and crazy."

"Whoa," Krissy said, and stumbled backward 'til her back hit the wall. "The marriage merger can do that?" she asked, totally ignoring the second part of what Marlene had said.

Heather and Jasmine just stared at each other as Marjorie slowly brought her hand to her mouth. Inez began walking in a tight circle, fanning her face.

"This is too crazy," Inez said. "If we're getting juiced up like this, it's gotta be for something scary-big, anybody feeling me? I'm with Marlene; we need all them guys from the clergy up in here, too. Like what if I find out I'm cock-diesel like Mike, and he's fast with a switchblade, like me? Oh, shit, y'all. You hear what I'm saying?"

"Yeah . . . completely," Tara murmured, her gaze distant. "This isn't like times before. They're acting like it's a last stand, and I don't even think they know why."

Damali walked in a circle raking her locks, total frustration claiming her as the puzzle numbed her brain. As much as she hated to admit it, fear for the safety of one half of the team had a headlock on her as well.

"Do you know where the capital city is for ancient Babylon?" Damali finally blurted out, unable to control the volume of her voice as her nerves frayed and snapped. "It's on the Euphrates River, south of Baghdad in modern Iraq!"

Unable to contain herself, Damali paced faster as the group's eyes widened before her. "Pray and pray hard, sisters—they're walking right into part of this whole Middle East madness. There's ground troops from however many nations over there, civilians . . . tanks, tracers, land mines, God only knows what, and our squad could accidentally come out of a whirl right in the middle of a firefight—who knows! And I haven't even begun to think about what demons are over there right now screwing with everybody, keeping the conflict going, holding humanity in a death struggle against itself . . . hell . . . Level Seven might be topside, for all we know!"

"I'll see if I can get maps, something to give us a geographic visual as we pray white light around where they are. It helps." Krissy jumped up and dashed down the hall, returning quickly with her laptop.

Jasmine, Heather, and Marjorie linked hands, making blue-white static zing between them with Tara in the middle to draw her vamp-locator knowledge to the fore.

"The old stones are screaming," Heather said quickly, looking up at Damali. "The region is not just white-hot topside, but underground. The holy cities . . . with the conflict going on near Beirut, Jordan, and north—Christian and Muslim and Jewish strongholds are in flames."

"But they went to Lilith's bedchamber," Tara said with a shiver. "To her main lair that has *never* been breached in history—even warrior angels couldn't find it . . . it is an insane move, a fool's quest." She covered her face with her hands and breathed into them deeply as though trying to keep from hyperventilating.

"Yeah, but Carlos is the only fool I know that ever sat in the Chairman's throne and lived to tell about it as a living human being," Marlene countered. "Even warrior angels didn't do that . . . and if he had an old link to Cain that didn't all the way die out, then if anybody could find Lilith," she added, glancing at Damali, "it's him."

Damali briefly closed her eyes, trying to find the silver lining in the mayhem surrounding her. "There's always a reason, there's always a reason . . . there's always something good that comes out of every bad for the greater good," she murmured like a mantra, trying to remind herself of that and calm her nerves for the sake of the team as another wave of panic threatened to sweep through her.

"Ohmigod," Krissy said, beginning to rock. "From where we are in the South Pacific, they're already into the next day, fourteen to sixteen hours ahead of us, just before midnight there by an hour, perhaps. What if . . . oh, shit, they're outta their minds!"

"I know, I know," Damali said, pacing. "They're nuts."

"Just like the prophecies," Juanita murmured, holding her hands up in front of Inez as both women's eyes rolled back into their skulls, showing only the whites the moment each seer went under.

"*And I saw the Lamb open one of the seals, and I heard, as it were the noise of thunder, one of the four beasts saying, come and see . . . and I saw, and behold a white horse: and he that sat on him had a bow; and a crown was given unto him; and he went forth conquering, and to conquer.*" Inez's head snapped up with a gasp. Her voice had been a gravelly, chilling tone that was not her own.

"Revelations one and two!" Marlene screamed, running into the bedroom and searching for Damali's stones. "Where're your stones, child? Your divination tool! This is the big one! The first seal is opened! Call Father Pat—this is not a drill!"

CHAPTER TWO

If she could just rest . . . if he would just relent so she could regenerate . . .

Lilith clawed at the thick ropes of sinew before her, barely able to lift her head to strike at his black nipples with her fangs. She'd wailed so hard and long with pleasure that her voice was now only a weak rasp. Twelve days, and he'd promised her a month alone . . . she couldn't stand it. He had to call in Jezebel and Delilah to take some of the abuse before she lost consciousness.

"No," he said in a wash of impassioned heat against her hair. "You're my favorite, and what you've done in this throne behind my back absolutely scorches me senseless." He sucked in a hissing breath. "Had I known the extent of your treachery, I would have come up here years ago . . . most certainly days ago." His voice dipped to a caressing whisper. "But I just didn't know."

Lilith's head dropped back as she pleaded with him through another blinding orgasm. "First it was the topside desert near the beginning of all history . . ." she gasped in an elongated wail, "I could barely take it—then near the burial tombs of the pharaohs that Rome overran . . . now this. I am vapor!"

"Yessss. . . . Now thiissss," he hissed, promising a huge serpent-shift in the offing that made her shriek.

Black tears of pleasure coursed down her face. He'd promised her his best and damn if he wasn't delivering. His huge spaded tail was wrapped around her and what had once been Cain and Dante's old throne. In his passion, her ecstasy-crazed husband had actually ripped it up out of the floor anchors, using his tail to repeatedly bring her into his every thrust while holding on to the Vampire Council's pentagram-shaped table for leverage.

Never in her existence . . . most assuredly never by a vampire that championed this throne . . . only the power that belonged to this entity could produce such near-fatal delirium.

Ruby blood splashed everywhere as his massive talons dug into the table's veins, causing the center fanged crest to close its eyes and shudder with need. Hot drool splattered the table, the floor, her hair, and shoulders. When she peered up, he was foaming at the mouth with his eyes shut tightly, images fluttering beneath his lids from all that his deceased heirs had carnally committed to that throne.

That her husband, the ultimate Dark Lord, had actually consummated a deal in the Chairman's throne, giving her co-rulership of it to prevent any further coups, had literally made her pass out when he'd generously offered it on a cumming gasp in *Dananu*. Bats were limp on the floor, spent, unfed, so frenzied for twelve unending days and nights of mating that they couldn't whirl themselves into a transport if they'd wanted to.

Scythe-bearing messengers were prostrate in the hall, exhausted and weak from the spectacle that created copulation frenzy in the corridors. The Unnamed One had never graced the council like this, not as long as Dante ruled it, and never during Cain's short reign. He'd brought a lover to chambers, here, as though it were his Level Seven lair, and marked territory, one level up closer to the surface? It was so incredible that Lilith's pleasure sob became bleating hiccup wails.

"Strike me, Lilith!" he thundered, beginning to shift.

Couriers and messengers swooned and passed out in the

cavern just beyond the chamber doors. Four exterminator guards flatlined, the energy that rippled pleasure across the marble floor was so great. Tortured voices rose to a piteous crescendo in the Sea of Perpetual Agony, begging to be able to feel just a fraction of that ecstasy just one more time. Frenzied rats ran around in circles, humping any surface they could find, including exhausted bats. Mating calls from the upper levels wafted down the dark corridor, coaxing the twisted sensual energy up to their realms.

"Do it now!" came the urgent command that made Lilith lift her head, yank back, and deliver a cobra-quick strike against his throat as he bent down for it.

The wail he released as they hit the floor and his coils swiftly wrapped her into a pulsing squeeze, crushing the throne with it against her back, caused her scream to bring down stalactites. Convulsing in a rhythmic pulse, the huge cobra head lolled from side to side, hissing, eyes sealed, then struck her jugular.

When she came to, he was lying on his side, propped up on his elbow, looking at her, but normalized in his gorgeous human male form. He stretched out a massive, black feathered wing and covered her with it, caressing her cheek. She turned her face into his rough palm and kissed it.

"It has truly been a long time since anybody has taken me there, Lilith," he said with a satisfied smile, still slightly breathing hard.

She snuggled closer to him and chuckled. "Wow."

"Better than Dante or Cain?"

Her eyes were wide with disbelief. "Of course—are you mad? Their throne is in splinters."

He chuckled an easy, satisfied laugh and then slowly rolled over to flop on his back, his wings spread-eagle on the battered floor. "I think I killed some of your messengers and a few Harpies. I'll do a body count later and replace them . . . I was simply overcome."

She slid up onto his chest, vastly flattered, and kissed him slowly, then licked the site of his oozing mate mark until he shivered. "Do not concern yourself with such trivial matters. I'm just grateful that you visited me like this after all these years."

He nodded, winded still. "It's been too long, Lilith . . . I don't even remember what came between us."

"Good," she whispered petting his huge, granite-cut chest. "Neither do I."

Without looking over at it, he began gathering splinters of the destroyed throne together, absently mending it with one hand outstretched and petting her with the other.

"Pitiful," he said with a smile. "I can't even think it back together right now without using my hands."

She sighed, but then tensed as she felt his body become rigid. "What is it?" Lilith sat up quickly, her gaze studying his as he looked up to the ceiling.

Her husband was on his feet in one lithe move, toppling her to the floor. His black feathered wings were wrapped around him and beginning to transform into leathery bat-wing membrane. His tail ripped through his back and he bellowed up to the ceiling, eyes beginning to glow. "Not fucking now!"

It took a second for the image to form in her mind's eye, and then she was on her feet with a screech. "My lair? They desecrated my lair with white light!" Horrified, she covered her mouth as she saw her familiar's multiple beheading. "My baby! My sweet, sweet baby—oh, Lu, they killed my hydra!"

"It's all right," he shouted. "I'll, I'll . . . don't worry—I'm so enraged and fucking energy-depleted, I can't even think, woman. Give me space! I need to eat, goddamn it—bring me some bodies, now!" He paced back and forth, leaving black plumes of sulfur in his wake. "My wife's lair? Never in all of history—this is unacceptable! It is a slap in *my* face; the gauntlet has been thrown down."

Transport bats attempted to stir but failed. Messengers crawled forward, unable to stand. Lilith backed up, her eyes widened.

"Adam was with them," she whispered.

"What!" The Unnamed One's voice blew out wall torches as his size began to rapidly increase in height and bulk. Fissures began to open in the walls and floor from the fury emanating from him like mini-earthquakes.

"How would Adam find your lair?" he seethed, his voice now deadly and his eyes slits of potential violence trained on her.

"He rode a white war horse," she shrieked, backing up, "and tracked the Guardian team. Adam would have never been there if the Guardians weren't at my door to retaliate for Cain's attack on their homestead in Mexico. Adam followed the male Neteru's energy tracer!" She quickly put the table between them as his gaze narrowed. "In all my treachery, I have never, ever, *ever* had a liaison with Adam; even I have a limit," she cried. "You're exhausted, husband, irrational—think. If Adam rode a white—"

"The first seal . . ." he said quietly, stunned and going to the righted Chairman's throne to sit down heavily in it. "I cannot believe they began the Armageddon without me, like this," he added in a tense, bewildered whisper. "I was sure that we had years after my mark had been upon the populations for a time . . ."

"The National ID Card mark that spread through Europe to the U.S.—they cannot buy or sell without it—was brilliant, beloved." Thoroughly undone, Lilith wrung her hands trying to console him. "It will take years for it to proliferate, and surely they cannot start the war without the mark of the beast? That will happen."

"In due time. It hasn't taken root yet, hasn't hit other continents!" He leaned back in the throne and closed his eyes. "While I was for once experiencing a sense of utter peace . . . and fucking my wife nearly to death . . . they do this? Low. Just foul, and so unlike Adam, but I must give him credit for that move. It was more like something our kind would do. If they ever catch on and battle like us, then we shall indeed have a long-term problem."

She stood watching her husband, frozen by the table, holding her breath lest his slow-moving wrath take a sudden turn to claim her.

"Lilith, darling," he murmured, causing her to back away farther as his tone dipped to a sensuous purr. "Raise the dark covens—dark witches and warlocks worldwide. Raise any vampire not slaughtered by an Isis or holy instrument. We need numbers, quickly. Bring Nuit's pathetic ass up from my torture chambers and put him in a chair—pick one. He knows this team best, regardless of what I think of him . . . and install two females at your helm. You must see that our heir in Nod survives. Midwives, make them strong and reliable."

Her husband stood slowly, rubbing both palms down his face and breathing out fire behind them. "I must strengthen all the realms above yours to the surface myself—just like the old days. I know I owe you eighteen more days of mind-melting ecstasy, but we will have to defer given the circumstances."

Absolute horror gripped her as she stared at her husband. This particular Neteru team had confounded even the Devil? Oh, yes, this was indeed the end of days.

She watched, incredulous, as her husband began walking toward the chamber doors, shaking his head and talking out loud to himself.

"I always envisioned Dante or my heir at my side when this time fell upon us—or initiating it myself, Lilith," he said in a tone that contained charged, repressed fury. "I must repair all the damage the Neterus have caused. . . . Always busy, always more work to do; when do I rest? Do you know what it takes to keep what I've built for us going, have you a clue?" He let out a roaring bellow that made rocks fall. "Kiss my ass! I never believed the Light would be so hasty! The realms above were always so methodical in the days gone by." He shrugged, eerily collecting himself to his former control. "Go figure—new millennium, new era."

"What else will you have me do?" she whispered, now deeply concerned for his state of mind.

He began walking, then turned and glanced at her over his shoulder. "I haven't decided yet. But I will tell you this— eventually I want to meet this Carlos Rivera Neteru and his lovely, Powers angel–Neteru hybrid wife. They absolutely fascinate me . . . and I may need a bargaining chip."

THEY WALKED THROUGH the folds of nothingness into Carlos and Damali's suite. Father Pat was shouting on the speakerphone when the pandemonium broke out. Dirty, demon-gook–splattered warriors were covered in ash and smoke, eyelashes crusted with black-blood cinders. They stood weary in the middle of the floor now that the adrenaline rush was ebbing. Shrieks made Mike and Inez cringe as battle-weary arms opened and bodies slammed against chests, forcing embraces to lock. Then just as suddenly, female Guardians tore away, pulled back, and began examining for nicks and demon-incursion skin rips.

"Anyone injured?" Father Pat yelled into the din.

"Every man in here is nicked up bad, Father," Marlene shouted, holding Shabazz's hand for a moment and then looking at Big Mikc's fist.

"Douse everything," Damali said. "Father Pat, we're gonna have to get back to the Covenant on the phone in a bit, after our healers work. Every one of these guys needs a full system purge, given where they went. Any opening, down in Lilith's foul lair, could have them dragging home who knows what."

"Good, good, you do that," Father Patrick said.

"We will keep the vigil in prayer," Imam Asula assured the group.

"We must come to you," Rabbi Zeitloff said, his tone strident. "You cannot fly here; we must meet somewhere neutral to decide how and when you can make it into Jerusalem."

The men on the team shared concerned glances.

"That is the wisest alternative," Monk Lin said. "Call us the moment you rise in the morning and your full team is assembled. We will send prayers your way that your purges are not painful and your healings swift."

"Bless you," Father Patrick murmured. "We shall close with a prayer just as we opened this transmission, for these are dangerous days."

As the group quieted and settled down to listen to Father Patrick, his mental voice entered Carlos and Damali.

I saw this coming, the elderly cleric murmured into their minds. *This is why, no matter how disillusioned I became on that airplane when we were all together before, I also knew the time was so close. Near death will bring clarity for a man of my years, and I wanted to be a part of this final battle . . . if I walked away, I would not be able to assist with resources that my organization, for better or worse, can assist you with. You have no idea how much I would have given to be with you at that historic battle against Cain. But I had to go with God's will, not my own, and put my ego and disillusionment behind me for those who will carry on beyond me. Do you understand?*

Yes, Damali murmured, closing her eyes. *We finally get it . . . and when you come, there's, uh, something I have to show you.*

I've missed you, Father . . . seriously, Carlos said, releasing a hard sigh. *Will be good to have you back with us, side by side again.*

I've missed you both, too, and wished I could have been there to anoint the dead and dying on the battlefield . . . there is so much team healing to be done. I have prayed over your spirits that they may be given respite and never broken. If just for a little while.

Both Neterus nodded as though Father Patrick could see through the phone. When he said "Good, now let us go in prayer," Carlos and Damali smiled as their eyes slid shut.

"Bless you, Father, Imam, Rabbi, revered Monk," Marlene said as the prayer ended. "Ashe."

Collective "good-byes" rang out and once the room was quiet, Damali clicked off the speakerphone, her gaze going around the beat-down team. She surveyed their ragged condition as did every woman in the room.

"We kicked their asses," Carlos said with a slow-dawning, lopsided smile.

Shabazz and Rider pounded his fist, and then Mike did, too, with his left, uninjured hand.

"We stomped dey asses good, y'all," Mike said, a sheepish grin peeking out on his dirty face.

"Shot the shit out of 'em," Rider said, shaking his head and raking his fingers through his hair. "But one of 'em was sweet on our boy—was a shame to kill him; he was kinda cute."

The male Guardians burst out laughing as Carlos playfully shoved Rider in the arm.

"This old warhorse did a vamp snatch on an incoming that was so freakin' lovely, I had to laugh—just gripped her up by the throat," Carlos said, miming the incident, and then glanced at Tara. "Slammed her ass down on the bar, and said, 'Not in the throat, bitch.' I thought I would lose it up in that piece, just bust out laughing and break character from that shit. Rider, man, where you learn that, holmes? You saw her coming like you had three-sixty!"

"No, you the one who's crazy, man," Shabazz said, taking center stage with a wide-legged stance. "This *insane* brother goes running—by himself—a half-mile into pitch blackness. My locks are standing up and shit because I can feel sure death slithering down the walls, bats inching along deciding to attack or not, 'cause they figure, his bold ass must have been called by Lilith."

Shabazz held the room for ransom, reliving the tale like a camp counselor telling spooky campfire stories. "So, I'm like lighting wall torches for dude from where I'm at, hitting it with tactical blue charge and making shit back up 'til we can get some brothers in there and cover him. Me and J.L. are hauling ass trying to catch up with him, when we skid to a halt because this huge-ass hydra, head the size of a VW, uncoils from under Lilith's bed."

"Her regular lay," Carlos said, shaking his head. "The bitch is twisted. Literally."

Shabazz and J.L. slapped him five, then pounded his fist,

and burst out laughing, ignoring the stunned female faces in the room.

"Nasty," Carlos stated with a shudder and making a face. "Snakes all in girlfriend's bed. I don't know how Dante or Cain dealt." He shivered and shook it off, causing another round of raucous male jeers and laughter.

"But C-los blew they asses up, yo. It was *too crazy*!" Jose slapped J.L. five.

"What about the damned dogs—shit . . ." J.L. said, beginning to walk in a circle.

"She had pit bulls?" Damali asked, her voice awed as she watched the post-battle, come-down hype sweep the male members of the team.

"Lord have mercy," Marlene murmured, glancing at the younger women's shell-shocked expressions.

Tara was standing stone still with her hand pressed over her heart, while Krissy and Jasmine hugged each other. Marjorie's hands were clasped tightly before her, as her focus ricocheted from one storyteller to the next, then she suddenly began folding and unfolding her hands. Juanita was pacing, and she would stop every few seconds to gape, and then start pacing again. Inez was leaning against the table, one leg jumping like she had to pee. Heather stood still, slack-jawed, hugging herself. Damali could feel the pressure in the room building like a thick barometric shift. These brothers had no idea . . .

"Aw, man, yeah, they had Hell dogs, boo," Carlos said, laughing, oblivious to the growing distress in the room. "But my man, J.L. his ass was *on fire*—dayum that brother was fly-kicking bullshit out of the air, stunning it dead aim. You go, boy!" Carlos play-boxed with J.L., who did quick dips and pivots, not allowing him to land a blow.

"No, Mike was the crazy one—strongest mofo on the planet," J.L. said, laughing and shaking his head. "I've never seen nothing like it! Just hurled a hay-maker, all the way up from Mississippi into a Harpies funnel, and stunned the little bastards so the brothers could pop 'em on the ground. That was insane, dude!"

"Hey . . . I tries," Mike said, grinning and flexing his fist, which was cut to the bone. "Just need a few stitches, or Berkfield's juice, and I'm good."

"Everybody lost it—on fire, I'll tell you what was on fire," Berkfield said, shaking his head. "Was when Jose and Dan were up on casino tables, blowing away vamps like lunatics, chips flipping from bullets. It was beautiful. You shoulda been there," he added with wide-eyed wonder. "The place was like a whole golden idol freakfest—absolutely outrageous—and that was just her bedroom. Can you imagine what it was like, for real, back in those days with whole cities teeming with demons 'til the Almighty just nuked entire areas?"

"It was over the top, D," Carlos said, agreeing with Berkfield. "Even for vamps."

Berkfield rubbed a hand over his bald scalp and shivered with disgust. "I now understand the biblical flood concept." He looked at Bobby with pride. "Thanks for pulling your old man up out of a canine lunge. You shoulda seen it. This old man is proud." Then he looked at Dan. "I gotta hand it to you, too, Danny boy. You can kick demon ass with the best of 'em. My respect—damn, you shoulda seen these two work with Jose."

"Naw, dad," Bobby said, slightly embarrassed from the compliment. "None of the ladies needed to see *any* of that. Man!"

"True dat," Shabazz said. "I need a mind purge, after that."

"You might need a little more than that," Carlos said with a half-grin, worry just starting to take root in his gut, now that immediate danger had passed.

Nervous chuckles passed around the male team members.

"Yeah, well," Shabazz said, running a palm over his locks. "A white bath, a strong purge, I'll be good in the morning."

"What happened?" Marlene asked, no nonsense in her tone as she crossed her arms over her chest.

"Baby, later, we can—"

"Oh, hell no," Marlene said, swiftly walking up to Shabazz and standing in front of him. "Everything. I wanna know what bit every one of you guys."

"Mar ain't said a mumblin' word." Damali argued and moved to stand in the center of the group. "We're glad you're back—you went, you conquered, and God bless your dumb asses, you came home." She wiped her brow in a theatrical display. "But now that you're home, the fun begins—like, trying to keep a retaliatory threat from nuking this resort. Purging everything out of your systems, and—"

"We're black-boxed at the Ausar level," Carlos countered, lifting his chin, indignant.

"Really?" Damali said, stalking him in a circle, causing him to turn with her. "That means it was *so bad* and *so ill-timed* that the Neteru Council of Kings had to give us *the ultimate* protection—something we've *never* had to have before, just so we can live somewhere to fight another day." When Carlos opened his mouth to speak, she held up her hand. "*Never* before."

"We had to send a message, D!" Carlos folded his arms.

"What if you guys couldn't get out of there and your energy dipped, huh?"

"Adam came for us on a fly-ass white war steed, toting a megadeath crossbow, crown tipped to the side, 'cause brother was hard ridin' and ready to die with us, aw'ight—my brother had our backs . . . him, Hannibal, Akhen—"

"The white horse . . . oh shit!" Damali bent over and covered her mouth.

The room went still.

"Baby . . ." Carlos said after a minute. "What's up with the white horse?"

"Try Revelations, verses one and two—the first seal is broken, the *big* war is on, my brother, and y'all were AWOL on a black-ops mission . . . no communication, us having mild coronaries . . . yeah, did I mention that's why we had *the Covenant* on the phone—after Inez's vision?" Marlene folded her arms.

Damali stood up slowly as male jaws went slack, and placed her hands on her hips. "You kicked off the Armageddon, Carlos Rivera . . . Oh . . . my . . . God. And, do you know whose wife you are jacking with? Oh . . . my . . . God. And do you understand that part of this whole Armageddon thing is linked to the—"

"Oh my God . . ." Carlos closed his eyes and began to pace, raking his hair.

"Yeah," Damali said flatly. "Me and the girlz," she pressed on sarcastically, making little quote marks around the words "the girlz" with her fingers in the air, "have been discussing this *the whole time* y'all were gone. But did ya think to ask us about it . . . ? Oh, noooo . . .'cause you guys got *a fight rush* that made your dicks hard and you rolled out of here insane!"

"That's ain't fair, D," Carlos muttered. "And you know it."

Damali swept away from Carlos, walking a hot path back and forth. Marjorie picked up where she left off.

"I want to know *everything* that bit anyone, especially what bit my son." Marjorie folded her arms over her chest.

"That's right, Jack Rider," Tara said, her gaze deadly as she held her body tight with a hug. "A vamp snatch, three-sixty sight. Uh-uh. You're nicked and nicked bad."

"But that happened before we even started the brawl, baby . . ." Rider opened his arms. "Oh, for the love of Pete. Would you tell the lady?"

"Yeah, T," Carlos said, trying to deflect the argument. "He was on it way before the first clip emptied."

"Oh, I feel so much better knowing that just the vamp energy in there could open up his old wounds," Tara spat, her eyes narrowing.

"Look at this," Inez said, going up to Big Mike and yanking his wrist to stare at his wound. "Harpies, baby? Cut down to the bone by those nasty little critters? Didn't we just get werewolf outta your system? I swear, Michael Roberts, if you turn into one of those gray little things with bat wings, even temporarily, you sleep by yourself, *forever.*" She dropped his wrist. "A sister don't play that."

"Oh, naw, suga, for real, that can't happen," Mike said in a panicked tone, trying to talk to her as she gave him her back. "Can it, Mar? Tell the girl, please, Marlene, that—"

"I don't know what it can do," Marlene said, flatly, giving Mike the eye. "We've never had to purge a Harpie nick on the team, because up until Australia, we didn't see funnel clouds . . . but one of our fearless leaders, who will remain nameless, seems to always piss off Level Seven. So—"

"Oh, shit," Mike said, rubbing his palms down his face. "Look, 'Nez, I'll get cleaned out real good, but don't go there on a brother."

"Yeah, yeah, yeah," Inez fussed, sucking her teeth.

"So, Jose," Juanita said from across the room, her tone icy. "What rolled up on you, when you was out there, brother? Anything I should know about—or maybe I should take a stake with me to bed?"

Jose closed his eyes and groaned.

"That's right, Bobby, you betta get it right in your head, boss man husband who doesn't have to listen to his wife," Jasmine snapped, talking so fast that everyone stared at her. "I'm not getting no freaky germie that came up out of Lilith's bedroom jumping on me like mites and—"

"Honey—"

"Don't you 'honey' me!" Jasmine shouted, pushing Bobby. "I'm scared to death, could kick your butt myself!"

"Daniel, I cannot believe you, of all people, the team's voice of reason, would do something like this," Heather whispered, tears rising.

Dan groaned. "Aw, baby, not the guilt trip, c'mon, I—"

Heather had crossed the room so quickly and struck him so fast that she rivaled a female vamp. "Guilt trip, guilt trip," Heather shrieked, grabbing his shirt. "My period's late and I didn't know where my husband was and I find out he went somewhere that might take Damali's Caduceus—if they give it to her—to get whatever's in him purged! Daniel

Weinstein, Jr., are you completely mad?" She dropped her hold on Dan, whirled around, and began sobbing.

"Oh . . . shit . . ." Jose murmured, echoing the entire team's sentiments.

Dan pulled Heather into an embrace and kissed her hair. "It'll be all right," he said, rocking her. "I promise." But his words only seemed to make her cry harder, and his gaze sought Carlos's.

Carlos nodded, despite the bad feeling he had in his gut, and then he closed his eyes. "Oh, shit, man . . ."

"And *this* is why we move out as a unit!" Damali shouted, her arm snapping toward Heather and Dan. "*This* is why we don't do any more solo missions. Ohmigod, Carlos," she said, suddenly breathing into her palms. "Baby . . . just tell me, why? What was it that took you guys over the edge?"

"I felt a jolt off the throne," Carlos said quietly, his gaze locked to Damali's. "I knew if I said that, it would freak you out . . . but I knew it like I knew my name. Lilith had taken a permanent seat after Cain." He drew a shaky breath and walked across the room with all eyes on him. "Once you sit in that chair, baby, it has you for life—you can feel things from it, even if you're severed from it. That's our secret weapon. Me and Cain were linked by the chair and his hit of your blood. So, impressions off it are real fresh for me."

Carlos gave the group his back and put his hands on top of his head. "I knew she was . . . ascending, getting her power on—you know?" He let his breath out slowly. "Could tell she'd been distracted . . . had even been topside . . . but preoccupied. I could also feel something release Fallon Nuit . . . but it wasn't until we got there that I realized what had preoccupied Lilith enough that we could just walk into her joint like we did."

Damali walked toward him, her voice quiet. "Oh, shit, baby, what was it? How bad? Fallon being stronger, legions she's raising . . . what?"

Carlos turned and stared at Damali. "Her husband."

Damali backed up ten paces as a collective gasp cut through the room. "What?" she squeaked.

Carlos nodded. "It was now or never. Dude who shall remain nameless never rolled through Level Six like that. So while he had her in his clutches, we flat blasted her joint and took out a lot of her players. While she was vulnerable—and you don't catch girlfriend like that too often, trust me."

"Wait, go back to the husband part," Marlene said in a tight, quiet voice. Her gaze bore into Carlos as he glanced around at the stricken faces on the team.

"He never christened Dante's throne while Dante was in it, or while Cain was in it. But when Lilith sat in it—hey."

"What?" Damali wheezed, bending over and grabbing her chest, then she sat on the floor.

"Yeah . . . uh . . . that's why we had a window. I just didn't know that going in, just felt her power dip for a minute," Carlos said, leaning against the wall with a thud. He spoke slowly with his eyes closed, remembering being impaled on the Chairman's torture wall not so long ago. "Her husband came up to chambers and power-fucked her in the chair—I thought it was Nuit, at first, but I could feel girlfriend's energy dip in a way no throne ascension is supposed to go . . . like, I don't know what was going on before, but last night, there was a shift in the realms. So . . . I thought, maybe somehow there was a double-cross, or maybe she'd been dredged for allowing Cain to get smoked. If she'd been flung topside for her offenses, I knew she'd go to her lair and lick her wounds—the goal was to smoke that foul bitch in her own house, old-school payback served ice cold."

"I'm calling for the Caduceus," Damali said quietly. "That's why Adam came and got y'all . . ."

"Yeah," Carlos said, hanging his head.

"Hey, it was gonna happen sooner or later," Rider said in an upbeat tone. "It's not like we didn't know, folks. Right?" He looked around at the group. "It's in all the books, not a big secret, the end of days are here."

"Yeah, look at the news," Mike said with a philosophical shrug. "Whole region's gonna blow, and the way I sees it, best be getting ahead of the firefight than be behind it."

"Sho' you right, brother," Shabazz said, giving Mike a fist pound. "That's why I got to a real cool place in my head, did my prayers, faced east and bowed to Mecca. Then I did my Aikido meditation and I asked all the earthly spirits that I had been at war with to accept my olive branch of peace . . . asked the ancestors to roll with me, and then I was ready, good to go. Ride or die. Can't do no more than that."

"'Bazz, man," Carlos said calmly, pushing off the wall. "Not to be in your business, but . . . the shape-shift. You wouldn't have happened to—"

"Shape-shift?" Marlene went up to Shabazz and touched his cheek.

He looked away and spoke quietly. "Yeah . . . I talked to the brother on the astral plane. He was haunting my dreams, so enough was enough—and the way the Brazilian team went out was fucked up, but righteous." Shabazz brought his gaze to Marlene and began to stroke her locks. "We needed to have a conversation as men. Said he'd ride or die with me, because if I crossed over before my time, you couldn't take it." The look in his eyes became distant as he searched Marlene's face. "I'm cool with it. Understand how much that brother loves you, Mar. He still does, his spirit is bound to protect you . . . he asked if he could give me a fusion when I needed it in a firefight. We came to terms."

Marlene stepped closer, shut her eyes, and wrapped her arms around Shabazz as two huge tears ran down the bridge of her nose.

Tara walked over and cupped Rider's face. "Maybe you got what I was before when my spirit couldn't leave yours?"

Rider nodded and pulled his wife into a slow hug and kissed her hair.

"I'm so glad you're all right," Marjorie said, her tone gentle and sad as she kissed her son's cheek but went to her husband.

"We did it for you and Kris, and everyone else," Berkfield said, caressing Marjorie's back. "If anything was to happen to you all . . . after what we saw at the casa in central Mexico . . . watching Hidalgo and Duke, Esmeralda, and everybody bury their men and women. The whole frickin' Brazilian team . . . My heart couldn't take it, Marj. I'd rather go out swinging."

"You know that, suga," Mike said, gathering up Inez and showing her his badly cut fist. "Swinging for you, baby girl. Don'tcha know that by now, for you and little Ayana, this team . . . and any more we make."

Inez turned her face into his chest and grabbed his T-shirt with her fists.

Dan was rocking Heather gently, his battle-splattered palm caressing the silk at her back. Juanita swallowed hard, went to Jose, and put her head on his shoulder. Jasmine threw her arms around Bobby's neck and almost knocked him off his feet and began sobbing. Krissy turned to J.L., and he pulled her to him and kissed her long and slow before she could start crying.

Damali stared at Carlos until his gaze met hers.

I understand, she mentally said, her voice tender.

He nodded. *I wanted to kill her so bad, D . . . wanted to cripple their side without putting you or anybody's wife in immediate jeopardy, so it would take a long time before they could slaughter ours like they did in Morales. Every day I spent with you, every night, all I could think of was what if something crazy happened again and my wife . . . and what if a baby you were carrying got . . . D, you talk about how you can't take it, shit . . . my heart can't take none of that ever again.*

She swallowed hard as she looked at his handsome, dirty face and then stared into his liquid brown eyes that were beginning to flicker silver at the edges. *I love you, too.*

Girl . . . you know how much I love you, right?

The exchange was too intense, and she had to look away. *Let's get everybody cleaned up and take advantage of Adam and Ausar's black-box cover to rest, heal, and recover.*

Yeah . . . I'm starting to feel every blow now. Carlos rolled his shoulders and rubbed the back of his neck with a wince. *In a minute, the rest of the brothers are gonna be feeling it, too, now that the battle hype is draining away.*

I'm sorry, she whispered in her mind. *You brothers kicked ass the way it's supposed to be done.*

Naw, you were right. Can't go on impulse like that again. He stared at her. *D, I really fucked up this time, didn't I? I started the big one. I swear I didn't know who was doing her in that throne—I'm crazy but I ain't stupid.*

Damali shook her head. *Maybe it was fate, Carlos? Maybe that's what you were supposed to do, who knows? Like Marlene said, you're the only one, alive, who ever sat in that chair . . . what are the chances of a Neteru doing that, huh? The Almighty wouldn't have let you start what wasn't supposed to be started.*

You think so?

She just nodded, and prayed she was right.

"Okay," Damali said quietly. "Everybody just sit down, chill out, and let me get the Caduceus . . . then everybody take a white bath." She blew a stray lock up off her forehead. "Now I see why Adam black-boxed us in here. We're gonna need it."

Damali stood to go to the bedroom to collect her silver necklace containing the seven stones so that she could privately commune with her queens. But a noise and a quick flash of golden light made everyone turn to stare at the coffee table. Just as suddenly as the light glinted away, the Caduceus staff clattered against the table's glass surface. She closed her eyes. "Oh, yeah, we're definitely gonna need it."

CHAPTER THREE

By the time Damali had administered the Caduceus to the last Guardian brother, sweat had formed a huge V in her T-shirt, and her clothes clung to her like second skin. Even though Marlene and Marjorie had repeatedly asked to assist, Damali declined for their safety. Who knew what the guys had dragged home? Foul and funky energy, some unseen spiritual parasite, who knew? The team had been there, done that, and Damali felt way better keeping an unknown agent, especially from the probable sources it had come from, contained within one team healer—her.

"Okay, J.L.," Damali said, slowly straightening and stretching her back. "You're good to go, man." She gripped the long golden staff that was nearly as tall as she, watching the dual serpents on it slither into place and settle down to become inanimate again.

J.L. peered up at her from the sofa with a sheepish grin. "They never landed a blow on me, D."

She gave him her hand and a smiling scowl as she pulled him up. "Yeah, but you oughta know by now that down there, they don't have to nick you—they can blow smoke up your nose with a phantom tagging along in it to have you acting crazy."

J.L. held up his hands in front of him. "You're right, my bad."

Rider chuckled. "Give it up, brother. We're outnumbered and outgunned. They think faster and hit harder."

When several of the younger Guardians gave Rider a quizzical look, Big Mike chuckled and shook his head.

"They'll learn," Mike said in a rumble, beginning to grin broadly. He pulled Inez against him. "Y'all don't fight fair—low blows, hit a brother hard. Dang, girl, you'd cut me off forever?"

Inez laughed. "Turn into something real crazy, hear, and see what happens."

"I rest my case," Rider said, beginning to collect his spent weapons. He glanced at Bobby and Dan, then over to Jose and J.L., finally settling his gaze on Berkfield. "You better tell 'em, medic."

Berkfield laughed. "Every man for himself. I'm already in the doghouse."

"Oh, no you're not," Marjorie said softly, going to him.

"You might wanna school some of us old heads on how you just pulled that coup, Richard," Shabazz said laughing, giving Marlene a hopeful glance.

"Oh, so now everybody's got jokes," Marlene muttered, but a smile escaped despite her clear determination to remain peevish.

Relieved laughter finally overtook the room, which Damali knew the brothers were angling for. Even Carlos had to laugh as they watched each man cop a plea and try to justify the previous bullheaded move that could have gotten him killed or worse. But now that the apparent danger was over for the moment, the bravado and banter were back.

"All right, people, listen up," Marlene said, rallying the group in a no-nonsense tone. "You senior squad know the drill, but I'm repeating this for the newbies. Strip at the door; drop your gear into a plastic bag that has my special anti-demon blend in it. Let your partner tie up the bag, pray over it, anoint the top, and set it outside so the sun will hit it in the morning. You don't bring that mess deep over your threshold before sealing it up, and you stop at the door and say out loud, 'No demon may enter in the name of the Almighty,' before your partner walks through that door to strip."

Marlene's gaze traveled to each male face, making sure they got it, but waited until their wives nodded. "Okay. This is critical. Shower that splatter off you first, and bomb the drain with holy water behind it. Use my special white bath soap—wash your hair, everything—then, and only then, do you step into that white bath tub."

Damali hung her head back. "Maaaan . . . as soon as you all leave I'm gonna have to smudge this whole suite out with white sage and be casting out vibes 'til dawn, practically." She looked at Carlos hard. "Sec . . . y'all just don't know."

Holding her purple silk robe up and off her body by two fingers, Marlene looked at each female Guardian hard. "Same deal with your clothes. We hugged 'em, don't know what could have been attached, gotta do the shower and bath routine, too."

"Aw . . . maaan . . ." Inez grumbled under her breath and then elbowed Mike in the ribs.

"Like I said, meaner and hit harder," Rider said with a sigh. "Okay, we know. This is not a drill."

SHABAZZ HUNG HIS head back and groaned as Marlene stood in the shower with him and scrubbed his locks down to the scalp. Shower spray beat on his chest as Marlene's soapy hands got down into the places that made him close his eyes.

"I swear you do this kinda stuff, man, just so I'll wash your hair," Marlene fussed, her body loosely spooning his as she reached up to be sure she didn't miss a spot.

"Can you blame a man?" he said, breathing out another soft groan and tilting his head as she paid attention to a particularly sensitive area. "Oh, yeah . . . right there."

She laughed and scratched his scalp harder. "You need to stop."

"I'm not doing anything," he said, reaching back to stroke her slick hip.

She swatted him and turned him around. "Douse."

She looked down and then quickly looked back up. He laughed.

"What can I say—I'm a tactical."

"Douse," she repeated, trying to ignore the shiver that claimed her stomach. "No exchange of nothin' in this shower. You still have to get a bath, and you know it—how many battles have we been in and cleaned up after?"

"Maybe that's why I go to war so much, ever thought of that?" he asked with a half-smile. "This is the best part . . . and knowing I can't act on impulse in here and have to wait, really messes a brother up."

She stared at him and fought a smile, also fighting the way his voice and the tone it contained had made a familiar ache creep between her legs. Just watching him stand there under the spray, eyes closed, thick arms lifted as he rinsed out his black-coffee locks, each muscle group a complex steel cable network that moved as his fingers scrubbed . . . water cascading down his ebony chest . . . each section a defined block of pure muscle right down to the bricks in his abdomen, and Lord have mercy anything lower, she had to look away.

"Turn around and let me wash your back," she said more quietly than intended.

He obliged and she slicked her hands with more lather that released eucalyptus and myrrh around them.

"Oh, man, Mar . . . this is the best part," he murmured, dropping his head forward while his voice bottomed out. He leaned into her touch as she pulled at tight muscles. "Yeah, right there, my draw-shoulder. *Damn,* woman, that feels so good . . ."

Her fingers kneaded down either side of his dark chocolate spine after she took her time pressing out the hard cords across his shoulders. As she made her way down his back, pressing her thumbs against either side of his vertebrae, she could see a blue-white arc beginning to flicker in his locks, but then die out as though he were trying his best to suppress it. Just witnessing that did something to her and she had to redouble her efforts to stay focused on the cleansing.

Despite her best attempt to remain clinical, the sounds he released almost made her forget her own instructions, especially when she hit the small of his back and he arched, placing both hands on the tile wall. She was caught up, and she knew it, yet still couldn't keep her hands from paying homage to that special dip he had in his spine, the one that came just before the high rise of his firm ass . . . all muscle. Then her fingers found the cord that began the rise, each thumb kneading in an opposite direction until he was breathing in short pants.

She had to stop when she saw the blue static take over his locks, and then flow down his back to cover her hands like blue lava. "I promise I'll finish the massage after the white bath, all right?" she murmured, stepping in close but trying not to press too much of her nakedness against him.

He nodded and pushed away from the tiles to turn and stare at her. "I'ma hold you to that, Mar, but I need to wash your back . . . and your hair, too."

"I don't think I can take your touch right now," she admitted in a quiet voice.

For a moment they both just looked at each other, listening to the spray. He didn't say a word, and didn't argue, but just gently moved her to stand under the water while he soaped his hands. She closed her eyes and braced herself. The moment his static-charged hands touched her locks, she moaned and hung onto the walls.

"C'mon, 'Bazz, you've gotta go get in the tub and let me wash my own hair. The water just makes it worse."

"Yeah, I know," he said on a warm stream of breath close to her ear, his hands working lather into her hair and then caressing her shoulders, down her arms and over her breasts—making her gasp.

He knew Marlene was right, but he couldn't help it. Her beautiful walnut skin, slicked and wet, her hands had done him in, then her gorgeous, knowing eyes had paralyzed

him . . . the way small runnels of water cascaded down her
regal face and over her lush mouth and breasts . . . Not
touching her felt like he'd severed a limb. His hands reveled
in the sensation of touching her, rolling her distended raisin-
hued nipples between his fingers with soapy hands. Blue-
white static charge spilled over her skin—he couldn't help
it, it was reflex, like breathing. Her heavy cone-shaped
breasts fit exactly in his palms. He stepped in closer as the
water beat down against her, needing to seal the space between her pelvis and his erection.

"We really have to finish the cleanse," she said, her
breathy gasp betraying her as she hugged him.

"Yeah, I know," he murmured, still sliding against her
slowly without entering her. He nuzzled her wet, clean,
velvet-textured locks, water splashing his face as his hands
slid up and down her arms then over her hips. "C'mon, baby,
let's hurry up and get in and out of the tub."

She looked up at him, breathing hard, and for a moment
neither of them spoke.

"Please, turn off the water," she said in a hoarse whisper,
closing her eyes. "I can't move."

Her admission almost made him take her mouth on impulse, but he complied with a shudder and stepped back as
the water nearly stopped. He was breathing through his
mouth now, trying in vain to occasionally take in a deep
breath through his nose. But the sensation of her hands going over his shoulders and down his back wouldn't leave
him. It was as though she'd coated him with liquid heat and
it was spilling over his ass, which had ached for the promise
of her caress, but was denied. His thighs were jonesing for
that feeling that she'd spread along his once-sore biceps, and
his chest needed it, too . . . yet not half as much as his abdomen did. His stomach clenched just thinking about it,
which made his erection bounce.

" 'Bazz," she murmured, turning her face up to him with her
eyes closed, softly touching his chest to try to back him up.

The simple caress made him let out a moan that stunned

him. His nipples were on fire, felt like they were stinging with the need for her to brush them, lick them, and pull them between her lips. It made no sense how bad the ache her touch there created. Worse, it raced down his abdomen straight to his groin, filling his shaft.

He was getting ready to turn off the shower and had flattened her against the tiles, but she pushed against him more firmly and that's when he saw it as she brought her hands away from him quickly—the blue-static discharge of a tactical. Pure reflex put his hands on her shoulders, and the shudder that ran through her opened his third eye.

She looked at him, stunned for a moment as they both shut their eyes tightly. "Baby, don't," she whispered in a tense plea. "Not 'til we get in the tub."

"I don't think I can make it, Mar," he told her honestly. "You're not a tactical, I'm not a seer, but blending this up in here right now . . . you have to be the rational one." He dropped his forehead against hers. "You have to do the prayers over the water—I can't even think about nothing else but making love right now."

"I know. C'mon, baby, just . . ." Her voice trailed off as the image of the first time they got together in New Orleans arced from his mind into hers with all the sensory detail that went with it. "Oh, God, 'Bazz."

But she turned her head away as he bent to aggressively kiss her, and hurriedly stepped out of the shower. His slow saunter behind her made her breath hitch. Moving like a madwoman, she grabbed the jug of holy water off the edge of the sink and poured three heavy splashes down the drain.

She practically skidded on the floor rushing to the tub to turn it on, and her hands were shaking as she dumped the white bath contents into it. Shabazz was standing just outside the shower, eyes closed, water coursing down his impressive six-foot-two frame in rivulets, taking in deep breaths, his erection dripping water and pre-cum arousal ooze, his hands in a tent before his mouth as though he was summoning every Zen fiber within himself to relax.

Glimpsing him from the corner of her eye, she could re-late. The way his erection moved up and down slowly with his breathing was just too much visual stimulation—she looked at the wall. This was so sacrilegious. She had to pray over this water, asking that it be a barrier to all things evil, that it cleanse the person sitting in it. *Yes, get back to center, Marlene,* she told herself as she dropped down on her knees.

Seeing her down on her knees, bent over the tub, he had to look away. Blue-static charge covered her whole body now. Before it used to just be in her hands, which was bad enough. But if her shapely, toned legs wrapped around his waist with that charge . . . and her entire torso hit his, and if her third eye locked with this new thing in him . . . he . . . would lose . . . his mind.

Shabazz raked his locks and turned away from her. Just like her hands had started to hold his charge, he'd been able to glimpse into her thoughts, but the New Orleans thing—damn, he was right there again like it was twenty years ago. No com-pound, no team, before their lives got complicated, when it was just the two of them hunting alone and surviving it all.

Bad part was, though, if two senior Guardians like him and Mar, the original foundation of the team, couldn't get it together to take a post-battle white bath, then he didn't even want to think about the predicaments of the newbies.

Right now he wanted Marlene so bad that tears were standing in his eyes. The woman had him so jacked up he practically couldn't breathe. So how were the youngbloods on the team gonna get through this process? Or maybe it was just him, tripping, after a crazy-ass battle. Maybe after a shape-shift . . . the first time in his life he'd ever experienced something intense like that. *Intense* . . . yeah . . . that was the word, that was the feeling, after he'd shifted, everything was too intense.

"Water's ready," Marlene murmured.

Her voice sent a shudder through him. He turned and looked at her and then came over to the tub, half-afraid to get in it with her sitting on the edge. Something indefinably primal made him study her and have to actively resist dragging her into the water under him.

"Thanks, baby," he said quietly, and bent to kiss her out of reflex, and then stopped short as he remembered. "I guess right now I've got a one-track mind. My bad." He chuckled and slipped into the warm water and then slid down all the way to his neck.

The sensation of the smooth salts, and heady frankincense and myrrh wafting off of it with Marlene's charge made his eyes cross beneath his lids. Only able to open his lids halfway, he watched the blue-static charge ripple across the surface and then arc to her hand, and finally race up her arm to begin a slow fan out across her body.

She looked down and then closed her eyes to keep her mind on the straight and narrow. But his chest rose out of the water like a dark, thick slab of polished, carved wood that disappeared into the milky substance, then the engorged head of his hard member crested the opaque water, the groove in it glistening, making her want to lean over and kiss it so badly that she gripped the porcelain to stay put.

It was clear as day that the more aroused she became, the more it turned him on, and vice versa, even though they were both pretending to allow him to peacefully soak in a cleanse bath. Neither of them needed to be a seer to know that. The charge was in the humid bathroom steam—thick. She tried to send her line of vision to something else and wrest her mind toward a quiet, meditative thought. Yet her gaze kept drifting back to that glistening place in the tub flanked by his thick, muscular thighs. When he captured her hand and stared up at her, it was all over. His charge entered her, imploding between her legs and pushing a deep moan out of her.

Next thing she knew, she was in the water, the floor had taken a huge tsunami-like splash, and a strong arm was around her waist. She tried to keep him from a hard rollover, knowing that would be all she wrote, but centrifugal force was against her.

"'Bazz, baby, *not in a white bath*—we can't!"

"We'll take another one, I don't care, Mar," he said in a harsh gasp against her hair, entering her hard.

She almost sat up from the exquisite sensation—him, the double-helix charge, the image in her head, the water, the smooth salts and oils making him seal-slick. Her hands found the high curve of his ass and followed it, causing his thrusts to come harder, more erratic as her legs tightened around his waist.

Water was everywhere, her locks nearly standing on end, her spine barely protected by his hand beneath it. Normally a more quiet and controlled lover, he sounded like she was murdering him. Shabazz's voice bounced off the tiles, making her crazy, making her think of things and remember things between them that she hadn't thought of in years . . . and the more she did, the more his fledgling second-sight absorbed it, bringing pleasure sobs to both of them the harder he worked.

His dominant tactical charge spilled over the edge of the tub, skipped across the puddles on the floor, and zapped in an arc to the shower, then climbed the walls. She clung to him, half to keep from drowning, when her hands ignited with his spinal chakra points and he hollered her name in waves—head back, eyes squeezed shut, one fist pounding tiles, locks swinging water and orgasm depth charge.

The convulsion that hit him stunned her womb with pleasure so deep and feral that for a moment no sound came out of her mouth. Then she choked out his name in a broken two-part stutter and collapsed.

His face was burning against hers. She could feel his jaw move and the muscle in it clamp down as though holding something back. Sweat rolled down his temple and back as he gave up trying to breathe through his nose and gulped air. Her hands felt it all, the way each massive half of his back expanded and contracted while he heaved in breaths. Flickers of aftershock static raced down his spine and she started to pull her palms away, but he tensed.

"Baby, don't break the connection . . . oh, shit, not yet, let it run its full course."

She didn't move, just allowed the sweet flickers to make her fingertips and canal tingle. But when he finally lifted his head to begin to withdraw from her, that's when she felt the huge aftershock that had been building.

The sensation rocked her so hard that she dug her nails into his shoulders and arched up, mouth open and face contorted. Sound exited her body that belonged to another woman, a banshee, as he flattened a palm against her spine, hit her base chakra, and released the last trapped charge. She almost banged her head on the edge of the tub she'd whiplashed-jerked so hard, and she couldn't have stopped moving against him until it was over if she'd wanted to.

Spent and half-dazed they finally looked at each other. Shabazz was the first to crack a smile. That was it. She burst out laughing with him, but that only made him wince from her tightening sheath around him.

"What was that, Shabazz?" she asked, kissing him with a huge smile. "Dang, brother."

"I don't know," he said, still breathing hard. "I guess that's what you call a brother losing his complete mind."

"Whew . . . you have to lose your mind more often, then," she said, leaning up to kiss him.

"Puts a new meaning to a white bath, though, don't it?"

She glanced around at the floor. "This don't make no sense."

He chuckled and then got serious, tracing her cheek with a finger. "You know, when I shifted, it sorta took me out a little, Mar."

All the mirth dissipated from her eyes as she cupped his cheek but remained mute to let him talk.

"All of a sudden I was burning up, like every cell I owned would explode. Then this vast . . . I don't know how to explain it . . . other than *incredible* power and raw energy just slammed me." His troubled eyes searched her face as he spoke in a low, private murmur. "I'd slipped out of my clothes, I don't even know how, and was free, primal. It felt like there was no division between me and anything—then when it was all over, I was standing with the team, dazed for a second, bloody and naked, dead demon bodies everywhere . . . and I had to go put my shit on. Find my pants, Mar, you know? The brothers were staring at me for a few with their mouths open, and for a minute I was so damned embarrassed that I almost wanted to put my own nine to my skull." He looked away. "Do you know what I'm saying?"

"Yeah, I do," she whispered, tightening her hold on him. "I had it happen to me, remember?" But the moment she'd said it, she instantly regretted it—because then that one teeny statement would unnecessarily remind him of how such a scenario came to be. Old lovers, dead or alive, were skeletons that had already leapt out of the closet, but that now needed to stay dead and buried.

No way to recover, she simply pressed her forehead to the center of his chest. "I love you . . . and I'm sorry. I didn't mean to go there."

"Water under the bridge," he said quietly. "Me and you are too old to rehash the past." He turned his mouth into her hand and kissed it as she touched his cheek, then captured her palm with his to place a gentle kiss on her ring finger, which was laden with a large oval diamond.

"Yeah," she whispered as he withdrew from her. The sudden loss was profound.

"Thing is," he said, climbing out of the tub and helping her out behind him. "I could feel the energy band connections in everything, Mar, does that make sense?"

She nodded and brushed his mouth with a kiss as an answer. This time she grabbed his hand and kissed his ring finger, toying with the thick gold band etched with Adinkra symbols that matched hers. If she didn't make this man understand anything else, it was that she loved him. Not that she wanted anyone to lose their life, but the man holding her close right now didn't need to be the one to die out on the battlefield in Morales months ago, or in Lilith's lair tonight, for that matter. God knew what He was doing when He gave her back Shabazz. She was just fine with that decision from On High.

"I . . . I don't know," Shabazz finally said when she broke their kiss. "When I agreed to allow an assist, I didn't know it would come like this."

Marlene nodded. "The bathroom is wrecked, how about if we go in the bedroom and I finish that massage?"

He kissed her long and slow and deep, not needing his newly developing third eye to know that neither of them wanted to talk about it just yet.

INEZ INSPECTED HIS hand as though she were working for the Feds and his fists were contraband coming in from a foreign nation. Amused, Mike stood just inside the door, stripped, a plastic bag at his feet, waiting for his new bride to complete her assessment.

"They were just cut up so bad before," she said, gently spreading his huge hand out in hers. "No matter how many times I see one of the healers do it, it just amazes me to watch the wounds go back to normal when they're done."

"Yeah, suga, sorry about that. Razor tails, vicious little fangs, straight-edge wings. Sucker-punching that funnel cloud was like I threw a punch into a switchblade blender." He sighed and stared at her. "Baby, I think she got it all out . . . but I wouldn't ever do anything to—"

Her kiss backed him up to the door as she stood on her tiptoes.

"'Nez, we ain't supposed to—"

Where her touch landed stopped his words and made him deepen a new kiss. Her curvaceous body fit against him in all the right places and her hands were causing delirium.

"I gotta get this battle off me, suga, then I swear I'll make restitution. I'm so dirty, you don't want none of this 'til I clean up."

"Are you kidding me?" she whispered. "I want all of it, Mike. What would I do without you?"

Kisses pelted his chest and shoulders and his Adam's apple as he lifted his head to try to keep his mouth from hers. He didn't want to go against Marlene's wisdom, but damn, this woman was driving him outta his natural mind.

Inez's hands splayed wide, her fingers stretching, huge square-cut diamond catching light as she pressed against him, letting her satin-finish tongue glide over every brick in his abdomen. A shudder put his back against the door; a warm whisper of a kiss caressed his navel until his groin contracted. Although she was just an itty-bitty thing by comparison, the places she could reach with her short, fine self were buckling his knees. When she kissed him there, right where it hurt so good, he slapped the molding.

"Suga, you gonna make me mess up Marlene's instructions, girl . . . c'mon now. You better quit while you're ahead." His protest sounded weak even to his own ears as his rough palms glided over butter-smooth, brown skin, and lush, squeezable curves when she stood.

"If something woulda happened to your big, crazy ass, Michael, I would have died," Inez said, closing her eyes to rub her cheek against his chest. "Damali would have been trying to restart my heart, but I swear to you, man, I would have refused to come back out of the Light." She smothered him with another kiss when he leaned down to receive it, and then threw her arms around his neck.

He lied to himself, thinking he had no other choice but to pick her up and take her into the bathroom with him. That's what he was saying in his mind the whole time her microbraids teased his shoulders and her plump, juicy behind made him stupid while he kneaded it as he walked them across the floor. He remembered something Marlene had said about them both having to get doused, and after doing purges a hundred times over the years, half-memory kicked in, and he functioned on autopilot.

It was just that somehow he forgot to let his baby girl get out of her pretty teddy. The shower went on and she went in with it. And somehow it was impossible to make himself actually put her down. She was in charge of soap, he was doing the heavy lifting, the soap was working as greased lightning against friction, and the quick prayer they'd both said at the door would have to handle the rest.

"DON'T TOUCH ME!" Dan nearly shouted as he hopped around in a circle stripping down. "Don't even hold the bag, back away from it, honey. Oh, shit, your period is late, and I brought this home . . . remind me to kick my own ass once I'm out of the tub."

"Dan . . . it's—"

"No, no, sweetheart, I swear I'll take care of everything. Don't you worry," he said, frantic, yanking off combat Timberlands and stuffing his clothes in a bag. He didn't understand how women could just smile and be cool at a time like this. He looked at her for a moment and stopped struggling with his clothes. "You are so beautiful . . ." Then he returned to his crazed stripping.

"There's so many things I gotta do—gotta call my parents, gotta make sure I have a living will and set up a trust fund, and make sure there's enough in an IRA, should something happen and—"

"Daniel," she murmured, coming close to him.

"Ohmigod, are you crazy, Heather! Don't touch me!" He bolted away from her and into the bathroom, jumped in the shower, then peeked through the glass door when he heard her come in.

Panic sweat mixed with the shower spray as he looked at her gorgeous gray eyes and profusion of auburn ringlets that fell to her toffee-hued shoulders. But he couldn't stop staring at her.

"Oh, God, Heather, I love you so much and wanna hug you so bad right now . . . If I had known . . ."

"I love you, too," she whispered, touching the edge of the opened door. "But you were supposed to go with the other men, or you would have never been able to live with your-self, Dan. And then, how could I live with me for not allow-ing you to live with you?"

He closed his eyes and hung his head, the slight accent of her sweet Scottish brogue washing through him and making him want her. She was so open and giving and so everything he'd prayed for . . . correction, everything he'd begged Heaven on his knees for, and now she might be carrying his child?

For several seconds he just stared at her, allowing the shower spray to pelt his back. It was too much to absorb af-ter the night he and the fellas had just had. And his wife, a woman who loved him enough to take his name and bear his children was this gorgeous redhead . . . her Scottish mother providing the luscious silken tresses and startling gray eyes, her Ghanaian father giving her skin a perpetual, stunning tan, and the Creator designing her voluptuous body by his dreams and the stars . . .

Daniel shut the shower door, ashamed of his body's reac-tion to the beauty on the other side of the glass, and began soaping. Just as soon as he closed the door, he heard it open, and he turned to see Heather naked and joining him.

"What . . . what're you doing?" He backed up, trying to make himself fit into the far corner so he didn't touch her.

"They said we both had to wash, right?"

"Yeah, but you're pregnant." He glanced over his shoulder at her. "You can't be in here."

"*Might* be pregnant," she said with a sigh. "True I'm late, but a lot of things can throw off a woman's cycle, not the least of which is battling demons, stress, and—"

"So, so, that means that until we know for sure, we should be careful . . . and this isn't being very careful. We have to stop all kinds of risky stuff, like taking showers together when we're supposed to be purging, and, and, other stuff. You know?"

She fought not to laugh and a smile held it back. "Women can still make love while they're pregnant, you know, love?

You don't have to wait nine months and then six weeks more . . . like a year before you touch me again."

He turned slightly in the spray to half-face her without straining his neck. "Really?"

Heather covered her mouth with two fingers, the laughter brimming and ready to pop out at any second. He was so dear and so charming that she wanted to run her hands through his thicket of blond hair as she stared into his crystal blue eyes. Panic was etched across his handsome face, but after the stories of heroism she'd heard and knowing that she could have easily been sobbing her eyes out as a brand-new widow versus a honeymooning bride, he had no idea how much she wanted him right now.

"Really."

They both stared at each other.

Had he any idea how long she'd waited for a man of his caliber to come into her life? A decent, honest, honorable soul who had befriended her and caressed her spirit long before he'd ever touched her . . . and when he did touch her . . . *gracious*. Heather briefly closed her eyes as a quiver overtook her belly. The fact that Dan was trying to hide an erection from her because he thought she'd be offended, simply because she *might* be pregnant, drew her to him despite all his fears. Didn't he know that his tactical blue-arc gave him away? His body was practically glowing from the waist down.

"Daniel," she whispered, backing him up against the tiles and taking his mouth. "Let me wash your back, love."

THE AGREEMENT WAS implicit as they both stripped by the door. Jose glanced up at Juanita, their eyes met at the same time, and they both shook their heads.

"Uh-uh, that's how we met."

She nodded. "In the shower. Too hot."

"You know me, 'Nita," Jose said with his hands held up in front of his chest. "When it comes to you, baby, I ain't got that kinda willpower."

"Me, either," she said quietly, her gaze raking down his body. The man was built like a brick house, and she had to wrestle her line of vision away from his dark caramel skin that was stretched tight over hard-packed muscle. But his intense gaze caught her breath in her throat. Jose's deep brown eyes and thicket of unruly black hair made her take a step closer to him.

"Don't start," he warned, the tone much gentler than the strong one he'd had in his mind.

"I never stopped," she murmured.

He tilted his head, inhaled deeply, and allowed his eyes to briefly slide shut. She'd gotten wet for him and the sensory awareness contracted every muscle in his groin. Just looking at her in the buff was making the muscle in his jaw work. Big brown eyes in a beautiful face, mouth that would make a man stupid, dark brown hair that felt like silk flowing through his fingers . . . milk-in-tea–hued skin so soft he was almost afraid to bruise it. His gaze slid down her body and stopped at her naked breasts. When she lazily trailed her fingers over her pebbled cinnamon nipples, he let out his breath in a hot rush like he'd been punched.

"You wanna get in the shower first so you can start your bath first?"

She shook her head slowly, and then turned to saunter over to the tub, glancing at him over her shoulder. "Uh-uh," she said quietly. "You go first so you can watch."

THE MOMENT THE last article of clothing hit the bag and the offending garments were sealed away, he got body slammed. It was so fantastically unexpected that his arms and legs functioned on mental remote. With Krissy's mouth on his, her long flaxen hair spilling over his shoulders as he heaved her up to his waist and her creamy thighs gripped him, he almost forgot to head for the shower.

The way her body moved against him as he held her made him stagger. Mentally reprimanding himself as being a senior Guardian, he tried to remember what Marlene had said. In order to do that, he had to at least stop kissing Krissy as he made his way across the suite. A jarring tactile difference in textures underfoot from rug to hard surface gave him a little perspective. He was finally able to tear his mouth away from Krissy's eager kiss as he crossed the threshold to cool bathroom tiles.

"We've gotta—"

A hungry kiss cut off his argument, just as her feral tongue dredged a moan up from his chest.

"You almost died, ohmigod, J.L.," she panted, raining kisses onto his forehead, lashes, and nose.

"Kris, I'm all dirty and—"

"Put it in, I don't care," she gasped, capturing his mouth again.

The request and her kiss imploded in his groin, but as turned on as he was, he knew better than that.

"We can't," he said, breathing like something was chasing him.

"You said they never even touched you," she moaned, dropping her head back. "You were too fast for them . . . oh, J.L., I can see it in my mind!"

The pitch of her voice connected with his spinal column, just like the request had zapped on his blue-white charge. He stumbled across the room blind with her in his arms, feeling for the shower controls in a series of frantic slaps against the tiles until he found them. Logic was edging away in nanoseconds, competing with Krissy's wet seal against his belly. Her slick need tortured his stomach, slowly seeping down it to pool at his base while her firm round breasts bounced as she moved against him, coaxing his entry.

"We can't," he finally said on a thick gasp, pulling one of her tight, pink nipples between his lips. "Just lemme get the crud off, then you won't be able to get me off you."

She felt like a crazy woman as she quickly grabbed the soap and lathered his hair, running her fingers through his jet-black silk. His almond-hued skin against hers made her feel dangerous as her druid gift of kinetic expression absorbed all the erotic impulses he'd had and shot them back at him. Her kisses forced him into the spray, water blinding them, soap rushing away, breathing in bursts of passion before mouths locked again. She loved him so much, this kind, gentle warrior with intensely private eyes and a razor-sharp mind, who'd chosen her . . . and he'd married her. Body friction more than soap had cleaned him off. But the moment her kinetic energy entwined with his tactical sensory capacity, he lost it.

"Kris, baby, right now—I gotta be in you." He backed her into the wall, a deep moan reverberating off the tiles.

She couldn't catch her breath, but seeing him come unglued sent a sliver of logic into her brain at the last second. "You sure, 'cause you said—"

"Yeah, yeah, I'm sure, baby, oh yeah, oh God, yes, oh . . . yeah, I think we're both clean enough."

HE USED A crystal rocks glass from the suite's bar to pour the milky white bath through her hair. Mesmerized by her long, blue-black ropes and how the opaque water drizzled through it, it was all he could do to not touch her flawless ivory skin.

But having been strongly rebuffed in front of the team by his brand-new wife, the last thing he wanted to do was add insult to injury. He'd followed Marlene's rules to the letter, as hard as that was to do while watching Jasmine's petite nude body move like a water nymph in the shower. However, the last thing he wanted to do was mess up some ritual as the youngest guy on the team—or be the loose link that allowed terror into the family.

So, he was gonna do the right thing, stay on his knees and wash her hair like she had so lovingly washed his first, even though he'd been in the wrong. And if he stayed on his knees and kept his body pressed close to the edge of the huge tub, then maybe the hard-on would die down before she got angry again. If he could just get his hand not to tremble as he poured the milky water over her gorgeous hair . . . and if he could stop staring at her cinnamon-brown nipples that played a bobbing game of hide-and-seek in the water with him . . . he had to also ignore the peaceful expression on her beautiful face and the way her dark brown, almond-shaped eyes almost hunted him as he worked.

Her small, heart-shaped mouth was nearly his undoing as her pink lips parted and she took in a sip of air. Her eyes slid shut as he massaged her scalp. Yeah, on his knees was just where he should be—in the right position to beg her not to be angry anymore.

Bobby swallowed hard and touched Jasmine's face. "You still mad at me?" he asked, hearing the toiletries on the bathroom counter begin to rattle.

"No," she said, without opening her eyes as she relaxed in the tub.

"You sure?" he murmured, noticing towels begin to slip from the racks on their own.

"I was just afraid," she murmured. "I never want to lose you. I've lost all my family in the Philippines . . . those that I knew, and then we lost Gabrielle—who was your aunt, but like a mother to me. But, Robert, I've never known love like this."

Jasmine sat up slowly and opened her eyes. His voice caught in his throat as she took his mouth. She'd used his formal name . . . the name that made him sound more like a man than the team kid the old dudes treated him as. He pulled her to her knees with only a short rise of porcelain between them as his hands caressed her hair to slide down to her shoulders and arms, then glide over her breasts.

"Say it again," he whispered against her neck, kinetic energy flowing through him so hard that her hair was beginning to levitate off her shoulders. He hoped she knew what he was asking as his grip tightened around her.

"*Robert,*" she said in a low, sultry rush of breath into his ear.

It happened so naturally, the sliding fall where she slipped over the edge of the tub into his arms and his back hit the floor . . . just as naturally as she fit against him and he fit into her and the water droplets in the tub rose and fell in kinetic ecstasy, dancing to the rhythm that naturally occurred in the middle of the floor.

SHE YANKED OFF his vest and ripped his T-shirt over his head. He bent quickly to unlace his combat boots and drop his pants. Her nightgown was gone in one deft move. They worked in tandem to get everything into the plastic bag and said a quick Hail Mary over it, then embraced.

His tongue was down her throat before she could gasp his name. Her hands raced up his back and then caressed his bald head. He began to walk her backward, and she almost fell.

"What about the shower and whole thing?" she said, barely able to catch her breath.

"Later. In about twenty minutes," he gasped.

"But," she said on a hard pant, breaking away from another ardent kiss. "Marlene said—"

"After being married for twenty plus years, Marj, raising kids, and being through all we've been through together— can anything come between me and you?" He pulled back and looked at her hard, gulping air.

"No," she said, the response almost a broken shout. She covered his face with kisses, dragging him toward the bedroom. "But Richard Berkfield, if you die on me, *ever,* I will never forgive you."

He guided her to the edge of the huge king-sized bed in their suite and then pushed her hand down his stomach while looking into her eyes breathing hard. "Does that feel like a dead man, Mrs. Berkfield?"

She slowly closed her eyes and stroked him. "Oh, no, Mr. Berkfield, no, no it most certainly does not. Sit down."

"YOU HAVE EVERY right to be pissed off, darlin'," Rider said, yanking off his favorite silver-toe, hand-tooled, demon-hunting cowboy boots and tossing them into the plastic bag. He kept a steady eye on Tara as he opened his belt and stripped down his black jeans and Fruit of the Loom boxers. "So, I'm not gonna try and make any excuses. Temporary insanity was the cause. Yep."

He watched her watching him with a smoldering hurt in her eyes. Even while furious she was gorgeous, perhaps even more so then. Low room light lit her Native American features within African-American parentage, making her smoky dark eyes darker, and her sculptured cheekbones create a breath-stopping profile. Then her mouth, good Lord . . . full and lush, a mouth to drown in, and her hair was like a heavy black, velvet drape down to her shoulders. His gaze swept over her scantily clad body, causing her arms to fold tighter.

"Aw, c'mon and get naked with me." He wiggled his eyebrows. "Might relieve some stress, who knows?"

"You, Jack Rider, are incorrigible," she said, pointing at him as she untied the sash of her silk robe and discarded the item in the plastic bag. But she slowed her movements down as she peeled off her long, flowing nightgown, seeming somewhat uncomfortable, or at the very least, unsure about stripping in front of him while still so thoroughly annoyed.

"Damn . . ." he murmured, allowing his gaze to pour liquid heat over her as it slid down her throat and over her breasts, following a trail down her belly before it slid over her mound and her long, to-die-for legs. "I am *thoroughly* incorrigible . . . no lie."

"And you haven't heard a word I've said," she fussed, covering her breasts by folding her arms over them to block his view. "In fact, I think you're crazy, is what it is—that's the root of it. Insanity."

"Wanna know what else makes me crazy?" he asked with a wry chuckle. He looked down, making her smile. "Guilty as charged. You make me crazy."

"Get in the shower, Jack Rider," she said, trying to stay in character and pretend to be piqued.

"Now, you know, it's only because you recently came back from the Light that I am minding my manners." He talked as he walked, watching her peevish expression mellow as he passed her. "I didn't wait thirty years for you to be my wife, sleeping in the same bed, to screw it up with some demon cooties."

From the corner of his eye he saw her quietly giggle behind her hand. He turned on the shower full blast and hollered over the spray as she stood in the doorway.

"See, I can deal with delayed gratification—so I can wait you out. If you need to stay mad at me for blowing away some bad vamp types with crazy Rivera, I can accept that. I'm philosophical. Because you see, I can recall a time when I was soooo horny for you, missed you soooo bad that . . . hey, darlin', I'd just about dry hump a haystack trying to pretend it was you."

"Oh, Rider, just stop it," she said blushing, but coming farther into the bathroom.

"I bullshit you not, lovely lady. I would go to sleep drunk as a skunk, and wake up hollering for ya." He looked down again and then grinned. "This ain't nothing, it'll keep."

Tara swallowed hard as he turned into the spray. She watched the water run through his dirty-blond hair and course over his muscular shoulders. She loved his voice and wished he'd say something else, just so she could hear it echo through the bathroom. He made her laugh, he made her cry, he made her shout, he made her gasp, he made her crazy— God, she loved her some Jack Rider.

It was hard to watch him soap himself down without going to him. His humorous banter always had a zing to it, and the way that man could turn a phrase when he was serious . . . whew. And if he said those wonderful things while he made her look into his intense hazel eyes, she might have to break down and jump his bones.

Butterflies had escaped in her belly and the dense humidity in the bathroom was making her hair cling to her neck and shoulders.

"All right, I admit it. You weren't alone in that missing-somebody department."

"Huh? What did you say?" Rider chuckled and spun around to peer over the door at her. "Miss you? No, wrong word completely. *Crave.* That's it. Tara, I *craved* you. That was insane. It was easy to give up thirty-five years or so of smoking Marlboro Reds . . . Jack Daniel's, too, no problem, compared to giving you up? Sheeit." He stared at her, smiling, but his eyes were serious. "That was like giving up a kidney, maybe a lung."

"It wasn't that easy for me, either," she said, her tone suddenly sad. She opened the shower door just to see him better, and so he could hear her. At least that's what she told herself.

But she wasn't prepared for his stone-serious expression that didn't match the upbeat tone of his voice. Nor was she prepared for the way his arms just opened up for her to fill them without anything being said. His shudder when she touched him said it all. And when his fingers tangled in her hair with soap, memory snapped back so hard she cried out.

"That's right, baby, our first time was me washing your hair . . . lemme do it again . . . this time over the side of the tub like before . . . with nothing between us . . . no jeans, no sundress." He nuzzled her neck as his hands aggressively traveled over her spine and the swell of her behind. "Lavender, oh, God, the lavender you wore . . . just a passing whiff from a florist gives me wood. You're right; I'm completely insane for you."

She took his mouth and kissed him hard, unable to forget a single moment they'd spent together before she'd turned, and so many moments after. She found the sweet spot on his neck where she'd marked him, and the sound that escaped him ran all through her. His wide palms were spreading heat through her body as they swept across her in slippery strokes. She wanted to climb up him, but he wouldn't let her and the frustration of his denial sent her hands over his hard body in a frantic rush.

But he took her mouth slowly, his tongue in charge, dancing in a slow waltz that made her go limp in his hold.

"Let me wash your hair and take my time, darlin', until you holler."

IT WAS GONNA be a long night. Carlos watched Damali march around the suite with a smudge stick lit, her eyes set hard and her tone resolute as she banished the potential of any demon essence. Every threshold had been salted and covered, every entry point anointed, and his clothes had been stashed in a safety bag with hers. He trudged to the shower like he was going to the gallows.

After the shit he'd seen, and they'd been through, he didn't feel like talking about it or arguing. He understood her point, and was glad that she finally understood his. But for the first time in a very long time, the real stress of being the team's head of household weighed him down. What if she'd been right? What if he lost a man in the firefight? His boy Yonnie was AWOL. Kamal's entire team had been lost, when it very easily could have been anybody on their squad. Now Heather was possibly pregnant and he felt like a nervous grandfather suddenly responsible for Dan's safety—and Heather's went without saying.

Damali slid into the shower behind him. "C'mere," she said gently. "Lemme do your hair and your back."

"Thanks, baby, but I'm all right. I'll get out of your way in a minute."

She didn't say anything for a moment but lathered his back anyway, spreading wide swirls of suds against it. "It's hard being the one everybody looks up to," she murmured, her touch soft as she attended his skin. "I understand that."

"At first you bit my head off, though," he said, still a little salty.

He expected a comeback but instead she pressed her body to his, fitting against him in a snug, warm seal.

"I love you so much, Carlos Rivera, that sometimes I have to back up from that just not to suffocate or scream." She turned him around and let her fingers cradle his cheek.

"How many times did I almost lose you, then lose you, then you came back from the dead, only to lose you and . . ."

He smiled; she closed her eyes.

"That's what I was waiting for."

He pulled her into a slow embrace. "I started the Armageddon, D . . . I'm a little freaked out, for real, okay?"

He stared at her without blinking as she pulled back. Water coursed down his handsome face, droplets catching in his long lashes. She slid her hand across his jaw to bring his face forward.

"Oh, *you did not*. It was coincidence," she said, trying to make herself believe that was true.

He sighed and pulled her into his embrace and she held him tight. "I didn't mean for it to go down like that, D. I was going in to smoke some vamps that had done our whole family wrong. In and out. Hit the targets hard and be gone."

Again, silence filled the void between them and she gripped his arms tightly. "You know what? Okay, maybe you did kick it off." She stepped back and folded her arms over her chest. "Who else to do it?" When he looked down and turned into the spray, she grabbed his arm, making him look at her. "My husband is the baddest shut-your-mouth on the planet, okaaaay? And my man is soooo wild and off the hook that he went in and did some crazy soldier shit, and kicked off the galactic prophecies of old. He's got sooo much juice, all right, that Heaven picked *him* to make it jump off." She smiled wider as a sly half-smile snuck out of hiding on his face.

"You think so . . . think they actually wanted me to do this?"

"Did you get a vibe?" Damali's hands were on her hips.

He turned to fully face her. "Yeah. For real, I did."

"Well, did Adam come and help you, no questions asked, like they dropped the Caduceus on me from just a shout out? They must have had a reason."

"Yeah, D . . . now that you mention it, there was no static about what went down."

They stared at each other for a long time.

"I am *so* proud of you, Carlos."

He traced her cheek. "That's only because you're insane, like me."

"Yeah, true," she said, her expression serious. "But I still love you so much."

"Baby, you know I love you," he whispered over the spray, his hands sliding down her arms. "I'm just glad you're not still mad at me, because, D, I couldn't have stopped myself from doing that drive-by if I wanted to."

"I know . . . because it was a prime directive from a higher source than this team." She touched his face, suddenly wanting to just be out of the water, dry and curled up with him, warm in the bed. "I've had a few of those prime directives. . . . Some I listened to, some, in my headstrong days, I missed and didn't listen to . . . but I only got angry because this is some scary bullshit—that's why we all had that reaction, at first . . . still, I am proud of you."

She took his mouth nice and slow and allowed her wings to gradually unfold. She wrapped them both away in her protective covering as his hug pulled her in closer.

"I'm sorry I'm always so crazy, D, starting shit . . . it's just who I am."

"I'd do lifetimes of crazy with you, Carlos," she whispered, closing her eyes as she laid her head on his shoulder, "rather than the alternative of never having done crazy with you at all."

CHAPTER FOUR

The team had begun to assemble in the main suite, and it was clear to Damali that the guys had no incentive not to go to war. From the looks on everyone's faces as they walked through the door, and the jubilant male camaraderie that was exchanged, and even more so, based upon the hot glances being passed between couples, it was clear that they'd been handsomely rewarded for their heroic, albeit foolhardy, deeds. They'd been lucky this time, and then obviously *really gotten lucky*.

Damali forced herself not to roll her eyes and suck her teeth when she saw them. She took a seat on the wide, white sectional sofa and tried to put it all into perspective. The only subdued one in the group was Carlos, and that made her sad.

"Good morning, Vietnam!" Berkfield yelled across the room when Mike came through the door with Inez.

"Yo, yo, man!" Mike said like rumbling thunder. "What it look like, people?"

Marjorie's face had gone beet red and her voice dipped to a private admonishment. "Oh, Richard, really . . ."

"Don't start talking dirty to me this morning, Marj," he said, laughing, with a wink that made her giggle. "Because if you say, 'Oh, Richard, really' . . . I can make it so, Number One—and you know that."

Marjorie slapped her husband's hand away from her derriere when he tried to pinch her as she passed by the sectional seating. Inez glanced away with a too-wide grin, beaming at Big Mike.

"It's you, man," Jose said, grabbing Big Mike's massive hand and then yanking him into a quick warrior's hug as he came through the door.

Mike threw his head back and laughed at Jose's rare ability to practically make him fall. "Naw, brother, it's obviously *you.*"

Jose play-boxed away from him as a rosy tinge crept up Juanita's cheeks. She slipped into the room, waved to everyone shyly, and sat down. "Hey."

When Shabazz walked into the suite with Marlene, Damali glanced at the floor to be sure he wasn't levitating. He'd strolled in so cool, with a smile so sly that even Mike had to shake his head.

"What it look like?" Shabazz murmured, chewing on a toothpick and smoothly sliding into a large leather chair like he was made of pure liquid.

"Damn . . . You tell *me,*" Mike said, laughing and signifying all at the same time.

Shabazz leaned back in his chair and stretched like a lazy panther, closing his eyes. "It's *all* good, brother."

"Uhmmm, morning, folks," Marlene said, swallowing a grin, hustling over to the coffeepot on the wide credenza to heat some hot water for tea.

When Bobby bounded into the room, it was like watching a Labrador puppy do a happy-dance greeting.

"Hey, yo, whassup?" Bobby hollered with his arm slung over Jasmine's shoulders.

His megawatt smile was infectious, causing the older men in the room to burst out laughing. The bright light of joy in Bobby's eyes made Damali lean back on the sofa and briefly close hers with a quiet groan.

"So, what're we gonna do today? Are we moving out, or do we have a coupla more days of R and R, or we going hunting tonight? Carlos, I'm down, we can doooo that shit, ya know?" Bobby stood looking at Carlos with a shine of expectation in his eyes, practically wagging his tail, and completely oblivious to Carlos's somber mood.

Before Carlos could answer, Berkfield had hailed his son from across the room with a thumbs-up, and then elbowed Carlos in the ribs. He leaned in with a private tone of pride. "Chip off the old block . . . *damn*. That's my boy."

Bobby turned just in time to see J.L. roll up behind him, and the two dropped their hold on their partners and play-fought into the room. The two young sisters-in-law hugged and giggled and dashed into the room waving and singing, "Good morning!" They flopped down into chairs and held each other's hands, intermittently sending a squeeze of support to each other.

J.L. ducked a mimed rabbit punch from Bobby and then fell back and opened his arms. "Whassup?"

"Whassup?" Bobby answered, laughing, making his voice go deeper than J.L.'s.

J.L. fell out laughing, and then said it again to crack Bobby up harder. "Whassup?"

"No . . . whassup?" Dan said in an alto that beat them all, entering the room with Heather, behind Bobby and J.L.

Big Mike fell off the sofa onto the floor, laughing so hard he was lying on his back, wiping his eyes. Shabazz sat forward and lost his cool façade and broke down laughing so hard he couldn't breathe. Jose was doubled over, and Berkfield was red in the face with belly laughs that were making him wheeze. The women in the group laughed and just shook their heads. Carlos cracked a smile but didn't say more or laugh. Bobby and J.L. were totaled against the wall, and Heather simply covered her face with her hands, laughing hard but mortified.

"You almost missed roll call, man," Jose hollered at Rider through simmering bursts of chuckles.

Rider leaned against the open door frame real cool, drew Tara against him, and kissed her slow, and then released her to enter the room. "Depends on which role you're called for, son . . . g'morning, gentlemen."

The room went silent for a minute as Rider loped into the room behind Tara. Berkfield released a slow, quiet whistle of appreciation aimed at Rider under Jose's whispered harmony of "*Daaaaaaaayum* . . . " Mike got up off the floor and pounded Rider's fist as he passed and sat next to Shabazz.

Shabazz gave Rider a cool nod and they exchanged a fist pound without looking at each other.

"Old school," Shabazz muttered.

"The only way it's done, bro," Rider said, looking at Tara, then calmly extracted a chew stick from his vest, slid it into his mouth, and bit down on it like it was a Tiperillo.

"Well, now that the gang's all here," Damali said, her nerves raw and not completely sure why. "Maybe we can decide where to go next as a team?"

She glanced at Carlos as female Guardians slid next to their partners, some sitting on laps.

Carlos stood and went to the window with a shrug. "Wherever you all wanna go is fine by me. I'll transport you, get a shield up. Y'all know the drill."

The room went still for a moment as Carlos's morose tone blanketed the team. Concerned glances passed between the brothers and their wives looked at Damali, searching her eyes for answers she didn't have or wasn't willing to share.

"Can you get a divination from the stones?" Marlene said, her voice reaching out to Damali like tender balm.

"No," Damali said in a far-off voice. "My pearl has shut down since Cain's death . . . that crazy she-dragon was in love with him, and when Eve beheaded him, she's been grieving so hard she won't respond."

"Maybe we can ask the Queens?" Marlene said, trying to keep hope in the room alive.

"Yeah. Let her ask the Queens," Carlos said flatly. "I'll check with my council, too, before I do anything else wild and off the hook."

"Hey, does it matter where we build?" Rider said. "Look, being real here, guys . . . there is no safe place, per se. No safe neighborhood. It's what you make it, and if the big war is in full effect, I say let's go somewhere nice."

"Heeeey," Shabazz said, rolling his shoulders. "Gotta take a stand, set down roots, fortify where we're at so we can have some peace, feel me?"

"Completely, man. How we gonna raise kids on the damned run?" Mike rolled his shoulders and began a slow pace between the seat he'd abandoned and the dining room table. "San Diego gets my vote. Military base nearby, in case we need to *borrow* a tank or two. Beautiful weather, beach, close enough to L.A. to drive up to handle our business there, on the coast for easy out, a stone's throw to Mexico."

"That could work," Jose said. "So, like a fly crib the size we'd need, whatduya say, twenty, thirty mil? How's your pockets, brothers?"

"I'm good," Rider said. "Joint build-out as always."

"Uh . . ." Bobby looked at his father with a question and mouthed twenty or thirty million.

"We got your back," J.L. said, glancing at Bobby. "Band made a mint; Dan handled the paper, still getting royalties. Family is family; we got you."

"Cool, wow . . . thanks," Bobby murmured.

Berkfield ran a palm over his gleaming scalp. "Yeah, geez, you boys don't mess around."

"Hey, we gotta have this thing on lock," Shabazz said. He looked over at Carlos. "Wherever we finally put down roots, Adam's black-box is a go, right man? An extra layer on top of what we insulate with."

"Yeah," Carlos said in a far-off voice. "He gave me his word. It'll also keep dumb humans messing with technology and weapons off our doorsteps so we don't have to cap one of those sonsofbitches."

"Don't even take my mind there, bro," Shabazz said. "I will lose my soul and smoke a motherfucker in a heartbeat if they come for Mar or anybody else again like they did when they blitzed our Beverly Hills joint."

"You ain't said a word," Rider muttered.

"Hey, the way I read it is, 'Thou shalt not murder'—note the word 'murder' was supplanted for the word 'kill' later on—two different meanings altogether, hence the problem with translations."

"Aw, shit, you know our team's paperwork man is on this," Jose said, leaning forward. "School us, Danny boy— you oughta have been a lawyer, man, for real."

"If you go to the old books and original Aramaic that was then translated into Hebrew *way* before King James butchered the book for his own political reasons," Dan said with conviction, "murder means unjustifiably taking a life— but self-defense and keeping somebody off your wife and kid or yourself by killing an aggressor, human or otherwise, will not keep me up at night. I'll sleep like a baby, believe that. I don't call that murder—so the 'Thou shalt not kill' part has caveats . . . we need a translation from the Covenant on this—but if fucked-up military types rush us to turn us or our loved ones into weapons, I'm shooting first and asking questions later. They could be human helpers of the darkside, and during the Armageddon, too? Shit. Game over, man. If you chose the wrong side."

Mike nodded and glanced at Dan. "We feel you, brother. I got the same situation."

Everybody's attention immediately shot to Inez.

"No, no, not like that," Inez said quickly, causing shoulders to relax. "But my daughter, Ayana . . . I need somewhere for my baby girl and my momma to be, if this mess is getting crazy worldwide."

"Oh," was released in a collective harmony as people slumped back into their chairs.

Damali just watched it all from a very remote place in her mind. The brothers were nesting—actually *nesting*. She'd never seen a male version of this before in her life, and it was eerily interesting as well as disturbing. She glimpsed

Carlos, who still had his back to the group, his emotions locked behind searing sterling and reinforced with an impenetrable black-box.

"I gotta get Rabbi on the phone," Dan said, beginning to pace as he raked his hair. "My parents think I'm on a kibbutz in Israel, and with that region at war, my mom and dad are gonna be freaking out." He stared at Heather, his gaze gentle on the surface with repressed terror only a thin layer beneath it. "I want them to meet you . . . and I've gotta update my living will, get everybody's wills in order, open another IRA, make sure I move some things around in my 401(k) . . . "

"Don't panic, man," Shabazz said calmly. "We're gonna make sure it's cool."

"All right," Dan said, leaning against the wall and taking deep breaths. "I'm good. I'm good."

"This joint in San Diego," J.L. said, "we find it on the other side of the fault lines, the ones dormant for years, and if something jumps off, our section of ground breaks whole." He looked over at Heather and Jasmine, then Krissy. "We're gonna need you ladies who do stone work to feel out the area before Dan negotiates a closing on a property."

"We got it," Heather said with pride. "Thank you."

"Hey, it's for everybody, kiddo," Rider said, pounding fists with Shabazz.

"We can go in with Marj and Marlene to see if we can see a good spot or primo property," Juanita offered, glancing at Inez, too.

"Definitely," Inez said, nodding and giving Juanita a long-distance high-five across the room.

"We'll wire the shit out of the joint, too," J.L. said, his gaze scanning the room. "I've been thinking about this ever since Mexico. I'm sure I can figure out a way to supercharge the perimeter from a bounce off tactical energy so Carlos doesn't have to take the energy drains all the time. Silver stakes deep in the ground around the perimeter, and me, Bobby, Dan, and Shabazz can square off that—each linked to a cardinal direction—to put a first-alert energy band around the property that will go off like a tripwire and hit all four brothers like an internal security alarm."

"You's a bad, boy," Mike said, impressed.

"Then I'ma link that to your audio, dude, going through the vibrations our earth energy folks on the team have," J.L. said, "and you'll be able to hear a fly catch in that net, Mike. I can hook up our noses like that, too."

"Damn . . . you go, boy!" Jose said, nodding and pounding Rider's fist.

"We use a combo of state-of-the-art technology rigged with our standards from the old compound days, like holy water sprinkler systems, UV floodlights and all of that, plus we rig this new joint with every gift we own. Mar's strong prayer lines, Damali's, the stones on the property, down to the bricks, supercharged by our ladies, the Covenant standing at the four corners consecrating the ground after they bless the interior like that, so we're on hallowed ground and can't nothing come up from subbasements. Paint the floors with colloidal silver for insurance. Fabrics ready to rip off furniture upholstery and go to work, if necessary, by Jasmine's hand-painted designs. Berkfield's blood in the paint mix over all doors, windows, anyplace anything foul could get in. Alarm plants by—"

"Alarm plants?" Inez interrupted in awe.

"Marjorie has that earth energy, white-lighter Wicca thing going with Kris, and with Bobby's wizard topspin," J.L. said with confidence, "plants, which are living organisms, should scream bloody murder if anything makes it into the yard, same with houseplants. Give them a voice."

"Now you done went deep, Zen master," Mike said with a wide grin. "What happened last night that took you all the way to the ultimate creative plane, man?"

J.L. laughed with the other brothers and simply shrugged. "I was inspired."

"Yeah," Jose said laughing. "Me, too . . . like . . . I think we should go on tour after we get this joint built."

The entire team looked at him hang-jawed.

"Our music is dying, yo," Jose said, not the least bit fazed by the group's reaction. "We need to be able to move around after we get situated to get our message out and let the darkside know we ain't scared of them, ain't hiding."

"The youngblood's got a point," Rider said. "Our primary mission is to go root this bullshit out. I'm with Jose. I say we get a good base camp established, one where there's an ironclad haven for us to return to at all times, or if we need to bring somebody in for safety reasons." He glanced at Heather and then back at the group. "Whoever has to stay home, can man the communications gear and keep us in touch with the Covenant, or coordinate logistics. Then we hit the road and do our thing."

"Keep moving and keep the pressure on while they're weak," Jose said, lifting his chin toward Rider.

"The music gives us energy, keeps us in touch with the Divine," Shabazz agreed, his gaze roving the group. "It also energizes populations who've lost hope, and we can drop some protection anointment on folks in the audiences like Mar used to do in the old days when she poured libations."

"I can definitely do that," Marlene offered. "And with all the juice on this team, now . . . puhlease, we could blanket stadiums of people."

"Good," Dan said quickly. "I'll see what I can start to arrange—a World Peace Tour, guys? Tell me the promo and PR angle, and I'm on it."

"Sounds good to me," Shabazz said, standing and stretching. "We are gonna have to start earning some cold cash to refill the deficit spending going on." He looked at the group. "We've been gone, what, two years—and have been lucky. So, I don't give a shit if it's the last days and the Armageddon, that bull ain't gonna go down in one day. It won't be one battle, but a series of battles in a long, protracted war. That's why we hunker down, get ready for the long haul." He strolled over to Marlene, who had yet to make tea, and pulled her near. He nuzzled her neck and made her blush.

"We take life one day at a time, do our job . . . work hard, play hard, you feel me?"

" 'Bazz, stop," Marlene said quietly. "I feel you. You had the same vision I did, baby?"

He chuckled in her ear. "Yeah."

"I don't know about y'all, but I'm hungry," Mike said. "Throw me that room-service menu, D."

"You're hungry again?" Inez said, shaking her head. "Dang."

"It ain't your cooking," Mike said with his nose in the menu once Damali had tossed it to him. "Don't stick to your ribs. That's why we gotta get that new joint soon."

"Y'all, can I design the kitchen?" Inez asked, her eyes darting around the room.

A group "Yes!" rang out, much to her delight.

"Hey, throw me that menu when you're done," Jose said, glancing at Juanita.

"Me, too, man," J.L. said, joining the developing food fest.

"Can we get a place that has a pool?" Juanita asked, her gaze going to Jose first, and then the group.

"Baby . . . if you want water on the premises," Jose said seductively, "I'll make sure there's one in the room."

She blushed and looked away as four Guardian brothers literally got up from where they were seated to cross the room and pound Jose's fist.

"We'll get the property already built, then go in, modular fashion, and retrofit it to whatever you want, ladies. So start thinking colors, what type of furniture—"

"And once you get a clear picture in your heads, I can save you a lot of time and burn it in as a special delivery," Carlos said without turning. "Place your orders."

"Much obliged," Rider hollered across the room to Carlos, seeming oblivious like the others to Carlos's darkening mood. "Throw me that menu when you're done."

Marlene caught Damali's eye. *Can we go into the bed-*

room and have a session, you and me, for a minute? she asked in a mental whisper.

Damali nodded and stood. "Y'all get something to eat. Me and Mar are going to the back where it's quiet to see if we can get a bead on a first location."

There was no objection as Marlene and Damali slipped away from the group. Marlene quietly closed the bedroom door behind Damali, as Damali crossed the room and sat down, hugging herself.

"Okay, what happened?" Marlene leaned on the closed door, and then moved in to prop her behind against the bureau.

"Nothing happened," Damali said quietly, staring at the floor. "We did the shower, and the white bath, and we talked, and I held him until we went to sleep. My husband is really freaked out."

"That process was just placebo," Marlene said in a sad tone. "Oh, baby . . ."

Damali's attention snapped up to stare at Marlene. "What do you mean *placebo*? We've all done that routine a hundred times, if once, coming out of demon battles where somebody got nicked. It's standard operating—"

"Not last night," Marlene said with a weary sigh. "Yeah, we do the baths—but after you hit every guy with the Caduceus, that's like nuking any demon buggies that could have latched on. Those guys were clean as a whistle when they left the suite last night, D. The baths were old traditional methods, good in a clinch if we didn't have the healing staff at our disposal—which is why they were a must before."

"Then I don't understand," Damali said, now talking with her hands out of frustration. "Mar, why—"

"It was to bring each couple closer, heal the trust and ego breaches that may have opened up . . . a little psychosexual therapy so that understanding, communication, and harmony would return."

Damali closed her eyes and ran her palms down her face with her head leaned back. "Glad it worked, Marlene. You're a genius, as always."

"But, from the tone of your voice and the vibe that Carlos is throwing off, it sounds like you two were the only ones that didn't take my medicine?" Marlene looked at Damali until she returned her gaze.

Damali shrugged and began picking at a nap in her jeans.

"You two are always so danged stubborn, D. Why'd you give that man the blues for doing what his natural impulse is to do?"

"I didn't," Damali said, staring at her jeans and watching them become blurry. "Not once we got alone. He's scared to death, Mar, but would never say it and I'd *never* put that in his face. He is trying so hard not to make a mistake now, feeling like he's got everybody's life on the line—plus babies, too—that the poor man is in shock. He was cool as long as it was demon to demon, an eye for an eye, a fang for a fang, street justice in full-effect type of thing—like he thought hitting Lilith's lair would be. He was ready for that, could handle it in his head, knew the ins and outs and had worked the best-case, worst-case scenarios in his brilliant mind down to the bone . . . But the moment he really dug it, really realized that On High had sent him that battle charge and it was for real on . . . I've never seen Carlos quietly freak this hard in my life."

Damali looked up and tried to fight back tears. Marlene pushed off the dresser and came to sit by Damali, moving a stray lock over her shoulder.

"D, baby . . . this was what he's been groomed to do all his life. His walk on the darkside and maybe even still owning his fangs so he'd be a hybrid, able to hit them while they were down, come at them like Adam never would, be sly, cunning, courageous, outrageous . . . Damali, you've *got* to make him know what every man in here knows—he was *chosen*, this time, to set the ball in motion, because only someone as wild and crazy as Carlos could do that—and do it with honor."

Damali slid into Marlene's embrace, her tears wetting Marlene's shoulder. "I tried to tell my husband that," she whispered through thick mucous. "But he keeps thinking of those who died in Morales, seeing their faces on the battle-field, hearing their screams, seeing their loved ones break down at all the funerals we went to. And I felt it turn like a hundred parasites under the skin of his brain, struggling with self-created scenes of what would happen if Armageddon forces swept down and took a very pregnant Heather— and then imagining what Dan would do . . . shit like that, Mar, is eating him up alive. He's got this kamikaze thing happening in his head, telling himself that he should have gone alone, he was the one that had a beef with Lilith, directly, and this time maybe—even for him—he'd gone too far."

"Aw . . . maaaan . . ." Marlene breathed against Damali's hair as she rubbed her back.

"His libido is shot to hell, Mar," Damali whispered, squeezing her eyes tightly. Thick mucous from tears collecting had formed in her mouth, slurring her words as she spoke in quick, urgent bursts. "After a battle . . . that they won? Nada. He kept walking around in a circle saying, 'D, I gotta think. Gotta figure out the best way to keep this team safe.' And you and I both know there's no surefire way to do that."

"But every man in here knows it's not Carlos's fault if something happens." Marlene held Damali back from her to stare into her eyes. "They all went, ready to ride or die, like Guardians. They're all celebrating the fact that they were there to kick it off and were a part of making biblical history, and *still* made it home from the first battle alive. That's why they're so cool about it—what other way is there to be? It was coming, sooner or later, all the signs were there . . . didn't really matter who started it, and truthfully, after Cain's plummet to a throne and executing Guardians on earth—it was seriously in the stars and close at hand, so . . . just tell Mr. Rivera, this time, it's not his fault."

Marlene tried to smile. Damali couldn't as she wiped her face.

"Yeah, well, this time, after all those times before when it *was* his fault, he can't shake the feeling down deep that it might be. Every mistake he ever made is kicking his ass, Marlene. I can feel it like a serpent right under his skin." Damali let her breath out in a frustrated rush. "I mean *all* the way back, Mar. To like getting his brother killed because he was in the drug biz with Carlos, and Nuit got to him."

"Damn . . ." Marlene whispered.

"Yeah. Damn. And my husband is in some type of self-gratification exile, trying to be a monk, focused completely on selfless sacrifice, and gets pissed off at himself if he even remotely thinks of anything that would just be about him." Damali stood and began walking, raking her locks, her voice low and frantic. "It's crazy. I sat up with him almost all night and listened to him telling me about how, after all the self-indulgent shit he'd done in his life, he didn't have the right to drag the entire planet into his beef, and definitely wasn't trying to lose a brother or sister-in-law to anything he'd done. So his way of trying to make up for it was to give up any of his vices."

"Oh, shit," Marlene said, standing and beginning to walk in a dizzying circle with Damali. "But you're married—even ministers—"

"Yeah, yeah, I know," Damali said, holding up her hands. "But he wants to save that for procreation, which we're not ready to do, okay?"

Marlene stopped pacing. "Are you serious? Carlos?"

"Would I lie about something that freakin' serious, Marlene?"

Marlene covered her mouth, gaping, eyes wide.

"He wants to stay in conference with Adam and Ausar. Wants to remain battle focused and alert to deflect any incursion. Wants to have committee sanction from the archon's table before making any moves . . . wants—"

"But his best weapon was the fact that he was unpredictable!" Marlene nearly shrieked and then monitored her voice. "He was our side's loose cannon, our machine gun of high risk, our ace in the hole because his ass was so damned crazy . . . you have to heal his mind, Damali. Put the Caduceus—"

"He wouldn't let me near him with it," Damali said between her teeth, panic roiling so hard and fast within her that she was becoming nauseous. "Said if the Unnamed One did Lilith in a throne, and he had an old tie there, he didn't want any possibility whatsoever of that blackening the Caduceus, or entering me through him, and—"

"Go to Nefertiti," Marlene said, breathless. "She'll know what to do, maybe her or Aset, and then they can get Ausar to scan him, check him—"

"If I do that without Carlos's permission, have you any idea the humiliation that could cause, and then the fallout from that shit, Marlene?" Damali paced away to stand by the windows, hugging herself.

"You're right, you're right," Marlene said, her hands up before her chest. "I stand corrected. It's just that my placebo was designed to bring back joy, a reason to live, a reason to focus on the here and now between each pair, with hope burning brightly for the future—no matter the circumstances or how dark it looks right now."

She slowly brought her hands down and used the gentleness in her voice to make Damali look at her. "Love was there, strong, but hope was dimming. I used love to take us to hope. Hope is pure silver, Damali, you know that," Marlene said quietly. "Add it with love and it brings back weakened faith, *white light* even at the darkest hour. Once I truly understood what we were up against I knew in my soul that those guys needed a prime directive, a mission to remain cohesive so that fear and blame wouldn't splinter the team. After we wigged and brought down their battle high, because we were so scared, I needed a surefire way to get all the nagging doubts to stop. They needed a shot . . . er . . . in the arm, so to speak—and the women needed to feel that confidence so they'd rally with them. One mind, one body, one spirit—unbroken. Last night, everybody but the main one who needed it, got that. Listen to them out there. Carlos's booming laughter should be leading the trash-talking fest."

Damali nodded and fought a sob. "He has no joy in him right now, Mar. Fear has eclipsed hope—not for fear of what will happen to him, but to me or the team. His faith that he's being guided by the right side is shaky at best. The only thing grounding him is love. Guilt from things past is eating him alive . . . he even told me not to open my wings around him, in case something that will remain nameless from that throne accidentally attached to him. He won't let me lay healing hands on him, and barely let me hug him to drift off to sleep."

Marlene let her breath out hard and closed her eyes. "Baby, the man cannot carry that kind of guilt trip on his shoulders. Carlos being overly cautious is just as dangerous as his being overly reckless. You have to get him to understand that it was because his instincts were razor sharp that he picked up on an opportunity to hit Lilith's installation while it was vulnerable . . . while, I guess for lack of a better way to put it, while she was being coronated as queen vamp."

"It's the retaliation he's worried about. They hit her resources hard, and as long as it was a Chairman from the vamp legions, or whatever, he was mentally ready. But when he found out Lucifer had personally throned Lilith . . . I watched my husband walk away from the cleansing bath in a daze. He just kept saying, 'Oh, shit, D . . . *That's* whose head I pulled up while he was getting busy? Oh, shit.' Okay, Mar. That's where he's at. Now he is bracing for a retaliation that will make Cain's battles seem like a schoolyard brawl."

"They'd be coming for us like that anyway, though, in the final days," Marlene argued. "The Neteru Councils have been preparing for this for eons, and it was destined to happen at some point on our watch in all likelihood. Plus, Carlos had to know that if he hit Lilith's lair and even got her, that there'd be Hell to pay. It's just the fact that he actually interrupted the Devil and his wife that has Carlos so freaked out."

"Ya think?" Damali said, not meaning to be sarcastic, but having nowhere else to vent her frustration. "Plus," she added, mellowing her tone toward Marlene, "Carlos now knows that the strength of the newly installed Chairwoman is unparalleled to anyone else who ever occupied that seat—Dante included. That also means that the making of the Antichrist is not far behind. That's why Carlos is bugging. He feels responsible for the timing, for stirring the hornet's nest at a time when we, as a team, weren't iron-clad ready for what would fly outta that sucker."

"Look, he didn't know what schemes the Ultimate Darkness had," Marlene said, throwing up her hands. "Who knows such things? The man took a calculated risk, temporarily won, and made it out alive with all his men— weakening forces at a time when they seriously needed to get hit." Marlene began walking again, scratching her head, deep in thought. "Besides, if *that's* who had to install that bitch on a throne, wouldn't that seem like we'd done our job by seriously depleting their power options all the way down to the core?" Marlene stopped and turned to stare at Damali head-on. "That's our job. Tell the general, he did his job like a master . . . like a councilman, in fact. Totally unexpected, but right on time."

"I tried to tell him," Damali whispered from where she stood, speaking more for her own benefit than Marlene's. "I tried to tell him that his fangs were given to him and left within him on purpose, just like my wings were . . . that his learning about the Dark Realms is our strategic advantage at a level never known before by the Light. I tried to tell my man that all his business savvy from the streets, his fury, his charisma, his double-dealing, sexy ways were part of the grand plan."

Damali drew in a shuddering breath and hugged herself

tighter as new tears rose in her eyes. "And I tried to tell him that above all things, I respected him to the last cell in his body, no matter how much I might fuss from time to time . . . Mar . . . that's my man . . . my baby, and he's bleeding to death inside. But I can't stop the hemorrhage because this time he won't let me."

LILITH STOOD IN the topside clearing in central Europe calling the covens of old. "From London to Romania to Transylvania, worldwide, those who still remain in dark spirit and able to hear my cry, I beseech you . . ."

Her dark energy swirled from her outstretched talons, icy winds viciously whipping her death-black gown about her legs and arms, her hair eerily floating out from her body in a chilling black charge. With her head thrown back and all the passion of fury within her, she called them to her like wayward children. It was time.

"Mine, those of the most powerful among you left who took the dark oath of the covens, arise!" Lilith shrieked into the starless night. "Make good on your evil oath to serve the Dark Lord. Come to me, those of my blood pact, dark warlocks and witches, do my bidding!"

A night-cutting energy bolt left Lilith's talons to sear the darkness with black flames, opening what looked like a seam in the pitch-black horizon. The sound of missiles whirring filled her ears and made her laugh and screech in ecstasy as dark, torpedolike shapes hurled ever closer as though they were black comets.

"Yes! Yes! Come my children, we have much work to do," she screeched, whirling around in an excited frenzy.

The first projectile landed with an explosion that forced her to step back. Brilliant orange, red, and midnight-blue flames shot up vertically ten feet, and then a tall, gaunt warlock stepped out of the curtain of fire, swathed in a black cape covering his royal attire.

"Sebastian, you came . . ." Lilith cooed, and swept over to the warlock.

He took her hand and passionately kissed the back of it. "I pledged that I would be the first to always answer your call, milady."

"What has it been?" Lilith whispered. "How many centuries?"

"Too many to count," he replied, embracing her. "Tell me your bidding while I am still rational."

Five additional blasts rocked the area, causing Sebastian to release Lilith and shield himself from the flames.

The first warlock to step out of his fireball did so with chilling grace, and then fluffed his long black tresses and brushed off his formal black-and-white theater ensemble.

"Machiavelli," Lilith gasped, her eyes going to slits.

"At your behest," he said, glaring at the first warlock, and sweeping over to Lilith. He took up her hand and then caressed her cheek and looked around curiously. "I had heard rumor that Fallon Nuit was returned?" He closed his eyes as a shudder of anticipation swept through him. "Tell me this is so."

"He may be available, he may not," she murmured seductively, teasing him. "I could be jealous, unless you both share."

Machiavelli chuckled softly. "Fallon taught me *Dananu*, you know . . . even though he never gave me the full pleasure of bearing fangs. Callous brute—tell me, is he about?"

"Bargain with me in my language," Lilith said with a sinister grin, "then I might tell you."

"Do you remember where you marked me so many, *many* years ago?" he murmured in her language, making her briefly shudder.

"Like it was yesterday," she crooned, brushing his mouth with a kiss that left him swooning with excitement as she ran to greet the next flame.

"Jezebel!" Lilith screamed, not even waiting for the witch to leave her flame capsule. She barreled into the inferno with her, coming out of it carrying Jezebel, who was locked in a deep French kiss with her legs wrapped around Lilith's waist and her arms about her neck.

"You called," Jezebel said, breathless.

Lilith set the amber beauty down gently, running her talons through her long, thick, wavy hair. "He called, you know."

"Noooo . . . The *master*?" Jezebel fell backward, her sheer, black and golden bell-dancer's outfit beginning to smolder.

"In Vampire Council chambers," Lilith murmured, twirling a long strand of her jet-black hair around her finger. "Was amenable to a visit with me, you, and Delilah."

"When?" Jezebel whispered, appearing nearly faint.

"Soon, beloved. Soon. But first we have a quest."

The warlocks gave each other distrustful yet conspiratorial glances.

"And he did not call for me?" Medusa said, stepping out of the inferno in a huff, thousands of her baby serpents snapping. "Lilith . . . it has been ages." She adjusted her black Grecian robe and tried to adjust her tone. "Thank you for calling me now, however."

A battle-ax sliced through the fifth flame and a thickly muscled warlock stepped out in full black battle-armor regalia.

"My queen," he murmured, looking at her with a sidelong glance.

"Genghis," Lilith hissed. "We must catch up very soon."

He nodded and looked at the others with curiosity. "So many missing?"

"So many slaughtered by the Isis blade and the blade of Ausar," Lilith spat, sudden rage making her dark eyes glow. "I await one more transformation, and then we shall convene with the six oldest of your kind who can be raised."

"What Lilith says is true," Medusa hissed quietly, her serpentine gaze roving over Genghis. "Perseus, like Hercules, was a Guardian, but not a Neteru, or I would not be here, either."

Lilith clutched her chest in relief as the last flame flickered out with a blue-black wave of energy. A nude being stepped forward, her long, platinum hair her only covering, then it instantly grew out black at the roots to change into a curtain of darkness around her. She air-kissed Lilith on both cheeks as they embraced.

"Siren . . . you came." Lilith held her back, pleased.

"I was lost at sea, Queen," she said, her voice sounding like it came from within the endless echo of a seashell. "Your bidding is my pleasure."

"I have a riddle," Lilith said, gathering the witches and warlocks around her. "Something to challenge your skills and that of all the covens that follow you."

Wicked smiles of glee surrounded Lilith as the winds began to increase to lift her gown. "Here is the prize . . . winner takes some," she said, laughing and teasing them as she turned in a slow circle. "I never give all. But, for those who can ensure this plot works, there is a council seat available on The Vampire Council—you are looking at the newly coronated *Chairwoman*!"

She screeched and ran between them as their shocked expressions met her, and they slowly, one by one, dropped to their knees.

"Yes, I am still the Dark Lord's wife and familiar—his favorite among all others, but a plot more evil than any I could have devised has left Dante slain, as well as his son." She nodded slowly as she walked between her subjects. "Yes. Hard to believe but true. They both died at the hands of a Neteru, their fates sealed with a beheading by an Isis blade."

Machiavelli was on his feet first, followed by the others. "No . . . heresy."

"Indeed," Lilith said in a low hiss. "So, as you can see, pardon the pun, the stakes are high—are you game?"

"Just speak the challenge," Sebastian said in a superior tone, looking down his nose at the others.

"I want a spell . . . a spell like no other spell," Lilith murmured as her eyes slid closed and her arms outstretched. "I want a spell that will make you believe I have taken leave of my senses when I ask you for this, and it must spread like a virus worldwide to all covens to permeate the atmosphere where it can be inhaled."

"A plague," Genghis whispered. "Done."

"Not so hasty—that in due time." Lilith clapped her hands with twisted joy. "You'll never guess." She swept away. "It is genius, just genius—so absolutely wretched the Light will dim when I'm done."

Walking in a circle in the middle of their ring, she spoke in a low, conspiratorial tone. "I have called for Sebastian for his expertise in poisons and potions; Machiavelli for his shrewd political mind and intrigue in this time of planetary politics, to embroil the Neteru Councils and the Covenant at war with themselves; Jezebel for her lustiness and idolatry— her ability to sway worship of things false; Medusa for her venomous jealousy that had taken over her mind like a thousand serpents; Genghis, you, my general, will provide me battle insight to lead legions under spells of Darkness; and my Siren for your voice to affect the music, and to call the Neterus to their ultimate demise."

"This spell," Sebastian whispered tensely, raw lust causing beads of sweat to form on his brow, "the elements you seek can be easily included, but the delivery system . . . I must know your requirements."

"Up to this point," Lilith said, one finger on her pursed lips. "Men have ruled the Vampire Council—and in their blindness, they attempted to create a break between the millennium male and female Neteru. A nearly impossible task where soul mates are involved." She walked away with her hands on her hips. "No attempt worked. They tried to impregnate her to make a daywalker," Lilith screeched, throwing up her hands in disgust. "Men! So egocentric. Of course it failed. Then they tried to go after her mate, Carlos Rivera, and turn him permanently dark—but that failed, because they didn't factor in the pure white light essence of love. He'd never be completely dark as long as he loved her, for Light would be in his dead, black heart—*there* of all places! Dante should have known when he couldn't break him on his torture wall for loving her so."

Lilith walked away, gown billowing out from her legs as a

sulfur trail burned in her wake. "Fools! That man loves the very ground Damali walks on; even a demon-child could see it. She is his breath, was even his heartbeat when he was dead! And it is the same for her—and now that they have married under the seal of holy matrimony, we cannot even see where they are all the time."

"Then, how . . . my queen," Jezebel asked, unsure and glancing around, "are we to destroy them?"

"Create an aphrodisiac." Lilith looked at the stunned faces and laughed in a loud, screeching cackle. "It is so mad, so completely insane, it is perfect."

When bewildered expressions met her, she allowed her voice to sing out her answer in teasing bursts. "I have a little blood in my keep, from when Cain bit Damali, and she willingly gave him her throat." She skipped over to Sebastian. "It wasn't rendered at V-point, but there's heat and need and desire for the exterminated grandson of Lucifer in it."

"Say that you are simply stoking my appreciation for you with mental foreplay," Sebastian whispered, swallowing hard.

"It isn't strong enough to spark the creation of new life," she admitted, looking at her nails, "but it's toxic, that I assure you." Lilith looked up at those newly incarnated who had assembled to do her bidding. "I want that team to implode from the outside in. I want her so desirous of her Neteru husband that she's like a bitch Hellhound in heat—worse than a natural Neteru female ripening. Pure lust to darken and taint any love bond there is. I don't want her simpering understanding, her willingness to work through his issues; I want her fucking pissed off when he doesn't screw her on demand. Crazed is what I want! Totally offended that her Neteru female charms don't move him. I want her ego crushed, and her focus attacked, and his understanding patience of her flaws pushed to the breaking point when she smothers him. Corrode his silver so it never gleams again."

"Damn," Jezebel murmured with appreciation and wiped her brow.

"Yes," Lilith agreed, her eyes glowing and her expression tense as she walked away from them. "The male Neteru also sat in Dante's, and subsequently Cain's throne—both shared a link to Dante . . . one by paternal seed, the other by the paternal bite. There is waning residual energy there from Rivera . . . but what we have we shall use!" She spun on the group. "Dampen his libido—use guilt. Use distraction. Use duty and honor. Use whatever, but put out that flame. Make him so good and honorable that he is sickening," she screeched. "Strengthen his good attributes so that the Light does not detect foul play."

Lilith stopped and cast a glare around the half-ring. "A wife hotly pursing her husband would not set off alarms to the Light. A husband pursuing lofty goals is honorable—would not set off a Heavenly disturbance."

"But they would be at odds, soon enough, as frustrations claimed them both," Jezebel whispered. "It would be a quiet, slow, painful parting that begins with them not seeing eye to eye, not meeting each other's needs, and then they'd look up one day and might still love each other, but would not be in love. All passion gone. Other lovers could then enter the house to make it collapse on its own—free choice."

"Cain almost broke the code on that," Lilith said with a cool chuckle. "But his own ego got in the way, and he rushed it. Had he held out a little longer and allowed her a bit more frustration, he would have had her." Lilith shook her head. "Alas . . . but dear dead Cain was apexing and hadn't been laid in eons, so he was thinking with the little head." She smiled. "I don't have that problem."

"And the Neteru female leads a team of female Guardians, her sisters who are cloaked to our dark visions by their bonds of matrimony. But this Neteru *is female,* and her sisters will be happy while she languishes," Medusa hissed with a wicked laugh. "In their human frailties, they'll be so caught up in their own joys and futures, that they'll miss her sad eyes, the tone in her voice, the tension in her as she puts up a good front to preserve her pride and to try to be happy for their good fortune as any dear sister should be . . . all the while they will be blinded to her silent cry for help. Soon quiet, insidious, slithering jealousy will creep into her heart as she weeps and wonders, why not her? It is only human."

Medusa's sick laughter rang out into the glen and drew conceding nods and applause from the others.

"You get it," Lilith said, opening her arms for Medusa and then nicking her throat. "I knew you would see the genius of my plan."

Medusa clung to Lilith and leaned her head back to receive more attention as her serpent hair squealed in delight.

"And as men blindly prepared for war, the primary goal to protect their village—especially any women and children in their midst— dissension in the ranks would make their confidence wane," Genghis said. "Their male Neteru general distracted, divided, cannot effectively lead and will make mistakes."

"Talk dirty to me—you *know* I love it," Lilith murmured toward him seductively, handing off Medusa to Jezebel. She approached Genghis. "I knew your expertise would titillate my sensibilities."

"Through this devious plot, you have worked with the Light, the Heavenly edict of the One we leave unnamed. According to their laws—what has been put together, let no man split asunder—so you are not in violation of any edicts from On High . . . it is free will if the Neterus create their own household demise." Machiavelli laughed with a sinister chuckle and raked his fingers through his long, wavy, dark hair. "*Bella . . . grazie,* and done so *lentamente.*"

Lilith pointed at him, and sent a pleasure charge his way. "Now there's a man who understands politics. Plausible deniability at every turn, especially during the onset of the Armageddon."

Machiavelli bowed with a shiver. "Always glad to assist, milady."

"It will affect her voice," Siren said in a faraway tone.

"Her words will become sharper, her attitude brittle as bitterness sets in. Her comments sarcastic. Her music riddled with anger, not hope. But her voice will also be trapped, for whom will she admit this devastation to? It would be shameful for a leader, a female general—a heroine who is supposed to embody all wisdom and compassion toward humanity—to be so mired in her own personal battle of such humiliation. Her Guardian sisters would be disappointed and hurt that she felt any resentment toward their joy for any reason whatsoever; her Neteru Queens would be aghast. In her pain and isolation, Damali will ultimately call her Neteru mate to his own demise as he runs headlong from his household to get away from her . . . which will make the rest of their ship vulnerable, their crew shark bait. I love this plan, Lilith. It is perfectly beautiful, just like you."

Lilith blew Siren a kiss that made her hug herself. "You are the last important piece—her voice." Lilith closed her eyes and made black static-charged fists at her sides as she spoke. "Put it in the air, in the water, in the food supply. I do not care the delivery system. That is your mission and your conundrum to resolve. I don't want it to affect a single human except Damali Richards. I want her to be the one climbing the walls and distracted, and completely focused on—"

"Things of false importance," Jezebel said in an impassioned whisper.

Lilith shuddered. "*Yes,* and you can have this night with me for the most profound understanding of this objective. You win the door prize. You and Medusa, for her deep, serpentine insight." Lilith smirked. "Tsk, tsk, Sebastian. It is not like you to miss out on ducal rights. I'm almost disappointed."

"My potion, which is what is required to collect the spells and blood remnants, regardless of specialty, will redeem me and make you wish you had chosen me as your first option. I will let my work speak for me thus." Sebastian flung his cape over his shoulder in a huff.

Sighing with complete satisfaction, Lilith looked at the

witches and warlocks and ignored the disgruntled first-night losers. "You know what the reward will be, something none of your wicked spirits ever attained before your deaths. But as a Level Seven entity with powers to confer your dark essences to a Vampire Council throne . . . do my bidding," she said in a low rumble. "And do it *well*."

CHAPTER FIVE

Damali and Marlene reentered the living room knowing that for them to stay gone from the group longer would unnecessarily raise worry. They could hear the strain in Rabbi Zeitloff's voice blaring in the speakerphone.

"Daniel, online conversion courses? Over the computer?"

"I want them to like her, and you gotta be the mohel at the bris if it's a boy." Dan paced, raking his hair while all the brothers drew in with solidarity.

"He needs a cover story to chill out his mom and pops," Jose said. "Bobby and Krissy are lucky, their parents are here. But like Inez's mom, we can't pull in the Weinsteins, so they'll need constant vigil over them, like Inez's mom and baby."

"Yeah, because if we go in and leave a tracer that could put his mom and old man in danger, none of us will be able to live with that—but this man has gotta be able to let his people know he's all right, happily married to a nice Jewish girl, and might be a daddy." Rider landed a heavy palm of support on Dan's shoulder as Dan continued to rake his hair.

"Thanks, Rider . . . Jose." Dan looked at Heather as the women on the team gathered around her. "I just need to be sure she's okay, Rabbi, and I want my parents' blessing . . . after all I've seen, ya know."

"Oy, Daniel, Daniel, Daniel, you make this old man have an ulcer!"

"It is for the greater good," Monk Lin said softly.

"What—my ulcer?"

"No, Daniel's ability to get a family blessing on his union," Father Pat said calmly with a slight chuckle.

"If there's a child in the offing, then family cohesion is paramount," Imam Asula said. "Honor thy mother and father . . . thus—"

"Okay, okay, I don't need you to quote Old Testament to me. I cut my teeth on Old Testament, Asula. Humph!"

"Listen," Carlos said in a weary voice. "I can whirl you, Dan, Heather, and me to his parents, black-box it, let them meet, and leave. I can pull up right outside their door. You be there as the cleric that they've been corresponding with all this time, they can meet Heather, then we drive off in a car, go around the corner, and be out."

"And who might you be, how do I explain you, Mr. Rivera, who looks like a G.I. Joe action-figure marine? Their son is supposed to be on a kibbutz! You all have me, a man of the faith, lying through my teeth—and at the end of days, I don't mind telling you people, this is unwise a thing to do—am I the only crazy one here? Is it me?"

"He was on a kibbutz, sorta, Rabbi," Rider said with a grin. "I looked it up to be sure I knew what it meant, as I'd hate to lie to clerics or have them lie . . . it's a—"

"Collective settlement," Dan said in a rush.

"In Israel!" the rabbi shouted.

"Does it have to be, or can someone who's Jewish be in it to qualify?" Heather asked, panicking.

Marlene cringed and placed a finger over her lips and stared at Heather, who had slumped back.

"Do you see the problem, here, Daniel?" Rabbi Zeitloff shouted.

"Ain't no problem," Shabazz said. "Do it like this. You go in, you say, 'Hi, Mom, Dad, I've missed you and love you. While I was away on the kibbutz I met this beautiful woman—her name is Heather. She converted for me, and you're gonna be grandparents. You already know Rabbi from the letters he was good enough to send with pictures.' "

Shabazz sat back in his chair when the speakerphone remained silent. "Then, you wait and let your mother scream, hug you, and hug Heather. You let your dad slap your back. Our man Carlos gets introduced as Special Services, Black Ops—the leader of your division—a division with no name. C-los rolls in there with five-star general gear on, leaving a mental suggestion, but never lying to your parents, and doesn't speak beyond a 'Nice to meet you ma'am, nice to meet you sir.' Then you say that you are not at liberty to say what you really do for a living but it is very high up, pays extremely well, and that you are working strategically for world peace—which is the only reason your wedding was so rushed and you denied your mother her big wedding glory. But your rank and mission give them bragging rights in their neighborhood." Shabazz looked at Carlos. "Then you glance at your watch and state that it's o-whatever-hundred hours it is, and time to move out. Let Dan and Heather hug and kiss their people—and be out, brother."

"That's a plan I can live with," Carlos said, pounding Shabazz's fist.

"That's some smooth shit, man," Jose said, and then checked himself. "I mean, stuff."

"Where's the lie?" Carlos asked, directing his voice toward the speakerphone.

"You sound like a vampire!" Rabbi Zeitloff shouted.

"But will it work?" Dan asked, wiping the sweat from his brow with the back of his forearm.

"It has potential," Rabbi Zeitloff fussed. "I can do it, but at its core, it's as rotten as—"

"At its core," Monk Lin coolly interjected, "is the honorable desire of two young people who have found love to make their parents a part of ushering in a new generation."

"Give me a break."

"Love," Father Patrick said.

Imam Asula chuckled. "I think we have a solution."

"Rabbi?" Dan asked, standing over the speakerphone. "Please. This is really, really—"

"Oh, all right! You put it all on my head; if I say no, then I'm against love, and you've ganged up on me. I do not appreciate this kind of group pressure for a man of my age. But I like Daniel, he's a good young man, and this Heather, I'll like her more when she converts and I don't have to lie to Daniel's mother and father that he married a nice Jewish girl. All right."

Dan's shoulders slumped in relief and he closed his eyes. Rider practically caught him around the waist to keep him from falling, but grabbed him by the shoulders instead.

"Thank you," Dan breathed out.

"Thanks. We'll call you when we get settled in San Diego," Carlos said. "Peace."

The moment all good-byes were said and each cleric hung up, Dan clicked off the call button, and pandemonium broke loose. Slaps on the back almost made Dan fall. Calls for beer to go with the room service order rang out. What had begun as a midmorning strategy meeting had turned into a raucous room party.

"I told you to call him, man," Jose said, laughing. "You gotta get that no-fear in the cojones."

Dan and Jose squared off, faced each other, and made ugly grimaces as their arms made huge, bicep-straining U shapes in the air. "No fear!" they shouted in unison, and then burst out laughing.

"Champagne and brew on the way," Mike hollered, holding up a phone extension.

Heather went to Dan and hugged him, hiding her face against his neck as he stroked her hair. "You did that for me . . . all of that just for me? The whole team, too . . ." Her voice wobbled and broke. "Thank you, Dan. I love you."

"Aw, man," Rider said with a broad smile. "We might lose

a man at the party, might go AWOL and back to his room—hurry up with the food, Mike!"

Bobby stood with his back against the door and arms outstretched, blocking a possible exit. "One beer with the team, dude. It's protocol."

"I'll go see what's holding up the food," Carlos said with a tight half-smile. "Maybe I can just go to the bar and bring back that part of the order."

"I'll help," Damali said, jogging over to leave with him. "You'll need extra hands to carry all those six-packs," she said, making excuses when he cut her a sharp glance.

"Cool." Carlos lifted his chin as Bobby stood aside, laughing.

"Bring back some natural juices for Heather, too," Bobby said as he rolled his body away from the door so Carlos and Damali could pass. "We gotta take care of our lady in waiting. No alcohol for her."

Carlos didn't answer, just nodded.

"I'll make sure to bring something up just for her," Damali assured Dan, and then slipped out the door with a sigh.

THE GOLDEN-FANGED KNOCKERS at the door didn't even ID check her with a strike, her power signature was so strong from her unprecedented coronation. Messenger demons had genuflected as she passed and strode down the long, narrow crag beyond the Sea of Perpetual Agony.

"Bring me that cowardly little satyr," Lilith commanded to her Harpies as she swept into Vampire Council chambers.

She sat with a weary but satisfied thud in the council throne that headed the blood-veined, pentagram-shaped table and drew a golden goblet of black blood into her clutches. Intense weeping made her peer over the rim of her goblet, and then the huge black marble chamber doors suddenly opened.

Four Harpies flew forward dragging a half-eaten satyr across the floor. They unceremoniously dropped him at

Lilith's feet and he immediately drew away to hide under the table, whimpering.

"Fetch him and hold him on the table before me, since he likes to hide."

The satyr covered his head, screaming "*No!*" as the Harpies dragged him out of hiding and flung him down on the hard surface, splashing blood. Immediately the vampire crest in the center of the table took offense and sank huge fangs into the satyr's spine that came out through the small, fawnlike creature's abdomen. A puddle of urine soon spread, causing Harpies to shrick in hot disgust.

"Do not make me get up out of this chair," Lilith said in a deadly whisper and then cleaned the offense away with a wave of her hand. She stood. "Now. Firstly, I bet you wish you'd never betrayed Cain and had remained loyal to the end?"

The satyr nodded quickly, blue tears running down his face.

"You Pan creatures are so fickle and given to such wasteful excess and mischief, but this time you've really gotten yourself in trouble, haven't you?"

"I'm sorry, miss. I didn't know. We just wanted to run and play, and didn't want to fight anyone," he whined, beginning to sob.

"See, that's the problem with being in the middle, not making a commitment, especially in the end of days—you were committed to nothing, so you must now endure everything."

"Oh, no!" he wailed and covered his face.

"If you had sided with the Darkness and Cain, you would still have a place . . . like my dear Harpies," she said, petting the largest one that fought to be near her. "Or my bats, or messengers. Even my pit bulls have a place in the realms."

When the satyr's cries escalated, she leaned over him with a hand at each side of his trembling body. "Silence!"

He sucked up a sob with his lip quivering.

"If you had sided with the Light, even if you were killed,

a highly probable thing . . . you would be in a place of utter bliss," she whispered and pulled back. "Completely boring and disgusting by my standards, but at least you wouldn't suffer."

Folding her arms over her chest, she peered at the terror-stricken creature impaled on her table. "But as a reasonable woman, I'll bargain with you for a do-over, a chance to make a wise choice a second time around."

"I'm on your side," the satyr said quickly, nodding. "You, miss, I choose you."

She shook her head. "Delightful." With a sigh, she sat down. "Now, I need to understand better how Nod works . . . you see, Cain's time there in the Light did not translate to our thrones. The data was garbled. Only his dark passions and lusts and plots did we receive, but the way Nod works, what fuels it, how things . . . grow there . . . we could not see for the blinding Light."

"Nothing grows in Nod," the satyr said quickly. "It is the same, ages very, very slowly over eons. It is pure energy, that's why we wanted to leave. There's no food or water, only energy to quench you, but stable, even energy and no procreation. We cannot even mate, it is all mental stimulation . . . so you see, Miss Queen of all that I'm bound to uphold, that's why we tried to leave after Cain."

Panic shot through Lilith and made her pace. Her mind quickly seized on the reality that, if nothing could grow there and could only remain in stasis, then her fertilized egg was simply languishing without a procreation or life-energy jolt. It didn't matter that it had been successfully couriered into Nod while the seals were breached and Cain was at war sending hybrids over the barrier between worlds. Nor did it matter that it was stored within a willing host. It would remain there, possibly for eons at a time when her husband had called for her to bring forth his heir.

"Are you sure, satyr?" she said, suddenly sweeping to the frightened fawn.

"Yes," he cried, beginning to sob again. "That's why we

followed Cain's energy trail out—only Hubert was strong enough. He was biggest and Cain's opening then was such a horrible tear that a few of us slipped out behind him. But the others are trapped inside because it takes a Neteru's call to be released." He covered his frightened face with his hands. "Only his warriors could pass both ways on his call while he fought. But once he died, they cannot get out, either. But those two Neterus, they can go in and they can bring out warriors for you, Miss Queen. They both went there and visited Cain . . . and he really liked her. His energy still resonates with her there, I'm sure."

Lilith returned to her throne quiet and intrigued. "A diversion," she whispered, talking to herself as she shut her eyes. Helpless refugees, angel hybrids, or soft, doe-eyed, confused little creatures would draw out the protection instincts of a team that had befriended their kind, she thought with a wicked smile. Human Guardians couldn't go in, but who could resist a little satyr begging for amnesty after having learned the error of his ways? . . . Especially one that is half-eaten and bloodied and brutalized? It would shock their sensibilities; it would be like mutilating a puppy or a baby seal . . . perhaps a small child. Neterus couldn't leave it. The satyr would tell them that angelic beings were being slaughtered by Cain's loyalists, and he'd picked up the beacon.

"She'll go because she's a Powers angel, a healer," Lilith murmured as a deep chuckle consumed her.

Suddenly she stood and screeched, making her bats whirl in a frenzy within the twisting smoke above her throne. "She will go," Lilith shouted, extending her arms and clenching her fists, "because she'll be all alone and heartsick and will cling to the need for a divine purpose to give her life meaning! She *will go* because where she is brings her such pain that she will want to redeem her dark thoughts through helping others! Angel hybrids like her! She will go—because Damali will want to heal all the injured and bring them to safety and build an army of feather-bearers in the end of days!"

Lilith threw back her head and laughed. "And she'll go and

jolt my near-dead host with a life-force jolt to make her live again, and unwittingly spark conception with the Caduceus in her hand and tears in her eyes—then Damali will bring my vessel out into earth's atmosphere where my heir can live!"

She spun on the little satyr and walked over to the table. She leaned down and stroked his belly, toying with his fragile life. "Isn't that brilliant? I guess I have to repair you a bit and let you live, even though I had my heart set on fawn-human for dinner tonight . . . I haven't had such a delicacy since Zeus's time."

"Please don't eat me, Miss Nice Lady Queen," he whispered, squeezing his eyes shut as Lilith allowed her fangs to elongate. "I don't taste very good."

A deep chuckle filled the chamber as she studied him and then licked him between his legs and up his belly as the table retracted fangs to drop him. She kissed the places that had been butchered and allowed the satyr to heal, giggling with the sinister knowledge that while she bided her time, she'd maim him again even worse before dropping him at Damali's feet one night. But for now, he had to remain alive.

Lilith sighed philosophically. "You like my plan to let you live so you can run and tell Damali that she must help the hybrids still trapped in Nod?" She ran her finger over his belly button, causing the hairy little creature to shudder with need, and cooed when a small, pink penis rose out of the hair between his legs. "Aw . . . how cute."

Harpies covered their eyes, squealing.

"I like your plan—it's brilliant, Miss Queen," he said, inching away from her as she brushed his tiny pink member with a huge fang.

"Good," she cooed, beginning to sway like a serpent. "Because only a woman could think of something like that."

The strike was instant; blood splattered several Harpies, and the piteous satyr's scream made bats fuss in flight.

CARLOS WALKED AT a pace that Damali could barely match. His eyes were forward and his jaw locked tightly.

"Hold up," she said, jogging to keep up with his long strides.

He ignored her, jaw pulsing. Finally at the bottom of the exit landing, she was able to jump down four steps and stop him with her hands against his chest.

"Whoa."

"We gotta get the beer and juice, D. People are trying to party."

"No. That shit can wait. I need you to just slow down and talk to me—please."

He looked away. "What's to talk about? The team is cool with the decisions that were made, they came to a consensus, we're moving to San Diego."

"But I never heard your opinion in the mix, baby." She folded her arms over her chest.

"I ain't got no opinion," he said, still not looking at her.

"Why?"

"Because all of this is a moot point, anyway."

"Why?"

"Because even though we hit her lair in what was already a topside, hot war zone," Carlos said, not using Lilith's name as he folded his arms over his chest and stared at the wall, "the entity that did her coronation almost broke down Christ—that's how strong that mug is. So, let's party, yo. I'm with Rider. What the fuck diff does it make at this point? Huh? 'Nita wants a hot tub in the room so she and Jose can get their freak on—I'll bring one in, pronto—she just gotta tell me what color. Dan wants to say good-bye to his mom and dad and get a blessing before his ass dies; I'm with that. It's the right thing to do. Mike wants ribs and whatever room service has—heeey. No problem. I'm so cool with all this shit, it doesn't even make no kinda sense, D."

Speechless, it took her body a moment to move when he began walking again. She understood Level Seven to mean the Nameless One, but dang, the way Carlos put it about that being the one to tempt Christ made her shiver. *That* was a bold mug, as Carlos called it. She ran to catch up to him and spoke in bursts from sidelong glances, passing other resort guests.

"You're right, I'm panicked, and me and you now have to work as one to do whatever we can at this point."

"I'll tell you what we can do," Carlos muttered. "After that dumb shit I just did, we can all bend over and kiss our natural asses good-bye."

"You're not giving up on me," she said, jogging to get in front of him to make him stop.

He shrugged. "Naw. I'm not giving up, just being real." He tried to round her but she body-blocked him, eyes wide. "Look," he said, glancing around. "You of all people know that we shouldn't even be having a conversation like this without a prayer seal."

"You're right, you're right," she said, holding up her hands. "Thirty seconds, let's do it, because brother, I need to talk to you—maybe reality is just sinking in. Will you give me that?"

He begrudgingly nodded while she closed her eyes and murmured a prayer for white light to surround and seal their private, marital conversation.

"All right, first off," he said, leaning in close and glancing over his shoulder as he spoke through his teeth, "you didn't take the charge off that throne, I did. So don't act like I'm some punk because of what I felt and how I'm reacting."

She touched his arm. "Baby, I do not think that. I trust your instincts to the letter."

He stepped in closer, held her arms, and closed his eyes. "I thought I had felt dark, or twisted, or depraved, but . . . oh, shit . . . there was no bottom to the blackness—and I'm ninety-eight percent disconnected. Can you imagine what would have hit me if I was still locked in? I'd be drowning in my own drool and fucked in the head for life." He stepped away from her, breathing hard. "They don't know. The brothers don't get it. Shit—I didn't know. I didn't get how evil the Ultimate Evil was, and *I had been to Hell on a throne.* You can't conceive it, can't wrap your mind around its vastness, just like the human mind is incapable of understanding the Ultimate Light . . . but as above, so below. My problem with all of this is, this time I dragged *that* to our team's doorstep."

She grabbed his upper arms hard, frantic, and almost began shaking him. "Carlos, you might have felt what you felt, know what you know—knowledge is power, like you always said and learned as a weapon from them . . . but, baby, please, please listen—you didn't drag anything to us that wasn't coming for us regardless. The Armageddon was gonna kick off, and we're a Neteru team, so we are in the path of the tornado, the funnel cloud. They were coming, it isn't your fault, and anything that happens to anybody on the team isn't on your head—it's fate. They were chosen to be Neteru Guardians and they answered the call. Honey, don't blame yourself," she whispered urgently, and then hugged him hard.

They both fell quiet as a maid walked by. But she stopped and grinned at them too wide and too long as she pushed her cart. Then a flicker of glowing darkness entered her eyes as she slowed to speak.

"Yes it was his fault," the maid said, laughing, and then hurried away.

Damali almost screamed. Carlos had her by the hand going in the opposite direction in a flat-out run. He was so shook that he couldn't even focus to fold them away, and she was on the border of such instant panic that her shoulder blades were bulging and threatening to present wings. They practically crashed through the door and made Guardians stand up in unison.

"Don't eat the food, center of room, evac now, leave anything behind!" Carlos shouted.

"What happened?" Shabazz moved fast, sending a credenza across the room with tactical energy to block the door as the team huddled.

Carlos opened his arms, adrenaline spikes making him dizzy. "They breached a freakin' prayer barrier between two married Neterus—that's what the fuck happened, 'Bazz. We're out!"

"YOU DIDN'T," LILITH said, laughing and shaking her head.

"I did, my darling. . . . And I told you I would flush them to you in a panic to begin our little dance," Sebastian murmured as Lilith reclined in his large, circular bed staring out at the Carpathian Mountains.

"But how did you manage to break *a prayer barrier* between two married Neterus?" She lifted herself up on her hands and knees and crawled toward him, stalking him for answers.

"Do you really want to know?" he crooned, taunting her.

"Don't toy with me, Sebastian. I am in a very dangerous mood."

He tilted his head to the side, unafraid. "Make me a councilman."

"Or make you dead—spit it out." She folded her arms over her naked breasts.

"All right, you're no sport at the moment, I see."

"I'm exhausted, having to think of everything and set wheels in motion . . . I now better understand Lu's lament about always being busy. He's not just a workaholic; there is vast incompetence that must be coped with. So, you were saying—so that I do not rip out your heart."

Sebastian folded his arms over his narrow, sallow chest and lifted his pockmarked face, indignant. "Am I not the greatest warlock you've known? Sleight of hand, my darling."

"Sleight of hand? I must understand this trick."

"Hunches, playing the best of hunches," he said, watching intrigue glitter in her dark eyes with great satisfaction. "Hunch number one: have witches the world over in the various covens hone in on where seven or eight wedding ceremonies took place in a hurried condition—same day. Not like Las Vegas that does hundreds, or a municipality. But the exact number all in the same facility. That was clue number one."

"Brilliant," Lilith murmured, easing down to lie on her side. "Tell me more."

He lay down beside her, tracing her arm. "Then track the silver. We wouldn't be able to see it, but it would appear like a blinding supernova to our dark coven forces blocking them—and in that blindness is where we should go." He sighed, his expression smug. "And once they found that, they should look for couples who have an extra Light around them . . . and listen to their conversation. If the witch or warlock was deaf to what they said, then it was one of them."

Lilith cradled his cheek. "You never disappoint me with your treacherous mind."

"And if a beautiful woman was arguing with a handsome man who fit the description that we all know . . . the familiar has only one thing to say: 'Yes, it was his fault.' To reinforce his guilt and hysteria and to rock his faith that even his prayer barriers with his wife can now be breached . . . And to make him think your husband can track him from the throne." Sebastian laughed when Lilith's eyes got wider. "But he can't, of course . . . however, our male Neteru doesn't need to know that." He kissed her as her mouth gaped. "You wanted dampened libido, worry, fear, self-recrimination. I delivered, Lilith—and I'll have your potion ready soon. So . . . what is my reward?"

"Two more days and nights of *hard* negotiation with me . . . how's that for starters?"

SHE'D NEVER SEEN her husband do a power foldaway with no clear destination in mind, and drop the team hard, off-course, in the middle of a public beach, then have to mind-stun civilians for a second until he could get himself together. He was breathing erratically, wild in the eyes as she stopped time with everything in her for a few seconds to give everyone a chance to adjust.

His heart was slamming into his chest, sweat drenched his clothes, and he hated the fear scent folded into it. The whole team stunk to high heaven like that for the first time because he lost his cool, the way he saw it. Lucifer's familiar was strong enough to break a prayer seal. His mind stretched and almost snapped from the concept. He grabbed Damali's hand.

"Me and you, open a channel to the Covenant. I need a location. A new compound location—seers on your mark. I want Father Pat in this mix. I need barriers up when we whirl again." His gaze raked Damali and Marlene, then the slithering memory that Father Pat had really broken from the church, had lost faith in the formal organization of it, and was operating as a rogue cell within it, made Carlos begin to hyperventilate. "Bring Imam Asula in as backup, with Monk Lin and Rabbi. Oh shit, we need a squad with no shaky vibes, right through here."

Marlene clasped Damali's other hand as the team drew in closer. "I'm going higher than that—I'm calling Aset."

ALL SCREAMING HAD ceased by now. Time meant nothing, there was no way to sense it, nor had he the inclination to do so. Once the Dark Lord had reached up his rectum to his skull, dug in claws, yanked, turning his entire being inside out, the pain that accompanied that vile act was beyond futile.

He'd learned that the gurgling noises his twitching body made only delighted the Harpies. The Master of all Darkness had left him to the feral little beasts that took great pleasure in ripping away bits of his soft, exposed flesh, turning him into their version of shredded beef. Master's Hellhounds were no better. They'd savaged his remains, growling and fighting over bones that they ripped away from tissue anchors as vermin and beetles, every pest from the Amanthra realms, took up lodging in exposed organs that now writhed from their invasion.

But in their depraved glee, the Harpies had made sure he missed none of it by slipping into the coveted abyss of unconsciousness. No . . . they took turns sitting at his head, sticking their long, flicking tongues into his exposed gray matter, gouging it and keeping it awake as they regurgitated black blood into it.

There was no peace. No respite. He tried to focus on the pain to keep from imagining the next horror the master would visit upon him when he returned—for surely the Dark Lord would oblige whatever fear scenario the Harpies siphoned from him.

The sound of cloven hooves against marble made his almost boneless body begin to convulse with the foolish but instinctive need to escape. Squeals of terror escaped his fractured larynx as both the sound and vibration neared him. Incessant, excited bickering and squabbling from noisome Harpies made him try to worm his fetid carcass away in a slow, slimy ooze across the floor.

The jolt that assaulted his rectum voided his bowels and made his prone form go stone rigid as the blast slowly dragged his body right side out one inch at a time. The moment the last crackle receded with a juicy pop and his lungs and Adam's apple lodged into place, the wail he released was so intense that the Harpies laughed and clapped for the master.

"You are fortunate," a low, rumbling voice said as the hooves began to sound farther and farther away. "I have much work to do to ready my armies and do not have time to devote to your torture. Thank you for keeping my wife's pets amused during my absence, Fallon."

Nuit's nails dug into the cavern floor as he pressed his face against it, quietly sobbing. His body was now only a disorganized sack of meat and flesh. Hell dogs had snapped away vertebrae and ribs, and bones in his arms and legs, leaving jagged pieces that now pierced his abraded skin. Only the small bones in his hands and feet remained with his skull that the Harpies had guarded to save his brain, bones obviously too small for the dogs to bother themselves with to squabble over.

"If you can stop being such a pussy," the deep voice beyond Nuit said with a languid sigh, "I have a job for you . . . now that you understand a small measure of my wrath."

"Anything!" Fallon bleated. "Anything, my Darkness, just, I beg you . . ."

"Yes, yes, I am well aware of your state of agony. Do not waste my time with entreaties—do my bidding."

Fallon nodded with his eyes squeezed tightly shut, too terrified to look up into the eternal darkness that surrounded him for fear that he might see the Dark Lord's eyes and draw his displeasure. "Yes," he gasped. "Your bidding is my every breath."

"Good. We have come to an understanding, then. An accord." The vast darkness breathed out slowly and methodically. "My wife . . ." it said in a thunderous echo, chuckling and then seeming to choose words with care. "She is the most treacherous bitch in all creation. She would turn on me in a heartbeat, if she could . . . this is what I so love about her. She keeps things interesting. However, I need a pair of eyes in council, eyes now so terrified of my wrath that they dare not make a mockery of this second chance to leave my torture facility."

"Beyond terror," Nuit said, pressing himself closer against the ground. "Stricken."

Deep thunderous laughter filled the cavern. "Good . . . very good, because she was never at this place of complete acquiescence. Despite her torture, Lilith had games embedded in her psyche so deep that even Harpies would never be able to siphon them all. Each one, however, was like a jewel just waiting for the moment to surprise me with one. Last month I found out just how much that is her core. Games, duplicity, thy name is Lilith. But trust me, Fallon, I will be so much less lenient on you than my beloved spouse. Are we clear?"

"Crystal, my lord," Fallon whispered.

"She holds up under torture so much better—I lashed out at her, personally, for a month. You could not endure twelve days with her pets during my absence . . . while I spent precious time with her."

Nuit gulped, unable to fathom what that experience might have been.

"No . . . do not try to comprehend the incomprehensible," the Dark One murmured, his voice soon becoming more distant. "Watch her for me and report all to me. Betray me and I will not be so lenient in the future. Fail me and I shall release eons of frustration upon your miserable carcass. I know she has a plan with my heir, but I want that monitored so that it does not become her heir alone. She is devious."

"I will be your everything and shall not fail."

"Indeed." Another hot, fear-generating breath filled the darkness and then wall torches lit. "Repair him."

Quiet surrounded Nuit and for a while he kept his cheek flattened to the dirt. Before long he could see the hem of scythe-bearers' robes. One stood beside him with a weapon held high, and the moment Nuit looked up, the demons smiled and brought the blade down midthigh, cutting half of the damaged stump off above where the Neteru blade had taken his leg.

A roar of anguish left him limp, and just when he thought he could bear no more, hungry Harpies raced to the new wound site and began to eat away at the exposed meat.

Screaming in agony, Nuit tried to pull back with his fingers, but with virtually no bones in his body, he was no more than a sack of quivering, jellied flesh.

"He said it was over!" he screamed, sobbing. "He said I was to be his eyes and ears—relent!"

They stopped. His wormlike body slumped in fatigue. But soon he saw their purpose as several Harpies began vomiting regenerative black blood into the wound site. He watched in awe as the bloodied nub began to slowly grow with new bone and tissue. Then a scythe-bearer bent and produced a cured human stomach filled with black blood from under his robe and brought it to his parched lips that he might drink.

Nuit greedily sucked at the regenerative substance, choking as he took it in as fast as he could. Spent from the first feeding in more than two weeks, he closed his eyes, feeling soothing warmth begin to invade his fevered body as beetles and pests exited through every orifice and pore. Slowly, damaged organs knitted back together, and missing parts grew out of the small scraps of tissue that remained. Broken bones mended but made him scream with agony as they snapped back into place.

Sweat covered the new skin on his naked body, and another scythe-bearer came to his side to feed him again. This time it cradled his head as he drank, its red glowing eyes gleaming within its hooded robe. Fallon trained his eyes on the vacancy within the robe and it showed him his old throne. Tears of relief slid down Nuit's face while he finished the offering, the sweet elixir of life coating his insides with ecstasy.

As the demon that held him stood, Nuit grasped its wrist for support to stand. His new leg was numb, but from all appearances, he wasn't marred. The face in the hooded robe went black for a moment when the scythe-bearer closed its eyes and nodded yes.

Without needing to be told it slowly lowered itself to the floor on its knees with the others, making a small circle around it and Nuit. The hooded entity then turned around and lifted its robe. Nuit glanced over his shoulder into the vast darkness beyond, but the need after regenerating from near extinction was too great to deny. No less than he could have denied the blood offering presented to him. He dropped to his knees, mounted the messenger, threw his head back, and wailed.

"I CAN WAIT," Machiavelli said in a smooth but annoyed croon, causing Sebastian to leave Lilith's body in fury.

The two warlocks squared off in a black-bolt challenge, but Lilith's hiss created a temporary cease-fire.

"You come into my bedroom, waltz in without an invitation!" Sebastian shouted, poised and ready to send a blast at the well-dressed intruder across his bedchamber.

"You Romanians are too volatile and impetuous," Machiavelli tsked.

Lilith's gaze narrowed. "You know how much I enjoy your company, my dear, but your timing was more than rude and threatens my patience."

"*Scusi,* but this is why I came, *bella.* You cut me off for Sebastian when his impetuous move could have backfired on your ultimate plan."

"Liar!" Sebastian shouted, drawing on a heavily brocaded burgundy robe.

"Why thank you," Machiavelli crooned. "Compliments like that might gain you the favor of even my company one night."

"Speak quickly," Lilith said, growing exasperated as the two Old World warlocks sparred with words. "Sebastian is a strong warlock. Your charges had better be valid this time, Machi."

"To be sure," Machiavelli said with a gloating scowl as he walked slowly back and forth in front of the large circular bed, speaking as though he were in an Italian court again. "Sebastian is indeed a strong warlock, his specialty potions and poisons—but that is where his expertise lies and should have remained. He does not know the twists and turns and outrageous complexity of the human psyche like I do."

"Make your point," Lilith said, growing nervous as the thwarted orgasm ebbed.

Machiavelli stopped pacing and stared at them with his hands behind his back. "Lilith," he said, curtly. "Have you any idea what striking complete fear into the male Neteru could alternatively do?"

He waited a beat. "Play with the concept on your palate."

Lilith slowly stood.

"Yes. It might kill his libido as he rallies troops, calls Neteru warriors from his King's Council—and it would draw his mate into battle cohesion with him, any potion to build her lust counteracted by her survival imperative."

Machiavelli walked away ticking off charges against his graceful fingers. "The team that was to be in bliss would panic, all lovemaking cease, as they prepped for battle to follow their Neterus to their deaths . . . so what would there be to be jealous of?" He spun and looked at Lilith. "Your entire plan could crumble unless you can re-create a false sense of security for these people. They need a period of normalcy for any of this to work. I can help with that, if you immediately remove him from our liaison—I'm sure you understand that I'd gladly share bodily fluids with him, but not warlock strategies."

Machiavelli shook his head and laughed with an evil scoff as Lilith screeched and flew at Sebastian, slapping and clawing at him while he covered his head and yelled, "You fucked up, signore. Move over, she's my conquest for the night."

CHAPTER SIX

Violet light began to overtake Marlene's third eye. Damali was so shaken that she neither complied nor objected. The team had such wild looks in their eyes that each and every one of them seemed about ready to keel over at any second. But the moment Carlos synched up to the fact that Marlene was summoning the Neteru Queen Council pyramid energy, he opened his fist, had the blade of Ausar in his hand, and rammed it into the sand.

"Aw, hell no!"

Damali's time distortion broke. Curious but amiable beachgoers looked at their team in passing and went on their merry ways, none the wiser that they'd just stepped out of a dimensional fold.

"We just got played," Carlos said, walking in an agitated circle. "You know what . . ."

Damali watched him, trying to remain calm as no one said a word. She could tell he was so pissed off that blue-white static was flickering at the edges of his nostrils. But it was good to see that—rather than the other way he'd been.

"Never again!" he shouted, walking a hot line back and forth in front of the team and drawing slight glances from the occasional passerby. "I'm never in my life again gonna be chased out of my own house or wherever I am," he said, talking with his hands and almost stuttering. "We take a stand, right here, right now—if this is the big one, so be it! We were chosen to be here to hang because *somebody* must have thought we could! I am so fucking pissed right now, you just don't know!"

Unblinking eyes stared at him. Nobody moved, nobody said a word, nobody breathed for what felt like very long seconds.

"Aw'ight, C, what's the plan, boss?" Shabazz said, the first to break the silence. "I'm down for whatever."

"It was a damned familiar," Carlos seethed and then spat. Confused glances passed between team members.

"Y'all wanted San Diego, all right, we're in San Diego— just a little ahead of schedule, aw'ight?" Carlos walked away and headed for the surf.

"Is he okay, Damali?" Marjorie asked in a quiet tone after a moment. "This doesn't feel Carlos-normal, you get me?"

"He's under a lot of stress, Marj," Damali said in a low murmur, giving her teammates the eye not to press for more right now. "Hold tight, I'll be back."

She jogged down the pristine strip of beach to where Carlos stood and watched him rake his hair with his fingers, drawing in slow breaths with his eyes closed and face tipped up to the sky, as though summoning calm with every fiber in him. Rather than interrupt him, she just stood as a soothing presence beside him—at the ready for when he was more able to talk about it.

Within her bubbled a very quiet prayer, one for peace and understanding, hope, and no casualties this time around. They were blessed, regardless of all the drama they'd endured. Carlos had brought them to a place that boasted of seventy miles of pristine beaches situated between the Laguna Mountains and the Anza-Borrego Desert where the northernmost point of La Jolla offered three-hundred-foot cliffs.

As wild as the last fifteen minutes had been, not to mention the last twenty-four hours or so, a sudden peace claimed her soul as she stood next to her very agitated husband. Going inward, she sensed the land and drew its elements of beauty to cloak her, sharing that vision with every seer in the group. Then she drew in the wondrous vibrations and scents of the nature around her, allowing that to pour as balm over the shattered nervous systems of her tactical and olfactory squad members, saving the gentle natural calls of the serene environment for her audio, Big Mike, for last.

Before long a certain knowing overtook her. Carlos had put them down within the oldest and most exclusive district of La Jolla. This place was an extension of Carlos's land homing pattern, where his regal spirit could claim residence amid his ancestral trails. It had Spanish and Indian vibrations in the very sand. It was all him—high, majestic cliffs from his old existence of owning a lair, and would befit a warrior's sensibilities by being surrounded on three sides by the sea with the steep slopes of Mt. Soledad at its back. At high enough elevation, one could be alerted to anything coming before it approached. He was, after all, a Neteru.

But she tried not to think of that right now, the very real issue of war, choosing to focus on the Mediterranean-like balmy temperatures and the way she could sense that the streets rolled up by midnight, all residents indoors and relaxing at home. Peace.

Yeah . . . Upscale boutiques, art galleries, restaurants, good elementary schools set in turn-of-the-century, stunning Spanish architecture and eclectic designs. University of California San Diego campus for all the newbies, and maybe even her, to get that chance to do something normal that they'd never done before. High-tech industries and state-of-the-art labs that would make J.L gasp. loaded with free-thinking geeks so prevalent that there'd be a supportive community for him and Krissy here, too.

Naturalists, herbalists, green-space folks who respected Mother Earth. Seabirds; Bird Rock. Protected marine sanctuaries and an idyllic crescent of sand sheltered from storms, a hang glider's paradise. Azure water, gleaming sand. Sandstone bluffs, natural kelp beds that drew gray whales and seals, with busy sea lion rookeries, a world-renowned zoo, beautiful family parks, museums, and an elegant presidio . . . oh, God, in Heaven, she was nesting, too—and her husband had found the perfect spot for everyone on the team, even shooting at it blind.

She understood his terror, because that's what he most wanted to do—nest, come in off the road of high stakes and high drama. To make it all just cease for a while, make it all go away.

Carlos took one look at her face then opened his arms not saying a word, and she filled them. He pressed his cheek against her hair and began to rock her gently to the pound of the surf. She understood, could feel it through his skin, his pores, his breath, why he'd been so angry with himself . . . why he'd gone after Lilith wild swinging—because of this. He wanted to preserve this. The peace. His right, more so than to bear arms, but also his right to a place where he and every other man he respected could raise a family in peace. He'd gone after Lilith swinging hard, swinging blind, and then realized that he might have actually drawn something worse than her his way . . . their way, jeopardizing more than his personal interests.

Damalie hoped that her gentle, steady caress at his back conveyed that she'd heard him, no words necessary. Her steady, calm breaths said that she trusted him, respected him, no matter what; he'd done what he felt he had to do. Finally she could hear his breath stabilize and he kissed her hair, slowly letting her go.

"I got us here ass out, no weapons, and no luggage . . . I guess I should go see if I can get everybody set up in a temporary hotel so Dan can work some real estate magic, and, uh, go back and get our gear from Tahiti."

He was looking down at the sand when he spoke, an embarrassed half-smile tugging at his mouth. She kissed him and tried not to smile too wide.

"I think I can get us set up in a hotel. We'll manage." Her

insides were screaming with a thousand wife-worry questions that all began with 'Are you sure,' but that was the thing—in order for him to be sure it was cool, he had to get back his confidence at the scene of the crime. Of course he wasn't sure, but the only way for him to reverse that was to face the thing that had shook him head-on. So she fell back, trying to keep her vibe easy and confident. "I'll let everybody know what's up, and by the time you get back, we'll be somewhere busting a grub."

"You sure?" he said, watching her retreat toward the group.

"Yeah, we're good," she called over her shoulder. She forced her tone to be light and upbeat as her mind bleated a hundred prayers at once—*Lord, let this man be all right, don't let the Unnamed One snatch him when he goes back.* From everything she'd learned from Marlene-the-wise, as well as her dear queen, Nefertiti, making the man lose face in front of the team by having to explain that he'd temporarily wigged was just as bad as putting a blade in his confidence. So she walked, glancing over her shoulder just once with a strained smile.

Concerned stares met her as she returned to the group several yards away, and she stood in front of Carlos's blade that had been rammed in the sand, body-shielding it from onlookers as it slowly dematerialized into nothing. The moment he was gone, team hysteria broke out, and they hit her with rapid-fire questions all at once.

"Okay, what's the deal with our boy, D?" Mike said. "He wigged. I ain't seen Rivera battle-freaked like that in my life."

"Took the words right outta my mouth, Mike—and probably just gave me a Bride of Frankenstein streak of gray hair on my head," Rider fussed and then spat on the sand. "Can't do that to us old dogs; our hearts can't take it. Sheesh!"

"I'm saying, D—sheeit, if there's something major going down at the hotel, we ride as a team. It can go down, you feel me?" Shabazz folded his arms and set his jaw hard.

"He blocked a transmission to Aset," Marlene said, her

gaze firm. "What was that about? The way he pulled us out was like a code—"

"No lie," J.L. said, unintentionally cutting Marlene off. "The hairs are still standing up on my neck from that shit."

"Ya mean?" Jose said, coming in closer. "What was it, D? What'd your boy track?" He looked around the group. "It had to be big—my boy wouldn't have—"

"We've gotta set up base camp, stat," Dan said, beginning to pace.

"Roger that," Berkfield said. "We've got how many hours of daylight left, folks?"

"Okay, okay, wait!" Damali said, outstretching her arms. "Everybody breathe. Chill for just one minute." When Dan looked like he was going to fire another question, she repeated the command. "Breathe." As the disgruntled team complied, she looked at Marlene. "We do this by the numbers. Seal this conversation with a prayer."

"I thought holmes said that's what freaked him out—that something was strong enough that a prayer didn't work," Jose said, outright terror starting to creep into his expression.

"All right, stop right there." Damali held up her hands with her gaze landing hard on each pair of eyes before her. "*That* is *the last* thing we want to get into our heads and spirits at a time like this." She allowed her gaze to travel around the semicircle again. "In the end of days, all you got is your faith—so you'd better water and feed it real good. We clear?"

Nods of agreement came back as her answer.

"Seal this meeting with a prayer, Marlene."

Damali waited until Ashé had been said, and then she folded her arms over her chest. She drew a deep breath to bring additional confidence into her voice. Her brief reminder to the group was as much for their benefit as it was hers—because she'd actually seen the thing get up in her and Carlos's conversation.

"All right, we can stand down. Here's what happened. We

were talking and a familiar made a side-out-the-neck comment that was a little too close for comfort and it freaked us out. Our bad."

When stunned expressions met her she pressed on. "All right, don't act like it couldn't happen to you guys. We're a little jittery, after the thing that went down last night—all right." Damali let her breath out hard.

"But a Neteru duo . . . D, be straight with us." Shabazz stepped in closer. "For real."

"I'm being real," she said, watching the team's shoulders relax. Every person had an expression on their face between relief and fatigue, as though the quick scare had taken ten years off their lives. "Look, as I calmed down, and Carlos and I talked and sensed for a tracer back there," she added, motioning toward the shoreline, "he and I realized that there were several variables that we had to consider, not the least of which was the fact that the familiar who'd spooked us could have been trolling the halls of the hotel, as they often did, targeting overly intoxicated guests."

"Yeah . . . they do that," Shabazz said, finally relaxing and getting a fist pound from Mike as he stepped back.

"Right," Damali said, gaining more confidence as her own logic ran full tilt. It had to be that, God, please. "Or it could have been slinking around those unfortunate victims who were always out looking for action that they wouldn't realize, until too late, they'd probably never recover from. Hindsight being twenty-twenty, the little resort parasite was most likely just picking up on Carlos's tension while we were walking to go get the drinks, so saying anything related to that once we were deep . . ." She rearranged her words to shelter the privacy of his guilt trip and their argument about it, but Marlene still gave her the eye.

"Once we were deep in convo about our next moves," Damali said, picking up where she left off, recovering on the fly. "We were talking under a seal when it slinked by us and said something smart—but because of where our heads were, we got hyped and processed it wrong. So the whole drama amounted to an old-fashioned, 'psyche your mind.'"

For a moment, no one said a word. No wonder her husband was pissed off at himself and embarrassed . . . how many daggone hotels had they been in and seen that basic type of demon? But under the circumstances, she could definitely understand his knee-jerk reaction to err on the side of caution.

Slowly, smiles broke out on faces and team members began shaking their heads, rubbing the backs of their necks, and running their fingers through their hair.

"Dayum," Jose said. "Aw'ight, I'm good now. But don't take a brother there."

"Whew." Berkfield just rubbed his face with both palms.

"I'm saying," Shabazz muttered, as the rest of the team muttered their relief.

The only person who remained a little edgy and distant was Marlene, like she was only half-buying the story. Damali wasn't about to tell her that there hadn't been enough time for her and Carlos to discuss all of that, much less reason it out. The team needed to feel like he was just erring on the side of caution, and that was it. Protecting his dignity was paramount right now.

"Okay, guys, here's what's up," Damali finally said, trying to wrest back cohesion and keep everybody cool, despite her own fears. "Just like old times. We find a hotel—base camp. Dan gets on the phone to do his thing, just like we had to do with the Beverly Hills mansion that got trashed; the old house and property gets donated to the Covenant as a tax write-off so we're open to buy a new joint. J.L. and Krissy set up the fax and Internet connection with the Covenant and bless the transmission in white light."

Dan nodded. "I'm on it, D. We get settled in, handle our business, and get the Covenant ready to do the purchase—this time, with us in a blind limited liability partnership—each couple with an equal percentage share and the Covenant with ten percent ownership."

"That's my brother," Damali said, hugging Dan. She knew he was always on point, but now more so than ever before, he had a purpose and would be on top of his game.

Damali let him go with a kiss on his cheek and settled her gaze on the women on the team. "You know the drill, ladies. All seers, you heard Carlos, start envisioning where there's an adequate property, and Dan can do his thing—cash. Wire transfer makes people stop haggling all the time. Carlos can bring in what you mentally shot him this morning, plus scavenge what we need from the old compound. So we dooo this. If I know Carlos, your bags will be at the hotel when we get there. Then we can all go find us a good restaurant to bust a grub."

"They've got a Ferrari dealership down on Prospect Street, I think," Jose said with a broad smile, looking at Dan. "Plus, down on Avenida de la Playa," he added, looking at Bobby, "They got surfing shops, glider-port joints—it's all you, man."

Damali just looked at him and didn't say a word. While she was glad that the team was starting to normalize, still, it was going to take a while getting used to all the newly hybrid team talents. She just shook her head as they trudged up the beach. A tracker . . . a nose . . . that could see? Jose? Who'd gotten it from his wife? Yeah, these were some very strange days and times, indeed.

"THEY ARE BOTH partial to the sea," Sebastian murmured as he stood over his poisonous batch deep within the Black Forest. Night creatures stirred, the moon was full, and he swept his arms over the top of the magic-charred kettle to increase the heat with a blue-black lightning bolt. "Call them to the water, Siren, where her oracle works best. They may still be in the Pacific." He stroked his familiar, and the gray tabby arched and hissed, then nipped his hand. "There, there, precious," he crooned. "You did very well."

Siren leaned over the dark cauldron that was angrily frothing and gazed into the swirling morass of evil intent with

opaque eyes and released her voice. Vicious tendrils of potion shot up and wrapped around the airborne sound that
turned sallow in their grip, strangling and grasping it to drag
it down into the bubbling hot mixture.

"Excellent," Sebastian whispered. He looked at Medusa
and for a moment she backed up. "Give it to me!"

She stepped forward with a scowl and closed her eyes.
"I'm sorry, my babies," she said quietly, and then yanked out
a handful of squirming, hissing hair. She dumped it into the
caldron and turned away as the baby serpents screamed for
her, repeating "Mommy," in high-pitched wails. The slurry
in the cauldron sent up a sulfuric stench and nearly bubbled
over, and she waited until the nasty brew had calmed before
she added her potion to the spell.

"Do your work," Medusa said, hugging herself. "Slither
into guilt and past misdeeds, home to unreleased agony and
pain and grief . . . and break her."

"There," Sebastian murmured, his voice thick and oily
with triumph. "Was that so hard?"

Medusa shot him a glare and hissed. Unfazed, Sebastian
turned his attention toward Genghis, who unsheathed a
blade, stepped up, and opened his palm over the batch.

"Yes, add your blood, General, that she will battle herself
and her husband as though she were battling your hordes,"
Sebastian murmured, and he watched with dark fascination
as Genghis slit his palm and a long, thick drizzle of oily-
black blood made the contents in the cauldron sizzle and
then flame up.

"Almost ready," Sebastian said in a low, pleased voice as he
jerked his attention to Machiavelli. His gaze narrowed on him
as he watched the competing warlock preen and straighten his
clothes after having just left Lilith. "You're late."

"I was here as soon as I needed to be . . . I'm sure you
know why I was detained."

"Add your element!" Sebastian shouted, rounding on
Machiavelli, who stood calmly, but with black-bolt charge
dancing at his readied fingers.

As Sebastian swept up to him, Machiavelli spat. "Add it yourself, or have none. You want my disdain—there, you have it."

Furious, but needing to quickly get the acidic saliva into the brew while fresh, Sebastian hurried over to the cauldron and leaned close to the bubbling surface. Angry tendrils of blackish-green potion leapt up and licked his face, making him cry out as the scalding substance raced over his skin. When he pulled back, breathing hard, Machiavelli smiled.

"Surely, you didn't expect a gentleman to endure that." Machiavelli adjusted his billowing sleeves. "Will that be all?"

Sebastian lunged, but Genghis caught him.

"Complete the batch," Genghis ordered. "Or I'll kill you both."

"We don't have time for this," Medusa hissed. "We must deliver it now, under the current auspices. If one fails, we all fail. You know what Lilith told us. Her wrath is tied to the master's wrath, and surely none of you want to experience that." She looked around the small clearing, and slowly order was restored.

"Jezebel, your share is the final element I need. My sweat has been added to steal her focus, to make her work hard and invest sweat equity in all the wrong things. We have all lined the cauldron with our spells. But, you, my dear, are literally the cherry on top . . . your element will drive her to insane lusts."

Jezebel smiled as she sauntered over to Sebastian. "Compliment accepted."

She slid into his embrace and threw her head back as he slid his palm down her stomach until it slipped beneath the edge of her sheer pantaloons. A deep moan echoed in the clearing, making bats take flight as his gnarled fingers thrust into her canal and came away with green, translucent slime.

"Perfect," he whispered, bringing it under his nose for a shuddering whiff and then submerged his hand into the cauldron.

The mixture went still for a moment and immediately

cooled. He laughed hysterically and began to withdraw his hand from the slurry, but just as soon as he did, thick, passionate tendrils whipped up his arm and tried to yank him down farther into the batch. Genghis immediately grabbed him around the waist and hauled him back. Machiavelli assisted at arm's length, sending sharp black bolts to cut the tendrils at their base. The moment the last one was severed, Genghis and Sebastian fell away and hit the ground with a combined thud. The cauldron sputtered, flamed up red hot, and then cooled.

"Call Lilith," Sebastian said to Siren. "Tell her to give it to the Harpies to dump in the Pacific Ocean—her potion is ready."

CARLOS WALKED BACK into the suite that they'd abandoned, sensing. It was definitely a familiar that had been the culprit. The nasty little thing had sniffed the door but couldn't get in because of the prayer barriers. He let out his breath hard, too frustrated for words. Dan could handle group check-out by phone. There was nothing left to do here but begin the boring task of dragging everyone's belongings together in its purest, subparticular state to help make the load lighter and to white-light blast it clean before dumping it back on the team.

The only thing he wouldn't deconstruct was Damali's silver collar. Who knew what that could do to the delicate balance of her stones, and right now, they needed all the divination help they could get. Plus, with Zehiradangra still grieving so hard, who knew what his so-called helpfulness might cause. He sure as hell didn't want to find out.

Crossing the room and double-checking again for any signs of incursion, Carlos picked up Damali's silver and gemstone necklace and clasped it in his fist. He briefly closed his eyes and nodded.

Yeah, baby, that's a good choice, he mentally murmured to Damali. *The Valencia . . . Old World charm, plush suites, in the center of the shopping district—cool. Yeah, I'm on my way . . . miss you, too, boo.*

What was he worried about? This run felt like he'd just gone to the corner store to pick up some milk and bread.

SHE HADN'T SAID a word when J.L. stood close to the reservation desk next to Dan, and mysteriously the computers found reservations for nine VIP suites. The fellas just shrugged with too-wide grins, and she made a mental note to tell Dan to somehow make quiet restitution with the establishment so they could make their soon-to-be highly inconvenienced guests whole. She suspected that the mansion they were seeking might have similar results—people oh so willing to sell the ideal place that they might not have even been considering leaving, and at a reasonable price. Damali sighed as the concierge came over, eager to help, and began handing out keys. She'd beg forgiveness later.

Yeah, but, D, think of it this way, Marlene said in a mental chuckle. *We're saving the world, so some VIP benefits come with insane membership into this club . . . a little courtesy, ya know?*

Damali smiled and rolled her eyes good-naturedly. *Just make sure Dan hooks those folks up some kinda way, please.*

From the corner of her eye, she spied Carlos smoothly mind-stun guests and workers in the lobby for a second and then slip next to the bellman's area with two large luggage dollies filled with the team's gear. He held up her necklace to her with a sly smile and then tossed it to her as she neared him. Laughing, she caught it with one hand, glad that the old him was gradually coming back.

LILITH WALKED INTO the midnight clearing, her long Vampire Chairwoman robes softly swishing over the dried grass and leaves in a light rustle. Pleased, she dipped her finger into Sebastian's deadly concoction and pulled out a dripping, oozing glob that she summarily popped into her mouth. The ecstasy spread over her face as she closed her eyes and murmured, "Excellent . . . Your best batch ever, I believe, Sebastian." With a cluck of her forked tongue, she called her pets to her robe hem. "Release it underground into the sea from Hell."

Bats in the barren trees squeaked in delight as barrel-chested Harpies opened a small cavern in the earth, grabbed the cauldron by its huge round handles, and dragged it into the pit.

Lilith looked at Sebastian and folded her arms. "I guess you've earned your keep, if this works."

"It will—"

Sebastian's words caught in his throat as he ducked and an Amazon battle-ax whizzed through the air, narrowly missing him but beheading Medusa. Black blood spewed everywhere as Medusa's hands futilely clutched her headless throat. Her hair began to flame with screaming serpents while her head spun wildly on the ground like a top out of control.

An Amazon war cry fused with screeches from demon bats, Harpies, and the assembled witches and warlocks to shatter the night. White-light arrows shot into the darkness, torching anything they connected with, and coming at the dark coven out of the unseen void. Black bolts whirred out into the nothingness like tracers, with witches and warlocks taking shelter behind trees and black charged shields, trying to get a directional bead on their attacker. Lilith had instantly transformed into her battle demon form, her huge leathery wings and spaded tail slicing at the darkness as her fangs lengthened and talons presented.

Lilith was off the ground, going airborne when another female warrior voice, an all-too-familiar voice, made her turn to glimpse over her shoulder. Then her body jerked, and Lilith released a furious screech. Out of the void stepped Eve with two Isis daggers that she quickly stabbed onto Lilith's tail to create leverage and, using strength that was unexpected, yanked Lilith out of the air, swung her hard, and made her collide with a tree.

The tree groaned, leaned, and snapped, forcing Siren and Jezebel to run in the opening. Nzinga was on Siren in a heartbeat, releasing a razor-edged boomerang that took Siren's head off before she could open her mouth to scream.

"My son?" Eve hollered, advancing on Lilith, while Nzinga and Penthesileia kept the others at bay. Eve released a battle cry that made lightning whiten the sky for several seconds, blinding the coven. "Tonight is our night to finish it!"

As Lilith flipped up, Eve opened her hand and Madame Isis filled it. Genghis sent a powerful black bolt into Eve's back, causing her to fall as he advanced on her with chain and mace. With a two-handed blow she severed his weapon, eyes wild, causing him to fall back. Lilith flew up for an aerial attack, drawing a funnel cloud of enraged Harpies and bats with her as she yanked the daggers from her tail and flung them at Nzinga and the Amazon Neteru.

The Amazon caught one of the blades and flung it sideways at Machiavelli, who was quickly advancing with a saber—catching him in the liver. He recoiled, holding the wound, stumbling back with electric charges sparking wildly from his right hand. But he stumbled into Nzinga's grasp—who had dropped to one knee, caught the other dagger, and promptly grabbed his long wavy hair to yank his head back and slit his throat. Just as suddenly, Eve had Genghis on the ground, Isis dagger over his heart. He sent a black charge into the Isis to deflect it, only to see Eve's eyes go to black glowing slits for a moment as her sword drank in his dark current and then ejected as pure white light, exploding his body beneath her.

Lilith shrieked in the air at the sight of Eve walking out of Genghis's embers. Whirling on Jezebel and Sebastian as they tried to escape, both Nzinga and her Amazon sister chased them and cornered them in a stand of trees at the edge of a ravine, while Eve ran after Lilith, lobbing white-hot death bolts at her from the Isis.

Backing off the cliff, Sebastian tumbled into a free fall, while Jezebel used the diversion to open a slit in the dirt to disappear. Frustrated, both Neteru Queens turned on the aerial battle Eve was waging with Lilith, deflecting any bolts aimed at their sister and drawing the funnel cloud toward them.

Instantly swarmed, both Neteru Queens locked elbows together and ran in a circle of ever increasing speed, battle-ax and boomerang edge extended until they were a blue-white blur that collided with Harpies and bats. The collision between the funnel cloud and the Neteru energy whirl was brutal, tossing out gray and black mutilated demon carcasses in sparking cinders, breaking the cloud's momentum. Injured and straggling Harpies attempted to get away, and seeing herself outnumbered, Lilith opened a yawning cavern in the ground and dove for the safety of the pit.

Eve's rage was white-hot, and the first Neteru summoned the natural trees to her advantage, lighting them with screaming Neteru fury. She rammed the Isis into the earth and then opened her arms and threw back her head.

"What was mine had thrice been taken—my husband's peace, and two of my sons' lives. I demand recompense, Lilith! Fry, bitch!"

Fury made Eve's Kemetian braids rise from her shoulders as her fingers spread, with arms outstretched, causing the huge ropes of underground roots to quickly grow and then knit together in what appeared to be a blue-white spiderweb blocking the cavern. Lilith was moving too fast to stop, momentum had become her enemy. The massive tree roots lit just as she tumbled into their giant network to become hopelessly snared.

Screeching and twisting in agony as the white light electrocuted her, Eve didn't miss a beat. Yanking the Isis from the ground as her sister Neterus joined her at the cavern's opening, Eve leapt over the edge onto the root network, scaling it with blade raised to get to Lilith.

Nzinga and Penthesileia guarded their sister as she perilously advanced, a bleating war cry in their throats the moment Eve put her foot on Lilith's chest, raised the Isis, and plunged.

But something stronger and darker than Eve had ever felt

ripped Lilith through the roots, forcing her to lose her balance and tumble into the abyss behind her. Frantic, Nzinga and Penthesileia immediately put their hands together, drawing an energy line between them that Nzinga drew into her fist and hurled over the edge, yelling Eve's name.

Swinging doubled-hand swipes blind, going down like a rocket, Eve sliced at unseen demons and scythe-bearers, backing them away from her hurling form. Lit tree roots held the slowly closing cavern open just enough for Eve to look up at the incoming Light beam. Demons that tried to grab it or attack it, fried. Still, she was hurtling too fast to catch onto it. But the intelligence within all Light dropped it down beneath her and then wrapped around her, slowing her descent so as not to snap her back, and then quickly pulled her up in the opposite direction.

She landed at the edge of the pit in the arms of her panicked Neteru Queen sisters, but the frustration of nearly conquering Lilith had put blood in her eyes. Holding the Isis blade like a cannon, Eve shot power pulses of Light into the yawning pit behind Lilith, screaming invectives that made the moon shudder.

"You whore! I will rip out your womb myself, for all you've done! I will visit a plague of Light upon your filthy throne and hand-carve my name into the top of it, you bitch!" Silver tears of fury streamed down Eve's face as cinders from exploding demons and sulfuric ash belched up from the earth.

But a slow, ominous rumbling made the Queens fall back, and within seconds the blackness that flowed over the edge of the open pit was so dense that the lit tree roots sizzled to charred black and fell away. Legions of scythe-bearers poured over the edge. Undaunted, Eve clasped Nzinga's hand and Nzinga clasped Penthesileia's hand, forming a trinity around the Isis. Violet pyramids opened on their foreheads, a blue-white bolt of shared purpose connecting them that quickly ran through their bodies as though they were ground wires, hit the blade, entered the dark earth, and sent a fast-moving white carpet of nova-energy to fan out from them. Demons melted, dying screaming, only billowing sulfur remaining. Then it went quiet, so still, that the Neteru Queens didn't move.

A low, warning snarl echoed up as the ground snapped shut.

Eve's eyes narrowed as she looked at her sisters. "This time her husband came. We must warn Adam and the others."

BURNING AND SHUDDERING from her injuries, Lilith clung to the huge leathery wings that surrounded her. A sinister laugh filled the cavern.

"Eve seemed upset," the beast mocked as he dumped Lilith on the floor of her Vampire Council chambers. "That was expensive, resource-wise . . . but she's grown stronger. Rage is gorgeous on her." He looked down at Lilith as he opened a vein on his wrist for her to siphon. "Next time maybe I'll ask her if she's game for a three-way."

SEBASTIAN AND JEZEBEL made it to a cave, breathless. They stared at each other for a moment, listening hard for any signs of the Neteru Queens.

"Four of our coven," Jezebel whispered with a hiss. "A sneak attack from the Queens of old like I have never witnessed—and this wasn't even the whole of their number . . . Lilith unable to defend us," she said gulping air out of breath from their flight. "What does this portend?"

Sebastian came to her side quickly. "Come nearer so that I might tell you," he said in a breathless whisper. He waited until she did, then immediately drew a poison-edged dagger and slit her throat.

Her stunned gaze met his sinister smile as she staggered back, gasping, the opening in her throat gurgling with blood. He watched her fall slowly to her knees, the shock of his attack still in her eyes.

"It means that the Queens helped narrow down the competition," he said smugly as he watched Jezebel die. "Machiavelli taught me that."

IT HAD TAKEN almost a full hour to get all the rooms properly prayer-barrier readied, and even longer for everybody to settle in, check their weapons, and come to a consensus about what to eat. Marjorie gave up refereeing and curled into a ball on the sofa while everyone finally decided to order in for the meeting.

In the remotest part of her mind she heard them talking. Yes, she agreed, it made sense to get something here, now, and then venture out a little later more rested. A lot had transpired. Rabbi was coming in tomorrow. Dan and Heather and Carlos would meet the Weinsteins. Shame they couldn't meet the whole team, she dreamily thought as consciousness ebbed. It was good for parents to know where their children were and who their friends were . . .

She was back home at her parents' house. The swing set she remembered was brand-new. She had on Mary Jane shoes and had long blond pigtails tied with blue ribbon; it was after Sunday school. Someone who made her smile was pushing her higher and higher.

Gabrielle! Her mind screamed it in excitement, but in her strange dream, her mouth didn't move. Her sister was young again, and they were laughing. But then Gabrielle's eyes got sad as she touched her face.

"I have to go soon, Marjorie," Gabrielle said. "You be a good girl and run home and tell them adults everything, okay? Don't keep secrets."

Marjorie shook her head. She remembered the secrets of how Gabrielle was touched the way no one is supposed to touch a daughter. It was too terrible and she squeezed her eyes closed, her mind screaming: *Don't leave me. You're my big sister and I love you!*

"I love you, too," Gabrielle said, cradling her face. "Look at me—you must hurry," she said in an urgent tone that made the child within Marjorie open her eyes. "They made a spell.

Dark covens. I could not hear it because of the barrier to darkness here in the Light. But tell the adults you live with that they must be careful. Tell them to get my . . . to get Jasmine and Heather to touch the stones and to see if they can know what trouble is coming your way. I love you. I must go. Mommy and the rest of the family are here."

Huge tears of disappointment filled Marjorie's eyes. *Can I come, too?*

"Not yet, little one," Gabrielle said.

But if Mommy's with you and all our sisters, where's Daddy? I don't want to be left with just Daddy all alone, Marjorie wailed inside her mind.

Gabrielle kissed her on the center of her forehead. "Don't worry, sweet pea, he didn't make it up here. God bless him."

Marjorie Berkfield awakened with a gasp and a sob. The team stopped talking and planning to stare at her.

"I miss her so much," Marjorie sobbed, covering her face as Berkfield and Bobby raced to her side with Krissy. "Oh, God, she's gone!"

Berkfield pulled his wife into his arms. "It's all right, Marj, it'll be all right."

"No!" she shouted, twisting in his hold. "She said this time I have to tell the adults. They made a spell."

Not a sound beyond Marjorie's forlorn wails and the team's breathing could be heard in the room for several minutes. Then, one by one, people took their positions.

"Me, you, Tara," Heather said quietly. "To the beach near the stones."

Dan shook his head. "Not in your condition . . . if there's a spiritual attachment or something, honey, please, no."

"I got your back," Juanita said, stepping in for Heather.

Damali stood. "My oracle's down, still grieving, but maybe if I get her some sea water and access Aset for a divination— hey." Without alarming the group or Carlos, she knew she had to break away to get to the Neteru Queens Council. She'd felt a power surge within her that made her fingertips arc with static. It was going down, and it was big. She knew it.

"I'm with it," Inez said. "If the bitches are spell-casting and working roots, oh then it's on. I got people in my family in Brazil and in Haiti on Grandma's side that don't play that. They won't start it but will finish the shit, guaranteed. You know, like they say, 'Don't start none, won't be none.'"

"Now they done jumped into my yard, hard—conjuring heifers . . . a dark coven, is that what Gabby said, Marj?" Indignant, Marlene tilted her head with her hands on her hips. "Your sister came in an astral visit and specifically said that? Now they're sending warlocks and witches, because we've slain all their vamps, huh—is that it?"

Marjorie nodded and sniffed hard, calming as she wiped her face. "Yes. But now I also know for sure she made it. I had hoped, but didn't know."

Marlene went to her and hugged her tightly as Berkfield eased back. "I felt like this with Christine . . . it hurts, but there's peace in knowing."

Marjorie nodded sadly and pressed her face against Marlene's shoulder as Marlene rubbed her back. "Thank you."

Krissy left J.L.'s hold and went to her mother to create a three-way female hug. "I'm going, too. We all loved her and what happened to her just wasn't right."

Damali glimpsed Carlos, but could tell he had gone somewhere very remote within. It was in the way the muscle in his jaw pulsed as he stared out the window in profile. But that was only right, given how Gabrielle had been tied to his best friend Yonnie . . . a vampire still MIA and behind enemy lines. Now she thoroughly understood why Carlos had freaked. The man hadn't overreacted at all.

PART

II

The Honeymoon Is Over

CHAPTER SEVEN

Trying to take everyone to the beach didn't make sense, but that was just what looked like would happen. She needed to get Carlos alone for a generals' powwow, and she could tell by the way he bristled that he was uncomfortable with the team's swift-moving tidal wave of emotion. They both turned and looked at each other at the same time.

"Hold it!" they said in unison, making the group go still.

Carlos crossed the room and folded his arms over his chest, blocking the hotel suite's exit. Damali came to stand beside him. He gave her the nod, silently yielding the floor.

"Look, the first Armageddon seal has been opened, and all of our nerves are raw. So, before we do anything that could put anybody on this team at risk, we need intelligence."

"D's right. If the dark covens opened up like Marj got from a spirit dream warning, then before any of the group touches some polluted stones, picks up an attachment, or anything whack that could go down, me and Damali need to find out just what's up."

Shabazz glanced at Marlene, who nodded. "No argument."

"Good," Carlos said, his line of vision going around the

room. "Then I suggest, since there's a funky vibe out there, me and Damali go check it out while you all keep moving forward on handling our team business.

"Dan, on getting us a base camp—stat, and Marlene on getting the Covenant over here . . . seems like we're gonna need backup."

"Roger that," Dan said. "I'm on it."

"Cool," Carlos muttered. "Then, we're out."

DAMALI CLUTCHED HER silver necklace, looking at the seven stones set within it that hadn't been active since Cain's demise. The oracle pearl that contained the she-dragon—Zehiradangra's pure spirit essence—almost seemed to have died.

"Maybe I should try to rouse her," Damali said as they neared the pounding Pacific surf.

"Hold up, baby," he said, grabbing her arm before her Tims touched the water's edge. "I cannot put my finger on what has me so jumpy." Carlos scanned the waves, watching families and surfers along the coast. "Find a tidal pool; don't put her in the direct waves."

Damali stared at him. "Why not?"

"All that surfer dude energy out there, families . . . ships, yachts. If Zehiradangra is grieving so hard and has gone so far within her own spirit that she won't come out and speak, you put her in a highly charged environment like that," he said, motioning with a wave of his arm, "and you could shock her system."

"Damn, I never thought about that," Damali said, and backed up, cradling her necklace in both palms. She looked down sadly. "The last thing I'd ever want to do is hurt her."

Carlos slung an arm over Damali's shoulder. "Yeah, I know. She was good people."

"Wanna try to see if both of us calling her might coax her out?" Damali looked up at him. "I know she really liked you."

"You ain't mad, that, uh, we used to be friends?"

Damali allowed a half-smile to slip out. "Nah . . . I married you, so hey."

He swallowed a smile. "Let's go find some water."

THEY WALKED HALF a mile down the beach until they found a small jetty of low rocks. Within the dips and crags there were plenty of small pools where tiny crabs and snails tried to ward off predator seabirds. Squatting down, they both cupped their hands under Damali's necklace and lowered it into the water. The shriek that came from the pearl made them drop the jewelry, stand quickly, and jump back.

Gulls went airborne as the pearl released a blood-curdling scream. Bewildered, Damali and Carlos simply watched in dismay as the pearl became gray and cloudy, then went black.

"Help, help, oooohhhhh! He's killing me!" the pearl shrieked.

Curious glances by passersby, who hesitated for a moment to be sure there wasn't a woman being molested, forced Carlos to seal the distressed pearl in a small, translucent black-box to hold back the sound.

"Oh, my God, get her out of the water," Damali said, now grabbing on to Carlos's arm.

He quickly complied without touching it, bringing the pearl to the sand using an energy drag.

"Okay, now I *know* we need to go see Aset and Ausar," Carlos said, still staring at the pearl in her necklace. It had begun to smoke under the California sun's brilliant rays.

Damali nodded, gaping at her pearl. "Ya think?"

IT WAS SUPPOSED to be a solo visit by each of them, just like always. Carlos had called down the golden obelisk to transport him to the Neteru King's Council, just as Damali had called the violet pyramid door to her Queens. But the moment both Light passageways opened, they merged, and suddenly Damali and Carlos were walking down a long white marble corridor side by side. The vaulted ceiling was shaped like a pyramid, and had glowing, silver hieroglyphic symbols etched in the marble. A strange violet fog gave the hallway a dreamlike quality that made it hard to tell if they were moving or standing still.

"This is too freaky," she whispered.

"I know," he whispered. "You ever been down this way before?"

"No. You?"

He glanced at her and shook his head. She peered at the black-box on the golden floor, drawing his attention. The pearl was now spinning wildly inside the box, which emitted yellowish, sickly smoke.

"What are we gonna do with that?"

Carlos shrugged. "I don't know—but I know one thing, you ain't putting it on your neck anytime soon."

"You got that right." Mesmerized, she couldn't stop looking at it for a few seconds, and then she looked at him. "What if I'd dipped that in the water while the team was there and whatever's making it sick got out?"

"I know, baby," he said quietly. "It's bad enough me and you touched it holding hands, so . . ."

"Yeah, I know. We could be carriers of something really foul to the whole group."

A roar coming down the hall made Carlos instantly bulk, drop fang, and throw out a shield in front of him and Damali as the blade of Ausar came into his hand.

"No, no, no!" Damali warned. "It's Aset's guard lions. Stand down, or they'll attack to the death from the perceived threat."

It took him a second to heed Damali's warning as two huge white lionesses that stood four feet at the shoulders, with saber-tooth incisors bounded down the hall, muscular wings helping them gain momentum as their silver claws raked the golden floor. He stood at the ready to shield himself and Damali again, should it be too late and the creatures already have been confused. But the lionesses stopped ten feet in front of them, looked down at the black-box containing the pearl, and snarled at it.

Hesitant, one of the lionesses batted the offending item away with a hard swat. When the sound of Zehiradangra's screams began to leak out, the other lioness snapped the box into her powerful jaws, pivoted off a wall, and took flight, headed back in the direction they'd come from. The remaining lioness issued a warning growl toward Carlos, then glanced over her shoulder and went airborne to follow the lioness that had retreated first.

"Aw, man," Damali whispered, practically singing the statement. "They really did *not* like that."

"No doubt," Carlos said, rubbing tension out of the back of his neck. "Plus, you get a whiff of that stink that came out of the box?"

Damali made a face. "Yeah. But now what? I've never called a council hearing and been—"

Dense violet and gold-hued fog instantly filled the chamber, surrounding the sickly yellow vapor that had escaped, and cutting off Damali's words. She and Carlos watched in awe as the chamber fog retracted into a lance and speared the center of the yellow mist, eerily causing it to scream. Then just as suddenly the multi-hued fog formed a tight pyramid around it, and began to shrink as though compacting trash until it disappeared.

"Now *that* was deep," Carlos said in a quiet, reverent voice once the pyramid was gone.

Damali never got a chance to respond before twelve heavily armed male and female warriors in glowing white-gold Kemetian armor strode down the hall toward them. At the lead was an unusually tall man and a woman. They looked like siblings. Both owned the same shaped faces, opaque eyes, gleaming ebony skin, and taut athletic build. The only difference was the male was slightly taller and thicker than the female, but their tight dreadlocks were of the same length, and wrapped in silver bands, like their arms. The entire retinue carried shields, broad swords, quivers on their backs filled with an arsenal of silver arrows, and daggers stashed in the calf-straps of their golden sandals.

"The joint session of Neteru Councils has commenced," the warrior pair said in unison. "Guardian spirits at the wall! Flank troops!"

In crisp military precision, the squad behind the lead pair took a step back to open the line, male warriors with their backs against the marble wall to the right, female warriors to the left, lining the corridor. The warriors that had led the retinue then spun on their heels and began walking down the row without another word.

Damali and Carlos looked at each other and then walked forward, not quite sure if they were supposed to. But from all indicators—since they hadn't been attacked and the warriors on the wall were sealing the space behind them— they could only assume that they were doing the right thing.

Guardian spirits? Damali mentally whispered to Carlos after they'd been walking awhile. She studied the strong, sinewy backs of every hue that walked before them.

Yeah . . . these must have been some of the baaadest mugs on the planet to be guarding Neteru Council, D.

They both shared a glance as they walked.

You think we'd get to keep our Guardian family intact when we cross over, because we're Neterus?

Carlos glimpsed her again, but didn't break stride. *Ya know, D, I was just thinking the same thing.*

THEY CAME TO an abrupt halt in front of a massive set of alabaster doors. Down the centers of each thirty-foot, one-ton door embellished with gold hinges, were moving, silvery hieroglyphics that seemed to tell a story that went back to the beginning of time. A war horn sounded and the doors then opened by themselves, but only after glowing in a flurried pattern and stopping like a whirling combination-lock on Damali's and Carlos's Aramaic names.

"Whoa," Damali said under her breath as the lead warriors bowed and then stood aside for her and Carlos.

Carlos couldn't even speak for a moment. His entire Neteru King Council was in session, each King seated on a high pedestal, white marble throne next to his throne-seated Queen, and holding her hand. At their wrists, a long golden sash of Kinte and mud-cloth joined each couple. In the center of the semicircle of thrones were Ausar and Aset and Adam and Eve. Those single Kings and Queens formed a U shape of support behind them, going back row after row, up like in a huge coliseum without steps, floors, or anything one could see with the naked eye holding up each row.

Damali felt her jaw go slack, just standing in front of such awesome power. The electric charge rippled across the floor and over their skins, making a tingly sensation of weightlessness enter every pore. She and Carlos simply gawked as the more aggressive of Aset's lionesses brought forward the offending black-box, roared, and dropped it at her feet.

Ausar looked at Carlos, then over to Damali, and finally at his Queen, before staring down at the box. "Council is called to order. Ashé."

Carlos and Damali looked at each other, their expressions plainly asking each other, *Now what?*

"We had to contain the warlock pollutant," Aset said as she stared at the box. "Our apologies for the decontamination chamber entrance. It is unbefitting of Neteru royalty, but we had no choice."

"We will have to thoroughly purge the dragon pearl oracle before we can return it to you," Ausar said, his voice sad. "We may even have to exterminate it . . . the creature's spirit is suffering so badly."

"What happened to it?" Damali asked, suddenly jolted into finding her voice.

"Yeah," Carlos said, as Damali's hand slipped into his. "Z was cool until . . ."

"Yes, I know," Eve said calmly. "Until I beheaded my son, Cain. It's all right, Carlos. I had to do it and I can talk about it in a more detached frame of mind now . . . I have to."

"We don't want to bring you pain, dear Queen Eve," Damali said, genuflecting, which made Carlos follow suit. "But there's so much going on right now, and we need a way to do a clean divination."

"One of our seers got a visit from her dead sister in the spirit realms of Light, saying something about dark covens rising," Carlos said, his gaze respectfully going between Ausar, Adam, and their wives. "Here's my concern. We just hit Lilith's joint hard, as Adam knows. But then I later found out that the only reason we got in as far and as deep as we did was because *her husband* was installing her on the Vampire Council's throne as the new Chairwoman—"

"I knew it!" Eve shouted, standing. Adam gripped her hand tighter to keep from breaking their bond. "When I took my sisters Nzinga and Penthesileia to her topside essence in the Black Forest, she was just finishing a dark ritual. I had no idea it was her coronation! I would have driven the Isis into her heart and right into the black throne that she sat on, impaling her wretched heart."

Carlos and Damali shared a glance.

Eve took a war party of Neterus to battle Lilith? Whoa . . . Damali mentally sent to Carlos, unable to contain herself.

Carlos's eyes just widened slightly, and he squeezed her hand tighter.

"My wife and her warrior sisters almost had her, but the kill was interrupted by the Unnamed One," Adam said, coaxing his wife to sit again.

This time Carlos and Damali looked at each other straight on.

"They sent legions of scythe-bearers over the cavern, but we incinerated them like the vermin they are," Nzinga said with pride, reaching over to clasp Penthesileia's hand.

"Yes," the Amazon Neteru Queen said proudly. "And we drove back her witches and warlocks that stood guard as witnesses. Only two escaped."

Carlos waited a beat before he spoke, gathering his words with care. "First of all, that's a bold and awesome hit on our side, but the coronation took place underground, Level Six in Dante and Cain's old throne. That's how it's always done for a Chair installation, and what had me buggin' so hard was, the installer was none other than Lucifer himself."

The great hall went silent for a moment.

"It's true," Damali said, holding Carlos's hand tighter. "My husband still gets residual imaging from that throne . . . from, uh, his old life—which we can use to our advantage and probably why it even happened," she added quickly, defending him as she pressed on. "And what he sensed almost fried his nervous system. I think that could be what's wrong with my pearl, too, because she was linked to Cain, and at his demise, grieved so hard that maybe she tried to follow anywhere his essence had been."

"If girlfriend went there," Carlos said, "as a being of Light, with no dark proclivities whatsoever, she's definitely going blind by now."

"The Caduceus may be the only way," Aset said quietly, as she glanced at Damali, then Ausar.

"Bigger issue is this, though," Damali said. "If you didn't interrupt Lilith's coronation—which you didn't, and there was a stand of warlocks and witches, topside, around a Vampire Council Chairwoman, then the combo of vampires and witches seems awfully suspicious."

"Like a foul spell going down, now that the first seal got broken," Carlos said, glancing at Damali, both of them nodding. "Plus, we kicked their . . . tails," he said, monitoring his language before the royal assembly. "The question is, who was at the hocus-pocus fest? Maybe if we know the players, we can decipher what kind of thing they're gonna use to come at us."

"Truthfully," Nzinga said, "we were slaughtering them so

quickly that who they might have been, dims in my mind's eye. My focus was their incineration."

"Focus," Eve commanded gently, turning so she could see Nzinga, whose gaze went to Penthesileia.

"I recognized Genghis," the Amazon said after a moment.

"Genghis, as in Genghis Khan?" Carlos rubbed his neck with his free hand. "Okay, we know they were making a war spell for sure, now."

"Truth," Hannibal said from his high post. "But I have something for Genghis—something his spirit shall cringe to witness!"

He stood quickly and put his fingers in his mouth, using his hand to create a loud whistle. Hoof-clatter filled the great hall within seconds, and a huge, prancing, ruby-hued stallion with massive wings entered, pawing at the marble floor, snorting fire. Its eyes gleamed like large translucent jewels, and its coat and mane shone as though made of the cut stones, the light shimmering in its crystalline facets.

"Behold, the stallion of power," Hannibal said. "If their armies of Darkness arise, I am authorized to break the second seal to take peace from the earth that they in the Dark Realms shall turn on and kill each other." He opened his arms. "The Neteru Council of Kings has already awarded you the great sword—it is your choice to call this steed to your service to escalate the combat. We are with you, my brother!"

"And if it becomes bleak for our side," Eve said in a tense murmur, "I have the right to call to Damali's hand the black mare, thus opening the third seal." She stared at Damali without blinking. "Take your time to call her, for a balance of weights and measures comes with her. She will raze their food, making the staff of life scarce, hurting not the oil and the wine."

"Why would I ever want to do that?" Damali said, dropping Carlos's hand and covering her mouth.

"To starve out their armies!" Nzinga shouted. "Then

Ausar can release the pale horse of hunger and death upon their weakened demon legions, death by starvation—then opening the fifth seal to raise armies of the fallen, those who were slain for the word of the Almighty, those martyrs murdered by evil. They will rise again, after a season, but the sixth seal must then be fulfilled."

"Yes!" Joan shouted. "Every army and every soldier in the fight of a just cause, and every person burned at the stake in their vicious inquisitions of injustice—the enslaved, the tortured, shall rise in victory!"

"The moon will go crimson, winds shall lash the land to sweep the vile assets of Hell from the planet . . . earthquakes shall move mountains and islands out of their lodging to shake them from every hiding place beneath the ground; the sun will go black to entice them out to fight against a battle they shall never win," Adam said, breathing hard with battle lust and leaning forward. "The battle is on!"

"After that, the twelve scattered tribes shall gather, a hundred and forty-four thousand Guardians in all, to be redeemed and—"

"Wait!" Damali and Carlos shouted in unison, holding up their hands.

They both began pacing, panic sweat making their clothes stick to their bodies.

"That's too much responsibility," Damali said, her voice shrill.

"Man, put that red monster back in its stable, brother—I ain't calling that shit to earth. We got people down there, families, and babies, and . . . aw, man, this is over the top." Carlos raked his dampening hair.

"Right," Damali said, almost hollering. "If the food gets scarce for demons, that's biblical plagues . . . a quarter of Africa has already been decimated, we've got bird flu in Asia and Europe reaching pandemic proportions, and old, already conquered diseases making virulent comebacks—we can't bring that on people!"

She spun and looked at Carlos.

"Naw, like, we just came up here for a simple divination, since the first seal was open and a funky spell was gonna go down. We ain't come up here for all of this, yo!"

Ausar and Aset sat back in their thrones garnering calm as the great hall quieted. Two Guardians led the snorting steed away, and Hannibal sighed.

"Our apologies," Ausar said evenly. "We have been waiting for this for a long time, and perhaps we got ahead of ourselves."

"Please don't break another seal," Damali said, her voice a dry rasp.

"For real," Carlos said, still too hyped to stop pacing. "Adam, man, I didn't even want the first one broken, if I knew it was gonna be all of that."

"Well this is why we've given you access to the Covenant!" Adam shouted, losing patience. "They are your earthly guides!"

"True," Eve said with a half-smile. "But Carlos did not directly ask you to break that first seal. You tapped into his energy and felt him headed toward Lilith's lair—and if you are honest with yourself, you—"

"Jumped the gun!" Carlos yelled. "I didn't ask for no seal breaks—just some assistance. Uh-uh, you ain't laying that at my feet in the end of days, brother—we cool and all, but uh-uh."

Adam stood, indignant, looking around at his fellow Kings. "All right! I admit it! My breakage was premature—but given the stress Eve and I have endured—"

"No one is blaming you, man," Solomon said in a conciliatory tone. "Sit. We are all here for the same purpose."

Begrudgingly Adam sat.

"I feel where you're at," Carlos said, drawing Damali under his arm. "But if we can contain the madness . . . I mean, we'll scrap to the bone, will battle whatever comes our way, but our main goal is to keep down the number of human civilian casualties."

"We would have said the same thing, during our incarnation," Aset said in a soothing voice, staring at Ausar.

"You would have, but I would not—I would have taken a hundred thousand men into battle and razed anything of the enemy in our wake."

"You see how these large, epic, Old World battles went down," Carlos murmured to Damali, "and why I don't come up here off the chain?"

"I know," Damali said, letting out her breath hard. She looked at Aset. "We can't roll like that and sleep at night. New plan."

"We can try to decipher the origin of the toxin that affected the pearl," Lady Fu Hao said quietly, smoothing back her long, black hair that was wound up in an elaborate bun. She spoke in a calm tone that was almost hypnotic. "Once we understand what they were trying to accomplish, we can advise you on evasive moves and battle patterns to keep you one step ahead of their plans, and this will minimize casualties."

"Cool. Now that's a plan I can live with," Carlos said, glimpsing Damali from the corner of his eye. "And just for the record, the Covenant hasn't been available to us for a while because of the ongoing human debate over Cain and what that means."

Adam held up a hand as though to say, *Peace, drop it.* Carlos nodded.

The Native American Queen leaned forward, her attention split between the Amazon and Lady Fu Hao.

"They have one of my lands on their team now, Tara, who might be able to help break the spell code—she has shaman in her, like the guardian Jose . . . and both had the capacity at one point to bear fangs." Estsantlehi sat back. "We will work with a blend of energies and see what we can determine."

The Aztec Queen stood and began to walk back and forth in front of her throne, her green jeweled robe glittering. "Could they not call their fellow Guardians, one hundred and forty-four thousand strong to them, making them know who they are?"

Chalchihuitlcue waited, her large, luminous eyes seeming to absorb the thoughts of the group before she spoke again. "This would allow worldwide, scattered teams that have been under siege—too much to be able to seek their own kind—to sense each other's energy tracers . . . Guardian signatures worldwide, for the first time could mesh. This would also be only the second time a Neteru team would make itself known to non-Neteru Guardians as a beacon, so that only those with the eyes of Light could find shelter amongst their own kind. They must gather unto each other for safety and to fight a collective battle, if their goal to minimize casualties during the end of days is to be achieved."

"She's talking about a worldwide energy grid, a larger one than we did in Morales, this time," Carlos murmured in reverence. "That's genius."

Damali nodded and bowed toward the Aztec Queen. "Before, we had to find regional Guardian teams through calls to the Covenant, or sometimes we'd get lucky and our joint Neteru call to arms could connect us. But in a firefight . . ."

"It would be nice to fold in some air support," Carlos said, pounding Damali's fist. He glanced at Adam. "That way no more seals need to get accidentally broken."

Adam looked away.

"How would they call that many humans together, without causing suspicion, or even risking an entire Guardian planetary force in a wipeout?" Aset sat back in her throne. "Too risky."

"We can hit every zone, twelve in all, with a World Peace concert," Damali said with a smile. She looked at Carlos.

"Oh, snap—Jose was talking about that and I thought the brother was losing it."

"Right," Damali said. "If we go to twelve locations worldwide, then twelve thousand of our Guardian brothers and sisters in that area can come, mixed with civilians, and we don't risk a whole Guardian population wipeout, while also spreading some peace, hope, love, joy . . . people gotta have something to hold on to in order to keep the faith."

"Then, it is settled," Aset said, gaining a nod from Ausar. "We will support this endeavor, as well as respect your request for our warriors to stand down—except in extreme cases. But we will do all that is within our power to provide an extra layer of protection to your team, given that Lilith has been installed by her husband . . . who shall remain nameless—while we also endeavor to ascertain the specifics of this putrid spell the dark covens have cast."

"We will get back to you with an answer," Ausar said, his voice seeming a bit pleased around the edges. "The base camp that you are presently pursuing will be readied to your specifications in short order. You must have a stable place to lodge, a palace. This living like nomads is unbefitting your station."

"But know that, if you are directly attacked by Lucifer, we will bring out the red steed," Adam said, still bristled.

Eve nodded. "We will never allow a Neteru team to be cast against that level of unfair disadvantage." She leaned forward, becoming more impassioned as she spoke. "If it is Lilith, as much as I want her head on a pike, I will heed your request to fall back . . . but *do* call me, Damali; just say my name, and I'll be at your flank with a battle-ax raised—*know that*, sister."

"But in the interim," Nefertiti said, causing the others to stare at her and Akhenaton—both of whom had been silent observers during the previous, heated exchange. She waited a beat, her beautiful Kemetian gaze stunning the group to calm, as her melodic voice dipped to a harmonious murmur. "Rest, replenish your weary spirits, and live in the present—it is a gift. Take respite when their armies cease fire, rest when they rest, that you may live to fight another day . . . and do not forget each other in your quests. You must claim peace as much as you must claim victory in battle, or it will escape you."

"Your living quarters have been barriered to evil; Adam and Ausar have pledged our support in battle as well as securing your lodging. For now Eve and her Queen sisters have decimated the darkside's coven forces, injuring Lilith and killing four of six witches and warlocks that had been secretly gathered in the glen." Akhenaton glanced at his fellow archons. "Whatever poison they'd sent is contained within the pearl. Nefertiti brings you wisdom not to forsake joy altogether, as this keeps hope alive. Otherwise, you and your team will go mad."

"I say we call in Merlin on this," a Guardian shouted out from the ranks on the floor that rimmed the hall.

"I agree," Arthur said, weighing in his opinion from his throne, leaning forward. "Merlin is renowned for his authenticity and spell expertise."

"Arthur's right. Merlin could be summoned. They have druid capacity on the Neteru team," another Guardian's voice rang out, quickly creating murmurs that echoed through the great hall.

"Protocols of this session will be observed!" Ausar said, quelling the sidebar commentary from any Guardians on the floor. A large Egyptian hooked staff materialized in his fist and he pounded it on the marble base of his throne, sending a loud banging shock wave across the hall as his intense, unblinking gaze scanned the gallery of Kings and Queens. "King's Council, speak."

"The Merlin question," Akhenaton said with a sigh of frustration, "is advice that we will take under advisement. But we want to be sure, first, that the pollutant is contained at the highest bands of energy. To release it to loyal spirits without knowing the nature of its potential would possibly injure one so good as Merlin. Whatever they sent to attack the Neteru household went to the spirit holding the most pain and grief at the moment, which would have been the oracle. Their team had begun to heal their individual losses . . . and their wise mother-seer had recently applied a spirit balm to everyone, before this spell was unleashed."

Nefertiti nodded. "Yes, my husband is correct. Their team was glowing pure silver aura and white-hot joy when this insidious spell was released."

Carlos gave Damali a quizzical look, and her eyes replied, *Later.*

"You know, however . . ." Solomon said, looking at David. "We need to check the due dates in the Akashic records of when the Antichrist is expected, now that the first seal has been broken. This could change the entire plan . . . if that's what Lilith was conjuring in the woods."

"Solomon and David are wise! Maybe until they know," Noah shouted out from the Guardian ranks on the floor, obviously unable to contain himself, "the new male Neteru should hold himself away from his wife—as we were advised to do on the Ark. This would cease all potential conceptions while that which is unclean is being swept away."

"I shall not call for order in this hall again!" Ausar shouted, standing.

Damali blanched. Carlos took up her hand.

"Y'all be sure to let us know, though, if we need to do something like that—or you find something crazy in the records." Carlos glanced at Damali again. " 'Cause, like, we've been down that road a few, feel me? Ain't trying to go there again."

"We'd all feel that presence, if Satan's spawn were on the earth plane," Adam grumbled. "As a counselor and judge, you are worried about a level of detail that does not currently exist." He looked at Carlos. "True, she has the recessive Powers angel gene, but after the battle against Cain and his hybrids in Central Mexico, Rivera's spirit and loyalties are no longer in question On High. There is no more talk of possible annulment of the union, so I see no reason to take such drastic measures to have a man hold himself away from his wife—if anything, Solomon, this could cause discord."

Ausar leaned around his throne and spoke in a low private tone to Solomon. "This brother doesn't have three-hundred-plus wives, understand? Do not stress our young brother during the Armageddon like this." He smiled and shook his head, chuckling. "The way I know Rivera, he might immediately call for the sixth seal to be broken, if you do."

"Yeah, man," Hannibal muttered, leaning in to privately speak to Solomon. "Rivera already helped bring that stolen seal back to us before he was even a Neteru, too . . . so now you're listening to Noah? He was an old man when he got on the boat. You need to ask his sons—"

"—I'm conservative," Solomon said with a skeptical but conceding nod. "However, I'd still like to have a sacred records review."

"In the meanwhile," Aset said, openly trying to stem what appeared to be the beginning of a long session debate. "Let us not filibuster over this hypothetical threat. Due diligence and research is warranted, and thus, what we shall employ. But our young Neterus have a wonderful plan to bring the world teams into contact with each other in preparation for any humanitarian threat that could be levied from the darkside—and we have controls swiftly being put in place to aid those efforts."

"Go in peace," Ausar grumbled. "Session adjourned."

"Can you say world tour, baby?" Carlos chuckled as a twelve-warrior escort team fell into formation before them. "I think you needed that anyway."

She smiled. "Yeah, I did."

"MAN, D," CARLOS said, swinging her around and laughing as they came out of an invisible fold on the beach. "I have *never* been *so glad* to get out of somewhere, girl!"

She threw her head back and laughed, holding his shoulders as he began running with her hiked up by her waist. "That was craaazy! Like visiting the principal's office in school!"

"Naw, that was like going to court, yo! Start the what? Call a red who? Oh, shit!" He made them fall in the sand with a thud, still laughing.

"Kinda puts it into perspective, doesn't it?"

Carlos just looked at her. "Girl . . . I ain't guilt-trippin' no more, not after that. I'll take Dan to see his peeps, we'll work on the concert logistics, get the Covenant over here, set up base camp here in La Jolla, sheeeit. I ain't breakin' no seals, though." He put his hands on top of his head for a moment.

She kissed him. "Good. 'Cause if you break a seal, I'd have to kill ya."

He laughed and kissed her back harder. "As long as you kill me like this."

She smiled and sidled up closer. "That could be arranged."

The smile left his face and he looked at his hands for a moment, tilted his head, and slowly closed his eyes.

"I can never figure out how you always do that to me," he murmured and then opened his eyes.

"Do what?" she asked with a waning half-smile, tracing his brows with the pad of her thumb, suddenly wanting to kiss his thick, black lashes.

It was hard to think as she looked at him now. Her fingers ached to skim the waves of his dark hair. She always loved what the sun did to his warm, golden brown skin . . . and he looked so damned sexy as he slid down onto his side, and propped up on one elbow . . . every muscle in his shoulders and arms and chest and stone-cut torso beneath his tight, army green T-shirt and black jeans had moved when he'd moved.

"You make my hands feel like they're on fire to touch you," he said after a moment, his voice becoming gravelly as he stared up at her. "I felt it the minute we walked back into the earth plane. I had to pick you up, touch you."

"I know," she said, her voice a husky murmur as she leaned down and her hands cradled his face. She didn't care if people walked by smiling at them, he was in serious peril of getting jumped right where he lay. "The second we came out of the fold, it spread out through my palms and ran up my arms." She swallowed hard. "Then it started coating my insides."

He leaned up and kissed her hard, his tongue straining against hers. "Maybe it's 'cause of what they said I might have to do—and got a reprieve. That crazy shit Noah was talking about," Carlos said, his words smothered by his own breath. He pulled her chin into his mouth as though devouring her, then sought just her bottom lip.

"Okay, we've gotta get a room."

"Ya think?" he said, breathing hard, no longer even able to laugh.

"Yeah, 'cause the whole team—"

Her back hit the inside of a hotel door.

"Send Mar a message—stat," Carlos said between deep breaths, tugging at her yellow tank top to get it up and out of her jeans. "Tell her we need a private debrief after being in council, so your husband doesn't lose his mind, but so she doesn't wig and mount a search party looking for two MIAs."

"Okay, okay," Damali said, almost sliding down the door as his hands finally connected with her bare torso. The sensation made her arch like she'd been electrocuted and forced a deep moan from her gut. She held his wrists as they swept up to capture her breast. "Touch me there, and I won't be able to home in on squat. The message will go to the lobby or some danged where."

"Then tell her later." He found the sweet spot on her throat and suckled it 'til her knees gave out.

"Whose room are we in?" She couldn't breathe, couldn't see, couldn't think, just needed to touch him, and her hands were everywhere.

"I don't know," he groaned, opening her jeans as she worked open his belt. "Por Dios, your skin is *muy caliente* . . . like hot caramel melting all over my hands."

"Can you at least block it out of the reservation system so nobody walks in here?" she gasped, arching as his fingers slid into her panties.

"I can't concentrate enough right now," he admitted, aggressively nuzzling her hair and shuddering as her hands pulled hard to free his T-shirt. "Best I got is a black-box—and I definitely ain't got a prayer seal in me right now."

The moment her hands slid up his spine, she knew it was all over. He dropped his head back, let out a yell like she'd scalded him, and every pulse point he owned lit up.

Nearly delirious and unable to speak, she helped him fight with his clothes as he struggled with hers, half-falling, needing to unlace Timberlands, forgetting the order of what made sense. His hands on her skin, anywhere they touched, made her feel like her bones were melting. It was as though he'd dunked her into a cauldron of white-hot, liquid pleasure. She was drowning in his scent, the feel of his skin, his voice making her gulp air, as her body contracted for him in pain.

Her essence literally ran down her leg as he rubbed himself between her thighs. Her voice hitched, faltered, ran the keyboard as he bent to suck her distended nipples. Then he stood up quickly, looking tortured, caught a fistful of her locks, and suddenly swept one of her legs up into the crook of his elbow.

She flat-hand slapped his shoulder; she didn't have to tell him what to do. He entered her hard on a wailing groan, making her see stars. Silver sweat slicked his body, and she hadn't even been able to get her legs to carry her the few steps across the room so they could fall into bed. His mouth was devouring her whole, every kiss that landed making her cry out until his attention became laser-focused, and he moved.

There was no way in the world she could meet his demanding tempo, composed solely of whole note, hard thrusts delivered on the downbeat. Her body bucked and thrashed wildly out of synch, out of time, in such urgent heat that she gave it up and gave it back a quarter note at a time . . . then half notes, eighth notes, whole notes, rests . . . sharps, flats, chords, her nails keeping time on his shoulders, her head and back colliding, creating a symphony with the door.

Her windpipe was scorched by the time his fist tightened

in her hair and she felt him grappling with the door molding, trying to pull himself into her deeper and faster, needing to anchor himself to her any way that he could. Then his rhythm frayed, snapped, and broke down to match her syncopated madness.

Frenzy entered his lungs, she felt it the moment it entered hers. It was something insane and spectacular, pleasure dominoes crashing one into the other . . . something so powerful it forced him to use her name like punctuation in his lyrics. Damali was a rapid-fired noun at the end of each mental sentence, more like a gasp; *Oh, God—Damali, oh, shit—Damali, aw, damn—Damali, por favor—Damali,* then he stuttered twice, losing her name between thrusts, and came hard, yelling, "Oh, baby," out loud.

If he pulled out now, they'd never speak again. Her hands raced over his body frantically seeking anchor, finding his hips, then settling on the tight, high, gorgeous swell of his ass—she was home! She pushed herself against him so hard that she'd moved them both back two inches from the door. But he knew her body like he knew his own, and God bless him, he dropped her hair, quickly wrapped his arm around her waist, and pulled her in hard twice 'til she was cuming in jags.

They fell against the door with a thud. He dropped her leg from the crook of his elbow and she almost slid to the floor.

"Damn . . ." she whispered, out of breath.

He just nodded, gulping air, sweat running.

"Your tattoo didn't even light," she murmured, kissing his neck. Then she traced it with her finger and watched in awe as it disappeared under his skin like it was hiding from her. "I've never seen it do that before."

When she glanced up, he was biting his lip, silver tears wetting his lashes.

"Baby?"

He shook his head with his eyes closed and then pressed both hands flat against the door on either side of her head with his fingers splayed. "Not yet. Don't touch it. I can't take it."

Her hands caressed his back and instead of bringing him

down like the after-lovemaking caress should have, it made him pant.

"Put your hands on the door," he ordered through his teeth. "Ground the charge, D."

Confused but more than willing to play, she complied. "Happy now?"

Relief made every muscle in his face relax, and he groaned as it then slid down his neck to his shoulders and his back, until his knees slightly buckled as the tension left his thighs.

"Whew, woman, I swear one of these days you're gonna be the death of me just like this," he murmured against her ear. "Your wings didn't even open and your tattoo never lit, and you still had me slobbering on myself."

She took his mouth but kept her hands on the door. When he pulled back she smiled. "You didn't even drop fang, brother, and look at how you have me—up in some room I don't know where, buck naked. Does that make sense?"

"You better call Mar, now, while you can," he warned, nipping her neck, but keeping his hands on the door.

"You better make up some yang on that computer, and book the room to us, or black it out of their system . . . while you can," she said, slowly bringing her hands off the wall and wiggling her fingers at him until he laughed.

"DO YOU SEE this?" Lilith screeched to Sebastian, holding his crystal ball out from her body with one talon above the crest of the pentagram-shaped table in Vampire Council chambers. "Do you!"

Fallon Nuit remained cautious and sat back in his throne forming a tent before his mouth with his fingers.

"They *held hands* when they touched a tidal pool to enliven her oracle! They're married, one flesh—so when I told you to make a spell that would only affect Damali Richards, did you not account for the one-flesh rule?"

"Your Majesty," Sebastian murmured, going to one knee, "I . . ."

"Kiss your ass good-bye, *mon ami*," Fallon remarked dryly.

"It has been so long since we've worked with married enemies that—"

"Silence!" Lilith shrieked, her robes billowing with smoke. "My wings were charred and shall never return because I risked my very existence being ambushed by Neteru Queens coming to the clearing—and *this* is what you give me?"

She hurled the crystal ball to the floor and let out a scream that made Sebastian and Fallon cover their ears. The bats above stopped their whirling cloud and took cover. She snapped her arm away from her body in a hard point, forcing the fanged crest in the center of the table to open. "Look at it and weep, Sebastian!"

Lilith swept away from the table and grabbed Sebastian by his cape to physically drag him nearer. "I do not have the power to see into a consecrated union, but look at them on the beach—do they seem unhappy? Does he seem disinterested in her!" Lilith began shaking Sebastian like a rag doll.

"But this spell allows us to find the Neterus, now," Sebastian said, sounding frantic. "This was a side benefit no one could have predicted."

"Yes, we tracked them to this room just by following the tracer from your spell that got on their hands," Lilith spat. "But in a day even that will vanish and be useless. They only got a small bit from a tidal pool, not a fucking tidal wave like they were supposed to! Or from her being poisoned by the pearl that absorbed it into her own necklace—damn you, Sebastian. Look at the other side of that hotel door. It does *not* take a dark arts elemental genius to understand that there is *nothing* wrong with that man's libido! The hinges are about to come off the door if the wood doesn't give way, first!"

She flung Sebastian aside and looked at Fallon. "Should I cut off his dick for this atrocity, Fallon? What say you? I'm too overwrought to decide."

Nuit held both hands up before his chest. "After being in

your husband's chambers, I must defer to your wisdom, dear Lilith."

Sebastian swallowed hard and began walking backward.

"I lost Jezebel, and dear sweet Medusa out there for a potion that backfired! Genghis and Machiavelli . . . oh!"

Fallon stood and materialized a black blade in his grip. "*Machiavelli* was lost to this incompetence?"

"Yes," Lilith screeched, walking in an agonized circle. "The resources we expended on this mission . . . and to have Rivera banging the hinges off a hotel room door is too much for even me to bear. I could go up there right now and—"

"Lose your head to both of them," Fallon said, stepping away from his throne. "Two rutting Neterus? Be serious, Lilith— and be advised." Nuit neared Sebastian with a deadly smile and slowly drew the black blade down his chest and over his stomach to come to a stop at his groin. He watched the smoldering trail the blade left. "Let us not be hasty, Lilith. Sebastian is a good resource, still." Then he leaned and sniffed, causing Sebastian to close his eyes. "Treason!"

Lilith tilted her head and came near Sebastian, both vampires dangerously circling the warlock. "You have every warlock and witch's power essence threading in your blood," she whispered.

"You even slit Jezebel's throat," Nuit murmured, lifting a thick strand of Sebastian's hair away from his neck and pressing the blade harder against his groin.

Both vampires' gazes locked as Sebastian squeezed his eyes tighter and made fists with his hands.

"Forgive me," Sebastian whispered. "I can still make good on my spell."

"Thissss . . ." Nuit whispered with a hiss, licking Sebastian's jugular, "is the most cold-blooded coup I've seen in quite a while. Shall we meet in the middle of his throat, Lilith?"

Lilith poised her fangs on the other side of Sebastian's neck. "To the victor go the spoils," she murmured. "Welcome to council."

CHAPTER EIGHT

Every time they'd said, "Okay, this is the last time, and then we're going back to the suite," one thing would lead to another, somebody would mess up and touch the other person, and the whole madness would start again.

Damali leaned up from the floor on her elbows with her knees bent, looking at Carlos, who was sprawled flat on his back. "We have to check in with the team before it gets dark," she said, heaving in air. "The sun is going down and this doesn't make sense."

He nodded with his eyes closed, trying to steady his breath. "You know we're gonna catch a ration of shit for this from everybody—so get ready."

Damali let her head drop back with a groan as her legs slid out into a V in front of her. "Awwww, maaaan . . . you know it."

Her foot accidentally brushed his arm and she felt his breath hitch in the pit of her stomach.

"Don't start," she whispered and began to draw her legs up toward her.

He reached back and caught her by the ankle, and then slowly rolled over as he pulled her down the rug, staring at her. "Just one more time, then on my word, we'll go check in."

* * *

THE MESS WAS so intense and ridiculous that she literally had friction burns from the rug on her butt and her knees. He was so spent that he couldn't pull them into a fold to get them back to the team.

Sure, they'd had plenty of great sex together, dead or alive, but it still puzzled her that it had been so intense that Carlos's fantastic silver didn't blaze once in his irises. The more she thought about it, he also hadn't even presented mating-length fangs. Not that she was complaining in the least.

As they slipped out of the vacant room at Hotel La Jolla and hurried to find a cab, she said a quick, silent barrier prayer so nothing could trail them back to the team. Safely tucked inside a taxi, her fevered mind finally had a chance to slowly come back to its own. Then it dawned on her, she and Carlos had been knocking boots until almost midnight without a barrier around them . . . and the first seal of the Armageddon was broken—were they nuts?

Carlos turned and looked at her at the same time she quietly freaked out. He grabbed her by her upper arms. "Don't worry, it's gonna be all right."

Where did that come from? Did it matter at all? His hands were on her arms sending a desire ache into her nipples. She kissed him so hard that she flattened him against the backseat of the cab. The driver looked in the rearview mirror and cleared his throat. Carlos broke the kiss, trying to be cool, then gave up the battle and pulled her to him hard again to put his tongue halfway down her throat.

"Listen," she said, flat-palming his chest as she whispered in a rush. She had to hold her hands in front of her in order to keep Carlos from flipping her beneath him and embarrassing her out of her mind. Unsure whether he might attempt it, she glimpsed the way-too-interested cabbie and tried to reason with the man next to her, who was breathing hard. "You're so exhausted, you can't even fly. We have to stop until we at least get to the suite. Okay?"

Carlos nodded and closed his eyes as her palms rested against his chest. She could feel his heart slamming against the heels of her hands as though trying to get out of his body. His breaths were so shallow as he tried to summon cool that she had to fight with her fingers and will each digit not to touch his pebble-hard nipples.

"Marines?" the cabbie asked brightly, seeming thoroughly amused. "Camp Pendleton? Get a lot of military types around here, newlyweds—can always tell. The guys drag their asses back to base too tired to fly, drive a Jeep, or a tank—whatever they do. But I think it's pretty cool, ya know. Congrats, kids. I hope you don't have to go back overseas for a long time."

THE INABILITY TO summon cool probably messed with him more than being temporarily too exhausted to fold Damali out of the hotel room and back into the suite. It was more than outrageous, beyond ridiculous, that he could barely get his hand down into his jeans to pull out cash to pay the cabdriver.

He had to chill, one breath at a time. He was not walking back into that suite sweating and carrying on. Oh, hell no. D just had to keep her hands to herself, just for a minute so he could get his head right . . . fine as she was . . . with that satin-smooth, caramel skin of hers, trailing shea butter and hot sex, velvet locks, mouth . . . Jesus . . . gorgeous eyes that could burn right through his to the soul . . . curves for days . . . He studied her behind with a tilt of his head as she began to open the suite door. And her ass, the way it fit right in his hands . . . he hadn't felt a jones like this since he'd been apexing—and even then . . .

"Hey, C—for the second time," Shabazz said with a smirk.

"Huh, oh, yeah, hey, man," Carlos said, glancing up and remembering to step into the room.

"You okay, dude?" Rider asked, frowning, setting his cards down slowly on the dining room table. "You look like something's been chasing you . . ." His nostrils flared slightly, and he and Jose stood at the same time.

"Good night, people," Rider said, glancing at Tara. She didn't say a word, just waved.

"Adios," Jose said, rubbing the back of his neck. "I'm just glad you're cool, man. We was worried. But it's all good." His hand slid into Juanita's, making her smile as he passed her.

"Night folks," Juanita murmured, and then just shook her head.

"Okay," Mike said, stretching as he stood. "'Nez, we can stand down. It's just like old times." They were out the door before Damali could say good-bye.

"Mar, you got our message, right?" Carlos said, trying to preserve a little of their dignity.

"Yeah," Marlene chuckled and then dropped her voice as the rest of the team moved out slowly. "It was a sputtering, garbled transmission saying, 'About in an hour or so my husband debriefed his mind. Can't talk, gotta run.' Now *what* was I supposed to make of *that*?" Marlene's hands went to her hips with a wide smile. "I guessed it was delayed-reaction balm . . . but after it got dark and you guys didn't come back, we all started getting nervous."

"I'm sorry, Marlene," Damali said, and then tucked her trembling hands into the bends of her elbows as she hugged herself.

Just seeing her do that made Carlos begin to walk in a circle.

"Me, you, Carlos, Shabazz—private meeting," Marlene commanded quietly.

"Not a long one, though, Mar," Carlos said, walking to the window, dragging in air as the team thinned out in their suite.

Shabazz shut the door behind Berkfield and came back deeper into the room. "Damn man, you're in here sweating like a junkie and got the shakes—ain't seen you look this bad since you got a vamp nick and turned."

"That's what this shit feels like," Carlos said, looking at Damali and unable to keep up the front any longer. "But the hunger ain't for her blood, and I'm about to vamp-snatch girlfriend in two seconds . . . so say what you gotta say quick."

Marlene and Shabazz looked at each other and then focused on Damali.

"Honey, your color is off. How's your appetite?" Marlene asked, trying to inspect her for bites.

"For him—outrageous," Damali said, wiping sweat off her brow with the back of her forearm. "But he never bit me, never presented fangs while we were, uh, out . . . ya know. Everything's all right, guys, in the morning—"

"You'll be sick as dogs." Marlene glanced between the two of them. "When you went to the Neterus—"

"We was cool there, Mar," Carlos said, his voice brittle. "Can't this wait until tomorrow?"

"Looks like Louisiana roots, if I didn't know better," Marlene fussed, crossing her arms.

"Haitian is my call," Shabazz muttered, sitting on the back of the sofa.

"Look at the whites of their eyes, getting cloudy, just a tad," Marlene said, speaking to Shabazz as though a doctor in a clinic.

"It's in their sweat. I can pick up the taint. Must have been dormant while under the intense white light in council, but went full blown the minute they came back to the earth plane."

"Oh, shit . . ." Carlos groaned, rubbing his neck. "I knew something came out of Lilith's pit—"

"No, you were okay, and so was every other guy on the team," Damali said, going to him. "The only weird thing we saw was the pearl, when we dunked her in water."

Carlos looked up. "Yeah . . . the way the lionesses attacked it."

"They went after your necklace?" Marlene asked in a tone of disbelief.

"Yeah, after the pearl in it turned black," Damali murmured, stepping closer to Carlos.

"Wait, D, a Neteru oracle went black in front of your eyes and you guys didn't tell anybody? That's a fucking team hazmat, folks." Shabazz was off the back of the sofa raking his locks.

"He and I both lowered it into the water . . . his hands touching mine, because I knew she always liked Carlos . . . we were trying to coax her out," Damali murmured, staring at Carlos.

"I remember," Carlos said in a low, sensual rumble. "In the water . . . my hands were touching yours, your hands were touching mine, then the charge ran right through me . . ."

"Like it's running through me right now," Damali murmured.

"Hold it!" Shabazz and Marlene shouted, breaking their trance.

"Step back from each other ten paces," Marlene said.

"Okay," Carlos said quietly, but he didn't move, just stroked Damali's cheek, making her shudder.

"It's in your hands," Damali whispered with a soft gasp.

"Okay, okay," Marlene said, taking Damali by the shoulders as Shabazz body-blocked Carlos.

"Put your hands out for me, hand—don't punch me, I'm outta your way in ten seconds, but do me that favor," Shabazz said, studying Carlos's aura.

Carlos closed his eyes when he opened his palms and spread his fingers. "I just gotta touch her, man."

"Tainted energy all in it," Shabazz said, surveying his aura. "Breaks at his tattoo, over his heart chakra, all the energy concentrating in primal meridians. This was some fucked up root work, if ever I seen it."

"That's what Marj was talking about," Marlene said, visually scanning Damali's hands without touching them and then pressing two fingers to Damali's third eye. "Damn, chile!" Marlene said, jumping back. "Warn your mother-seer, okay? You knew I was going in and I don't wanna know all that."

Damali covered her face with her hands and tried to breathe. "I'm sorry. That's what we're trying to tell you . . . it's that bad."

"Look, we'd appreciate it if this problem stays at the senior level, until we can figure out what to do, or if it's catching," Carlos said, putting his hands behind his back to keep from reaching for Damali.

"I need to get in conference with Marjorie, Heather, and Jasmine—Marj is a blood relative, the girls were either tight with Gabby or in a coven with her as her initiates, and I'm gonna need the power of three to figure out what's all in the spell to counteract it."

"I know what you're saying, Mar, but damn," Carlos said, closing his eyes. "This shit is embarrassing."

"They're looking into the pearl up in Neteru Council. Maybe can you just let Aset and Nefertiti know, and wait 'til they come back with a verdict before we break it to the team? *If* we ever have to break it to the team?" Damali's eyes furtively searched Marlene's and Shabazz's faces. "C'mon, guys, have a heart, like Carlos said, this shit is too embarrassing."

"Forty-eight hours," Marlene said, "with full disclosure to Aset—which I'll do tonight. But you guys try a white bath, and don't worry, I've got this room already barriered. Just stay in here, 'til . . . aw hell."

"White bath, never happen," Shabazz said, "unless you individually dunk 'em—which ain't gonna happen. The only thing you said that's plausible is for them to stay in the room for now." Shabazz headed for the door. "We got two Neterus down. Face it, baby."

"ALL RIGHT," ASET said, her eyes narrowing as she leaned forward on the oval Neteru Queens Council table, making the radiant colors in its opalescent finish shimmer. "What was your angle, Lilith?"

"A love spell to push the two together doesn't make sense," Nefertiti said, staring at the black translucent box.

"It does if you want the Neteru generals diverted," Eve said through her teeth.

Nzinga nodded. "So that you can create a sneak attack . . . something is planned, and it has been too quiet on the earth plane."

"Open the box," Lady Fu Hao urged. "We must dissect the spell, now that Marlene Stone has told us of its debilitating effects."

"I stand ready," Penthesileia said, holding an Amazon battle-ax. "If cauldron parasites emerge, they will be slaughtered."

The Aztec Queen removed a long, sharp, golden-handled dagger from her sleeve. "Anesthetize the oracle as you lower the black-box, Aset. It will be traumatic as I remove her from the necklace and submerge her into an alabaster bowl of Ma'at's truth elixir."

Aset nodded. "If she's beyond repair, then, Chalchihuitlcue, you have the swift hand of sacrifices . . . don't allow her to suffer."

The Aztec Queen nodded. "I shall indeed be merciful and make it swift."

"I KNOW THIS isn't normal," Damali said, racing across the room to kiss Carlos the moment Shabazz and Marlene shut the door.

Both on the same mission, he cleared the sofa in a one-handed hurdle and they bumped into each other and almost fell.

"I knew it wasn't straight up when my fangs didn't drop," he said between urgent kisses, cradling her face as she worked on his clothes.

"Or I didn't see your silver," she said, stripping off her tank top.

When her breasts bounced free, he covered them with his palms and leaned in, causing them both to release a long moan riding a shudder.

"Yeah, your wings didn't come out," he finally said, now

panting and working harder to get off her clothes, tugging on her jeans zipper while her hands set fire to his chest. "Dead giveaway."

"We should take a white bath," she said, devouring his mouth.

"Uh-huh," he mumbled into her mouth, pushing her back on the sofa. "In the morning."

"Yeah, in the morning."

"Oh, yeah, D, in the morning . . ."

"Oh, God, Carlos . . . in the morning . . ."

"Uh-huh, like that, in the morning."

SHE DIDN'T REMEMBER if she went to sleep or simply passed out, but Marlene hadn't lied, they were both sick as dogs. It felt like sunlight was chiseling a hole in her temple, and for a while she lay on her side hoping it might just be so the pressure inside her brain could leak out. Her entire body felt like it was purging, even her cycle had come on and she'd now have to deal with that, too, for a couple of days. When this was all over, she was gonna personally kick Lilith's ass.

Keeping her body as rigid as possible to stave off the dry heaves, she tried to sit up to move to the bathroom, but Carlos's grip tightened on her arm.

"Touch me again," she said through her teeth, "and I'll stab you."

"Oh, Jesus, don't move, I'm gonna hurl. Don't rock the bed."

"We're on the floor."

"Oh, God, the room is spinning."

"Breathe slowly," she said, sipping air with her eyes squeezed shut. "I'm gonna crawl to the bathroom and make us a white bath."

"Bring me the wastebasket on the way, if you can reach it."

"HOW YOU GUYS holding up?" Marlene said quietly, touching Damali's forehead and looking at Carlos with concern. "You still feel clammy."

Shabazz and Marlene shared a look.

"That's 'cause girlfriend is trying to be ultraladylike," Carlos muttered, sipping peppermint and ginger tea with his eyes closed. "I got all mine out—both ends. I'm way better this morning, Mar, trust me."

Damali dry heaved and covered her mouth, her eyes wide, and then dashed for the bathroom.

"She'll be good in twenty minutes," Marlene said philosophically. "Told y'all if you didn't catch it last night, you'd be sick as dogs."

"Let it rest, Mar," Shabazz said, trying not to smile as he stared at Carlos. "Baby, just let it rest."

"AS LONG AS I live, and for as long as I die, Damali Richards-Rivera, I never want to be that out of control over any substance again in my life—not even you."

"I hear you," she said in a faint murmur, holding on to the side of the bed with her eyes closed as he tied a Windsor knot in his uniform. "Just keep your voice down. I don't even know how you're gonna go with Dan and Heather right now . . . you know his mom is gonna feed you."

Carlos held up his hand. "D, please," he said, taking in a deep breath through his nose. "I just barely got my stomach back. I'll make it up as I go along."

She peeked up from the bed at him and had to admit that the uniform was blowing her mind. Under any other circumstances it would have made her try to get up and coax him to stay. The brother had more braids and medals on than made any type of sense. And although it was "borrowed" from some top brass owner for just a little while, the ruse was all for a good cause. If people knew the real deal, not a soul would argue that one Neteru general, Carlos Rivera, had definitely earned his stripes.

"You look good," she finally said, and dropped her head back to the pillow.

He kissed the top of her head. "Think I'll pass inspection for Mom and Pop Weinstein?"

Damali opened one eye. "Just give 'em the strong, silent, steely jaw—if-I-tell-ya-I-have-to-kill-ya look."

"Aw'ight," he said, glancing back and looking concerned. He stood in front of the mirror, then put his hat on, then took it off and whipped it under his arm, standing at attention a few times, practicing. "Okay. I'm out."

From a very remote place in her mind as she drifted back to sleep, she caught that nervous anticipation in him—saw and felt just how much he wanted to do a good job for his team brother and not mess up. It endeared him to her even more, because by rights, with everything else that was going on, Carlos could have begged off and no one would have argued. But he didn't. Because it was important to Dan and Heather, it was important to him. That was just one more thing she added to the list of things she loved about her man.

"YO!" JOSE SAID, laughing. "You clean up real good, brother." He walked around Carlos and let out a long whistle.

Carlos laughed and opened his arms, then looked at Dan. "I pass inspection?"

"Whoa . . . Rivera . . . My mother will have a coronary and then tell the entire neighborhood that I work for the Pentagon."

"Well, get the story straight, dude, before you go in," Rider said, laughing. "Rivera can make you a Black Ops agent, Bond—as in 007—or a Secret Service aide to the president of the United States of America, in that uniform."

"Generals can do that, you know," Mike said with a wink, teasing both Carlos and Dan.

"You better work it, brother," J.L. said, shaking his head and laughing as Krissy came over to kiss him. "And here you introduced me to the Berkfields with fangs. Where's the justice? No wonder they gave me a hard time about marrying their daughter."

"Honorable fangs, though," Tara said with a smile.

"Yeah, but Mom would have taken it a whole lot better if

she'd seen Rivera in Heathrow Airport in that getup—right, Mom?" Bobby said. "Be honest."

"He does look very handsome in that uniform," Marjorie crooned. "Just dashing, Carlos. Almost as handsome as you looked in your wedding tuxedo." She glanced at Heather. "It's going to be just fine."

Carlos bowed and gave Marjorie his most professional rendition of a general's voice that he could muster. "Ma'am, thank you, ma'am." Then he started laughing. "Oh, maaan, what have y'all gotten me into?"

"Impersonating an officer is how many felonies?" Berkfield said with a grin, causing the color to drain away from Marjorie's and Heather's faces.

"The man is fine," Inez argued, folding her arms over her chest. "Dang, Carlos, just imagine if you'd gone that way years ago."

"'Nez, why'd you have to mention that?" Krissy fussed. "Geez!"

Carlos looked down at his duds, refusing to get sad about the things he couldn't change. "Naw, Inez is right," he said, looking up with a half-smile. "But see, 'Nez, if I had this on years ago when I met your girl, guaranteed she wouldn'ta been no virgin by the time she reached twenty-one."

With that said, the group burst out laughing as Shabazz, Mike, Marlene, and Rider grabbed Carlos and Dan by the arms and hustled them out the door.

"THIS IS NEVER gonna work!" Rabbi Zeitloff said as he met everyone at the airport baggage claim.

"Please keep your voice down, Rabbi," Dan said, looking around nervously. "Let's just get your luggage, go to the real far end of long-term parking, and let Carlos do his thing."

Dan glanced around nervously as other military personnel slowed down, stopped, saluted Carlos, and kept going. Heather squeezed Dan's arm and also squeezed her eyes shut when another high-ranking official rode up an escalator and hailed Carlos.

"Before someone puts a camera in my face for a media comment—because it would be just my luck that something major's kicked off in the Middle East while we're standing here—ya mind if I wait in the car?"

Dan, Heather, and the rabbi said no in one voice.

Carlos turned on his heel in a military pivot, keeping in character as he got out of Dodge. The threesome watched his back as he melted into the crowd and disappeared toward long-term parking.

"See? What'd I tell you, huh? This, Daniel, is never gonna work!"

HIS NERVES WERE already shot by the time he folded them out of the parking lot, and Rabbi Zeitloff's constant complaining only frayed them even more. But when Dan pushed him and the rabbi to the top steps of his parents' home, it wasn't until Mrs. Weinstein started screaming and almost fell on the floor that they realized what she probably thought.

Carlos's first impulse was to touch his jaw to be sure that during the transport he hadn't dropped fangs—his energy had been off. However, seeing the look in the woman's eyes, remembering the uniform, a cleric at his side during wartime, he caught her before she hit the foyer tiles.

"He's my only son!" she screamed, slapping Carlos's face and knocking his hat off. "My beautiful baby boy!"

"Mom! Mom!" Dan shouted at her side, but his mother was too hysterical to even know who he was.

"Frank!" she shrieked with her eyes closed. "They took my Daniel!"

"Ma'am, your son is alive!" Carlos barked in a military voice. "Home on leave!"

He sat her up so that she could see Dan's face. Her husband had hustled into the room. Dan was on his knees in front of her, and then she began shrieking again, this time strangling him with a hug. There was no use in trying to introduce anyone to her. The woman was rocking and sobbing and petting her only son's hair. Dan's glasses were askew on his face as he stroked her back and tried to glance at his father, but it was of no use, his mother's meaty arms had claimed him.

Ever so calmly, Carlos walked over to retrieve his hat. Rabbi Zeitloff stepped back with him as Dan's father joined his wife and son on the floor. The reunion made them both stare out of the window until Heather's quiet presence caused the crotchety old rabbi to put his arm around her shoulders.

"Most times," the rabbi said, "when I come to homes like this, it isn't a good thing, Carlos. It is not a happy reunion like this. So, I should thank you for making an old man have hope."

Carlos nodded and kept his gaze on the horizon. "He's a lucky man. My mother never got me back in the daylight . . . so she could do that. Woulda given my eyeteeth for that."

"I hope they'll like me," Heather whispered, clasping the rabbi's arm.

"What's not to like?" the old man said, his voice unusually soft. "You're a beautiful girl . . . smart . . . and you make Daniel happy—I hope he makes you as happy." Rabbi Zeitloff leaned in. "I don't do this sort of thing for everyone, you know."

Heather giggled, and that made the rabbi and Carlos smile. They looked over and finally saw Dan and his father helping Mrs. Weinstein up. Carlos secured his hat better under his arm, quietly chuckling at the wasted practice of taking it off with military precision only to have a hysterical mom slap it off his head. But not to let all of his practice go to waste, Carlos made the pivot turn on his heels that he'd worked on all afternoon to face Dan's parents.

"This is Rabbi Zeitloff," Dan said, "the one who you've been corresponding with." He looked anxiously between his parents and watched his father and mother collect themselves.

"See, Stella—I told you the boy knew what he was doing, and all this fracas before you even heard the man out. Rabbi, my apologies."

"No harm done," the rabbi said, waving off the offenses. "You're parents; she's a mother."

"Rabbi, I don't normally behave this way, but he's my boy . . ."

"Yes, yes, a son is a lovely thing . . . and so is a daughter." The rabbi glanced at Dan to urge him to make the introduction.

"Oh, I don't have a daughter, Rabbi," Mrs. Weinstein scoffed. "I wasn't so blessed with a girl, too. But I have my boy."

"And, uh, this is the guy I work for, uh, General Rivera," Dan said, looking at Carlos with a plea in his eye.

"Nice to meet you, ma'am. Sir." Carlos extended his hand and said no more. It wasn't his place to introduce Heather, and if the rabbi passed, then hey. Dan had to man up and tell his momma he'd gotten married without her being there . . . although he didn't envy his Guardian brother at all, in that regard.

"Our son works for *a general*?" Mrs. Weinstein whispered, glancing at Dan and then her husband.

"Is it important, what you do? Dangerous?" his father asked, seeming skeptical.

Against Carlos's better judgment, he stepped in to give Dan a little more family cover.

"What he does, sir . . . ma'am, is of the highest importance to world security. Not national security, but *world* security. Because you don't have clearance at that level, I am not at liberty to discuss more."

Carlos waited a beat for theatrical effect and then tried to think of any incendiary words he'd heard in the media that might help Dan's parents just accept what he said on face value. His mind locked on "the axis of evil," wondering if people really knew what that meant. True, Dan was fighting an axis of evil with the team, but one that had a whole different meaning—not the one where there were a bunch of humans with disputes over land, oil, weapons, or any of the other material concerns the darkside had manipulated them to go to war over. He just wondered how long it would take for people to wake up and stop bombing each other, especially when it seemed the targets mainly included old men, women, and children. But he had to tell Dan's people something that they could wrap their minds around. Demon hunting wasn't such a thing, so he kept it to world politics as the closest analogy he could come up with.

After a moment, Carlos pressed on, knowing that the well-timed pause had probably engendered awe in Dan's parents. "What your son does is dangerous, is important, and is part of . . . eliminating the axis of evil. He has indeed been invaluable to our special forces." Carlos looked at Dan and gave him a crisp salute. "This is why, as his commanding officer, I wanted to escort him to his parents' home and to personally meet the fine people who made him who he is. We know this is hard on families, not knowing where your loved ones are or what they are doing, but we appreciate the sacrifice."

Carlos gave Dan the eye when his mother practically swooned with pride and his father's chest puffed up, that *now* would be a good time to explain a quick marriage. An elbow in the ribs from Rabbi Zeitloff helped Dan spit it out.

"Mom, Dad . . . because things were so hectic, and abnormal, and dangerous as Car . . . uh, General Rivera said—and I met someone who works with me in the same unit, who also can't discuss what she does," Dan said, bringing Heather closer to him with a hug, "I want you to meet Heather, my wife, and uh—"

"Wife! Frank, did he say wife?" Mrs. Weinstein's voice hit a decibel like fingernails down a blackboard as she covered her mouth with both hands.

"That's what he said, Stella—wife," Mr. Weinstein said with a smile.

"Mom—"

Mrs. Weinstein looked at the rabbi, ignoring her son. "Is she—"

"*I* married them. What do you think?" the rabbi said in a feigned huff, cutting off Mrs. Weinstein's question before she could ask if Heather was Jewish.

"She's beautiful," Mrs. Weinstein said, coming up to

Heather to look her over. "My son married a girl this gorgeous? *My Daniel,* who in high school, wasn't able to—"

"Mom!" Dan said closing his eyes.

"He was too smart for those other girls," his mother said, preening and kissing Dan's cheek. "But I bet they'd be sick now to see our Daniel with such a *lovely* wife," she added, holding Heather back and then hugging her.

"And smart, too, don't forget, Stella—she has an important, high-security job like Dan . . . the two of them have the same shtick. Cut from the same cloth."

"Yes, sir," Carlos said, now fully enjoying the role. "She works in Dan's same unit."

"I'm so pleased to meet you both," Heather said in a quiet, relieved tone as Mrs. Weinstein released her. "I've heard so much about you both. Dan loves you so." She looked at Dan, and he touched her hair.

Dan's parents hugged her again, taking turns handing her off to each other and then embracing their son. Dan's father gave him a huge smile of approval that made Dan seem to stand even taller.

"So, when was this wedding, and we have to meet your parents; I have so many questions," Mrs. Weinstein said in one run-on sentence. "And you want children, right?"

Heather's eyes filled with terror and she glanced at Dan, who'd lost the color in his face.

"I just have one question," Mr. Weinstein said, making everyone turn. "Why are we standing in the foyer? Why haven't we come into the house like normal people?"

"Yes, yes, we should come in and everyone just relax for a very short while," Rabbi said, already staging the excuse to leave as he and Mr. Weinstein deflected Mrs. Weinstein's probing questions.

"But you *have to* have dinner." Stella Weinstein looked around at everyone as though mortified by the concept that her son could visit, bring home important guests, and even a rabbi, and not eat. "If I'd known you were coming," she said, covering her chest with her hand in mild shock, "I would have cooked. General, make my son eat—he doesn't eat."

The thought of food made Carlos's stomach roil, but he knew better than to decline. This was family.

Dan and Heather looked at Carlos with such appreciation and affection that Carlos looked away.

"Thanks, General," Dan said. "I'll never forget this. *Ever.*"

HE THOUGHT THEY'D have to give Mrs. Weinstein smelling salts when it was finally time for them to leave. Carlos kept breathing back dry heaves—it wasn't that the food wasn't fantastic, but rather the volume on a shaky stomach. Each time his plate was three-quarters cleared, a heaping dollop from what should have been a military-chef's spoon dropped more on his plate. The argument Dan's mother gave was relentless: "Eat. You should be glad a mother is cooking this instead of the government—not that I'm casting aspersions on the government, but who knows how clean army food is?"

Who could argue?

VIOLET BEACON LIGHT filled the bedroom and mingled with the late afternoon sun's rose-orange beauty. Damali lifted her head, feeling a bit better, but still wrung out. At least the headache had gone, and the nausea had slightly calmed. Her white tank top felt slightly damp and another shower was calling her name, but there wasn't time.

Damali pushed herself up and then got out of bed, yanking on her jeans and shoving her feet into a pair of flip-flops. If the Queens had called her like this, then there was important news to be had. It didn't take long for their warm light to surround her and bring her to their opalescent table.

"Damali," Aset said, walking up to her quickly and dispensing with all formality. She air-kissed Damali quickly, holding her by her upper arms and then hurried back to the table. "Look," she said, showing Damali the thrashing tentacles that fought to get out of Carlos's black-box.

"Eiiiw," Damali said, glancing at the writhing morass, and then she looked at Aset and the other Queens. "That came out of the oracle? What the *heck* is it?"

"Medusa's contribution to the spell," Nefertiti said. "If I tell you what Jezebel added, you will be positively ill."

Damali held up her hand. "I'm already queasy enough, ladies, so—"

"It got on her," Nzinga said, drawing the Caduceus into her hand and tossing it to Eve.

Eve caught the golden rod that was ensnared with golden serpents and rammed it into the floor by Damali's feet. Instantly a golden carpet of light spread out along the white marble floor, washed over Damali's flip-flops, and entered her body through her feet, causing a warm, peaceful sensation to overtake her. After a few moments, Damali opened her eyes. The residual effects of last night seemed to dissipate. Right now she would have paid five bucks for a stick of gum, though.

"It wasn't that bad, because her husband caught some of the charge—it only got their hands," Eve said. "But it was a vile spell, indeed."

"Nasty," the Amazon Queen said.

"We'll elaborate to you later, who all the culprits were," Aset said, "but we were able to save your oracle."

"Pearl!" Damali said, hugging herself. "I was really worried and was trying not to even go there . . . but I figured Zehiradangra might be strong-willed enough. But, still, I didn't know."

Aset guided Damali by the shoulders to a small opalescent bowl filled with azure liquid. She could see some type of crystals, or perhaps undissolved salt at the bottom holding the pearl in place.

"Hi, Damali," the pearl murmured quietly.

"Zehiradangra," Damali said in a gentle tone, going to the bowl and leaning close to coo to the traumatized oracle. "Oh, honey . . . I am so sorry. I wouldn't have dunked you in the sea, had I known."

"I know, Damali. Your heart is always pure . . . unlike that, that . . . oh . . ."

"Shsssh, don't talk. Rest," Damali said. "When you're ready to come home, I'll come get you. But you're safest here, with the Queens. Okay?"

"All right," the pearl murmured. "I'm just sooo tired."

"Sleep, honey. Just rest."

Damali stepped back, raking her locks as Nefertiti covered the pearl with a panel of white Egyptian cotton.

"What did they do to her?" Damali asked through her teeth as the Queens drew away from the pearl and back to the table.

"They were trying to make your husband impotent and your lust for him to cause strife, and hit you with jealousy against your team sisters, and—"

"What!" Damali put her hands on her hips. "First of all, that bitch is crazy if she thinks there's anything she could do to make Carlos—"

"We know. It was outrageous, but could have worked if you both hadn't learned your lesson with Cain and hadn't strengthened your bond. That's what she was banking on, for there to be some residual unforgiveness—it would have slithered into your systems that way. The only reason it adhered at all was because Carlos felt guilt for something he didn't do—breaking the first seal." Eve looked at the other Queens. "That's how they get in. They find a weakness in your spirit or psyche and exploit it."

"It was so toxic," Lady Fu Hao said, "that if it had somehow gotten into the rest of your team, there would have been a full-scale team meltdown. A mutiny. Old jealousies, bitterness, hurts unspoken of but not forgiven . . . coveting those things one did not have. It would have been horrible and could have done years of irreparable damage to friendships, marriages, psyches, and spirits. It would have started with you two, then trickled down."

"How do I make sure none of this got into anyone else?" Damali said, her eyes frantic. "My team is just healing from all sorts of personal drama; it's like an arm just out of a cast or a wound still tender after they took out the stitches."

"You couldn't heal it unless you recognized it," Aset said. "But now you know."

"So the moment you see any dissension, don't let it fester. Stamp it out," Eve warned. "Bring it into the Light, get it up and out of that person and bring the parties together to heal."

Damali closed her eyes. "Last night . . . it was simply ridiculous. We couldn't even think. If the team were to lose it like that—"

"They can't be allowed to. It would stop all rational thought," Nzinga said flatly. "Then when the first part of the evil spell wore off, the next wave of it would come— Medusa's serpentine jealousy."

"Then Machiavelli's duplicity—backstabbing, talking about others on the team behind their backs, forming secret alliances," Chalchihuitlcue said in a low, concerned murmur.

"They raised *Machiavelli* for this?" Damali began pacing.

"Yes," Nefertiti said. "Added Jezebel's . . . er, essence, to make you lust and—"

"Oh . . . just . . . *stop it!*" Damali hollered, looking at her hands. "EeiiiLLL . . . that skank!" She whirled around, flapping her wrists. "I need to wash my hands—essence! As in *essence*?"

"You shouldn't have told her that part," Nzinga muttered. "Too much information."

"Sebastian's twisted mind, his evil thoughts, to poison and skew how you think . . . clouding perspective and blocking reason," Nefertiti continued, undaunted. "Genghis Khan's warring nature to make you and the team battle yourselves relentlessly . . . the war within a household can never be won . . . and then they added Siren's voice to block the voice of reason, to make you say things that could not be withdrawn once said, to beckon couples to seek solace on far shores . . . anywhere but home."

"This is what they would have visited upon your household, Queen sister," Eve said, rage kindling in her eyes. "But you were strong; it backfired on them because your house-hold was on firm foundation when this foul wind blew against it. The pearl, bless her, was grieving so heavily at the time that most of it went right into her."

Aset nodded and swept around the table to sit on her throne. "They miscalculated and thought you and Carlos would be the ones mourning greatest, possibly having no knowledge of your oracle's heartbreak as a magnet. They also forgot about the one-flesh reality, and never suspected you to come to the sea touching your husband to douse your necklace. They would have made your necklace a carrier of this nasty spell into your household . . . right around your very throat."

"You know whaaaat?" Damali said, cocking her head to the side. "We oughta hand deliver this mess right back to Lilith's door and let it explode in her realm. I *know* them bitches down there couldn't shake this if they wanted to."

An angry grin slowly dawned on Eve's face. "Sealed in a prayer that whoever sent it should have it back tenfold . . ."

"Praying that whatever they prayed for Damali, they should also have back, many-fold . . . karma," Lady Fu Hao said in a dangerous whisper.

"A household breach, the old-fashioned way," Nzinga called out, grabbing Penthesileia's forearm in a warrior's grasp as the Amazon threw back her head and released a war cry.

"Bring her house down," Nefertiti said between her teeth. "A house divided cannot stand. Now that the first seal has been broken, we can breach their realm, if reprisal warrants—and *this* does!"

"They have sown the dragon's teeth!" Penthesileia yelled.

Chalchihuitlcue drove a dagger into the black-box so that Damali could hear the twisting, fighting tentacles scream. "I'll cut off sections to bomb every level."

"Every level?" Aset asked.

Damali nodded. "Yeah."

CHAPTER NINE

She couldn't stop it. Didn't want to stop it. Once her Amazon Queen sister threw her head back and released a battle cry, the fight command had popped off so fast and so furiously that it felt like a lightning bolt tore through her system.

Call Carlos how? She was in battle fury's grip. It was going down.

Every indignity that Eve felt, she'd experienced. All of it threatened Damali's sanity. By any means necessary; no justice, no peace—until Lilith felt her household violated and crushed the same way she'd come after hers; it was on!

Damali stood in the Black Forest clearing with her three Queen sisters, Eve, Nzinga, and Penthesileia. They'd brought her to the last place Lilith's essence had scored topside, hoping that Damali could use her past experience to open the chasm of Hell.

"No problem," Damali muttered, walking around studying the charred earth. "Harpies and scythe-bearers opened it right here." She squatted for a moment, putting her hand over the sealed crevice. "They locked up shop, but I know how to get 'em to open the door." She stood up quickly. "Stand back, take cover, and when the first funnel forms—or when demons slither over the edge—let her rip, Nzinga.

That will get us down to at least Levels One and Two. I just hope the spell vaccination Lady Fu Hao gave us works."

"It will work, she is the best at counteracting forces of Darkness that have been delivered through potions and evil elixirs," Nzinga said, lifting her chin higher.

Damali backed up from the site, keeping her eyes on the ground. "Yeah . . . whatever she gave us was strong enough to make me see silver and make my cycle go off. Girlfriend ain't no joke. So, let's do this."

The older Queens nodded, but Eve hesitated. "What if Lilith comes up in the funnel? I want her head."

"Lilith won't come up in this funnel," Damali said with a tight, angry smile. "Because I'm not calling that bitch."

The Queens shared confused glances as Damali leaned back, took a deep breath, and began yelling.

"Fallon! Fallon Nuit! Bring your punk ass up here and fight like a man!"

FALLON STOOD UP from his throne so quickly that he almost toppled it. Lilith and Sebastian hissed.

"It could be a trick, Fallon," Lilith screeched. "Be still and listen, send up—"

"It's Sebastian's potion," Fallon said in an even tone that barely concealed his excitement.

Sebastian weakly nodded with a smug expression. "So, it would appear that my work was not all for naught, then? It would stand to reason that she'd call . . . the first real master vampire she knew, descended now to council level—after her human Neteru was depleted." He leaned forward, his gaze narrowed on Lilith. "Potions are delicate chemistry and take time to snake their way into the human system. Listen to her frantic calls above."

"With Cain gone, her last near-vampire lover," Fallon said, sweeping away from the table with a flourish and staring at the vaulted ceiling, "who would be able to satisfy her proclivities more than I?" His vision became laserlike as he stared at the swirling funnel cloud of transport bats. "Look at her," he murmured. "Eyes wild, her blade raised, fury making her tremble, and my name on her gorgeous mouth." He closed his eyes for a moment. "And you ask me to wait . . . after losing her twice?"

"Do as you like!" Lilith screeched. "I sense a setup, but have no problem in using your worthless carcass for cannon fodder, Fallon."

Nuit tilted his head with his eyes closed. "Listen to the distress in her beacon." He drew in a slow breath. "She said, 'After Cain, how dare you leave me like this.'"

Sebastian chuckled. "As good as a ripening, my fellow councilman. So now you owe me."

Nuit smiled. "Well worth the price, indeed."

THE CHASM IN the earth opened and a hundred massive scythe-bearers flowed over the edges. Nzinga stood hidden in the stand of trees and began swinging the silver energy tether in a whirl of circular motion and then released it so that the glowing white orb containing the reversed spell passed the demons and fell into the abyss. The scythe-bearers hissed and screeched then went after the offending light before it descended too far into the pit, not realizing that the moment it hit anything down there, it would detonate like a grenade.

Damali took cover as huge tentacles reached up from the yawning opening in the ground and snatched down scythe-bearers with an angry snap. Their blades were of no use. Each time the guard and messenger demons hacked away one squirming limb, the black-green slime that splattered them entered their systems and made them lustily turn on their fellow demon soldiers. Those demons unable to reach another one of their own connected with the spell's thick ropes of tentacles, tree trunks, exposed roots, anything they could rub themselves against until the spell pulled away the groaning carnage to go deeper into the pit. The Queens squinted in disgust as the tentacles finally dragged away writhing demons, and disappeared.

"Never in my born days . . ." Eve murmured, shocked. "Not even in Sodom and Gomorrah."

"I'm just pissed off that they tried to bring that shit to my door—my household," Damali said through her teeth. "Well, hold on for phase two. The door is open. Watch my six."

Quickly moving to the edge of the precipice, Damali made her voice as seductive as she could. "Fallon," she said, listening to it echo down through the unguarded first and second levels. "How could you show me all those hot images, taunt me outside of la casa in Morales, and then disappear? I didn't realize chivalry was dead, *mon dieu.*"

Damali rolled her eyes and put her hand on her hip, but kept the Isis firmly in her right grip. She could just imagine the devastation the spell was having with the ghost gangs and incubi and succubae, not to mention the poltergeists. Lilith would be busy for weeks cleaning up that madness and restoring order, and if it got down to the serpents . . . the Amanthras might strangle themselves in frenzied mating balls. The were-demon realms on Level Five might not even come out to hunt on the full moon.

An urgent mental jolt from her Queens made her ready for the soundless mist behind her. Damali didn't turn around; she knew male vampires and what they craved like she knew the back of her hand. The moment Nuit materialized she spun, had his hair in her fist, and bit his jugular.

"What took you so fucking long? Do I look like a woman who wants to be kept waiting?"

She smiled. The surprise in his eyes and the hard shudder that passed through him made her wonder for a moment if he'd busted a nut.

"Damali . . . for years," he crooned, nuzzling her neck.

"Yeah, what can I say? I finally came to my right mind, I suppose . . . besides, you know what marriage does to a girl."

"No, tell me, *cheri,* in excruciating . . . mental . . . detail."

She fought not to tense at his cool, clammy touch and gave a French kiss her all to stun his mind. There was just something so foul about having a being without a soul run its hands over her ass, but this was war. Carlos had always been white hot against her, even while dead. The soul factor, she supposed. But the fact at the moment was she needed Nuit to take her down through the tunnels so she could seed the levels with glowing time bombs, let them quietly detonate, and then her squad would be coming in as backup once the tentacles consumed everything in their wake with lust.

"You got a throne?" she murmured, coming out of the kiss breathless for maximum effect.

His hands were in her hair, tears of desire in his eyes, and she could feel him about to totally lose his composure to present bat wings and a spaded tail. "Never could I have imagined what the scent of you this close could do to my reason, *cheri,* much less the taste of your mouth and the spill of natural confection your skin is in my hands—"

"Listen, while I'm flattered," she said, not wanting to have to kiss him again, or worse. "Stop humping my leg and answer my question—do you have a throne?"

"Of course I do," he said, nuzzling her hair and sliding a glistening fang up her throat.

"Then can we get our swerve on down there? I'm horny as hell and really don't feel like being out here in a pile of leaves and bugs and whatnot," she fussed, staying in character, doing everything she could to make him believe the spell had taken her mind.

He just stared at her for a moment as though she'd slapped him, and she could feel his mind trying to blunt fuck hers to pry information out of it. She smiled and allowed her eyes to slide shut as her hand slipped between their bodies and she stroked his groin.

"Oh, *yeah* . . . that's it, lover. Just do that in a throne and I'm yours," she murmured and then pulled in a deep hiss between her teeth. "I remember when Carlos used to be able to do that, baby."

A dark transport cloud swept her up so fast that it knocked the air out of her lungs. In the dense blackness, she had to remember how to sense the descent, flying blind, with eyesight useless and Fallon's mouth on hers . . . but dropping small charges from her pockets while he was extremely preoccupied.

She landed on his lap and immediately jumped back before the throne itself could start to invade her. For a moment, he was slightly disoriented and she needed a cover to buy time.

"I didn't know she'd be here, and who's he?" Damali said, pointing at Sebastian.

Lilith hissed. "Fallon, are you *insane*?"

"Hey, Lilith," Damali said, ramming her Isis into the floor and watching the marble smolder. "I would have given you the ride of your life in a throne, Fallon, but not with that bitch watching—she doesn't deserve it. Put her out or I ain't dropping the silver—him, too."

Damali quickly turned back to Nuit, who had ironically battle bulked on Lilith. She didn't bother to fight the smile and allowed it to come out on her face looking just as sinister as she felt.

"The legendary one. Ahhhh . . . I am Sebastian, greatest of spell-caster warlocks and newly installed councilman at large," Sebastian said with a bow toward Damali. He spun on Lilith. "If you ever challenge one of my spells again, I will remind you of this moment." He began to sweep away to the council antechambers. "Nuit, you lucky bastard, I want a mental video of this when you're done." With a puff of black smoke, he was gone.

"I will ask you again, Fallon," Lilith said, hissing and spitting as she transformed to meet his physical challenge, "have you lost your mind?"

"En garde!" he shouted, producing a Black Death blade.

"Girl . . . you know how they are when they want some, right?" Damali said, studying her nails.

Damali ducked the black bolt that Lilith sent her way, and was pleasantly surprised to see Nuit put a black shield between them with the Isis still on her side.

"You owe me this, Lilith!" Nuit shouted in *Dananu*. "After all I've done for you—this one indulgence is all I ask!" His fist hit the council table and broke off a corner of the pentagram.

"I owe you nothing but my wrath!" Lilith shrieked back in the negotiating language of their kind while leaning over the table and meeting Nuit eye to eye. "But it will be a first in chambers." She pulled back and shook her head, and then laughed.

Damali froze. That was not the expected reaction.

Nuit leaned over farther and brushed Lilith's mouth with a quick kiss, and then closed his eyes. "Thank you, Madame Chairwoman. Forgive my outburst."

Lilith swept away from him and waved her hand, chuckling in a low rumble. "The pulse of that erection, Fallon, is enough to make you deaf, dumb, and blind. I hope I find more than your ashes when I return."

Nuit glanced at Damali and dropped his black safety barrier from around her. "If it is thus that I am ash, surely it will be because she has scorched me."

Damali smiled a tight smile, watching Lilith slowly walk away, and knowing Lilith did have eyes in the back of her head. She drew her Isis blade into her palm, ready.

"Now, where were we?" Nuit crooned, walking around his throne and beckoning her to him with a look.

Anything she was about to say to stall him came to an abrupt halt as the marble floor began to rumble and Lilith and Sebastian whirled into the chamber. Damali began backing away from the central vibration point that seemed to follow her around within seconds of her every move. Wall torches were falling along with rocks. Fallon Nuit was trying to get to her like a valiant lover. But she made it appear as though she was falling from his grasp, too—knowing full well he'd jettison her somewhere she'd never been in the pit, and wouldn't know how to get out.

Then just as suddenly as the underground earthquake began, a swarm of vicious Harpies came up from the wide fissure that opened in the floor. They rushed at her, screeching, causing Fallon Nuit to foolishly attempt to come between them and her as she butchered the little beasts with her blade.

"Call them off, Lilith!" Nuit shouted as gook from Damali's swings splattered him.

"I didn't send them," Lilith screeched over the din. "My husband did! Something's wrong!"

Oh shit. Damali's mind screamed for an out as she gripped her Isis like it was a baseball bat and swung wildly, decapitating ugly little fanged faces from squishy demon bodies. Soon to be overrun, she had only one option left, the one she was saving for the Vampire Council as soon as the odds were even but the best laid plans sometimes never stood a chance.

Fumbling as she hurried, Damali dug a hand into her jeans, pulled out the last grenade, and lobbed it over into the abyss to hit Level Seven's sentries. The moment the orb of Light went over the edge, Harpies screamed and dove after it. Lilith flew at her with a blade poised at her heart, and Sebastian whirled on her with black lightning charges from behind that temporarily stunned her.

"She had to defend herself—your Harpies made her fight! She is a Neteru, it is her nature, Lilith," Nuit shouted in a standoff with Lilith, blade drawn. "Harm her, Sebastian, and know that—"

"Did you see what she threw into the Ultimate Darkness's lair?" Lilith whispered, staring at Fallon Nuit like he was insane.

"You can fuck her when she's dead, my friend, after you make a blood sacrifice of her—but if you do not address this breach, you may find yourself unable to enjoy it if she lives." Sebastian turned to Lilith for approval and then slowly drew away. "Oh . . . noooo . . ."

"What?" Lilith screeched, spinning to look at Sebastian.

Damali flipped up, took a fighter's stance, and kept her eyes on the pit and the three vampires before her.

"They reversed the spell! Take cover!"

Huge, monster-sized tentacles vomited up from the floors, its various-sized limbs undulating with messenger demons and Harpies in their grasp. Damali began running toward the door as the long ropes of spell lashed out, twining around thrones, wall torches, and the table as Lilith, Nuit, and Sebastian tried to escape each grab. Funnel clouds of transporter demons in the vaulted ceiling drew vertical tendrils to shoot up and snatch the teeming mass of mating bats down into the fissure in the floor.

Black charges from an infuriated Nuit chased Damali across the floor like machine-gun spray. But a bolt of blue-white energy resembling C-4 blew council doors off the hinges, followed by a battle-ax lodged in Lilith's throne hurled by Eve. Dodging a charge from Sebastian, Damali flipped to corner his escape to the antechamber, shattering his blade in two. Nzinga and Eve had Lilith's attention temporarily hemmed in while Penthesileia ripped through Fallon Nuit's Armani suit at the chest with a machete.

However, the battle temporarily ceased when a black-fire–snorting, golden minotaur the height of a six-story building climbed out of the fissure, exploding the floor and walls, and quaking the vaulted ceiling to start an avalanche. It still had souls twisting in its jagged, blackened teeth like white maggots as it rose with a roar and leapt into the center of what had been Vampire Council Chambers. The great beast spun and pawed the earth with cast-iron, razor-sharp cloven hooves, its spaded tail a bullwhip against the cavern walls.

Cornered, the Neteru Queens were backed onto the narrow crag that had once separated the Vampire Council Chambers from the rest of the portals, with the Sea of Perpetual Agony's bubbling, lava surface separating the divides. The furious Vampire Council members were nearly hidden by the massive girth of the huge beast that suddenly lowered its head with black, gleaming horns pointed at the Queens and charged.

One mind—all four Queens moved as swift mirror images of one another. Damali's blade replicated into the hands of her Queen sisters. Penthesileia quickly thrust her blade into the cavern dirt, reached over her shoulder and drew an Amazon bow and arrow, and fired with a silver energy rope attached to her arrow. The arrow burned into the rock surface behind the beast as it lunged and cleared the lava sea. The Amazon Queen immediately grabbed the end of the line, and yanked her blade from the foul dirt to pass the beast gouging out an eye.

Eve covered her, sending power pulses like mortar fire into the wide open and unprotected Vampire Council Chambers, while Nzinga grabbed the blue-white energy line as it swung back to propel herself past the bucking, injured beast to maim it again, shearing off one horn.

Taking flight, Damali's wings lit the cavern, further pushing back Lilith, Fallon, and Sebastian. As the angry entity thrashed in the cavern, she was able to grab hold of its ear, flip herself onto its back, and drive her blade into the other eye. But when it leapt and smashed its back against stalactites, goring itself in its agony and rage, Damali flattened her body to its smelly, oily, scaled skin. Only narrowly had she missed being crushed to death, were it not for the jagged rock formations in the cavern ceiling that dug into its huge shoulders while she hid between the kneading sinews.

But opportunity was opportunity. Seconds mattered, and Damali slipped off the raging beast as it bucked against granite and struggled to free itself, bleeding black blood. Her Queen sisters were in an unguarded portal area, and Damali headed toward them. The spell tentacles had rushed up over the edges of the now wide-open Level Seven fissure in Vampire Council, and had Lilith by the leg, Nuit in a full coil, and only the outline of Sebastian's struggling form could be seen. The corridors were cleared, as entities on every level were temporarily trapped by the spell, and massive, seeking tentacles were reaching out with yearning toward the huge minotaur.

"We're out," Damali said, glancing around quickly for

any landmark she knew, and finding none. Even the Sea of Perpetual Agony was writhing as tentacles came up with tortured souls in their clutches before submerging again into the inferno.

"Let us go out with a blinding reminder to never screw with Mother Nature," Eve said, her gaze hard but satisfied.

The four Queens smiled, touched their blades together, and raised the combined Isis as a column of light shot up, creating a vacuum opening.

But Damali's smile was the widest. "We kicked their asses tonight!"

"YOU DID WHAT?" Aset whispered, looking at the four dirty, demon-splattered Queens as she walked behind her lionesses in the decontamination chamber. She shook her head as she stared at Damali's wings. "You look more like a Valkyrie that escorts dead soldiers to Valhalla on the battlefield than a healing Powers angel that is—"

"We slayed them," Eve said, unable to contain her joy. "All the way to *the bottom*."

"You should have seen Fallon's face—he actually bulked on Lilith!" Damali threw her head back and laughed. "I so owed them both that shit, Aset, if I don't live twenty more minutes, it's all good . . . just to see *that*. In council, too!"

The foursome laughed and exchanged back slaps.

"It was like old times, Aset," Nzinga sighed. "The young Queen was awesome."

"Like the best of the Amazon battles, only better," Penthesileia said. "I wondered if I might even bump into Achilles while there, but no."

"They will feel our wrath and be quite disorganized for a while," Eve said, wiping sweat from her brow with the back of her hand. "Nary a sentry twitched. They were too consumed in their frenzied mating to even guard their own corridors—and to think this is what they'd sent to our sister's home."

"Speaking of which, ladies," Damali said with a bright

smile. "Can I get a shower and a quick Light blast . . . then, uh, some clean clothes and a lift home? I gotta break this to my husband real easy."

HE WASN'T WORRIED about where Damali was. Marlene had said the Queens had called her, and left a violet tracer so there'd be no concerns. It stood to reason that they might have cracked the code on the problem that had been contained in the black-box he'd left in the great hall, and he was curious to find out what Damali had learned.

Plus, after Dan and Heather's good fortune of parental acceptance, albeit along with a little overeating indigestion, he was in a really good place. Peace had claimed him for once in a blue moon.

Carlos chuckled, listening to the crazy banter in the main suite. But he was just glad that, at the moment, everything was cool . . . man. Rabbi Zeitloff was at one of the Covenant's synagogue safe houses awaiting Father Pat, Imam Asula, and Monk Lin's flights that were coming in soon. Dan's rendition of everyone's reaction as that brother held court in the living room and told the story with so much yeast that it rose, was hilarious. When Dan started doing different voices, Carlos almost rolled out of his chair onto the floor.

Finally, Jose was the one who just got everybody going. He started in with teasing them about being secret agents, and then J.L. got into the mix.

"Check it out," J.L. said, turning his laptop around on the coffee table. "You need to let me and Jose pimp this ride out for D, and I got one for you, too, C."

"Aw, man, get out of here," Carlos said, laughing. "What is it?"

"See, every secret agent in the flicks has to have a cool ride, and since you scammed Dan's parents, I was saving this for you," J.L. said with a wink. "Check it out, the Bugatti Veyron, pretty bitch pushes two-hundred-and-fifty miles per hour, rockets from zero to sixty in two-point-five seconds, and accelerates so fast you can drive her upside down—feel me?"

"Daaaayum," Jose said, nodding with approval. "We mighta just been playing around, but . . . hey."

"I was thinking the same thing, dude," Rider said, coming to look at the car. "What's the price tag on that lovely, sexy, make-you-wanna-holla female, J.L.?"

Every woman in the room groaned.

"Oh, no, please don't get them on a tech bender," Marlene said, flopping into a chair in defeat. "I thought we were gonna go look at real estate before the sun went down."

"A cool one-point-three," J.L. said, answering Rider's question and ignoring Marlene.

"That ain't bad, for all-a that," Shabazz said, pounding Carlos's fist.

Marjorie just leaned her head back on the sofa and closed her eyes.

"Are you all crazy!" Juanita fussed.

"A million dollars for a car that you know Carlos is gonna crash up or run something over with?" Inez said, sucking her teeth.

"That's crazy," Krissy said, plopping down on the edge of J.L.'s chair, leaning in to see better. "But it's gorgeous."

He looked up at her and smiled. "Wait 'til you see this one. The Bugatti is for D, she needs the extra speed to get out of a jam . . . and when I weapons-kit it . . ."

"Yeah, when homeboy pimps her ride," Jose said, leaning in for a fist pound, "it's gonna be—"

"*Da bomb*," Carlos, J.L., and Jose said together.

"You see why I don't argue about some things?" Marlene said in a resigned tone, glimpsing Heather and Jasmine's wide grins. "It's not because I'm psychic. It's just because I already know how this is gonna go. We found the property this afternoon, so now all the technology and toys to go in it—and filling up the garage goes with that territory—is their thing."

"Aw, now, Mar, don't get all salty. We gonna get you some snazzy-jazzy stuff, too," Mike said, laughing. "Maybe put some GPS locators in your—"

"The old-fashioned way works for me," she fussed with a smile, but had to also stand and go look when those assembled around the table released a collective groan.

"Aw, look at her," Bobby said, tracing the screen with his finger.

J.L. swatted his hand away. "Uh, uh, look but don't touch and don't drool on my laptop."

"I hear you, son," Berkfield said in a near whisper. "Damn, . . . she's a beaut."

"The Saleen S7 is all you, Rivera," J.L. said with a smile. "Damn, I wanna funk that lovely lady out with some machine-gun turrets, RPG launcher, side lasers along the running boards to burn out and blow tires, you know?"

Carlos stared at the flawless, metallic red finish on the car that had shark gill doors that opened in a vertical hatch. "Aw, man . . . only point three seconds behind the Bugatti."

"The lady oughta get there first," Rider said, making the guys laugh.

"She's built like a missile with cockpit interior," Carlos said, mesmerized, leaning in farther to read the small print as J.L. continued to enhance the images. "V8, seven-hundred-fifty horsepower, zero to sixty in two-point-eight seconds." He looked up at Shabazz. "No airbags. Once you're in her, you're totally committed. You can't second-guess—it's 'til death do you part."

The male contingent in the room fell back against whatever available surface in utter appreciation.

"A death machine, dude. They gotta fill her tank up with pure testosterone blend—whew! Just like a Harley." Rider pulled out a chew stick. "After hearing that, I want a cigarette."

They all laughed, and everybody shook their heads.

"Yeah, but the Lamborghini Murciélago LP640 ain't no punk, either," J.L. said. "That's all you, 'Bazz. Bet your tactical class one charge could hold that boy to the highway at a hundred fifty miles an hour while changing gears ... scissor doors."

"Oh, yeah, that's me, brother—manual shift, hey." Shabazz smiled and rolled the toothpick in his mouth.

"Okay, okay, we give," Marlene said, holding up her hands. "Yeah, all right. It's been a long time since we've had a real compound for an extended period of time, much less a garage. Fine. Buy the toys."

A collective whoop filled the air as high fives and fist pounds got exchanged.

Marlene couldn't help laughing. "I don't know why y'all are acting like what I said meant a thing—you were on a mission and gonna get this stuff any ole way."

"But, Mar, it's been a really long time since we could funk out the whole compound with state of the art, you know. My creative energy is dying, Mom, it has been cramped," J.L. said, his tone wistful.

"J.L., if we turn you loose on the house, we're gonna need a floor plan for every button and whatnot you install in the rooms," Marjorie said. "I don't want to accidentally detonate my shower, or start a code-blue evacuation sequence that levels the house."

"You know what ..." J.L. said, his gaze becoming distant. "That is *genius,* Marj. I never had a melt-down, blow the joint, code-embedded—"

"Whoa, whoa, whoa, whoa whoa!" Rider said, laughing. "Take us slow, and by degrees, J.L."

"I feel where he's coming from, though," Jose said, supporting J.L. with a handshake. "Like, I was trying to get us back to touring, and nobody was feeling the music."

Carlos looked at Jose for a moment, remembering to bring that to the forefront of the discussion. The night before everything had been so murky, clouded by the condition he and Damali had been in, then it was time to pull it together and do the run for Dan, as promised.

"We took it to Neteru Council, and the man is on-point," Carlos said, pounding Jose's fist.

Carlos held the group in thrall, explaining only the necessary elements of getting the worldwide Guardians to know how to track them, and made the point that, since their cover was already long blown with the darkside, that wasn't a concern. Prayer barriers and evasive tactics would have to keep the heat off of them in the future.

"What about those madcap scientists that snagged us before?" Shabazz said, looking at Marlene with concern.

"They're still out there, just like every other human helper to the vamp empire. But those are rogues, and we still have the squads that helped us in Tibet. Both Neteru Councils are gonna try to give us Light support and cover, keeping whatever domicile we settle into covered. Just like to buy all this fancy equipment, we'll have to run it through several layers of holding companies with the Covenant cleaning up the trail, so we can stay on the down low."

Carlos pushed off the wall he'd been temporarily leaning against. "The only thing that concerns me about the World Peace tour is the fact that every time we move, we're vulnerable to a new, hostile environment. But if you guys wanna tour while the new compound is being built, then I'm down for whatever."

DAN WAS RIGHT in the middle of explaining how they might be able to get some of their old endorsements back, after J.L. had discussed the types of security they'd need at various stadiums around the world, when Damali walked out of the bedroom.

Everybody looked at her and fell quiet. Carlos studied her closely. He knew his wife. She had victory fire in her eyes.

"Hey, y'all . . . what'd I miss?"

No one answered.

"What did *we* miss?" Carlos asked, folding his arms over his chest.

She began walking in an excited circle, talking with her hands. "It was crazy! Ohmigod! Sit back and lemme tell you what went down."

"DOES THIS MEAN we should still buy the property Marlene was talking about?" Dan said quietly, the first to speak when Damali was done. "Or should we just update wills and wait for the response to this latest adventure?"

"Danny boy, you're beginning to sound like me," Rider said, dragging his fingers through his hair. "You see why I used to smoke."

"But at least now we know what was in that spell . . . and what we have to do to keep our bonds strong," Marlene said. "What if that mess had gotten into our household?" She rubbed her palms down her strain-weary face. "The Queens are awesome, and that was the best slingshot, spell-reversal-by-prayer move I've ever seen in my life. Damn, sistah—well done!"

"Comeuppance like a mofo, foul karma boomerang delivered all pro, D. I'm proud," Shabazz admitted. "You're scary, but I'm proud."

The rest of the team sat wide-eyed and mute, their stunned gazes going between Damali and Carlos and back again.

Carlos chuckled. "D, didn't I just catch a ration for doing something like this?"

Damali blew him a kiss from across the room. "Oh, man, you should have seen my sisters work it, though! I had Nuit backed up in a throne, and Lilith hissing—then he bulked on girlfriend."

Carlos held his hands up in front of his chest. "As long as you had your clothes on, I've got no beef." Then he smiled. "You backed the brother up into his own throne? Damn, D, you're vicious."

"We bombed all *seven* levels," Damali said in triumph.

Shabazz and Mike looked at each other and mouthed the word *seven*. The gesture rippled around the room, rendering everyone mute for a few added moments.

"And, I've been thinking," Damali said, starting to walk. "Ya know, when we do this tour, I'm really not feeling peace—per se."

"Sleep on it," Marlene said. "You're still battle-high."

Carlos laughed. "Yeah, D, adrenaline is all in your sweat."

She gave him a glance that said *Later, but definitely,* and ignored the protests. "Nah, I'm feeling more like a Take A Stand: End the Violence Against Humanity concert. There's a difference. One is more passive, and my music isn't flowing in me like that." She looked at Jose for support. "Like, we have the old standards that built us up over the years as the Warriors of Light . . . and some new stuff that we can refine and get out there . . . I don't know, like, 'Wounded Lover,' and all that, for the love portion of the show. For the part that gets into what happens when the madness continues."

"I feel you, D," Jose said. "Like, the concert in L.A. and during the early days, when we'd call evil out, and you'd strut across the stage with the squad, ready to rumble, holding up your Isis."

"That was some of your best stuff, D," Carlos admitted, looking at her and almost forgetting the team was there.

"Yeah, then you'd drop back and croon about those that got lost in the battle, and what missing them was like— Sydney, redux," Jose said, glancing at Carlos. "It was awesome. And we'd end on a note of hope with something bangin'."

"Then, I suppose, while we have a little hiatus, we oughta get back to seriously trying to lay down some closing tracks," Shabazz said, glancing at Rider, Mike, and Marlene. "Maybe we can get some serious choreography going to include some of these newbies, just like before."

"Oh, no, I'm strictly paperwork and backstage," Dan said.

"Me, too," Bobby said. "I'll be on security detail in the wings with the Covenant and Mom and Dad. Forgetaboutit."

Shabazz smiled. "Aw'ight, not everybody is meant for the limelight. But we'd work you in, if you wanted to."

"I don't sing," Inez said, laughing.

"But you can dance your butt off, sis," Juanita said. "How about you, Kris?"

"Uh . . ."

"I'll teach her," Inez said.

Tara held up her hands. "I'll carry an Uzi in the wings. I'd feel less scared doing a tunnel run than stepping onstage."

"No lie," Carlos said, shaking his head.

"Oh, man, no—I am *not* accepting that from you," Jose said, laughing hard when Carlos's eyes widened.

"What'chu talking about, Jose—be serious, man."

Damali covered her mouth and laughed.

"I am serious," Jose said. "If this is a worldwide call to arms, you have to get out there and—"

"Do what?" Carlos said, talking with his hands as the older Guardians began to stare at him as though considering Carlos insane. "I don't sing, I don't—"

"You can spit, brother. I've heard you," Jose said with triumph.

"What!" Carlos crossed the room, pointing at Jose.

"He talks more trash than a little bit," Damali said, now laughing so hard she was bending over. "Roll them Rs, baby, when you're talking cash-smack a mile a minute, drop it down low, all up close in the mic, war-jones running through your veins, you'll—"

"She's still battle-high, Mar!" Carlos said, laughing and walking away. "I do almost everything this woman wants, but not that—no!"

"Give him a beat, Mike," Rider said. "Jose, J.L., on percussion."

"Don't act like y'all ain't used to stand on the corners spitting lyrics, out shit-talking the others, just messin' around. You're from east L.A., holmes," Shabazz said with a wink. "Land of Krunk."

"Not to be confused with the dirty South," Mike said, beginning to make beats on the table as Shabazz started mouthing a heavy bass line.

"It all starts like this, and you know it," Damali said, strutting over to him and getting in his face. "Battle of the bands began with a battle of the blocks. Don't act like you don't remember."

"I remember, but I'm not doing no concert in front of a hundred thousand people, no matter what you say, D."

Carlos folded his arms over his chest and fought not to smile as Damali held an invisible mic and leaned up in his face with a street challenge, one hand on her hip.

"Oh, so now you scared, running blind, trying to act like you ain't hearing me, ain't got the time?" Damali said, just pulling a line from the air to start the battle.

"No, *you* got played," Carlos said, snatching at the air as though he'd just yanked down an invisible microphone. "They took your mind. Women, children, babies, now you're killing your own kind—psyched you out as a hustler—got you believing the hype—but your ass is straight-trippin' like you're smokin' a crack pipe!"

The room erupted in cheers as Carlos stepped back. Damali laughed hard, nodding.

"Aw'ight, aw'ight," Damali said, smiling. "Mad props. But, take this." She grabbed the invisible mic again and got in Carlos's face. "Ghetto bravado, brick-selling macho, bank-rollin' cash hits, steady talking cash—whoops, who's your daddy, don'tcha momma know? Best get hip real quick, learn how this lesson go—ain't only 'bout the knot you got, this joint's 'bout to blow."

"Whooooowe!" Rider said, falling back on the sofa as Shabazz slapped him five.

"Yeah, okay," Carlos said nodding. Then he took a deep breath and snatched the air mic again, rolling so hard and fast on Damali that Jose almost lost the beat laughing.

"Beef between brothers and blocks, nations flaring like dropped rocks—drama with crazy chicks, babies dying—they sick, what you ain't wit it—oops who's your baby's daddy, don't you really wanna know, why she go on Maury's show—jus' ask a brother how he know. Yeah, like I said a

quick minute ago . . . they took your mind—turned you in,
turned you out, got you blind to what it's all about—stole
your peace, robbed your pockets, jacked your future, your
mind—women, babies, old folks—why the Darkness need
to come at cha', when you killing your own kind?"

"Oh, shit!" Jose shouted, jumping up from the sofa and
abandoning the beat.

Shabazz was on his feet, fist pounding Mike so hard they
couldn't keep the beat steady, either. Damali was nodding
and laughing as the group erupted in general chaos.

"That was the nastiest spit I've heard in a loooong time!"
Jose said, shaking his head and rubbing the back of his neck.
"Damn, C."

Carlos laughed, breathing hard from the no-breaths-
between-words exertion. "I don't care what y'all say, I talk
trash, but I don't do in-concert. The living room is one thing,
but I'm not standing on a stage in front of all them people
forgetting what I was gonna spit."

Damali rubbed his back and he laughed when he moved
away from her.

"Nope, girl, don't even try it."

Everybody laughed harder, and then Mike and Shabazz
picked up a hard, military cadence, with Shabazz doing verbal bass line, and Mike on table percussion. They looked at
Jose, who immediately jumped in and started making up
lyrics.

"Roll call, Guardians. Sound off!" Jose hollered.

Damali repeated the line and looked at Carlos, making
him shake his head harder and fold his arms over his chest.

"Who's ready to roll?" Mike said in a deep, threatening
baritone that made Inez sit up in her chair and lean toward
him, listening hard.

Shabazz was right on his next sentence and he glanced at
Jose to be ready to take it after he spit. "Git down and dirty
wit it, leave no stone unturned to win it."

"Roll to your last breath, take no prisoners fast death."
Jose looked at Carlos.

"Ride, like you're gonna die, don't even ask no questions why."

Damali smiled at Carlos when he was done. "Who's ready to roll—uh-huh, what you say? Who's ready to ride—uh-huh, what you say? Who's taking a stand—uh-huh, what you say?"

"Just get your gear and move out. Draw the line—what you about?" Carlos said in the same steady-beat baritone as the brothers had, but then changed up the tempo to a syncopated, Latin influence that made them all shake their heads with appreciation.

"Who's down for whatever, whenever, whoever, however it's gotta go, yo? Who's willing, and able, and ready to go back—back to the hood, back to the block, back to backing this bullshit up while holding your Glock? My beef starts right at home, 'round the corner all alone. Who knows enough is enough; ashes ain't ashes 'til dust is dust, *man*? You gotsta be crazy letting this madness up in your mind, up in your hood, up in your woman, up to no good—inviting in evil at every turn, you're like a wide open virgin about to be burned—but I'm school ya now, brothers, so you all can learn—the insanity you're fighting can't be won, 'til you man up, and face up, and stand up, and be done. Roll call, who's ready, tonight I'm getting my gun."

Mike slapped Carlos so hard on the back he almost knocked him down.

"Ooooh, maaaan!" Jose hollered. "That was ridiculous, C!"

"We definitely can't bill this as the World Peace concert—I'm not even sure Stop the Violence applies," Dan said, impressed.

"Hey, go with Take Back the Block, then," Shabazz said with a wide smile, "'cause this brother definitely took that shit."

"Didn't he," Inez said. "Damn, C, I didn't know you could spit like that."

"That was pretty awesome, Mr. Rivera," Marlene said,

"and I've been in the biz for a fair piece of time—raw talent, brother. Mind like a razor to be able to come up with lines on the fly that fast—which also tells me how fast you can lie," she added, making the group erupt again in laughter before she hugged him.

"You definitely have to use a God-given talent like that, especially if it's calling Guardians to take a stand right in their own neighborhoods," Marjorie said, looking around. "You're calling people to say no to craziness in their own lives, first, and to monitor their own blocks and stop the insanity in their own homes before going anywhere else to stop it."

"Marj," Berkfield said, rubbing his palms down his face. "We're not in showbiz, leave them to—"

"But you used to say that all the time when you walked a beat," she argued. "I know what I'm talking about. This is true."

"I just didn't know you had it in you like that, dawg," J.L. said, laughing.

"Neither did I," Damali said quietly, unable to keep how proud she was from seeping into her voice.

Embarrassed by the attention and Damali's breathy tone of appreciation, Carlos walked over to the minibar and hunted for a beer, quickly realizing that the team had been in their suite for a long time and any stash that had previously been there was long gone.

"I was just adding-in here in the living room. Onstage takes the pros and I ain't that," Carlos said offhandedly, but still very pleased that he'd made Damali proud. It didn't mean he was down for a concert, but that he finally felt that he could relate to a part of her world that had felt so foreign before. That felt good. Really good. Maybe too good, given that it looked like the team was gonna probably be dug into their suite, concert planning for the duration.

An unexpected knock at the door gave the team a start. Bobby cautiously answered it as the room became quiet and tense, everyone's weapons concealed but at the ready.

The concierge stood at the door, his face solemn. "I am sorry to disturb your gathering," he said, glancing around with disapproving eyes. "But our other guests have asked if it is at all possible for you to keep it down just a tad?"

CHAPTER TEN

Yonnie looked down at Lorelei and withdrew from her body in disgust. He'd bedded another damned witch, who looked more like an imp begging to be made a vampire—and not one of them worthy, couldn't even come close to his Tara, or Gabrielle, for that matter.

"Why not?" she asked quietly, clutching the damp sheets to her rail-thin body.

Yonnie didn't even turn around as he buttoned his shirt the energy-saving way by hand. He didn't want to look at her sallow complexion and dyed black hair with its garish streak of purple running down the left front panel. His temper was such a short breath away from becoming murderous. With every thrust against her piteous frame his body had cried out—*not Tara*. There was no lavender, even though the wash of purple hue in her hair had drawn him to her . . . maybe that was it. Or it could have been the initial wide brown eyes that reminded him, but then only to find out as he'd moved in closer that she was a fraud . . . all games and deceit as any dark coven witch would be . . . except Gabrielle.

"Make me tell you no again, and that's your ass," he said through a sudden presentation of fangs. He had to get out of her room and pull it together.

"Why don't you just do it, Yonnie?" she said, challenging him as she stood.

"Because you don't have tits," he said, turning to leave. Rather hurt her self-esteem than her. But as she walked up closer, dangerously close, he wondered, why not? His chances for the Light had died long ago . . . his boy had left him hanging, had sided with a Guardian, Jack Rider, over him. So what if his turn bites would make her instant cinder? She'd rimmed his asshole with her lovely tongue, and that was worth something.

"You wanna take a walk on the permanent wild side, and can't take no for an answer." He smiled and began circling her. It had been so very, very long, and she had no idea.

"I want to be the undead," she said, looking up at him and trembling as he made her keep turning to hold his line of vision.

"Your treacherous ass is already the undead. Your soul probably fled your body years ago with all the foul bullshit you did." Yonnie stopped walking and then pushed her away from him so hard that she fell. "You dumb bitch. My bite would incinerate you on contact. That's the only reason you still got a throat. I'm out."

He was breathing hard, the urge to feed from her suddenly so visceral that he couldn't immediately retract his fangs. She stared up at him with a wide, foolish smile.

"I'm from the coven of Jezebel—we go back a very long time." Lorelei stood, letting the sheet fall away from her petite frame. "Don't you know that all banishments have been rescinded, because the Darkness needs to quickly amass power?"

Yonnie stared at her hard, but her information had stayed his leave.

"That's right. A spell by Sebastian got reversed in the realms. The Dark Lord is pissed, and he's calling his own home with more power. I'd heard through the grapevine that Nuit had tried to make you a councilman when Cain was temporarily installed. All the girls were looking for you to do the honors. I just found you first."

He crossed the room, needing space to think. Dark coven witches were known to lie, that was their specialty, but the truth registered in Lorelei's statement like fresh blood. Yonnie quickly opened his mind and concentrated, mentally seeing down vacant level after vacant level, the realms' portals wide open? He began to pace, rubbing his palms down his face. Carlos had bitten him as a councilman, elevated him to master—but had never relinquished the elevation bond. Each time Carlos went up in rank, so did he—when Carlos was chairman, he'd been a councilman and didn't even know it! How?

"Oh, shit . . ." Yonnie murmured, stopping by the window to stare out into the night.

No wonder Nuit could only save him from Rider's hallowed-earth-packed shell at dawn, but not run him. They were peers. Equals. But when Fallon presented him to Cain, lifting the turn ban on him, so much chaos immediately erupted that no one, not even Lilith, had recalled Dante's old edict. The ban had never been reset. He saw it all, even Lilith's installation—now also understanding why he'd spent days in an L.A. coven brothel tagging everything in there that he normally would have passed on. It also threaded guilt through his veins . . . yes, Nuit might have played him, but he'd flatlined Tara while at councilman-level strength. No wonder his boy let her go into the Light without him. Tara was safer with Rider; he'd known that all along but it stabbed him.

"Where are you going?" Lorelei said, beginning to panic as Yonnie's form started to disappear. "I gave you something, good information, and fair exchange is no robbery!"

"I gave you something, too, bitch, so don't ask me for anymore." Yonnie's voice echoed into the room where he'd been.

"What was worth what I just told you?" she shrieked, raging around the room at the nothingness of Yonnie's mist that remained.

"About ten inches for twelve hours and your miserable life."

"RIGHT HERE, IT says it," Solomon replied, drawing the Neteru Kings closer to the large, open, gleaming papyrus scroll before him. "*1 John 2:18, '. . . it is the last time; and as ye have heard that antichrist shall come, even now are there many antichrists; whereby we know that it is the last time.'*" He stood and looked at Adam and Ausar.

"Yes," Adam argued, "we have seen many in our vast times. Several attempts. That doesn't give us accuracy."

"No one knows the exact hour, just like their side cannot predict when our Neterus will be born. It was a clause on both sides that was agreed upon when the great bargain of free will was struck," Ausar said, looking at both Adam and Solomon. "We cannot act with haste on something so delicate."

"But when has there ever been a rapid trinity of Antichrists?" Solomon allowed the gleaming sacred text to roll up slowly on its own accord and sat back. "Think. Most recently, Dante, son of the Unnamed, rose to the earth plane . . . then one split off from Rivera's DNA and entered the sacred space, then Cain, until Adam's beloved wife beheaded him. If there was ever a time for our Guardian teams to remain childless, it's now."

Ausar closed his eyes. "One of Damali's Guardian sisters is late in her menses. This is why Rivera needed extra cover on his transport to courier his teammates to their parents for an after-the-fact union blessing."

"You know what Eve might have to do," Solomon said, his tone sad and heavy. "I bring this matter to the table at only the highest levels because the Guardian in question was once of a dark coven."

"But she has redeemed herself through free will and positive actions," Ausar said, beginning to pace. "We cannot cast aspersions or hold on to the past that is no more."

"It will break my wife's heart," Adam said. "It would also leave Damali destroyed, after all that she herself has endured in said regard." He walked away from the archon's table. "She, like Eve, would try to save it until they knew for sure."

"And by then it could be too late," Solomon said flatly, no judgment in his tone.

"A womb-purge is not in our province . . . and even if the Queens performed it, how would we know? Would any of you want that on your heads? An innocent baby's life, like the days of old when Kings swept through their empires killing firstborn children?" Adam's impassioned plea made Solomon close his eyes. "Are we not seeing genocide in the Motherland now? Peer down from the table and witness the Sudan, my brother. I can point out more horror, but feast your eyes there, first, and then tell me to lobby this unnatural cause to my wife!" Adam walked closer to the wide marble pillars that rimmed the inner chamber and held on to one for support. "After losing two of her own, my Eve would never countenance such an atrocity without unwavering proof."

The two Kings before Adam fell quiet for a moment, their expressions conflicted.

"For now we inform the Queens and simply watch the developments without action," Ausar said, quietly. "But if we see it enter the earth plane, we'll have no choice but to allow Hannibal to release the red steed."

THE NETERU GUARDIANS took the party to the beach and were even bold enough to build a fire. Their prayer barrier was set up like a big tent under the stars. Tactical Guardians kept authorities turning a blind eye to permits and beach curfews. Carlos had brought in a full complement of grub and beer, from the Dungeness crabs and chicken that Marlene and Shabazz fussed about, to sweet corn on the cob and everything in between. It all went on the fire, got blessed, and happily consumed.

Greasy hands found guitar chords and bass notes, beat drum skins and ran keyboards—the music was consuming them as much as they'd consumed the food and beer. Every instrument that had been brought in and salvaged from the old Beverly Hills compound was treated to a warm reunion with its owner.

It was a defiant display of taking back the night. Those gifted with music in their souls searched for song hooks, rapped and wrapped sixteen lines and sometimes twenty-one around thumping refrains—the audience of nonmusical Guardians being just as important, all energy blending one mind. Enjoy life. Live. Give. Share. Rejoice. Appreciate. They called the present the gift that it was. They carried that message to the sky above as they carried on down on the beach, blanketed in the effervescent light of creativity, laughter, love, and family, barbecuing crabs and corn and washing it down with ice-cold brews. Who knew what tomorrow would bring?

They'd finally run out of energy by dawn. The fire was now just embers. Cities and countries had been roughly chosen. A general outline of a stage plan and a plan of action had been loosely mapped out. Dumpsters and recycle bins far away got several deposits.

Slow-moving but smiling Guardians stretched and watched another new day roll in, feeling blessed.

"I SAW HIM," Lorelei whispered into her crystal ball. Her beady little eyes were narrowed to slits as she sent the message into Sebastian's throne. "Where are you, Master? You're the only raised one left of the dark covens of old . . . the rest have been turned to ash. We need your energy to continue to empower us. Now we all do your bidding." Receiving no response, she began to worry and she made her attempts more urgent as her coven sisters gathered closer.

"He should have heard us by now," she said, looking at the five concerned gazes around her. "He is a full sorcerer; his rise was felt by all as Lilith raised him—and now, there's nothing."

"We should contact the displaced covens of New Orleans that were forced to flee with the general population," a hissing blonde whispered. "Perhaps there was foul play, and they could get us close enough to summon Fallon Nuit's energy."

"Or we could simply go directly to Lilith to ask—"

"Are you crazy?" Lorelei almost shouted, breaking the séance. "Over Sebastian's head? Never, until we know for sure that he's been incapacitated."

"Then hone in on the spell he cast," a brunette murmured, her eyes shimmering with evil. "If something has gone awry with his spell, then he may be in danger and need assistance . . . that is the only reason he wouldn't respond to a coven call of this magnitude."

SEVEN HOURS OF peaceful sleep did her body good. As she stretched and yawned, Carlos's familiar warmth spooned her, making her bones lazy all over again.

Hotel life was getting old. The yearn for being in their own house again, their own kitchen, their own space was threatening to steal her peace. Rather than allow it, she snuggled deeper into Carlos's embrace and dozed, listening to his steady breaths of slumber and loving every minute of the way his heartbeat thrummed through her back.

As she drifted in and out of sleep all she could think of was seeing him spit lyrics, the way it had totally taken him over . . . then how that caught fire at the edges of the team, burning everybody, setting them on fire with creative energy that they hadn't experienced in a long time. Carlos stirred behind her and she pressed his arm closer against her belly.

"Thank you," she murmured.

"Good morning," he said in a drowsy, sexy voice, kissing the back of her hair. "For what?"

"For doing what you do," she said quietly, making his arm hug her tighter. "For being you—the fire for the group. The catalyst."

He chuckled softly against her hair. "That's just your nice way of saying I'm always the one starting some shit."

"I'm serious," she said quietly and swallowed hard, suddenly overwhelmed for no reason, and unable to even explain to herself why.

"Hey . . ." he murmured, hugging her more closely. "I didn't mean to make fun of what you were saying, baby . . . but if you want me to start some shit, you know all you have to do is ask—and ya don't do half bad yourself, you know."

He made her chuckle, even though she hadn't felt a laugh in her. It didn't really matter that he didn't know what she was talking about; she wasn't sure, either. All that mattered was that he loved her like he did, the way he loved her—that he stood for something she was proud of, and had brought back her real Muse . . . not an imposter. She'd been so afraid of her music after Cain that she almost killed it, so had her team. But leave it to Carlos to talk some trash to make even something that scary feel safe again.

"I want to go see the house today," she said with a sigh. "I just want to be able to see it, walk through it, in more than a mental picture—so I can save it like a postcard."

He nodded and kissed her hair again. "Yeah . . . the hotel life is getting old for me, too. Let's go put down some roots while they clean the room."

IT TOOK LONGER than they'd really had the patience to endure, but getting all those couples up, waiting until everyone got dressed, fed, and out of their rooms on their own recognizance to meet in the lobby was a logistical task akin to moving out a platoon. Then there was the debate about which of the several properties to see first, and finally they decided to allow the Covenant-approved Realtor to lead while they followed in a small caravan of assorted SUV rentals. Carlos and Damali looked at each other and the same mental question leapt into their heads—*Was it worth all this?*

They both nodded. *Yeah.*

CARLOS KNEW IT was all over when his wife's voice hit that pitch that generally turned his eyes silver. It was that

gaspy, "Oh, wow . . ." let out on a long breath thing that
women did when they saw something they really wanted,
that did him in. Third house, yeah it was a wrap. Every
brother got out of his vehicle with that look of resignation in
his eyes. Their women had obviously slaughtered them, too,
with the breath sigh. What was the point in haggling with a
Realtor? Poor Dan was outnumbered and needed to give it a
rest. The Realtors could smell a sure kill just like sharks
could smell blood in the water. Prices went from flexible to
firm, since the women's eyes said price was no object.

*Can you ladies at least find something wrong with the
house as we walk through it, so the ooohhhs and ahhhs don't
add another million to the tag?* Carlos tried to walk away
from Damali when Inez saw the kitchen and screamed.

"Oh, my God, thank you, thank you, Jesus, this is just
what I wanted," Inez gushed, grabbing Mike by the arm.
"Isn't this just how I told you I saw it—stainless steel everything, overhead pot racks, windows all around—facing the
beach! Look at the flowers just spilling over the window
boxes. Oh, Michael . . . a center island, Jenn-Air range, real
restaurant-sized burners and double oven, stand-alone
broiler . . . oh, good Lord, a real brick oven for pizzas and
breads, and look at the industrial-sized fridge—hand-laid
Spanish tiles!"

Mike squinted and then nodded with his eyes closed.
"You like it, baby, I love it."

Carlos looked out the window. *Cha-ching.* They were
done. If Inez kept working on the team's big audio-sensor,
they'd probably have to ask the Realtor to throw in a baby
nursery for free.

Stop, Damali mentally fussed. *Get into the present joy
of it all. 'Nez never had her own spot like this, and this is
gorgeous . . . look at the blues and yellows and oranges in
here, would ya? Wow . . .*

He would not say another word. His lips were sealed,
Carlos told himself as they passed through the huge eat-in

kitchen already situated to accommodate a long oak picnic table with sliding glass doors that opened out to a huge deck.

"Security issue," J.L. muttered.

Carlos nodded. "I'm right there with you, brother."

"Oh, but look at the pool . . ." Krissy gasped, racing down the deck to gawk with Juanita at the view.

Carlos gave J.L. a supportive shrug. "I know, man. What you gonna do?" He almost laughed when Jose closed his eyes and shook his head.

"Oh, Jose," Juanita said, her voice modulating between high-pitched squeals and breathy awe, "if you're in the water you can look out over the surface of the pool and see the waves down on the beach." She smiled at him, and it was a brilliant, dazzling, heart-stopping smile. "Won't this be so romantic at night?"

When Jose didn't immediately answer, Carlos slapped him on the back in passing. "Stop drooling, you're making the Realtor add it to the bill."

"I don't know how we're gonna wire the pool for under-the-stars swims," J.L. said, rubbing tension out of his neck.

"You're not," Carlos muttered, "unless you silver line the hole in the ground, which means excavation and then putting in a whole new pool—or else Amanthras will be swimming in there with—"

Krissy's squeal made the group hustle down the deck, and to Carlos's dismay, the Realtor had walked the ladies past the sauna, hot tub, and spa area with multishowerhead stalls and a changing room to a ground-level technology room.

"This is what I call the engine room, folks," the Realtor said with a triumphant grin. "The master controls for all air-conditioning and heating zones are here, the indoor sprinkler systems, sump pumps, motion detectors, plumbing, pool filters, multiple garage door openers, lawn sprinklers, you name it." He walked over to several flat screens and flipped a switch in the large ten-by-twelve open area. "Each system can be monitored by grounds crews with wireless intercoms from the main house—all bedrooms are wired, as well as the kitchen and family room, and the complete grounds can be seen by flipping through zones. The mainframe is on its own backup generator with direct alarms to police and fire, and—"

"J.L., J.L., look at this!" Krissy said at a pitch that might shatter glass. "It's all here, one room—our room, oh, J.L., look at it, do you know what we could do with the basic technology they have in here?"

Carlos just sighed. Another good man lost to the cause of negotiating. In the far recesses of his mind he'd heard the Realtor balk about it being basic technology in the room, but he was trying to keep his eyes on Damali. However, he threw in the towel when she saw the theater and studio. He couldn't even fake it, when she'd spun around in the studio screaming, his eyes were near silver.

"You're flickering at the edges, brother," Shabazz muttered with a grin, teasing Carlos as they passed into the next room.

But Shabazz couldn't even play it off when they all walked into a huge, blond-oak-floored dance studio where the floors gleamed like glass. Mirrors and dance bars rimmed the room on three sides, but the fourth side was a wall entirely of glass that faced the mountain landscape. Marlene put both hands together in a silent prayer and mouthed the words *Thank you*. When she opened her eyes the look she gave Shabazz made him slowly hold on to one of the bars for support.

"This is a perfect training room," Marlene said quietly— and that was all she said as she left the room.

Shabazz looked at Rider. "I know. Don't say it."

Rider held up both hands. "My turn is coming. I'm not hatin', as the youngbloods say."

Before they could get out another complaint, Marjorie's enraptured voice made them hurry to help their fallen comrade, Berkfield.

"Oh, Richard . . . look at this family room—it's like a

dream . . . what we used to always say we'd do if we hit the lottery."

Berkfield just opened his arms as his wife filled them and hid her face. He nodded and rubbed her back as she took in and released deep, shuddering breaths.

"We're so blessed," she whispered. "Our children . . ."

"I know, honey, I know, don't cry . . ."

"Ohhhh . . . Richard."

"I guess by now you know we're buying the house, right?" Carlos said from a side whisper, glimpsing Dan.

"Yeah, it's a matter of points and price at this juncture."

Carlos scoffed. "Yeah, right, even if I could negotiate in *Dananu* our position is compromised."

"I heard that, Rivera," Damali said, threading her arm around his waist. "Why are you guys always like this— except when you're at the car dealerships?"

He smiled and allowed her to pull him along. "Because y'all are always like we are here at the car dealerships. Bored and watching for sticker shock."

"We are not," Damali fussed.

"Are too," Carlos said laughing, and then had to simply shake his head when Jasmine saw the private bonsai gardens and meditation paths that had been created outside each bedroom suite.

It was such a sweet kill that Carlos saw it happen in slow motion. Jasmine covered her mouth, then closed her eyes, and walked toward Bobby blindly and hugged him. She didn't say a word; Bobby's face spoke volumes for her. Two down, felled by one garden and a carp pool. The thing was, Shabazz wasn't far behind them, just like Big Mike was having trouble breathing in the kitchen, probably imagining what Inez could whip up for him in there while wearing a teddy. J.L. had been lost on the ground floor forty minutes ago, just like Berkfield was lost somewhere between the thirty-foot cathedral ceiling of the sunken living room and the walk-in fireplace of the family rec room that had broken Marjorie down into tears. They had already called "man down" for Jose, when Juanita saw the pool. As far as Carlos was concerned, the only brothers still holding the negotiating line were him, Dan, and Rider.

At least that's the way he'd envisioned it until the Realtor pointed out that the house was set on seven acres of pristine land with stables, should they want horses. Carlos thought for sure he'd seen Tara's knees buckle and Rider catch her around the waist as she simply stared out at the mountain.

"All of that's ours?" Tara whispered, the sale obviously already final in her mind. "Untouched land the way it was meant to be . . . free."

"All the way down to the beach and personal yacht docks," the Realtor said proudly.

Rider didn't swallow hard; he practically gulped as she turned to him and signed "man with a good heart" over his chest.

"Remember those days in Arizona, trying to get there across all that country?"

"Yeah," Rider said in a gravelly voice. "All that wild lavender in the wind."

Too done, Carlos walked away. The Realtor was fingering his Montblanc pen like it was a switchblade.

Seeming pleased, their Realtor prattled on. "We can walk the grounds at your leisure to see the tennis courts and golf driving range in a bit, but I think you might enjoy seeing how we've designed private quarters for sixteen guests at a time—and yet some of the rooms could be turned into offices, quite naturally—even though we do have a central technology area on the second floor."

The Realtor kept a brisk pace, and the team followed, each person ogling the double-high windows and domed skylights, then suddenly realizing the security problem they presented.

"This is a unique cultural blend . . . In keeping with the sleek Swedish lines and minimalist Japanese design that has eclectically blended the Swedish spa experience with the healing stone and bath therapy wisdom of Japan, we've created master suite spas . . . incorporated them into the whole look and feel of each suite. Natural stones—"

"Natural stones?" Heather whispered. "Mr. Gerhart . . . these aren't just finishes?"

"No, ma'am," the Realtor said proudly. "Each fixture, like the double-wide tubs are carved from pure granite and lined with healing-property stones."

Granite. Wonder whose idea that was? Damali mentally whispered to Carlos and then chuckled when he looked away. *Uh-huh.*

"For example," Gerhart said, unaware of the sidebar commentary in the room. "Malachite tiles line the tub, just as you'll find an array in the sinks and showers. According to gemologists they're soothing, calming, and promote inner peace, balance the physical body, and are excellent for meditation or dream work. This stone is said to be aligned with the heart chakra and solar plexus, I believe. The entire house is based upon the principles of feng shui and each bathroom tub fixture has running wall fountains that recycle over the stones for a soothing effect, as well as to keep good humidity in the rooms for the ferns."

"Dan . . . look at the stones in here," Heather murmured, running her hand across the sink and closing her eyes.

Lost our chief negotiator—slaughtered in his own bathroom, Carlos mentally shot toward Damali, raising an eyebrow. *Guess we're buying, huh?*

Damali shrugged and then nodded.

"Okay, how much?" Carlos said, rubbing his palms down his face.

"But you haven't seen the rest of it," the Realtor said too calmly.

Carlos looked at Damali. *You know he's just saying that so he doesn't seem too eager, right?*

The Realtor chuckled. *Twenty million. I was sent by the Covenant, and unless you're blocking transmissions to all seers, I can read minds.*

"Well if you were sent by the Church," Carlos said, truly

salty, "then—" He opened up his arms. "Come on, you guys are supposed to play fair."

"A," Gerhart said with a sigh, "fair is that you can afford it. B—have you ever been in negotiations with the Church over property?" When Carlos couldn't immediately respond he smiled. "The Covenant has bills to pay, too, you know, since your team is prone to blowing up anything you get your hands on . . . and for the record, we have already silver-lined the pool. Don't dig it up and mess up our prayer barriers."

"Give the man a check, Daniel. We never stood a chance."

FAIR EXCHANGE WAS indeed no robbery, and Damali could only laugh once inside the exclusive dealerships. Every man, including her oh-so-smooth husband, needed a bib to keep car-appreciation drool off his shirt. Correction—fantasy machine appreciation. She didn't care what they bought, at this point, as long as they would hurry up and get something to eat.

But neither she nor any of the team's female Guardians could be the ones to hurry them along, not without hearing about the infraction until the end of time. It had taken them nearly five hours to look at three mansions and for Dan to plunk down a hefty deposit to take it off the market. So, a few hours in the dealership was something to be endured. Once J.L. and Jose started designing weapons for the rides, then . . . oh, yeah, she'd be on it. For now, they had to nod and give platitudes of "That's nice" or "That's awesome" or "That's all you, baby," as their men spoke in hushed reverence near a stunning vehicle, or simply squeezed their eyes shut.

Don't even laugh at us, D, Carlos said, laughing himself. *We've been listening to you ladies do this all afternoon.*

I know, I know, I ain't hatin', she said with a wide grin. *I'm just hungry.*

Yeah, me, too, quiet as kept, but . . .

Yo, solidarity with da bruthaz, right?

"But look at her, D . . . she's got *a Swarovski crystal windshield,* yo . . . oh, maaan . . . a lacquered bonsai shift with *solid gold* knob inlaid—get this, with narwhal horn—right on the shift lever . . . dove-skin upholstery, *baby* . . . can you see her in all silver? D, she's fionne, *damn!* Look, look, right here, check it out—special launch mode—insanity mode, to drop her suspension to keep her from lifting off the ground like a rocket . . . a thousand and one horses under the hood . . . shifts in a hundred and fifty milliseconds, D . . . *I'm in love.* And they're gonna make me wait for her for *a whole year*—I'm *dying.*"

"You're cresting fang, baby." She glimpsed him for a sideline smile and then glanced at his crotch. "Just checking to be sure the Bugatti wasn't taking my man."

He pushed her away from him, laughing. *You ain't right, D. No. I'm not. I'm hungry . . . Lord have mercy, Carlos.*

Aw'ight, aw'ight, I'll see what I can do to hurry the process along—but don't out me, D.

She made the sign of zipping her lips shut, causing him to chuckle harder, and then walked away.

Carlos glanced at Shabazz. "Why don't we call this a wrap, brother," he said, leaning in to speak confidentially in Shabazz's ear. "We can go bust a grub, let every man in here place an order for whatever he wants—do the thing wire transfer, but the bottom line is, we go get some food. Maybe some bubbly for the ladies, since we just bought the house of life, and break camp . . . since they are very appreciative that things got wrapped up so fast."

"I was trying not to blow the groove, myself, brother," Shabazz whispered back. "I'm hungry, and uh, could use some space from the team—feel me?"

Carlos nodded. "Cool. Pass the word. We're out."

"WE DO, TOO, make decisions faster," Carlos said, backing into their suite laughing and blocking his chest from her pulled blows.

"How can you say that?" she said, fussing and laughing at the same time, kicking the door shut.

"You said you were hungry, and within five minutes, me and 'Bazz had marshaled troops and were out. Every man went into that VIP dealership knowing pretty much what he wanted down to the color—whereas y'all couldn't even decide what to eat. All we said was no sushi, and we were cool."

"Yeah, well, sometimes you have to take your time and think things through."

"I *know,* after you stabbed a minotaur from Level Seven in the eye, you are *not* going there." He ran from her as she chased him for a few paces.

"See, I knew I'd hear about that 'til the end of time." She folded her arms over her chest with a big grin. "You ain't right, Carlos Rivera."

He held up his hands. "All right, aw'ight," he said, laughing. Then his smile slowly faded. "But some things didn't take me no time to figure out . . . and I was dead-on about it."

"Yeah . . . like what?" she asked quietly, leaning on the back of the sofa and studying him from across the room.

"It took me about three to five seconds for my mind to catch up with what I was seeing—then I knew."

She cocked her head to the side and listened to his voice dip, letting the sensual sound coat her insides with a slow heat.

"I saw this beautiful, crazy, wild chica square off on my boyz, who were trying to rob her . . . and it only took about two seconds to pull my nine and fire it in the air for them to stop . . . 'cause, see, I had to get closer, had to be sure my eyes weren't playing tricks on me," he said quietly, stalking her.

"Go 'head, man, you need to stop." She tried to look away, but his intense gaze brought her eyes back to his.

"I'm serious," he said, moving closer, but taking his time, going the long way around the furniture to get to where she was leaning. "She didn't just look terrified, she was pissed off . . . loco. Her skin had this sheen to it . . . like you ever see the metallic shimmer underneath a serious paint job, looks like diamond flecks or crystals are in the paint?"

She landed a hand on his chest with the intention to playfully push him away, but didn't. "Oh, so now my skin is like a Saleen S7's custom paint job." She shook her head.

"You're blowing my rap, baby, but what I've gotta tell you is profound," he said, smiling and tracing her cheek with the pad of his thumb. "I meant no disrespect, señora. That's a six-hundred-thousand-dollar car and I just came out of the dealer . . . but your skin is priceless."

He brushed her mouth with a light kiss. "What I was trying to say before my rap got interrupted is that, it didn't take a whole long process for me to make up my mind. I saw the glow . . . saw your eyes. Watched your braids you had then swinging up and off your shoulders as you threw a round-house that flattened my boy. Saw your breasts bounce under that little tank top you was wearing," he murmured, tracing her collarbone with his index finger. "Saw your thighs flex under your jeans when you stepped back fast in a fighter's stance . . . and maaan, that booty. Case closed. I was sold. I knew that was my future wife."

"You are crazy," she said, kissing his chest and laughing softly. "And you guys on the team, collectively, make us crazy."

"That's a matter of perspective," he said, finding the sensitive side of her neck. "You all go back and forth and have to go back over it all again."

"Yeah," she whispered against his neck, and then licked his tattoo back and forth and went over it again. "We do, but you told me you liked that."

His breath hitched. "Not fair." She did it again and he closed his eyes. "But, yeah, I love it when you do that."

"Not trying to be fair, trying to win."

He smiled and nipped her neck. "What's the negotiation?"

"If I told you that, you'd have the advantage."

"Can I guess?" he murmured, beginning to trail his hands down her body to capture her breasts.

She shuddered as his thumbs grazed her nipples through her tank top. "Uh-huh." But to even the score she leaned into his chest and began suckling one of his through his T-shirt until his breathing changed.

"No fair," he said in a gravelly tone.

"What did I tell you about fair, señor?" When she looked up, his eyes had gone silver, and that was most assuredly her undoing. It had frightened her when that didn't happen before, and to see it again was more than comforting; it turned her on.

"Then give me something to go on," he said in a low, sensual rumble as she lifted his shirt and kissed each separate muscle in his abdomen until it clenched.

"It's been something I've really wanted for a long time," she said, breathing out the statement against his stomach while opening his pants.

For a moment he didn't say a word, just tightened his grip on her shoulders.

"Now that we have the house coming soon . . ." he said quietly, his voice trailing off as he lost his train of thought when she slowly lowered his zipper. "If . . ." Her touch interrupted him again and he planted a kiss on the crown of her head.

She looked up with a mischievous grin, holding him tightly in her fist. "Give up guessing?"

"Naw," he finally said, wresting back his former control. "I'll figure it out, and then we deal."

"Okay," she whispered, flicking her tongue down his groove, then making a lazy, spiraling circle over the head and slowly drawing him into her mouth.

"I don't care what you do, D, I'm not giving up without a fight."

"Ummm, hmmm," she mumbled, slowly shoving his pants over his hips.

When she looked up again they both chuckled.

"You are *so* wrong, girl . . ."

"I know, but I was just messing with you," she said, kissing up his stomach until he bent to take her mouth. "Want me to stop?" She wiggled her eyebrows.

"No, but you know I'm no good when you do that," he whispered into the next kiss, slowly pulling her up to stand so he could peel away her clothes. "I gotta feel your skin."

"You know *I'm* no good when *you* do *that*," she said, practically melting as he slid off her tank top as though making her shed skin, the side of his face a light nuzzle over her breasts until the fabric was tossed on the floor. "Oh, damn, Carlos," she said in a breathy whisper. "You don't fight fair."

"Not trying to be fair, trying to win."

He kissed down her breastbone, down her torso and bent to pay homage to her belly. It didn't matter that he'd opened her jeans. He ignored what was aching inside them, his hands gliding down her inseams until he reached her sandals and slid them off. But the look he gave her as he slowly stood made her pull her jeans down and leave them in a pool at her feet without his aid. Her seeking kiss stopped him from bending to unlace his Tims, and her voice nearly broke when his hot torso collided with hers.

"Let me do it," she said in a husky whisper.

He gripped her shoulders and shut his eyes as she melted down his body in a searing slide, bringing his pants down, her tongue right behind it, and then she stopped to worry about getting him out of his boots. She was gonna make him start wearing flip-flops as long as they were in San Diego, if she didn't hurry. Her kisses were pelting his calves, causing his thigh muscles to contract with each one. She'd opened his legs with a gentle shove of her soft, graceful hands, and the moment his boots and jeans came off with his boxers, it was all he could do not to hard-roll her over the edge of the couch.

But the way she'd slipped off the back of the sofa to settle between his legs on the floor looking up at him, promised so much more . . . if he could just be patient. It was a promise conveyed in her eyes, and in the soft touch that set his inner thighs on fire. It was also in the way her hair grazed one leg while her lips found that sensitive skin just outside his sac . . . *oh* . . . *Jesus,* she'd pulled the whole thing into her mouth, didn't even nick him, just sent her tongue over it in a maddening circle until he was pumping against air.

"You win," he breathed out.

Her hand slid up and found his base. "Uh-uh."

What did she mean, uh-uh? She already had him dripping. He held on to the back of the sofa and dropped his head forward. He could feel the blood draining away from his knuckles, he was gripping the edge so tightly. Slow down, don't push, and he could hang . . . maybe . . . but her tongue was making him stupid. "Baby, listen . . ."

"Uh-uh." She wasn't hearing it, wasn't having it, he needed to understand. This wasn't about negotiation, it was appreciation sublime. The hollow challenge was just thrown out to get him to submit to being loved in agonizing increments until the tattoo on his base smoldered.

She found that spot, gave her tongue over to it wholesale, and felt his groan implode in her belly like a subsonic charge in the atmosphere. But this was about her appreciation for him just being him, for all the drama that he'd endured, all the madness that he'd suffered with her family, for all the times he could have walked and didn't. The fact that they'd both lived through a spell that could have destroyed them, had both recently gone places that they didn't have to come back from—she had to let him know he was her world.

Her hand slid over the wondrous swell of his tight, clenched ass as she held him steady to draw him into her mouth. For every time her tongue had lashed out in anger, she took it back one swerving roll and flicker at a time while suction-pulling hard, holding him in a tight pulsing squeeze, making him acknowledge her silent apology with a deep moan.

Just hearing him that close put her tattoo on fire, had it practically screaming up her back she wanted him inside her so badly. But this was for him—he always took care of her first. She had to hold him with both hands as he started losing the ability not to follow instinct and thrust hard; she wasn't gonna pull up until she saw silver sweat. But she'd looked up at the same time he'd opened his eyes and looked down, and the visual connection did something crazy to them both.

His body gave off a spontaneous, erotic, tactical silver charge that ran all over her, up, down, and through her. If he hadn't been holding on to the edge of the furniture, he might have choked her half to death by accident with an erratic deep thrust. But the current that linked them brought her so close to the edge, right where he was, that she had to quickly stop for a second to be sure she didn't inadvertently bite down. When he slipped out of her mouth, he buckled in the middle like he'd been punched, and the sound that ejected from his lungs was similar to when a person gets the wind knocked out of them. She covered the engorged skin with both hands with the intention to quickly pick up where she'd left off, but the way he held her shoulder made her look up at him knowing he couldn't take it and needed to be inside her.

Again their heavy-lidded gazes met. His solid silver irises were slowly going gold, just like his sweat was alchemizing right before her eyes. His hand cupped her face and next thing she knew, they were in the next room in bed.

Tell me what it is, baby, his mind groaned. That same deep sound came up through his body, her body, and out into her ear. "Just tell me."

The exquisite feel of him entering her in one hard thrust made her legs instantly wrap around his waist . . . what were they talking about in the first place? Appreciation, yeah . . . Her arch began the conversation in earnest.

You. That's all I want, her mind shrieked as her breath caressed the heated skin of his neck.

"You've always had that," he said on a gasp, not realizing she'd surrendered.

She had to make him understand that she wasn't playing any longer. She was dead serious, wide open; all the walls and pride she'd ever had were torn down and gone.

At first I was gonna tease you about doing the concert, then it became so much more . . .

I thought you wanted to start a family, I . . .

I do. Screw the concert. I want you, just as you are.

Aw . . . D . . . you always had that from the door.

I know—I just didn't appreciate it sometimes . . . let me make that up to you . . .

Baby . . . you're blowing my mind, debt paid in full.

No . . . I surrender—you win, I win, one flesh, oh, baby . . . don't you see, you always win, so do I?

Her palm flattened against his spine and she let him feel the total acceptance jettison from her chakra system to his, lighting a path up his back until he arched with a holler, dropped fang, and began to pant.

Oh, Damali, one flesh is killing me, corazon.

Then let's die together, okay?

Yeah, oh, yeah, okay . . . oh, D, it's too hot, drop the connection!

Uh-uh, you said it in church, 'til death do us part.

Tears stung her eyes and then fell without shame as she lost all technique and rhythm, put a hump in his back, and made his tattoo solid gold.

"I love you so much, want you to be safe, want us to be one, want a home, Carlos, a family, everything in this life, just with you," she said, beginning to cry. She didn't care if she was babbling, didn't care that she was bordering on hysteria—didn't he understand, she wasn't playing. "I wanna grow old with my man, see our babies grow up, I wanna still be your baby when I'm sixty-five, and wanna love you like this 'til the end of time."

He couldn't piece together even a mental reply. Everything was coming out of his mind in short bursts like his breath. Her admission wrecked him, took him to a place where there was no game in him. Core meltdown, her angel touch was dredging pleasure paradigms unfound, hidden cells within cells, loading in his shaft with pressure, unreleased, unrelenting, his body tethered to hers, unable to spend itself without her, filling his sac with such need that tears wet his face as his mind emptied first.

"Whatever you want," he gasped, "I want." It felt so good he was delirious, straight babbling. "Wherever, however, whenever, it's yours."

Air scorched his lungs as he held her tighter, silver-gold sweat now flinging off his temples and hair with every hard stroke, running down his back, tickling the crack of his ass, wetting his balls as they swept against her. Then suddenly it felt like time had stopped, holding him hostage on the edge of a blinding release, his sanity was ransomed, and beneath him was the only person in the world that could set him free.

"Oh, God, Damali baby, I love you, I want all those things too, *tesoro*, everything, *all of it*. Just let it go!"

His voice broke with a wail as he felt her start to fall, pulling him, dragging him over the edge of the largest precipice he'd ever scaled. His fingernails ripped down the sheets as he fell; the pleasure bolt left his skull and his sac at the same time, thundered down his spine and imploded in his shaft. The first wave of what hit him was so intense that he couldn't even bite her, his body just jerked like lightning had struck him and was melting him down into white-hot protoplasm from the inside out. Everything within him poured out into her. Hot, sticky Neteru essence that made him holler as it left his body in strobes of ecstasy. She was sobbing when the second wave hit, and soon he realized she wasn't by herself. Feathers were everywhere; his tattoos were running from ice-cold silver to white-hot gold, pulling more seed up and out of him with each phase-shift until he buried his face in her shoulder ready to beg her to make it stop.

Soft hands slid down his wet back and dredged the last of it up and out of him with a shuddering moan. He dropped against her body so hard he was afraid he'd crushed her.

It took a minute for his orientation to come back. That was the thing that he loved so much about making love to her, he could never tell how it was gonna go. V-point, creation-point, a chakra-bending experience, lit pulse-point foreplay that ended in him seeing stars . . . or a mind-meld, talk-dirty-to-me-baby, hard roll in the hay, or something profound just like this. He was half-scared of the places she could take him, truth be told. But he wouldn't give that part of their relationship up if a nine were at his skull.

"You okay?" he finally murmured between heavy breaths as he peeled himself away from her just enough to roll them both over.

"No," she whispered, hiding her face against his chest, sobbing hard. "It was so good . . . I'm devastated."

CHAPTER ELEVEN

If someone had put a gun to his head and asked him out-right why was he sitting in the hotel lobby bar only a few hours after making crazy love to his wife, he wouldn't have been able to answer.

"You'd be one dead motherfucker," Carlos muttered into his Rémy, setting the short rocks glass down hard on the bar.

One thing for sure was he needed space. They'd set up shop however many times before, built compounds and safe houses, even had lairs, and watched them be burned or sold. But there was something real different and real permanent about the way each woman on the team looked at that prop-erty in La Jolla . . . their eyes had hope, future, possibility shimmering in them, especially his wife. That was a lot of responsibility for any man, but seriously no joke for men with a bounty on their heads.

But he also understood the need the team had to invest in the mundane. It made the crazy reality they lived somehow seem sane. To buy a house, a car, go out to dinner and eat . . . to laugh, make love, think about starting a family, visiting parents—none of that could be taken for granted by a Guardian Neteru team. It was probably as far-fetched as any regular Joe or Jane going to the corner store and wishing they had a hundred mil or so in the bank to play with. That's how the mundane felt for them, so no wonder every team member was turned on, turned out, and celebrating when Dan inked the papers. Same deal with the cars.

Thoughts of home collided with Carlos's next slow sip of Rémy, neat. If it weren't for his boy, Yonnie, he wouldn't even have been able to come to the table correct earlier this afternoon. Carlos briefly closed his eyes and ran his palm across his jaw. He'd just gone into the Light coming out of Sydney back then, when his boy, a master vamp with Rider's lady, had stayed with him, regardless, planned for his future, and had made the fucked-up digit the government had left him multiply into a hundred mil, very large, in Swiss accounts. *That* was a *friend*. Because his boy had been a realist, he had a future. Now he was supposed to deny his main hombre access to his house? Damn!

He knew why it had to be that way, understood it all intellectually—the Neteru in him got it. But the street code of ethics, the honor even amongst thieves, the never-leave-your-boy-ass-out, ever, street code of conduct was at pure war with his inner Neteru. Carlos said another prayer in Yonnie's behalf. What else could he do? Might even be too late, but Damali had shown him, it ain't over 'til it's all the way over.

Carlos lifted his glass. "To anybody upstairs listening, this is one for the brother who ain't make it. Watch his six, even if I can't." Carlos downed his drink, spun the glass on the bar, and then slung it down to the bartender for a refill. "Damn."

It had been good looking out on Yonnie's part, back then. Otherwise, Damali's resources would have been strained. Girlfriend hadn't been touring in almost two years, CD sales had slacked off, endorsements dropped off—because who could use a star that didn't come out for photo-ops, interviews, or paparazzi to shine? Only Dan had a real clear picture on how the accounts were aligned, the portfolio spread. If Yonnie hadn't hooked a brother up, then he'd be like Berkfield and Bobby, trying to figure out how to buy a four-bedroom ranch in the burbs—and *not* in San Diego, at that.

Carlos accepted his drink and briefly shut his eyes.

"Rough night, buddy?" the bartender asked.

Carlos quickly scanned him. Not a demon, not a familiar. "Yeah. But I'm cool."

"Lemme know when you need another one, then," the bartender said, wiping out glasses with a white cloth.

Carlos just nodded. What was there to say? Yonnie had gone to war with him; had been on his mind since he'd seen him at la casa . . . he'd just kept that to himself. Rider was his boy, too. He understood both men's positions. Would have been cool if the Light could have cloned Tara. Carlos took another slow sip of his drink. He needed to talk to Yonnie, but what could he say to him, truth be told? Right now, all he had to offer him was his blade . . . Yonnie was still his boy and he'd always have his brother's back.

A tall dark figure with a familiar gait caught his attention in his peripheral vision. Carlos looked up and set his drink down slowly as he saw Shabazz approach the bar. He glanced at his Rolex—eleven P.M. Shabazz alone *at the bar*? Oh, shit . . . whassup?

"Yo, man," Carlos said, pounding Shabazz's fist as he slid onto a stool. He watched his Guardian brother grumble a greeting and order a Jack Daniel's, and said nothing until the bartender left.

"So, what's going on, man?" Carlos asked, cutting right to the chase after Shabazz had taken the first sip from his drink.

Shabazz winced with the sip. "Can't a man just chill and have a drink?"

Carlos stared at him. "No."

Shabazz's face relaxed into a slow half-smile. "Then why're you here?"

"We ain't talking about me, right now. We're talking about you."

Shabazz lifted his Jack Daniel's shot to Carlos, downed it, and slid the shot glass back to the bartender so accurately that it hit his palm like a bullet. "One more."

"All right, what happened, man?" Carlos nodded for a refill. "We can either play cat and mouse and go back upstairs snot-slinging drunk—which is always an option . . . but the morning consequences and the domestic fallout are high—or we can just be real."

"Aw'ight," Shabazz said, accepting the new shot. "Seal the area, brother . . . 'cause I've got some deep questions to ask you."

For a moment, Carlos didn't move. If the team's philosopher had some deep questions to ask him . . . then shit . . .

Accepting his new drink, Carlos silently complied and then leaned in to Shabazz. "Talk to me."

Shabazz let out a hard breath and set his drink down carefully as though studying the dark amber liquid in the shot glass. "When you cross over into the Light, man, you come to understand a lot of things. You make your peace with things you never thought you could deal with, feel me?"

Carlos nodded, understanding the reference to Kamal without either man needing to speak on it. From the way Shabazz had taken a shell at point-blank range that had blown his back out, no doubt he'd been to realms within the Light he'd yet to fathom. 'Bazz had his full attention.

"Yeah, well, that past experience that I don't wanna go into was a part of her, and his protective energy transferred from there to become a part of me." Shabazz took a very careful sip of his drink. "It's hard to think about it, much less discuss, especially understanding how much he loved her . . . and feeling it, as a tactical . . . the passion that went both ways. But like I said, you get real cool in your head about what was and what is, after you see the other side."

"Okay," Carlos said after a pause to collect his thoughts. "Then . . . if you're cool with it, and the shape-shifts help you out in a firefight, and the team is cool with it, ya mean . . . then . . ."

"Then why am I here?" Shabazz rubbed his palms down his face and looked at the shelved bottles behind the bar. "Lemme ask you somethin', man. And don't laugh."

Pure curiosity made Carlos lean in closer. Laughing was the last thing on his mind. He'd only seen Shabazz this shook when Marlene was recovering from near-death experiences. What the hell could be funny about that? This older Guardian brother was normally the definition of chill. This wasn't normal.

"Yo, man, you oughta know me better than that," Carlos finally said.

Shabazz nodded, but never looked at Carlos. "Upper and lower canines, man. Lost it right at the moment of truth. Swore no matter what, that bullshit wasn't coming into the bedroom with me—only on the battlefield, aw'ight. So . . . how you . . ." He tossed down his shot of Jack Daniel's hard and slung the glass toward the bartender.

Carlos took in a deep breath through his nose to keep from smiling. "How you hold 'em back?"

Shabazz didn't even answer, just nodded once and accepted his drink.

"The truth?"

Shabazz stared at Carlos.

"I never could, man. D turns me out. Plain and simple."

Shabazz closed his eyes and rolled the shot glass between his palms. "Yeah."

"It didn't freak her out, did it?" Carlos took a calm sip of Rémy, glimpsing Shabazz from the corner of his eye.

"No. That's the problem." Shabazz took a fast gulp of Jack Daniel's.

"Suggestion," Carlos said, catching the shot glass as Shabazz slung it. "Slow down, deep breaths, brother." He waited until Shabazz nodded and he held up his hand to forestall the bartender. "If you don't fight it, you own it, and if you own it, you benefit from it."

"That sounds like some Zen rhetoric I woulda told you," Shabazz said, staring off into the distance.

"You know she had a past." Carlos looked at Shabazz from a sidelong glance.

"Yeah."

"Aw'ight . . . and she loved you hard without the canines, waaay before they presented, right?"

"Yeah."

"And, she's dealing with this new . . . uh . . . aspect of you real cool, actually. I mean, c'mon, man, she's a seer." Carlos looked at his older Guardian brother straight on. "She didn't wig because she could probably sense what was about to happen before it did."

Carlos watched Shabazz's body begin to relax, and he sent the shot glass down the bar in a hard slide with a nod to okay the refill. "If it turned her out to see the canines, it was probably only because she realized that you'd lost it—flipped, bugged, wigged so hard that you ain't have no control left—something probably unusual for a brother known to *own* control . . . and she was the one who took you there—so naturally, she'd respond in kind. It ain't have nothing to do with no other motherfucker from the past. Rest his soul in peace, man."

Shabazz lifted his shot glass to Carlos when the bartender put it before him and clinked the side of Carlos's rocks glass. "Rest his soul in peace."

"Right, man." Carlos took a sip of Remy and then rolled the near empty glass between his palms. "Didn't I just go through this?"

Shabazz let out a hard breath. "Damn, man, all this shit runs in cycles."

"Yeah it does." Carlos smiled. "Why don't you go take your ass back upstairs so you don't start the other bullshit cycle none of us wants to be caught in, namely, being in the doghouse."

Shabazz chuckled. "I'ma finish my drink."

"Brother . . . you know *what* . . . you just left your lady up there after probably turning her out with a canine drop like she's never seen, and when she comes to and rolls over and you come strolling back into the room an hour later smelling like the bar, I don't need second sight to tell you how the thing is gonna go."

Laughing harder, Shabazz knocked down his shot. "I ain't rushing. She don't run me, aw'ight," he said, standing.

"Yeah, I know . . . I'm just saying . . ."

Shabazz extended his fist and Carlos pounded it.

"For da bruthaz," Carlos said, finally laughing.

"If I hear about this again, I'll shoot you," Shabazz said with a wide grin.

Carlos held his hands up in front of his chest. "I don't even know what you're talking about."

"Yeah, okay," Shabazz said, glancing at Carlos over his shoulder, and then he stopped and turned slowly, the smile disappearing from his face. "Why were you down here? You all right, man?"

Carlos looked up from his drink. "Yeah. I'm cool."

Shabazz didn't move.

"Just thinking 'bout my boy, that's all." There was no way to explain it to Shabazz, so Carlos forced a smile. "I'm good, man. I just came down here for some headspace. I'll see you in the morning."

Shabazz nodded. "I understand more than you know, just like you just understood my shit a second ago," he said in a quiet, concerned tone. "Remember—been there. Nobody understands what losing your ace is like, unless they've lost theirs, especially when you take the blame for how it went down. Survivor's guilt is a nasty bitch, like none other, brother. Don't forget, I shot my own man by accident in a vamp alley attack . . . and had ten years of headspace in the joint to think about it when authorities didn't understand." Shabazz extended his hand for Carlos to shake and held on for a second in a warrior's forearm grasp, sending tactical support into Carlos's system. "When you gotta leave one of your own, that never gets outta your head, man . . . so, if you ever wanna talk about it—I got your back."

"That's good to know, man. Thanks," Carlos said when Shabazz let him go. The support charge made him feel better, but he still wasn't ready to talk about it. Still really didn't see what good that would do anyway. It was what it was, fucked up beyond repair. "Go get with your lady—I'll see you in the morning."

HE'D BEEN CALLED before, but never like this. Two polar-opposite probes splintered his mind. Yonnie put both hands to either side of his head and yelled as pain erupted inside his skull. He stumbled along the edge of the Venice Beach pier and vomited up blood as the searing pain moved from his skull into his fangs. Sweating and only able to go a few feet before stopping, he knew he'd never be able to transport himself to a safe lair by sunrise.

"Carlos . . . help me, man," Yonnie choked out, gasping.

When he wiped his face, he brought his hands away quickly, staring at them in horror. Putrid flesh replaced what had been smooth, manicured hands, and was quickly aging to his actual two-hundred-plus, dead human years. Rooted where he stood, a dark magnetic force had him in its grip as the ground opened. He didn't even fight it; this had been coming for him for years.

"I WAS ABLE to deactivate the spell," Sebastian said with his head and gaze lowered. "I knew the portions of each element and separated them out, one-by-one, once we were able to gain clarity."

"You cannot blame us, husband," Lilith said on her knees with her gaze lowered and wringing her hands. "Every level, including ours, was in a mating frenzy. Their side deceived Fallon, who let it in."

"I had the female Neteru in my clutches to bring to you, Your Majesty," Nuit said, keeping his head down.

"Enough!" a thunderous voice railed. "You allowed my minotaur, my favorite golden calf, to be slaughtered by those Neteru bitches . . . the calf that they set up in the desert during Moses's time—do you know how long I've had that animal?"

Slow-walking hooves echoed within the complete darkness that even vampire sight could not penetrate.

"And you cower before me, quivering and naked, caught in the tentacles of a spawning spell . . . my legions fucking their brains out instead of making war—major cease-fires were almost put into effect topside on earth while this outrage occurred. If I hadn't pulled you three out of your frenzied coupling this would have gone on until the spell burned itself out—or my entire realm perished from starvation in its tentacles! I demand retribution!"

Flames of rage scorched their backs as the unseen beast released a mighty roar. "No animal or human sacrifices have been made during those hours, no tragic deaths *for hours* on earth. No werewolf howlings and it was a full moon! No vampire turns, no phantom citings, no possessions—no Amanthra treachery, all because you allowed a backfired spell returned to us from the Light to pollute my domain. Such a breach is a sign of weakness, Lilith! An intolerable condition for our side in the end of days. Something so insidious could lull humanity into a false sense of security, thus breeding hope—and hope encourages faith, and should worldwide love blossom, I'll have your heads in my teeth!"

"Never, never, my Dark Lord," Lilith whispered.

"Then gather mine unto me using my dark force from Level Seven, Lilith," a disembodied voice of fury whispered. "I want all vampire resources, the smartest of our kind, to devise a strategy—a patient, skillful one that will not jeopardize my heir."

The shift of the ominous presence around the endless black space made the three vampires on the pit floor draw themselves up smaller to avoid an unexpected lashing.

"I have called the first one, the one who goes by Yolando. He was the only one of our kind not polluted, because he was not in our realms when the incursion struck. I want the topside dark covens aligned as one force, ready and able to spellcast. Lorelei led me to him—reward her with power, but do not give her the kiss of the undead. We need forces that can withstand the Light to do our bidding day or night," the great voice rumbled and then trailed off in a sinister, hissing whisper. "I will call the men of science and manipulate them."

"We will crush the Neteru team," Sebastian promised with an unsure voice.

"I want them to have time to think we've been conquered so that we can see how best to turn the blade within their minds," the beast murmured seductively. "Didn't Machiavelli teach you anything before the Neterus murdered him?"

"*Oui*," Fallon Nuit said with a tight voice. "He and I . . . strategized together for years. Sebastian should have *never* taken such risks with a resource of that magnitude from our realms."

Sebastian hissed and the darkness went still for a moment, again causing the vampires on the cavern floor to cringe.

"I agree," the beast finally said in a weary tone. "When I have more time, I may devote myself to raising him. For now, Sebastian, know that you owe me—which is never a good thing . . . so do make excellent use of this Lorelei."

Hoof clatter began to retreat from the void. Relief washed through the huddling vampires. "Do not believe that you haven't incurred my wrath. I am patient, and will release my frustration in due time. However, the only reason you are still whole is that my other entities are nearly ruined, and it will take me days to go level by level to sort out the destruction . . . my werewolves are still stuck together and cannot disengage. My serpents hopelessly entangled, and my phantoms are a shrieking mess—insane and unguided. My dear Harpies may even be beyond repair, as they've clawed each other nearly to extinction trying to grab hold of any body part to mate with that they could while whirling in a funnel." A deep sigh echoed off the walls. "Lilith, have you any idea how hard I truly work to keep all this going for us, my dear? You are *such* a high-maintenance bitch, I swear!"

"THIS IS VERY disappointing, Yolando," Fallon Nuit crooned, walking around Yonnie as he lay shuddering and aging on the marble Vampire Council Chamber floor.

The veins in the marble pulsed with blood that fed the table, and Yonnie pressed his lips to the floor trying to siphon any nourishment he could, but his brittle fang broke off at his withered gum line. Too weak to fight, he dropped against unforgiving floor, scrabbling at it to no avail, his nails peeling away from his bony fingers like paper.

"You heard the Dark Lord," Sebastian said, growing weary of Fallon's unnecessary display of power. "Feed the poor bastard. We cannot waste any more resources."

"I will decide when he eats," Nuit said with a hiss, stooping down to snatch Yonnie's head back.

"Careful, Fallon," Lilith crooned. "He's brittle and has already lost a fang. Pull back too hard and you'll be on my husband's torture chamber floor again. I don't think Lu would be too thrilled to find out we've lost another valuable resource, do you, darling?"

Nuit stood, letting Yonnie's head hit the floor with a groan. "He's betrayed us, remember! I want him to feel what it's like when the wrath of this council has risen. The Dark Lord's call for one of ours is a travesty, that a master vampire heeds not a *councilman*? Sacrilege . . . treason—under any other circumstances, he would have been put to a slow and agonizing end in the Sea of Perpetual Agony!"

"True," Lilith said, studying her nails. "But so would you." She looked up at Fallon coolly. "The bastard did no more than you or Sebastian—he hedged his bets. He sided with then-Councilman Rivera, which was a pretty safe bet, a wise one I respected, until the asshole went into the Light." She looked down at Yonnie and clucked her tongue. "I would have run, too." Her gaze suddenly narrowed on Nuit. "Make him handsome again. That bag of bones and dust is a crime—a real waste of male vampire resources, if ever I saw one."

When Nuit backed away from Yonnie and sneered, Lilith flung a goblet of blood from the table to land and splash Yonnie's face. All pride gone, he licked the floor, gaining strength with each swallow. The next goblet she hurled at

Yonnie, he weakly caught, sloshing it as he brought it to his mouth to greedily consume. Blood ran from the corners of Yonnie's mouth, over his chin, his hands, and down his chest. Fallon Nuit spat on the floor and stalked back to his throne, and as Yonnie brought the goblet away from his mouth, he hissed at Nuit. Sunken skull, red glowing eyes studied Nuit. Skeletal hands covered in rotting flesh clutched the golden goblet. Tattered fabric that once belonged to burial clothes hung from Yonnie's gaunt, starved frame, but defiance wafted off him in roiling waves no less lingering than his putrid, dead-flesh stench.

"You should leave him in this condition, Lilith. Once a slave, always a slave," Nuit said through his teeth with bourgeois, antebellum entitlement. "His kind worked my plantations for years, and even now, after you've fed him from the floor, he dares hiss at us."

Lilith eyed Nuit, then tossed Yonnie another goblet, and watched Yonnie greedily consume its contents. "You did override Rivera's bite, *oui*?" she asked, teasing Nuit.

"Of course I did!" Nuit railed, pointing at Yonnie as he began to slowly regenerate. "The ungrateful sonofabitch owes me."

Lilith tilted her head to the side watching new muscle, flesh, and skin begin to overtake Yonnie's weathered skeleton. His hunched spine elongated and straightened as his sunken cheeks, chest, and stomach filled out—new sinew giving his chest and shoulders definition and strength. Gnarled fingers and claws became graceful, long hands. Spindly legs and hooked feet suddenly metamorphosed into athletically honed muscles, strong thighs and well-shaped feet covered in glistening, brand-new, dark walnut skin. Yonnie arched and cried out as his old fangs fell away and new ones split through his gums, while old, brittle hair broke off like dead pine needles off a dry tree and new, vibrant, flexible kinky dark hair sprouted from his new scalp.

A youthful, handsome face now replaced the garish nightmare that had been before them. Red glowing eyes normulized into intense, dark brown irises that surveyed everything and trusted nothing. The only evidence of Yonnie's recent torture was that he was naked on the floor and breathing hard from the transformation process.

"That is *definitely* Rivera's handiwork," Lilith said with appreciation, her gaze raking Yonnie to settle on his groin. "And has a bit of the old attitude still resonating within him, too . . . good." She blew Yonnie a kiss from her throne. "Don't ever trade that in, lover. I don't care who you become beholden to."

"If she wanted a pet we could have gotten her a puppy to play with in council," Nuit muttered to Sebastian, who subtly nodded.

"True," Lilith said, tearing her gaze from Yonnie and paralyzing Nuit with it. "Or I could just dog you." She stood and walked over to Yonnie but kept her withering gaze on Nuit. "Do not *ever* forget who I am, no matter what you may think of how I got the position. I'll crush you, Fallon, if you cross me."

Lilith held out her hand to Yonnie and chuckled when he declined it and stood on his own. She let her gaze rake him and spoke to his groin as she leaned in and whispered into his ear so softly that the others couldn't hear. "I'm not sure, but you might have been made a councilman in absentia. Was it Fallon's premature bite, never rescinded because Cain was injured and too preoccupied to do so, or were you made by Rivera's elevation bite . . . and are you now a lost rogue because your maker didn't formally get extinguished with his essence still in our realms? Without a title transfer to the next councilman in power that would have taken Rivera's place, no one would own you, per se. So, is that it? Are you a floater, Yonnie . . . a vampire without a maker in Hell?" She brushed his unyielding mouth with a kiss. "That would make you a free-floating radical. A variable. Something new that even I have never seen. But something dangerous."

She flounced away from Yonnie with a smug smile when he didn't answer. "You don't know yourself, do you?" Ignoring the curious glances from Nuit and Sebastian, Lilith crooked her finger at Yonnie. "You've never actually experienced a throne, have you?"

Yonnie looked away, a hundred emotions competing for dominance in his mind as he stared at a vacant seat. After what he'd just gone through, one thing was clear—something Carlos always told him—he couldn't be down in the bowels without owning a position of leverage. Knowledge was power. If Lilith didn't know for sure who'd made him, and obviously couldn't read his mind because something even he couldn't comprehend was blocking that . . . then he needed to play along, pretend that Nuit still held check.

"No," Yonnie finally said. "He just bit me in the casino."

"Aha!" Nuit said, standing and pointing at Yonnie, vindicated, as he looked at Lilith. He turned and narrowed his gaze on Yonnie. "I ought to make you get down on your knees and suck my dick for the offense of hissing at your maker."

Yonnie battle bulked, allowing his fangs to drop nine inches. "Open your fly and you'll draw back a nub."

"Imposter!" Nuit sat with flourish, gathering his robes about him.

"He allowed my mate to go into the Light! He let Rivera betray me and give her body to a fucking Guardian team!" Yonnie shouted, using all the game he had in him to twist the facts. "He let them bury her on consecrated ground, in a fucking church—and on the battlefield in Morales, Mexico, he allows my second mate, Gabrielle, to be blown away by her own sister. They used hallowed-earth shells," Yonnie railed, walking up to the pentagram-shaped table to pound on it, but the frustration rang true. The heartbreak was no act as tears began to flow from outrage.

"They beheaded Gabrielle on the field, prayed over her, and sent her soul into the Light, before I could grasp it." Yonnie's voice broke as he sputtered his complaint to Lilith, pointing at Nuit. "That lowlife, double-dealing, bargain-breaking, mother*fucker*! I might have to do what he says, but it's gonna take the Dark Lord on Level Seven and me puking up my guts before I come to him, unless he addresses the shit he did!"

Lilith looked at Nuit as he turned away. "The man has brought a valid series of complaints to chambers, Fallon. You elevated him to councilman status . . . I don't believe Cain ever followed through on rescinding your offer, given his state when you brought Yolando here. And, as a councilman, he has, indeed, experienced a number of offenses that by rights could make him not feel whole—as none of what you bargained with him was ever delivered." She sighed and stared at Yonnie hard with an unreadable smile.

"He never answered my calls!" Nuit challenged.

"You ain't call me, bitch, except when the Dark Lord came into chambers to drag your ass to prison —so like I'm supposed to show up and do what? Go down witchu when you ain't never have my back? Aw hell no. Po-po was on your ass, not mine, so hey. Read the clause, get the old blood contracts out—if your maker offends the Dark Lord, you do not have to be canon fodder." Yonnie leered at Nuit. "And you know why? Because the Dark Lord ain't stupid—why would he want a bunch of motherfuckers fighting against him and burning up his energy and resources to protect one of his own that offended him? That's the first order of business. So, no, while you was down there screaming for help, I didn't have to answer shit." Yonnie mimed turning an imaginary switch off at his ear. "Click, bitch . . . I switched the channel."

Lilith leaned back in her throne and laughed, glimpsing Sebastian's smile. "Oh, Yolando, I can feel the Rivera influence in you so strongly, it's beautiful." When Nuit folded his arms and looked away, Lilith swallowed some of her mirth. "Okay, gentlemen. So. We have an impasse. Nuit, by rights, owns you as your maker, but due to his negligence in fulfilling his multiple bargains, thus costing you two mates in quick succession. . . . Hmmm . . . he can either win you back from me, the one who fed you back to life—and your chairwoman, the holder of all disputed property claims, or he can strike a bargain with you that you agree upon."

"That is my property, Lilith, and you know it!" Nuit was out of his throne, but didn't advance on Yonnie.

"I am so going to enjoy holding you in escrow, Yolando," she murmured, licking her lips.

"Then, what shall it be?" Nuit raged. "We have business to conduct, and he has to make a decision!"

"I don't have to do shit for three nights," Yonnie spat. "You all better get another attorney on this council, which should be real easy since we got a million of 'em down here."

"I believe that is his right," Sebastian said, unsure.

"Shut up!" Nuit yelled, and spun on Sebastian. "You haven't even remained in your throne for twenty-four hours and you presume to know Vampire Council law? When did you acquire such skill, Sebastian? While rolling on the marble fornicating with Harpies?"

Yonnie made a face. "C'mon, man . . . that's nasty. How'd you make council, handlin' your business like that?"

"It was the spell!" Sebastian shouted, making Lilith cackle. "And the three of us agreed that whatever happened in the caverns stayed in the caverns while under the spell! Now I see why your own made man has no respect for you, Fallon! That was unnecessary!"

Lilith sighed. "Fine. Yolando has three nights to decide what is in his best interest, given his duplicate losses. But his loyalties aren't with Rivera, either, that's clear."

"You got that right," Yonnie said and spat. "I don't know who I'm more done with—him or Nuit."

"Pick a vacant throne, Yolando," Lilith crooned. "We need a man with your New Age thinking and an intimate knowledge of the Guardian team, especially the Neterus, on our council during these turbulent times."

Yonnie studied the choices before him, moving to the throne farthest from Nuit and leaving one open between him and Sebastian. He had to know what just went down. What kind of spell could have had enough topspin on it to invade all the way down through the realms to Level Six, and still have enough juice to have a councilman humping Harpies? Damn! Oh, yeah, something was crazy-wrong, and the more he thought about it, it definitely sounded like his boy's handiwork. He glanced at Sebastian, wondering as he took his time making a selection. That bitch Lorelei also said something about the dark covens rising, he just wished he'd paid more attention and remembered before the agony of the ultimate call hit him.

"Don't worry, Yolando," Lilith said with a sinister smile. "I know what you're worried about."

Yonnie froze, his gaze slowly going toward a very smug Nuit, as he wondered if somehow they'd seen through his game.

Lilith waved her hand down her gown, causing it to vanish. "Since you're now in my escrow account, when you come up out of the throne ecstasy daze, I'll do the installation honors, not your maker."

CARLOS PUSHED AWAY from the bar, settled the tab, and stood. He needed to follow his own damned advice, he told himself, but for some reason the hair was standing up on the back of his neck and his legs had propelled him out of the hotel to take a walk.

The night air smelled good. No, it smelled *fantastic*. Wood burning in fireplaces mixed with the surf, the breeze was steady and cool . . . some things would simply never leave him. They were as much a part of who he was as the Light. But it was all good. He'd learned how to appreciate the past without hankering for it to create chaos in his life. Tonight he was thoroughly appreciating how fine-assed midnight strutted out in rhinestone-studded blue-black, slit up the side with gray clouds, flossing a full moon.

Carlos suddenly stopped walking for a moment and laughed. That's what was wrong with Shabazz. "Oh shit!" He laughed harder as he started walking again, shaking his head, and glad the streets of La Jolla rolled up about this time. Yeah, he was talking to himself and crazy. So what? Three-quarters of America looked like him, talking on ear cellular phones that nobody could see.

He slowed his pace as he got to the beach. His laughter had died away blocks ago. There was something so peaceful about watching the surf at night. Something about the enormity of the vast sea of sparkling black surface, and hearing it thunder while the stars reflected off it. The white foam of the breakers was the only thing that interrupted the vast dark carpet. Until daylight came, it was so hard to distinguish where the Ultimate Darkness left off and the Heavens began, and just a sliver of gray horizon lit by a heavenly body was wedged in between . . . just like the gray zone—earth.

"I know," a deep and familiar voice said behind him. "Profound, ain't it?"

Carlos spun. "Oh, man!" He laughed. "Brother . . . I been . . ."

Something in Yonnie's eyes made Carlos stop his advance.

"What happened to you, man?" Carlos asked quietly, scanning his friend in earnest. "You're—"

"Stronger. Yeah. And not the one you want to fuck with right now. I thought you had my back, motherfucker!"

Carlos nodded. The pain had to bleed out, first. "Yeah. You're right. I couldn't get to you and I fucked up, man." He opened his arms and braced for the black charge. "But you're still my brother."

The black charge blew Carlos back ten feet and he landed on the sand flat on his back, dazed, with his chest smoldering. He rubbed the now very sore spot, glad that Damali's old accidental brand made taking a direct hit, black-chest charge like getting shot while wearing a flak jacket. It took a moment, but soon he was able to roll over on his side with effort and stand on wobbly legs.

"Aw'ight, man," Carlos said, speaking in jags between breaths. "I had that coming. But I need to drop some science on you 'bout what happened."

"I don't wanna hear a fucking thing about what happened!" Yonnie shouted. "I want my wife back!"

Carlos didn't move as a ring of fire ripped open the sand around him.

"Speak! Where's Tara?"

"You gonna have to chill so we can talk about this like men, brother," Carlos said, deflecting another charge and putting out Yonnie's fire ring with a hot silver gaze. "Nuit burned you, not me."

Yonnie began to pace. "I know, but you shoulda told me."

"Can I seal this conversation without you blowing my head off?" Carlos folded his arms over his chest and waited.

"Yeah, fuckin' A, seal it."

"Me and you, black-box—can't put a prayer around you, Mr. Councilman, you'll fry."

"Just do it."

Carlos put the translucent seal around them, adding a double layer of thickness to the flooring.

"When'd you learn how to do that, man?" Yonnie said, testing the walls gently with his fingertips.

"Came with the Neteru gig . . . nice suit. When'd you elevate, man?" Carlos lifted his chin, trying to keep the concern out of his voice.

"When you briefly became chairman," Yonnie said, staring at him. "That night you elevated me, you said when you moved up, I'd move up . . . you never rescinded the command. I just never sat in a throne, so I didn't have the knowledge to go with the power."

Carlos just stared at his friend for a moment. "What?"

"You saved my ass, man," Yonnie said quietly. "I owe you that . . . always had my six, even when you went into the Light." He walked away and swallowed hard. "That's why they couldn't break me, because I had a chairman's mark—those don't get taken away, ever, unless the Ultimate Darkness does it." He chuckled sadly. "And here I came to knock fire from your ass tonight."

Carlos raked his hair. "I am sooo sorry about what happened with Tara."

"Yeah, well . . ."

"Naw, hear me out, man," Carlos said, waiting until Yonnie turned to look at him. "If I ain't never lied to you as a vamp, why would I start now, supposedly as an honest motherfucker in the Light? Does that make sense? Study it, hombre. Think."

Yonnie nodded. "Then what happened?"

"You might not wanna hear this, but just like you told me before, as your friend—it ain't my job to make you feel good, it's my job to watch your back and make sure you survive. Telling you the truth is part of that."

Yonnie looked out at the ocean.

"I know this is kicking your ass . . . but I didn't have any control over bringing Tara back. Neither did Damali. *We don't have that kind of power.* Something happened when Nuit double-crossed you and layered in a kill bite over your love bite. Tara flatlined and I saw the spirit of Padre Lopez literally come into your lair as a ball of white light and take her." Carlos was so impassioned with the truth that he began talking with his hands as Yonnie stared at him. "I didn't even wanna fold her body away in a Neteru transport, for fear that the Light would speed up the decomposition process . . . she'd been gone forty some years, man. Rider had lost it so bad that Shabazz had to knock his ass out to get him to drop the body."

Yonnie swallowed hard and stood very, very still, staring at Carlos.

"We black-sheeted her, man," Carlos said quietly. "Brought her to the beach in La Paz. Wouldn't let Rider look at her—he didn't need to see that vamp aging thing happen to her."

Yonnie closed his eyes, tears glistening in his lashes. "No man should see that happen to his woman . . . especially not to one that beautiful."

"Right," Carlos said, dragging his fingers through his

hair. "Some hybrids got out of Nod with Cain's crazy ass. We had a nymph . . . a healer. Sara . . . Rest her soul in peace."

"What happened to her?" Yonnie whispered, breathing in steady, controlled sips.

"Sara attended Tara's body, so it would hold against decay until we buried it. We were under siege, couldn't do it right away. Lilith or Cain, who knows, had opened up old team wounds, we had Guardians flipping. But the hybrid stayed with Tara's body and preserved it."

Yonnie opened his eyes, sniffed hard, and turned away. "You buried her beautiful?"

"We never put her in the ground," Carlos said, his voice so quiet that Yonnie turned to stare at him.

"We took her with us, because we were under siege and didn't want her to be desecrated. She was your wife, your lover, our Guardian sister . . . Rider's common-law wife and lover . . . shit . . . nobody could believe she was gone."

Yonnie nodded, unshed tears threatening to fall. "Nobody could believe that, man. You did what was right, tried to keep the Harpies off her. Fucking vermin."

"My Light foldaway, at the distance we had to go, would have undone what Sara did to hold her intact. So, we let the hybrids carry her at their slower speed, and told them to put her down safe on hallowed ground so we could do the thing right . . . man, I would have brought you over the prayer lines to see her, would have opened a path with your name— *you know that*—so you could see your woman one last time." Carlos punched the sore spot on his chest over his scorched T-shirt. "I wouldn't deny my boy a right like that."

"I just thought—"

"You thought wrong!" Carlos hollered. "You're like a brother—we are blood brothers, man, shit!" He walked away, breathing hard, trying to pull himself together. "Nuns laid her out on a granite slab, Damali said . . . did I don't know what. I wasn't there, but twelve nuns praying hard, a hybrid healing nymph, and my wife, a Powers angel on real old consecrated ground . . . add in a man who'd loved her for over thirty years down on his knees begging any power above that will listen. The woman came back. A miracle happened, and it was outta my hands."

Carlos turned and looked at Yonnie. Their gazes locked in silent understanding.

"I understand miracles," Yonnie said slowly, his voice suddenly weary and sounding very fatigued. "She was my miracle, saved my ass when the empire was tracking me the first go 'round. If it wasn't for her . . ."

"I know, man, but you've gotta let it go. She's married." Carlos walked to the far side of the black-box and rubbed the back of his neck.

"You always said you'd have my back—"

"I did, man, don't put me in a position between you and—"

"Hear me out," Yonnie said as Carlos gave him his back to consider and folded his arms over his chest.

"My days are numbered. She ain't safe with me. I just wanna see her."

Carlos turned and stared at Yonnie full on. "If your days are numbered, why you look so healthy, like you just took a throne, man? Come on, brother . . . I still know *Dananu.* Don't play a—"

"I would never bite her, wouldn't turn her," Yonnie said without blinking. "She got a second chance. You've been there. You know what this is. Hell."

"I know," Carlos said without judgment in his tone. "I know."

"I had to elevate tonight because they finally caught me. Got the ultimate call and it broke my ass down so hard I was licking blood off the floor at Fallon's feet."

"Oh, shit, brother . . . the ultimate call . . . *I've* never even . . ."

"Yeah. I ain't proud—I'm just glad Lilith did the installation." Yonnie released a hard, brittle laugh. "But in that moment, right before I started regenerating, I didn't give a shit who installed a brother. Feel me? *That's* why I would *never* drag her back into the life."

Carlos nodded, not sure what to say. "Man, I'ma always have your back . . . I just . . ."

"It's cool," Yonnie said in a philosophical tone, and then released a hard sigh. "You took me as far as you could. Did all you could do. Took me places and gave me power I'd only dreamed of, man. You also gave me something that even while they were about to stomp my ass into a black puddle on seven, they couldn't take away from me—for a minute, she was mine. For a minute, she was my wife. For a minute, she cared if I lived or died. And, really, because of the way you rolled, one of my lovers went into the Light and came out whole. The other, Gabby, went over as spirit, but they can't touch either one of 'em."

Yonnie walked away from Carlos to place both hands on the translucent box as he stared at the sea. "Women and children first. Get 'em out first. You did that, homeboy. Got the ladies out. And I got a three-night pass, just like you had a while ago," he said with a sad smile as he turned back. "I'm on escrow account with Lilith because Nuit fucked up a legit bargain with a fellow councilman. Even after your ass left Hell, your smooth criminal ways was all in the thrones . . . I just got a hit, and I'm feelin' kinda reckless. So, hey, they can't read my mind over your mark, maybe they don't know where I am . . . as long as I can I'll send you images, locations, plots, schemes, whatever."

"You don't have to bargain with me to see her, man," Carlos said, so quietly hurt for his boy that the horizon was the only place he could send his gaze. "That's a suicide mission you're talking about."

"So, you be the one to dust me," Yonnie said, opening his arms until Carlos looked at him. "Put your blade in my heart and then take off my head clean—after I do my work."

Carlos just stared at him.

"Fair exchange is no robbery, Mr. Chairman," Yonnie said, slowly dropping to his knees on the sand. "I'm not negotiating with you. I'm begging you as your line-brother, your blood-line, to do the extinction honors when the time comes . . . scatter my ashes in the Light, let your blade do the job, because I've seen it make the impossible happen. It was only 'cause of you that I could keep Nuit and Sebastian off my ass, and got a chance to interest Lilith enough to buy me three nights." Yonnie stood and walked over to Carlos, tears streaming down his face.

"Pull it from my head!" Yonnie shouted. "Like old times, if you don't believe me." He yanked Carlos by the arm when he tried to look away. "I've only got one chairman! Only got one brother to the grave and beyond! I only had one crazy motherfucker have my back like you—so who else's six would I watch? Theirs? Fuck you, man, if you think I'm gaming. I woulda did this shit for you regardless!"

Carlos gripped Yonnie's arm in a Neteru warrior's hold and pulled him into a firm embrace, talking hard and fast. "I got your six, man. Blade for blade, bullshit for bullshit, we ride or die together—you hear me, man?" He let Yonnie go, trying to hold emotion in check. "I done lost Alejandro, Juan, Miguel, Julio . . . the list is long. Me and you, we been places none of them ever conceived, man." Carlos shook his head, sniffed hard, and kept his eyes on the sea. "The Light don't even understand what this is—I'm like, give the brother a fuckin' break, but it ain't my call, man, and I been asking 'em every day, yo, but they don't seem like on this petition they hear what I'm saying, you feel me . . . but I ain't step off, ain't do you foul. That shit been on my conscience, man, like a brick. Then you wanna come and tell me you're about to do a suicide mission, take one for the team, and I can't guarantee that—"

"I ain't ask for your guarantee!" Yonnie shouted.

"What? I ain't supposed to give a shit what happens to my brother on a torture chamber wall? I been there!" Carlos said, slapping his chest.

"Let me do me," Yonnie said quietly. "Just like you need to do you." He wiped his nose with the back of his hand. "I love you, too, man. But maybe after two hundred years, you know . . . my shit is too far gone. So let me do something that I can say I was proud of along the way. How many of us get out of the vamp game, once bitten? Eventually, you gotta give the devil his due. Torture comes with the whole lost soul imperative. So, taking a page out of your book, and a hit off your old throne . . . hey." Carlos stared at Yonnie, stunned and eerily pleased. "You took *my* old throne?"

"Who else's, man? Come on," Yonnie said with a shrug. "Might as well give them something to really kick my ass for. It ain't like if I don't they're gonna be nice and leave me alone. You know how this goes. And, who knows, if I game hard enough I might make it past three nights double-dealing for a while."

Carlos nodded and rubbed his palms down his face, feeling every muscle in his back and shoulders absorbing the strain. "Okay, man . . . and I'll do whatever I can to keep both sides off your back—my blade, though, only used against the darkside." He stared at Yonnie. "I can't make her see you, or have a hand in lying about where she's going, if Rider asks me."

Yonnie shook his head and held up his hand. "Yeah, yeah, I know—you gotta maintain position. Even while chairman, you know, there were some things you couldn't do, based on position . . . wouldn't seem right. Sends the wrong message."

"Exactly, and stop working me in broken *Dananu*."

They both looked at each other and smiled.

"But on the real," Carlos said, his smile fading. "For all this help, all this insider info—which is invaluable . . . and I can't deliver Tara, or the Light, no guarantees. I might not even be able to get to you before they snatch your ass to make it quick . . . and even then they'd have your soul . . ."

"All true," Yonnie said, studying his new manicure with a half-smile.

Bewildered, Carlos opened his arms and stared at his friend. "What are you getting out of this, man? I'm not supposed to say this, but, in your situation . . . like, you could save yourself, make an existence you could deal with. You know as long as you lay low in my territory and don't do crazy kills around me and the team . . . I'd . . . if you was cool." Carlos looked away, unable to say it, and half-disbelieving he'd even considered that he'd turn a blind eye to Yonnie's coven kills if he needed to do human feeds as a councilman. "Scratch that, man," he muttered. "You know what I'm saying."

For a while they both fell silent, then Yonnie's quiet voice brought their lines of vision together.

"Since you said something that you're not supposed to say as a Neteru," Yonnie murmured, his focus locked on Carlos, "then I'm gonna say something that I'm not supposed to say as a vampire . . . but since we're both breaking it down to street code—that we would do for a brother we loved down to the blood like we'd do for no other, I'll say this." He swallowed hard and walked away from Carlos, his breathing labored as he battled with his emotions. "You asked what I am getting out of this . . . why I am doing this."

"Yeah," Carlos said, his voice distant and thick.

"You give me something I never had. Something that doesn't exist where I'm trapped now." He turned and looked Carlos dead in the eyes. "Hope."

CHAPTER TWELVE

Tara's eyes popped open and for a second she didn't breathe; then she gently removed Rider's arm from around her waist as she listened to him sleep. She sat up in a smooth, fluid motion to allow him to rest, and went to the window.

She hugged herself as she listened to the familiar voice inside her head. It wasn't a sexual request, or even one delivered with rage, it was just a fervent bleating of her name in a tone so melancholy that tears came to her eyes. Her initial instinct was to just open the door and run toward the voice in her nightgown. But not wanting disaster, she became very still inside herself and remembered how to answer a master vampire's call. Her message was basic as she moved toward her suitcases to find a top and jeans: *I will come to you so we can talk, but promise me that you won't hurt him.*

A shudder ran through her as she quickly stepped into her clothes. Once she'd responded, the energy that reverberated inside her head was stronger than she'd ever recalled. Deeper, more sensual, more robust . . . denser. She had to find her shoes. Flip-flops. Then she stopped and stared at the bed. She had to let Rider know so he wouldn't wake up, panic, come out to the beach, and get hurt.

Hurrying to his side, she kissed him and gently roused him with several soft shoves. "Rider, honey, wake up," she said quietly, trying to monitor the urgency in her voice.

"Oh, hey . . ." Rider murmured, sleepily trying to pull her back into bed. "I woulda run down the hall to get some more—"

"No, no, listen to me," Tara said, holding his face with both hands. "I love you, okay?"

His hands covered hers as he leaned up to kiss her. "Same here, just come back to bed and I'll show—"

"No," she said, holding his face tighter. "I have to go. This is something I have to do, and you can't follow me. I wanted you to know so you wouldn't wake up and—"

"Oh, shit and oh hell no!" Rider was out of the bed like he'd been shot at. He pointed across the room at the bedroom door that led to the larger part of the suite. "If a master vampire is outside this door, I'm gonna cause an international incident and unload a goddamned bazooka in here, Tara. So what the fuck is going on!"

"He did not violate our room, but he is outside on the beach. And yes I'm going to go down there and bring closure to this situation once and for all," she said in an eerily calm voice. "No, I do not intend to get bitten again. And no, because I'm a grown woman, capable of making my own decisions—free will—you are not barring my exit from this room like I'm a child."

"You have *got* to be kidding me," he whispered through his teeth. "After all we've been through?"

"Especially because of all we've been through." She looked at him calmly, but her gaze was resolute. "He deserves that—no less than if Gabrielle was out there."

Rider walked across the room and yanked back the drape so hard it ripped partway off of the rod and anchors. "Last time we saw Gabby, as you recall, it took two Neterus to subdue her." He spun on Tara. "So, I'm supposed to just let my wife—a woman who I almost lost to this life forever—

just waltz out of this suite without a fight to go back into the arms of the very thing that killed her?"

Hot tears had risen in Rider's eyes and the anguish in his voice was as heartrending as the call that was splitting her skull. She covered her face with her hands and took a deep breath and then drew them away to look at him.

"Gabrielle was bitten by Lilith, and too far gone. We have been over that a thousand times, if once, you and I. But if she hadn't been, if she was still here and trapped like I had been, or like Yonnie is now, could I look you in the eyes and tell you, no, you can't go finish it?"

"Yes," Rider said quickly, nodding and walking to stand in front of the door. "You could tell me, 'Jack Rider, I forbid it—because I'm your wife.'" He slapped his bare chest and walked over to find his pants and his gun. "You could tell me, 'I have loved you since the beginning, and if I lose you to a nick, I'll die, Jack Rider.' Then I would have to fucking respect your word as my wife." He hoisted up his pants and stared at her, then checked his clip.

"Did you respect my word when I said that just the other night? When you wanted to go barreling into Lilith's lair with half the team? A place where, given all the nicks you've sustained over your lifetime of war with vampires . . . could have made you wake up on any given night and flatline me, or worse, make me have to drive a stake into your chest," she said quietly, "man with a good heart. Did you ever stop to think how afraid I was then, until now?"

He just stared at her.

"Move away from the door, Jack."

"Don't ask me to do it," he whispered, shaking his head. "Please."

She went to him and filled his arms and laid her head on his shoulder as his hand became filled with her hair while hugging a gun against her back. "Please don't ask me not to. It's the only way we can all rest from this."

He pulled back and looked at her. "Honestly, I know I

can't stop you; if I did tonight, there'd always be the next night and the next until you went to him . . . but how do you know he won't take you away in a whirl, stun your mind, and nick you?" Rider's eyes searched her face. "I'm asking because if that was the only way I could be with you again, and I had eternity in front of me alone without you—I would."

She closed her eyes and touched his lips to stop him from telling the truth. "I know . . . because I felt Carlos's embrace signature in his call. They met and Carlos wouldn't allow me to go to him, if he knew. But as a bystander, a man caught in the middle, he left it as my choice. He didn't barrier Yonnie away or wrap an extra layer of silver energy around the room. He left it up to me." She sighed and looked up at Rider. "And he loves you and me both enough that he wouldn't allow me to be in harm's way."

"Then ask him to go to the beach as your escort, since I pose a battle risk. Do me that favor."

She withdrew from Rider's arms with care and slipped around him to open the door. "Leave the man his dignity, Rider. You won. That's all Yolando has left."

"I FOLLOWED YOLANDO's trail to the beach," Lorelei said, looking into her crystal ball as she consulted with Lilith, Sebastian, and Nuit. "He is truly on your side. He attacked the male Neteru, sent a black charge into his chest. And when the Neteru stood to go to him, stumbling forward, dazed, Yolando sealed him close to him in a black-box."

Lilith threw her head back and laughed as she paced behind her throne. "Perfect! Yonnie has already injured one of them and he's just been installed." She glanced at the image of Lorelei's séance that swayed within the sulfuric miasma wafting out of the opening in the table beneath the fanged crest. "Show me his injury and his containment . . . I must ask Yonnie about this skill to produce a black-box."

Lorelei quickly brought the image of Yonnie's attack into her crystal ball for the vampires to see and then showed them Carlos inside the translucent box with Yonnie.

"He must have seduced him into a false sense of confidence, because the male Neteru never drew his blade of Ausar or used any of his other weapons. Look here, as Yonnie gives him a clear shot to take his heart, but when he stands, he is able to get close enough to embrace the Neteru."

Sebastian nodded and clapped. "Well done, Yolanda." He glanced at Lilith. "And look at his retreat. Rivera is broken, his shoulders slumped, energy depleted . . . he's been psychically attacked."

"*Oui*," Nuit said, skeptically, "because as we know, Neterus cannot turn from a bite."

"But all he needed was to get the big male Neteru to stand down, to remove barriers for him, then Yonnie can get to the others through this one," she said gleefully. "His former mate."

TARA HAD GENTLY closed the door behind her and then prayed down the length of the corridor that Jack Rider would give her ten minutes and stay put. It had become a mantra as she picked up her pace, willed herself not to run, and then hit the fire exit, practically jumping flights, all the while her mind was screaming—*Stay in the room, Jack. Please, baby, I'm begging you.*

Breathless as she crossed the lobby, every conceivable thought pelted her mind. Top of the list was, was she insane? The message came back to her instantly. Yes.

But she couldn't stop herself. The night was like a grappling hook, pulling her out into it, deeper and deeper, the surf of its endless midnight drowning her as she began to run, hoping with all her heart that Rider wasn't at the window . . . wishing there'd been time to shower their lovemaking off her. She'd made her choice, but Yonnie deserved her respect, if nothing else, and she didn't want to literally rub his nose in her decision.

She slowed to a stop, tears streaming and not sure why until she felt the presence behind her, his touch now cool on her bare arms.

"Thank you," he murmured into her hair.

She turned and hugged him but didn't speak. She couldn't.

"You're so warm now that you're alive," he whispered against her hair and then drew in a deep inhale.

She tensed and he shook his head.

"I know . . . I've already separated out that scent of him being with you and discarded it. That's not what I'm remembering . . . it's you . . . your lavender, your . . . personal signature." His voice broke as he fully enfolded her in his arms. "A scent that I never thought I'd ever have this close to me again."

He lifted his face up and away from her as his fangs started to lower.

"Yonnie," she whispered, her hand at his chest. "I did care."

You made the right choice. I have a bounty on my head, he said into her mind, knowing the beach had eyes. *I have to play this like I'm infiltrating your team, one-by-one, ask Carlos under a seal . . . but know that I always wanted this for you. The best. The Light. I couldn't give it to you. I just wanted to see you, feel you alive and warm and in my arms one more time.* "I gotta go."

She stepped back and held her hand to her neck in keeping with his ruse, but also to stem the old ache that being in his arms had put there. But that made him turn, study the spot that she covered too long for comfort and brought a flicker of red to his normally brown irises. She began to walk backward as he slowly stalked her.

"Tara, answer me this, baby. Did you ever love me, really?"

She stopped retreating and held her ground. "Yes. And I fought with my husband for the right to come out here and tell you that," she said quietly. "What I never got to say was thank you."

He tilted his head and then looked at the sea. *Tell me in my mind, they cannot read my thoughts . . . it's more inti-*

mate that way, anyway. Might be the last time we get to do this, too.

She let out a deep breath of relief as she saw his eyes normalize. *Thank you, Yonnie, for protecting me and honoring my request not to be violated in Jack Rider's home. Thank you for elevating me so I could protect myself, for being a gentle, caring, awesome lover . . . for feeding me, hunting for me, and loving me so hard that . . .* She looked out at the sea with him, now standing beside him. *This isn't gratitude. This is deep, abiding respect and friendship, and I love you for that, loved you during that time.*

Yonnie lifted his chin and swallowed hard but when he spoke, his voice was composed. *But you were always in love with him.*

Yes, she said gently. *But I never lied about that—and you knew that going in.*

He chuckled sadly and turned to her to draw her into another embrace. *I taught you too well. That's supposed to be my line.*

I miss you, too, Yonnie. And I'm so glad you're alive . . . made it and aren't hurt.

He closed his eyes and brushed her hair with a kiss, then allowed her blue-black silky tresses to fall through his fingers in waves. *Don't you believe it. I'm hurt to the bone, girl . . . to the marrow I'm fucked up.* He bent and brushed her mouth with his despite her initial tense resistance, and deepened the kiss, not caring that use of a slight seduction trance helped. *I have to let you go before I forget I have to let you go, and violate one of the oldest codes between me and my homeboy—never turn each other's marks.*

Tara came out of the kiss dazed, her body on fire, her brain nearly liquefied. He was stronger and his build was more solid . . . the fangs he withheld packed his gum line with energy that still resonated on her tongue. It was impossible not to stare at him, as her eyes frantically searched every facet of his face, his hair, his body, trying to understand.

"You look good, too, baby," he murmured, his eyes beginning to flicker at her visual invasion.

She covered her heart with her hand. "You took a throne." Her voice came out as a strangled whisper.

He nodded and stared at her, feeling the urge to let his gaze become hypnotic, but then looked away. "'Bout an hour ago . . . would love to have celebrated with you—but your husband would object."

She felt sand beginning to whirl and sting her skin as she sheltered her eyes. She watched him, squinting, as he pulled his cuffs down from under his black Armani suit, and brushed off his lapels, then was gone.

It took a while for her to will her legs to move, but eventually she stumbled forward. She knew what was going to happen when she got back inside, the brawl for it all, the verbal WWE smackdown session would be in full swing—either that or her husband's suitcases would be gone.

HIS MIND WAS SO wrung out from the shit Yonnie had dropped on him, but also so relieved that his boy was okay, Carlos just leaned against the inside of the elevator and closed his eyes. The walk had done him good. He needed to clear his head, let Tara know . . . get Rider right, run it by Damali . . . there was just too much shit going on. His line-brother was on a suicide mission and he couldn't do shit about it—and that fucked him up no end.

Tonight, if D would just not launch into a thousand questions trying to develop solutions or a strategy . . . if she would just use her healing hands to wrap her arms around him and let him think, just quietly breathe right next to him, he'd be good to go. Because there was no way to put into words without just breaking down, how deep the knife Fate had stabbed into him was turning in his chest. His brother was straight fucked. There was nothing he could do. His brother was bleeding, fucking hemorrhaging, heart ripped out . . . and there was nothing he could do. And all he could think about was if Damali had ever died, and he couldn't even see her body to make it real, get one last look to say good-bye right and proper, he, like Yonnie, would be losing his mind. Then to find out she was alive and had married some other bastard?

Carlos shook his head as he walked down the hall to his suite in a daze. *Please, God, let 'Mali be cool when I go in here. I can't deal, if she ain't.* Carlos fumbled with the room key and kicked the door when the credit-card key didn't make the little light turn from red to green. Trying to pull it together, he closed his eyes for a second, took a deep breath, and was about to try again when a hard grab spun him and a cinder-block punch dropped him.

Up in a flash, Carlos blindly dove into the midsection of the male who had dropped him, crashing them both through the adjacent suite's door. Mike's voice and the distinctive sound of a pump shotgun engaging made Carlos pull back the two-finger throat jab he had poised to remove an Adam's apple, and then jump up, thoroughly confused.

"Rider . . . what the fuck . . ."

Rider got to his feet, fury dulling the probable rib fractures he had. "What the fuck?" he shouted as Guardians filled the hall. "I'll tell you what the fuck! What the fuck gives you the right to tell some vampire motherfucker—friend of yours or not—he can call my wife outta my fucking bed and into his arms on the fucking beach—*that's* what the fuck, Rivera!"

"Baby, hold my gun," Big Mike said, handing off the pump shotgun to Inez. He looked at Shabazz, who braced and got ready to grab Carlos. "Rider, man, let's take this convo under wraps—not in the hall, old-school security."

"Old-school security?" Rider shouted. "She got nicked! I fucking saw it," he yelled, making a lunge for Carlos as Mike lifted him off his feet. Hysterical, he twisted in the huge Guardian's arms. "I'll fucking kill you—you brought this bullshit to my door and she wouldn't take an escort because your hug signature in his call was safe! You lowered her resistance, her barriers, her natural instincts. And that sonofabitch put his hands in her hair and she came away holding her throat!"

Hot tears and spittle flew as Rider raged and younger Guardians helped Mike get him into Damali and Carlos's suite. Damali stood with her hand over her heart as they subdued Rider on the sofa, half-sitting on him as he yelled.

"Black-box the room, baby," Damali whispered.

"I'll get a purge ready," Marlene said quietly and then nodded to Berkfield. "The man might have a herniated disc, ribs fractured from going through the door with Carlos."

Berkfield nodded. "I'm on it."

Bereft Guardians stood around the main sofa, and then watched as Rider was able to almost throw Mike and Shabazz off him.

"Oh, goddamn, my wife can't take another nick—never again in life! You let her go to that sonofabitch, violated family, all that we stand for, because of what? Tell me!"

"Let him up," Carlos said quietly.

Damali shook her head, as did Mike and Shabazz.

"Let him up," Carlos repeated calmly. "Because I didn't do what he thinks I did, and what he thinks he saw didn't happen."

The rage yell that Rider released and the surge of strength that went with it made the two senior Guardians have to redouble their efforts to hold Rider down. Only Tara's image on the other side of the black-box made Rider cease struggling. That's when Shabazz and Mike heeded Carlos's command. Weary, Carlos opened the translucent enclosure for her, and then he sealed it.

Rider was on his feet but didn't go near her. Fury and fighting had made his face beet red and his eyes bloodshot. She stood calmly staring at him with her chin lifted and shoulders back and then spun slowly with her arms out.

"Not nicked," she said quietly. "Ten minutes to say good-bye to an old friend who deserved my respect, then I came back, as promised, unharmed."

Rider spat on the floor. "I didn't deserve your respect?

Ten minutes could have meant another whole lifetime for me and you, darlin'. Mar, scan her. Old-school. She stepped out of the embrace holding her neck."

"I'll do it," Damali said, quietly. "Sorry, Tara, team policy, unless you're a Neteru."

Rider's gaze narrowed on Carlos, but Carlos folded his arms over his chest.

"I'm going into your head, man," Carlos said, "because some of this shit I gotta say can't be said in front of the team . . . shouldn't be."

Without even waiting for Rider's okay, he bludgeoned his mind with the truth. He let him see the entire conversation between him and Yonnie, and then feel it—every nuance of the pain. Then without warning, he flipped him to the scene on the beach, and showed him everything he was quietly monitoring, except the last kiss.

You think I'd let Tara go out alone with a newly made councilman, even if he was my boy? Carlos walked up to Rider and pushed him hard in the chest, backing him up a few paces. *I got a wife, too, man, and I've been a councilman—and I know how my boy feels about Tara! That's why I stayed outside, kept walking so if it got crazy, I could get her! Just like I wouldn't let you disrespect him, I wouldn't let him disrespect you—aw'ight? So don't you ever come at me like that again without hearing my side. Tara's my sister; you act like you were the only one getting your heart cut out when she was laying under a black sheet, decomposing on that beach! Me and 'Bazz didn't want you to see her go to maggots—but you think it wasn't fucking us around? So after seeing you go down the aisle with her, I'd allow her to get a nick? I'm done. Fucking offended!*

Too upset to wait for Rider's response, Carlos stormed out of the living room and headed for the bedroom, then slammed the door behind him. His breaths were entering and leaving his body in hot bursts of rage, hurt, and disbelief. He knew where Rider was, knew where Yonnie was, and seeing Tara torn only reminded him of where Damali had recently been. Right now, all of that was too much coming down on his head at once, and he stood away from the wall, palms flat, arms outstretched, trying to breathe.

He heard the door open, and Heaven help him if it was anybody coming at him with some more bullshit tonight . . .

A pair of soft hands caressed his back. A pair of warm arms slid around his body. A feminine cheek leaned against his biceps . . . and he didn't calm down until a downy blanket of feathers swathed him.

She mercifully stood there like that for a very long time, not saying a word, just shock-absorbing all the blunt-force trauma to his psyche. He would have stood there in that position of bliss if Big Mike hadn't knocked on the door and blown the groove.

"Yo, man, sorry to interrupt but the hotel is gonna have a problem with the door," he said, cracking the bedroom door open to speak through it without looking or coming in. "Any suggestions?"

"YOU SEE?" LORELEI said with a wicked smile. "It worked. Yonnie got to her, and she went inside—Guardians began battling each other in the hall, and then we lost sight and sound."

"That's all right. I've seen enough. Their rooms are prayer barriered, you won't see more—and you cannot see into the marital unions." Lilith walked back to her throne and sat. "First mission—accomplished. Create dissension, mistrust, infighting."

"The dissension spell worked, then, Your Grace?" Lorelei asked anxiously. "I affixed it to Yonnie days ago, and made it adhere to anyone human who was seeking him. Then it would pass slowly and subtly to anyone in the carrier's inner circle, going to places where there were the darkest crevices in the mind first."

"Done very, very well as a plan B, since as we know," Lilith said, her gaze narrowing as it landed on Sebastian, "plan A failed. Miserably so."

"What is your bidding now? I am at your disposal," Lorelei whispered with expectation.

"I don't suppose we'll need her to continue visually skulking around the beaches," Nuit said in a jealous, bored tone. "You might service the new councilman, should he stop by your coven brothel, and while he's there you might adhere him with more of your potions and deceitful spells, since he obviously came away denied a full reunion with his mate." Nuit looked at Lilith. "Something is wrong."

"He is employing patience, subtlety, biding his time," Lilith said. "I love a man who has self-control."

"I've been down this path a time or two, and Rivera's spawn, Yonnie, is cut from the same black fabric as his first maker." Nuit refilled his goblet. "But what do I know?"

"All right. Point taken," Lilith said calmly. "We'll watch more closely, but it's too dangerous now to risk a topside thorough investigation by one of us. The Neteru King and Queen Councils of old have grown bold and prone to earth-plane hunts with impunity. They have even breached the Dark Realms." She sent her evil gaze toward Sebastian. "Therefore, we work through the witches until we can strengthen our vampire ranks—the only truly worthy preda-tor for a Neteru Guardian team."

Sebastian smiled and glimpsed Nuit with smug triumph. "As you wish, milady."

"HE TOLD YOU, didn't he?" Tara said, standing just inside her and Rider's hotel suite door.

Rider looked across the room at the suitcases, the muscle in his jaw pulsing. She walked forward and he held up his hand without a word to stop her.

"Yeah, he told me," Rider muttered. "He was with you the whole time, at the ready, just in case."

She froze and then covered her shock. "Good."

Rider's gaze suddenly snapped toward her. "He had his hands in your hair . . ." Rider closed his eyes and lifted his chin toward the ceiling. "He had his hands in *my wife's* hair—a fucking vampire," he whispered.

"Yes," she said quietly. "And like a true gentleman, he let me go . . . so that I could come home to you, where my heart lies." She moved toward Rider and placed her hand on his shoulder, caressing it. "I won't lie. Yes. He wept into my hair and said good-bye . . . because my choice was to be here with you. And I told him he always knew that going in."

Rider opened his eyes and traced her jaw line with the pad of his thumb. "I thought it was starting all over again, and I just couldn't take it," he whispered.

"I wouldn't do that to you," she said, going into his embrace. "Ever, *ever* again."

Rider stroked her hair. "Your hair . . . that's the part of you that led to the first time we made love." He swallowed hard. "I never wanted him to touch that part of you, does that make sense? Of all things, your hair . . ."

Tara took his mouth in a slow, deep kiss. "Come help me wash my hair, man with a good heart. He never ever washed it for me. That I swear on my old grave."

DAMALI LAY ACROSS the covers, her arm slung over Carlos's side, just listening to him breathe. Tomorrow couldn't come fast enough. The Covenant clerics would arrive, they could have keys to the mansion, maybe bring in the furniture, get some tracks laid in the studio while Dan and Marlene haggled with show promoters to quickly get their world tour under way. Her man had been through the mill, Rider was on the verge of a mental breakdown if Tara couldn't tell that man something reasonable, the team's nerves had been shattered, and just a few hours ago, it had all been good. What the Hell had happened?

She was way beyond chalking anything up to coincidence. Uh-uh. If the dark covens had risen, in the morning, when it was safe, she and the girls, sans Heather, needed to do a divination. But it wouldn't be some buck-wild crap. They'd have a war room meeting in the suite, figure out who was going, who was staying, what kinds of possible barriers they'd need, and go in before the Covenant could get there to delay the process with witch-policy issues.

They needed answers, pure and simple. There wasn't a whole buncha time to cull through the Church's dirty laundry of killing thousands of innocent women who were healers, naturopaths, midwives, plus Native American and African American herbal geniuses in the name of Salem's lot. Most of those left burned at the stake would have been like Krissy, Marj, or Inez, any woman on the team, really, including her. Any female showing knowledge and strength at a time of persecution was toast. Marlene wouldn't have stood a chance. Nah, they had to do this thing fast and dirty, in and out, the Covenant could be backup at the concert and on the battlefield like chaplains, but right now, this was guerrilla warfare. Ugly.

Her mind drifted in a lazy pattern of admonishing herself that she really needed sleep, especially after healing broken ribs and fractured egos. But adrenaline was still coursing through her. Carlos's steady, even breaths of slumber helped created a comforting metronome that was beginning to lull her, but still, her senses kept scanning the beach. Then she saw it and shot bolt upright, grabbing Carlos by the back of his shirt.

"Oh my God," she said, trying not to yell. "We have to go get it, put it out of its misery."

"What, what?" He was sitting up, rubbing his face, shaking Remy and sleep out of his mind.

Damali closed her eyes and put her hand over her heart as she got out of bed. "The little fawn. Yeah, he was a traitor hybrid, but the little guy was just scared, didn't wanna fight . . . and after what happened out there to Sedgwick, Hubert, and Sara, I can't blame him. Those hybrids were gentle creatures—the ones on the good side, anyway. And to be thrust into the kind of action we saw in Morales, no wonder they headed for the hills."

They shoved on their jeans, quickly found T-shirts and sneakers, and headed out the door.

"Baby, he looks like Harpies half-ate him . . . I don't think he's gonna make it. And you can't bring him inside to compromise the team."

"I know," Damali said sadly as they made it down the hall. "I've gotta heal him on the beach, or . . ."

"Yeah. Put him out of his misery."

WHAT SHE SAW when she got to the small body being battered by the edge of the surf made her briefly turn away and cover her mouth. The poor little creature's eyes had been gouged out, and his small, childlike chest ripped, flesh shredded, as though huge claws had simply raked him for the fun of it. As his pink skin became a thicket of fawn hair she saw his genitals were mutilated, and the poor creature's right leg was half-eaten away, the left leg only hanging on by a compound fracture and gristle.

Carlos shook his head and quietly drew his blade of Ausar into his hand as the small creature moaned and began to blindly slap the sand, reaching for the presence he felt near him.

"Help me," he gasped. "They're slaughtering our kind, here and in Nod. The angel hybrids and those of us who are good. Please, nice angel lady, help me," he wailed and began to sob. "Don't make me go back to her."

Damali laid her hand on his head, siphoning away the pain until tears streamed down her face. "Oh, you poor little thing. Who did this to you?"

"Lilith. She's mean . . . evil, and told them to slaughter any hybrid that didn't stand with Cain, here or in Nod. She got the message back in with retreating troops. They've started the massacres." The fawn gasped and then blindly grasped around to hold Damali's hand.

She held his hand, tears brimming and falling on his chest. He sighed and his body relaxed as her healing began.

"Can you send me to the place that's always sunshine and fields?" the fawn whispered.

"I can try, and I will pray over you—so will Carlos."

Carlos stooped down and covered Damali's hand. "No matter what you did, or how afraid you were, you didn't deserve this."

Carlos slowly stood, removing his hand as the fawn followed his voice and Damali petted his head, kissed his forehead, and backed away.

"You should be in fields of clover with your own kind, romping and head-butting and enjoying perpetual spring," Carlos said in a smooth, calm voice. "You should see your parents again, and feel light, and whole, and warm, and safe, and—" Carlos swung hard when the fawn smiled, removing his head from his shoulders. "You should dance in clover forever. Amen."

SHE WASN'T SURE who was more shaken, she or Carlos, as they wrapped the small body in a sheet brought from the hotel and folded away to the nearest church. They both helped dig the grave for the little creature they didn't know, but didn't have to know. All that was important was it was at peace.

So much had happened under one full moon that there was no need for them to speak on it—not that they'd really know what to say, if they could. The fawn's information before it died would just be one more thing to add to the morning war meeting. Dawn would be here soon, and both team generals were still human and needed to rest.

However, there was one thing they didn't speak on, maybe because they already knew that to open that particular can of worms would take a lot longer than the five minutes of energy they had to endure. But how could they sleep at night knowing that the balance of power, oddly, in Nod—Cain—had left, and now innocent angel hybrids and multiphyla hybrids were being slaughtered wholesale? Wasn't that part of their mission, to protect the innocent, if they had souls? Where did one draw the line? What made one life or one soul more valuable than another, just because of geography or DNA? When did one turn a blind eye and say it's not happening here, so hey? Or when did one jump in and say if it could happen to them, it could happen anywhere, and wherever there's genocide, it must be stopped?

Now, *that* required a call by the Covenant, because neither she nor Carlos really wanted to wind up in a battle in a biblical banishment zone . . . not again. Mitigating circumstances had been on their sides before, but hoping that would keep them out of trouble again was like hoping lightning would strike in the same place twice.

Her mind was so weary she practically fell through the door with Carlos. What had started out as a really cool day just devolved into the utterly ridiculous. She took great comfort in how he headed for the sink to wash his hands, shaking his head.

"I know, baby," Carlos said quietly. "You ain't gotta say it. I know."

LILITH STROKED TWO of her battered Harpies' heads as they squeaked and squealed for her attention, climbing up onto her lap in her private chambers. She kissed them and cooed to them and clucked her tongue.

"My poor little babies," she said with a sigh. "Your wings are torn and you've been so abused, but you still did my bidding and the Neterus bought it hook, line, and sinker."

She scratched behind their ears and shooed them away. They looked at her with longing and then fled her bed to scramble up the marble posts to stand watch. "I'll bring you a tasty morsel soon, my pets. Just as soon as Momma regenerates and can go topside, a small child will be yours."

PART

III

The Battle at Masada

CHAPTER THIRTEEN

Daylight couldn't come soon enough, but at the same time, she felt like she could have used twelve more hours of sleep. The emotionally harrowing night was over, but then after such things always came a cold-light-of-day review. This morning, like no other in recent months, she was ready for the whole team. They were gonna squash the internal drama once and for all. She could feel a spirit of dissension wafting about the atmosphere around her like an unseen slurry of negativity that literally made the air thick.

Damali patiently waited as Marlene sealed the room with prayer. Carlos went right for logistics, and she gave him a moment on the floor before jumping in. That allowed her a chance to watch body language, see how bad it was, where people's heads were at. Damali folded her arms, not liking what she saw at all.

"All right," Carlos said, clearly exhausted. "The Covenant came in yesterday. Rabbi Zeitloff got 'em all situated at their safe house so they can summit. That gives us a day or two before we need to meet up and thoroughly debrief the clerics, and in my opinion, we need to get out of this hotel. I'm feeling boxed in."

Damali watched as no one agreed or disagreed. It was as

though everyone's hackles were up for no reason at all. Carlos glanced at her, but pressed on.

"So, all right . . . Dan said we can pick up the keys any day—the place was for immediate availability and a full-cash-on-the-barrel-head wire transfer means we own the joint. We just gotta furnish it and—"

"How we gonna furnish a joint that big that fast? Be serious. It'll be weeks, if not months before we can get settled," Berkfield complained.

Carlos frowned. "What are you talking about, man? We do like we always do. The Covenant seers have a blueprint from the images you all sent me. They go to their local donation warehouses and pull from that or dredge from estate sales that have been left in their charge."

Clearly not understanding the bad vibe, Carlos looked around the team with his brows knit. "What's new about this process? We wire transfer the money so they can refill their coffers and help folks that really need help. They bless every stick of furniture, linens, technology they've purchased for us to spec, whatever comes through the door, so nothing slithers in there with it—and it comes to us by their vans to haul off and place, or we can do it the efficient way and let me drag it in by energy transport. Either way, it gets a white light blast and I've got a visual on how you want the new joint set up, room by room. Isn't that why we did a full team walk-through?"

"Yeah, well, you better leave it to the vans to bring it, because right through here, man, you ain't looking like you can do all that," Mike said, folding his arms. "Means me, Rider, and Shabazz will be muling furniture for about a week."

"How about a month, when the ladies keep changing their minds about where they want a damned couch set," Rider muttered, his gaze going out of the window.

"Hold it!" Damali was off the sofa and she immediately gave Carlos the eye to stand down as she walked into the center of the room. "We sealed the room, which means that anything else that's in here with us that ain't right is blind and deaf to us." She allowed her gaze to land on each face for a moment. "But I want you to all get real still and pray for peace, clarity, and understanding . . . and I'ma watch the room. Tacticals—on the ready."

Begrudging glances met hers, but as she drew her baby Isis dagger and unsheathed it, slow awareness replaced the resistance.

"Three minutes to breathe deeply and still yourselves," Damali murmured with her eyes closed but her second-sight wide open, scanning the room. "Find that very mellow place within, the you that is a spirit of Light energy, positive, attract the good, compassionate, be willing to help, want the best for all, for the group, where laughter emanates, where love flourishes . . . where you heal rifts and forgive and touch the Divine spark that creates all life and created you." She drew in a deep, steady, calm breath through her nose and released it through her mouth. "Now each in your silent communion in your own way and in your own religion, bond with the One Above All and ask that the spirit of dissension be removed from your being."

Within seconds Damali heard a high-pitched screech and her eyes snapped open. A greenish-yellow crablike creature the size of a football with small hooked claws, roachlike antennae, beady little red eyes, and jagged yellow teeth exited Rider's back. It scrabbled up his spine, ran through his hair like a giant louse, and jumped onto Tara, screeching, then leaped with flea-hopping buoyancy over to Berkfield and his wife.

Guardians were hollering, chaos was rampant, Carlos had grabbed at the pest, knocking over furniture and leaving silver glare scorches everywhere. But the thing was too fast and once it got on someone, it hung on for dear life, every jagged hair and part of its crablike legs catching onto skin, fabric, and hair.

The fat, oily-bodied thing stank to high heaven, too, making it a revolting experience to have its touch make contact in any way. Its hooked claws were nearly impossible to dislodge once they grabbed on, and Juanita almost knocked herself out trying to run from it but colliding with a door frame. Krissy had gotten up on the dining room table and was doing a screaming wiggle dance as it found her hair.

"Tacticals up!" Damali shouted, jumping across furniture to get at the thing. "Pen it in, blue charges!"

Male Guardians were in the middle of the floor practically knocking themselves out trying to swing at the nasty little critter. Inez was doing a strip jig in the middle of the floor, screaming and thrashing wildly as it clung to her microbraids and then slid under her tank top.

"Get it off me, get it off me!" Inez shrieked hysterically.

Damali turned just in time to see Jose draw and she roundhouse kicked the gun out of his hand. "No conventionals! You'll hit your own team and if you shoot it, the little sucker will divide. Everybody stop, let it crawl on you for a second, and we'll pen it in with blue charges."

Inez covered her face, her leg bouncing but trying to be still. "Get it off me, y'all—like right now," she whispered in a faraway voice that was reminiscent of a person quickly becoming deranged.

"Buzz her," Damali said, looking at the three closest Guardians near Inez—Dan, Shabazz, and J.L. "Three united on three. One . . . two . . . now!"

The moment the tactical charge hit Inez, the defiant little creature bit Inez's thigh as it came out of her shorts, trying to burrow back under her skin and hold on like a tick.

"Pray, girl!" Damali said, her blade held tightly in her fist. "I want all of the little bastard out of you."

Inez was hiccup crying and it messed Mike up so bad he rushed over, but Damali held up her hand.

"No, Mike, these little beasties are crabs in a barrel, hon. They move through a group real fast, mate, and multiply real fast, and I have to get the head out of her leg or the damned thing ain't dead. A new body will grow right out of her."

Damali looked at Mike hard to get him to respond and spoke with no nonsense in her tone. "I don't wanna cut her leg you've gotta back up and trust me. Hold her hands and say Psalm 91 with her or something, but back up off me while I'm working, hear?"

"C'mon, baby, give me your hands," Big Mike said, trying to coax Inez's palms away from her face. *"No plague will come near my tent . . . a thousand will fall at my right side, ten thousand at my right hand, but—"*

As soon as Inez's mouth began to murmur with the same words Mike was saying, the creature pulled its head out of her thigh, threw its head back, and hissed. Damali got it in the forehead with the tip of her blade and then grabbed the smelly loose skin of its back.

"Keep the charge with me, fellas," Damali said as she sneered at the squirming creature. "Hit me with some city-strength juice for this nasty bug, Carlos."

Carlos squatted and looked at the demon, silver heat making its skin bubble and sizzle as it squealed.

"With the power of the Almighty, I banish the demon spirit of dissension from my team," Damali said, adding her charge to its body through her blade as it lost its grip on Inez's leg.

The moment it let go of Inez, Damali held it to the floor and Carlos put his Timberland on its back.

"Crush it slowly," Damali said, pure fury in her eyes. "I want a name of who sent this."

Carlos began putting more pressure on the bug, making it twist and squeal louder.

"Somebody bring me some holy water," Damali muttered, her gaze never wavering. "It *will* talk."

Marlene tossed a vial to Carlos and the moment he opened it the little beastie began to scream, "Lorelei! Lorelei!"

Heather and Jasmine covered their mouths and gasped.

"You know her?" Carlos asked, looking up with Damali.

Heather nodded. "She was second in command of the

New Orleans covens . . . after Gabrielle—but Gabrielle never approved her methods. There was a feud."

"She hid in Denver until we lost Gabrielle," Jasmine said, her eyes frantic as she stared at Heather. "She would do something like this, has the skill. Tries to seem like she doesn't and plays dumb, but is more vicious than she looks."

"Thanks, ladies." Carlos nodded. "I'ma run this name by my boy, Yonnie, for more details. He needs to know what's operating in his territories, and definitely not get himself jacked in one of the brothels."

"Douse it." Damali rammed her blade all the way through the small creature's forehead and removed her hand quickly from its fat little body as Carlos doused the head and squashed the demon under his shoe. Green gook squirted out around its eight legs and anus, and then the whole body went pop. Smelly, sulfuric gook came out in a splat.

The entire team made a face and muttered, "Eeeiiw."

"Damn, that was a brand-new pair of Tims, too!" Carlos wiped his foot off on the carpet with a grimace at the stench. "You know this is gonna be a helluva bill in here, between this and Mike's door."

Damali held her hands out away from her body and headed toward the dining area sink, yelling over her shoulder to the group. "Somebody open the windows!"

IT TOOK A few minutes for the group to settle down, and everybody agreed without any dissension whatsoever that the meeting needed to resume in Shabazz and Marlene's room—any room but the one that had the dead demon stench. Carlos looked at Damali, and she looked at him.

"You wanna school 'em, professor?" Carlos said, still seeming pissed off about his ruined Tims. "Or you want me to teach this morning?"

"Nah, I'll go," Damali said, hands on hips, but making a face at Carlos's boots. "Baby, you gotta take that down the hall and put on some sneakers or something."

Jose and Rider pounded fists while Tara and Juanita shielded their faces with their hands.

"Please," Juanita gasped with tears in her eyes from the fumes. "He's already tracked it onto the rugs—let's go to our room, and don't come in there 'til you change shoes, Carlos."

Carlos laughed. "Meet y'all back in five. I tell you, I ain't feeling no love. I help kill the bug and now it's, 'Oh, Carlos, could you wash your hands before you—' "

"Man, stop givin' the group noses the blues," Damali said, laughing. "Change your shoes. We're out."

CARLOS JOGGED DOWN the hall, but wasn't offended. The Tims were going in the Dumpster; it smelled like he'd stepped in a hot pile of fresh dog crap, and Juanita was right, the scent was following him everywhere as long as he had on those boots. But as he reentered the room, he watched the bug essence decompose in the sun. The claws and feet and mouth flared first, and then some of the green gook splattered. It burned the way vampire ash would. Much as he hated to, Carlos neared the bubbling ooze and sniffed, and then shut his eyes, grimacing. His old vampire capacity to know a blood tracer kicked in. Yeah, the damned thing had been feeding off Yonnie, then probably jumped to him, didn't get Damali because knowing his wife, she'd said a prayer before she drifted off or while he was down in the bar.

He stood, backed away, staring at the mess on the floor and unlaced his shoes. Yeah, he needed to warn his boy. That shit he'd picked up from Lorelei at a dark coven brothel was one *helluva* sexually transmitted demon.

"ALL RIGHT," DAMALI said, "we just saw it with our own eyes, and how many times have we seen mess like this in one form or another?" She waited, walking around the room with her hands on her hips. "No shame in the game—we're human. We laugh, love, fight, argue, throw pity parties, whatever, ain't nobody in here perfect." She let her breath out hard. "But that's why we have to have solidarity, one household, especially in the last days, because who knows?"

Carlos nodded and sprawled out in his chair. "D ain't lied. I go there, get down, start thinking about woulda, coulda, shoulda—but like my wife said, all that does is leave you wide open for something to slither into your psyche that shouldn't be there . . . and it's easy to forget to give it a white light jolt of prayer to get it up outta you once you've started to spiral."

"Word," Shabazz said, glancing at Carlos. "And Jack Daniel's don't help." He leaned forward and pounded Carlos's fist. "Mighta come in through me, my head wasn't right."

Marlene gave Shabazz a tender glance. "It doesn't matter where it came in, baby. All that matters is that we got it out before it multiplied and hurt the team."

"Hey, man—I'm sorry I went there last night," Rider said, looking at Carlos. "That's a whole scenario that pushes my buttons . . . detonates 'em like nuclear warheads."

"I feel you," Carlos said, reaching over to pound Rider's fist across the coffee table. "No harm no foul, man."

"Good," Damali said, letting her breath out in relief. "Here's the thing we have to keep in front of us at all times. Family might get on our nerves, but they are not the enemy. That nasty bug we killed in there is. Stuff like that can have us at each other's throats. So, if we see a partner spiraling emotionally, we have to support and spread the love—just like we would if somebody had a gunshot wound. I can't always do it . . . shoot, I might be trippin' that day myself, and have, upon occasion," she said with a slow smile, glad when everyone chuckled and began to relax.

"C'mon, y'all, at this point we've seen each other's dirty drawers. We've been beat up, tore down, sick as dogs, mad as wet hens, done heard some stuff . . . that uh, I *know* nobody wants to speak on, riiight?" Damali leaned over, bending at the hips to look at people, making a funny face.

Everybody laughed and waved her away.

"Uh-huh," she said, bobbing her head and mocking the team, but not excluding herself. "*Oh, baby*—Arizona was some tight quarters."

"Girl, shut up," Inez said, falling over on the couch as several male Guardians hooted and slapped each other five.

"See . . ." Damali said. "After all of that, c'mon, folks." She looked around, her smile going from ribald to gentle. "I thought I would die when Carlos did," she said quietly. "When Jose was so sick back in the old L.A. compound that he was in intensive care . . . Lord. Marlene and Shabazz," she said, tearing up, and then she put up her hand. "No words." Damali drew in a shuddering breath as the team sobered and couples slowly slid closer and arms and hands threaded together. "Yeah. Mike, how many times we sew your big, burly ass up, huh? That deck rail through the gut, though—I thought I was gonna lose you, man. If I did . . . uh-uh."

"I love you too, baby-girl. 'Member them early days before you could take a nick, D?" Big Mike looked at Rider, then Shabazz. "We used to make bets while playing cards about who'd put a nine to their skull first if you came home bit."

"Sure did," Shabazz said, drawing Marlene closer. "Was some tense times, but we made it."

"Guess I have lived long enough to see a few miracles," Rider said, glancing at Tara. "We've been blessed, despite it all."

"That night I got made—got brought to the team," Dan said, first looking at Carlos and then Damali. "It was the most terrifying ordeal of my life, but also the most . . . I can't explain it. The whole thing was like walking through a doorway in the universe. I felt my old life and reality leave my body, and when Mike and Damali pulled me out of that car, alive, unnicked, when vamps had ripped the freakin' roof off . . . then we survived a firefight—I knew. I knew I was blessed, put here for something, some reason."

Murmurs of agreement coated the room with warmth and

love and bonding as each team member recalled their defining moment and who had helped them through it, who made a difference. Berkfield openly wept when he detailed for the group for the first time how he was abducted from his previously serene, staid suburban life into the clutches of a master vampire, and held captive like a POW in a coffin on a yacht.

Emotional scars bled but also healed. Everyone listened, everyone shared one small piece of their soul, and respect for each man and woman's journey was reestablished in full.

"Some healing . . . angel," Carlos finally said, pulling Damali against him. "I think we all needed that."

"Sometimes we have to look back just to see how far we've come," Damali said quietly, kissing him gently and then looking at the group. "I might have wings," she said with a self-deprecating chuckle. "But I've got a potty mouth, and ain't been no angel. She closed her eyes and laughed at herself. "Oh, the many offenses I'll have to answer for on judgment day . . . the many asses I've kicked, whooo ha."

Carlos laughed with her and the team. "Me, sheeeit. I'm jus' looking for a plea bargain. I *know* I've gotta fall on my sword for my shit."

The group erupted into rowdy cheers and high fives.

"But that's why, after they sent that nasty spell shit in here, I wanted to do this," Damali said. "Get us back to center. They can't break us—right?"

"Mighta messed our heads up for a minute," Carlos said. "Like Damali was saying, we're human. But we're family. We're one team, one love, we're strong."

"Yeah," she said, hopping up to pace. "We're blessed. Don't ever forget that. How many times has this team cheated death?"

"Many," the team shouted in one voice that rang out.

"How many times we been to Hell and back, y'all?" Carlos said, standing.

"Many!"

"How many purges have we done—nicks healed and sealed?" Damali said with a wide grin.

"Many!"

"How many places we lived, roads we've traveled, shit we overcame at the eleventh hour?" Carlos folded his arms over his chest.

"Many!"

Damali and Carlos looked at each other, smiling.

"So the next time a brother or sister Guardian gets on your nerves, you're gonna remember the many times they might not have been here—'cause if it wasn't for Heavenly Grace, they ain't have to be," Damali said, her gaze roving the group. "You're gonna imagine what life on this team could be like if their aggravating ass wasn't here. You're gonna do a self-check, put your bullshit on hold, and step back and get perspective, and pray that demon up outta you before it affects the team, your partner, or you."

"That's right, baby!" Marlene shouted, waving her hand from where she sat. "Tell it like we used to do! That's right! We've gone too far to turn back now."

"Our jobs may be hard, not like the average person has— but we've been blessed beyond measure along with that, too . . . what'd they tell me, when they snatched me up and out of the pit? To whom much is given, much is expected—I got a lot of shit in the transaction, so a brutha gotta work . . . that's how I see it." Carlos shrugged and opened his arms. "Ain't no use in whining. Ya saw what happened to me when I wasn't grateful. Do as you like, but I'ma tell ya, you *don't* wanna go there."

"That's the stone, cold truth," Shabazz said, glancing at Rider.

Rider slapped Shabazz five. "My bad. My *serious* bad, brother."

"*Hey,*" J.L. said, looking around the room. "Many are called, few are chosen, and even fewer step up."

"No, lie—might be your choice, but that's a bad move," Jose said, shaking his head. "Real bad move not to heed the call from up there."

"How we gonna complain about anything, even this insane

job description, when we've got an embarrassment of riches?" Berkfield asked, glancing around the group.

Marjorie's head bobbed up and down. "There are people who never did anything wrong, per se, who haven't been blessed with good health, or can't find that special someone to love . . . or are destitute due to no real fault of their own."

"Or are living in war-torn lands in refugee camps," Jasmine said sadly. "If they live long enough to make it there."

"Or have family so crazy and mean-spirited," Heather said quietly, "they never knew this . . . this oasis of love from people that they weren't even blood-related to." She glanced around the team and then at Dan. "I d'not know I was already fighting demons, didn't understand they were inside people, I mean *really* inside them. But I would have still signed up for this tour of duty to get you all as my gift."

Dan pulled Heather into a hug. "When I think of how it could be, I'd take this any day."

"I hear you," Inez said quietly and then looked at Mike. "This is it, for me."

"Me, too," Tara agreed in a near whisper, her gentle gaze going to Rider.

"It's easy, especially when things get tough," Bobby said, looking around the team, "to start bitching and moaning about what isn't right, instead of looking at all the things that are. Guess we're all guilty of it . . . and having a demon jumping around the family like head lice definitely doesn't help."

"That's why you *gotta* guard your head," Carlos said, looking at everyone.

"I think I finally get it, what you always meant when you'd tell us that, Carlos," Krissy said, looking at him straight in the eyes. "During early training, I didn't get it. Not until I saw it today."

"Better late than never, girlfriend. Ask me how I know— and I'll definitely tell you *all* about it. Had me acting real crazy, I won't lie," Juanita said, her gaze catching Krissy's and opening to a new bond.

"Aw'ight, then," Carlos said, nodding as he scanned the

group. "You're gonna realize that if you can do Hell, loading some furniture into a new house ain't shit," Carlos said, new energy making his fingertips tingle. "You're gonna say, *Thank you, God,* that I have a house, 'cause some folks are homeless."

"Now you ain't said a mumblin' word, brother," Mike said.

"Yeah," Carlos said, patting down his body theatrically. "You gonna say, *Thank you,* 'cause not only am I healthy, alive, able-bodied, and whole, but even got a few extra gifts that the average bear didn't get."

"Aw' right, brother, preach," Shabazz said with a wide smile.

"Uh-huh," Damali said, nodding as she walked. "You're gonna say, *Thank you,* because not only do I have a really gorgeous roof under which to lay my head, and my health and strength and gifts . . . but I got me a family, yo . . . a lover and spouse and life partner and best friend all rolled into one, somebody who is my *soul mate* to go with me into any battle, got my back, watches my six, is my confidant, helps make this raggedy-assed world whole—so when I go out there to do my danged job, and I come back all beat down and twisted around, I gots me a place of peace to lay my weary burden down. That's when you really say, *Thank you, good God!*" Damali shouted, pointing up at the ceiling with her eyes closed. *"That's who's my daddy!* Don't get it twisted. No disrespect—just be clear—*that's* where *every-thing we got* comes from!"

"Lay it down, D!" Jose hollered. "That's concert track, sis! Get me some paper, somebody! She done crossed over to hip-hop gospel on us!"

Guardians were on their feet cheering and hollering. Hotel management was knocking on the suite door again, but who cared? They were out.

"I DON'T THINK I've ever seen the team move that fast, in such lock-step coordination when we weren't in a firefight,"

Carlos said with a smile as he set the long, butter-toffee-hued, leather sectional sofa down hard on the Persian rug in the living room part of their bedroom suite, positioning it to face the flat-screen, wall-mounted HDTV and Bose stereo system. "Where you want the bed?" he asked, slightly winded.

"That's 'cause you took 'em to church," she said with a smile, beginning to unpack suitcases. "Ummm . . . under the skylight," she said offhandedly.

Carlos stared at the solid oak, king-sized, four-poster bed, and then glanced at Damali. "Two minutes, look at the room, get a good look and be sure, boo. For real."

"Over there's cool," she said, not looking up.

"That's what you said about the sofa, until you decided the feng shui alignment to the door was off. C'mon, D. Help a brother out—I've been moving stuff all day."

"Okay, okay, I'm sorry." She looked around. "I'm sure. Under the skylight—but, oh, yeah, the cedar chest and armoire have to fit without blocking the energy vibe from the windows."

Carlos stopped struggling with the furniture for a moment and stood up, wiping sweat from his brow with the back of his forearm. He was gonna remember today's sermon on being thankful. "Energy vibe from the windows . . . the wife wants the room politically, energy correct."

Damali chuckled. "Of all things in the room, you want *that* piece of furniture placed well. . . . Hmmmm."

"I'm remembering better now why it's important not to have a spirit of resistance."

She laughed. "I'm sorry the pieces they sent from estates are so heavy. The good stuff always is." She looked at him, concerned. "Can I help?"

"I'm good. Inspired by the pep talk," he said, putting his shoulder against a post with a grunt.

"You pulled the team together," she said, leaning on the long oak dresser behind her. "You're the one who took the team to church, not me. That was really inspiring to watch, all joking around aside."

"Naw, D. You took 'em there. I just opened the door. Got a part of the conversation started. You were officiating." He stood and stretched his back once he got the bed in the exact position under the skylight, then looked up. "I gotta double seal that breach point, girl," he said, muttering to himself. "If something crashes through that glass while I'm with you under the stars . . . *man*."

She stopped sorting clothes and looked at him. "We were officiating . . . as one, then."

"Huh?"

"The team meeting," she said. "We rallied everybody together, me and you, for the first time, really."

He stopped pacing the perimeter of the bed, trying to figure out how to securely reinforce the room and gave her his full attention. "Feels kinda weird, doesn't it?"

She nodded. "I'm sorta used to Marlene and Shabazz always pulling the team together when we get attitudes or splinter."

"Bound to happen sooner or later . . . you know, getting the baton passed. They told us, as Neterus, we'd be heads of household, but I never really felt like I was until today."

"I know what you mean," she said softly. "It's kinda scary, too."

"A lotta responsibility."

They both looked at each other.

"Think having kids feels like this?" she asked, searching his face.

Carlos rubbed the back of his neck. "Yeah . . . I guess. Never really put all that together, you know?" He looked at the bedroom door. "Dan must be wigging right now. Settling into a house, wife possibly pregnant . . . a lot to think about."

"Yeah," Damali said, and then began sorting clothes again. She blew a stray lock up off her damp forehead. "Soon as we get the bedrooms in shape, one more meeting about the concert basics, then maybe we should just let people fall back . . . chill, bring in some grub. It's been a lot to absorb. Inez got the kitchen done with Marlene, then Mar

broke off that detail to work with 'Bazz, Heather, and Dan
on tactical sensors, double prayer barriers, and the works.
J.L. and Krissy have the tech centers pretty much up and
running for a second level of security. Mike is on weapons
with Berkfield, getting our war room righteous. Jose's working on the studio with Rider. Tara's good to go with Marj on
the family room, living room, dining rooms; they got some
cool stuff to—"

"Damali," Carlos said, drawing her attention with the
gentle tone of his voice. "We're gonna have to blow the
groove sooner or later and tell 'em about the fawn."

Damali briefly closed her eyes. "When we have breakfast
with the Covenant tomorrow morning, okay?" The plea in
her voice made him come over to hug her. "Carlos, just one
night in our new home, family all tucked in safe around us,
breaking bread, laughing, making love, whatever, just peace,
be still, man . . . before we have to go back out to war."

"We gotta count our blessings, even if they do weigh a
ton." He kissed her forehead and tried to get her to joke
about the weight of things every woman had selected for the
house, but she only gave him a sad smile.

Damali looked around their partially furnished bedroom
suite, forlorn. "I am truly thankful for everything, but I'm
also being real about what's ahead. I know we're gonna have
to go to our councils on this. I may have to revive my oracle,
even though she's not fully healed. . . . The Covenant will be
in it, because it involved Nod banishment edicts, we've gotta
track down this Lorelei heifer . . . I feel like I should be
saying, 'Hi, new house. Bye, new house,' because we're maybe
gonna get a shower, change clothes, pick up weapons, and
be out again—and I'm praying to God this time when we
come home, the house is standing."

"With no demon habitation." Carlos kissed the top of
Damali's head. "No argument." He pulled back and looked
at her and smiled, pushing her locks over her shoulders. He
dropped his voice and gave her a mock-serious expression

that made her laugh. "Hannibal would tell me, 'Brother, sometimes you must water your horses.'"

"What?" she said, laughing.

"Sometimes," he said, kissing her nose, "you have to let your warhorses rest. You have to stop, give them water, chill . . . heal, replenish. Even vamps regenerate. Then live to fight another night." He kissed her again. "But you can run me into the ground, until I get this bedroom *exactly* the way you want it . . . then you've gotta water me, baby. Oh, yeah, I'll be your warhorse."

She hugged him hard and closed her eyes as she pressed her check against his chest. "Thank you."

"WHEN DID YOU do all this, 'Nez?" Marlene asked in awe. "Girl!"

"I wanted to have the first real sit-down meal when everybody was up in here be real down home, since who knows when we might have to hit the road again," Inez said, beaming as she brought another huge dish to the table.

"Makes every piece of furniture I moved," Mike said, closing his eyes and shaking his head, "every time I had ta move it again," he added, making the group laugh, "whooooo, worth it all, baby."

Inez hugged him from behind and whispered in his ear. "Made you a peach cobbler."

"She's talking dirty to me at the family table, about peach cobblers and such. Woman, stop."

They laughed, they ate, they communed. They said thank you a hundred times, blessed every corner of the huge house and every plate that got passed. They gave themselves the right to be human and partake in butter-dripping macaroni and cheese, greens, cornbread, corn on the cob, snap beans, limas and rice, fall-off-the-bone baked chicken, pan gravy, and Inez's audacious desserts. Those in the group who had sworn off meat and dairy were spoiled just as well by her vegetable lasagna, baby asparagus so sweet it would make you cry, and her tofu garlic teriyaki stir-fry, and dips, chips, and fruit plates dripping with natural fructose nectars.

Inez put down love hard in the kitchen, the way Marlene put down her prayers . . . and J.L. put down security with authority, no less than Carlos and Shabazz put down weapons check, and went over security again. This was home; everyone contributed their best, their all, and invested heavily, mightily with their hopes. Damali looked across the table at Carlos, so glad he'd agreed to hold the news about the fawn. They all needed one night to say thank you privately, too.

Absently munching and just feeling the mellowness of the vibe that surrounded her, Damali picked up on a strand of conversation that she really hadn't been listening to. What was being said wasn't all that important, what was being felt at the moment between everyone was paramount. If things could just stay this way . . .

"Yeah, I know," Dan said. "International travel right now sucks for getting the band through all the security measures—even with our special connections. Like, they've even gone so far as to ban books on flights at Heathrow, and we'd been negotiating to do London as a major stop."

"Maybe we're going about this all wrong," Carlos finally said, leaning back in his chair with a stretch. "We wanted to do concerts in the twelve hot zones so our people could pick up our tracers, right?" He waited until everyone nodded. "But we've got typhoons sweeping China, and we did Tibet already. Teams there know us. We've done Sydney under deep cover circumstances, but we hit 'em hard there, so our ground forces are strong all the way to Melbourne. We got South America covered—got back in Brazil, even though we lost a squad."

Carlos fell silent for a moment, and leaned forward. "It's gonna be hard to go into India, with the bombings picking up, just like we can probably get into Japan easier than North Korea right now, due to the nuclear standoff drama there. From Japan, though, we can go down through Malaysia, the Philippines, Indonesia, but just like India and Pakistan, the political tensions are making it hard to move or gather people there . . . don't want to put innocents at risk for a Bali event to happen at a concert."

Damali watched her husband's logic hold the group in thrall, and just the sound of his voice as he dissected the problem calmly, resolutely, without tension, just stating the facts, talking with his hands as though envisioning it in his mind in the air, then moving dishes around on the table so the others could see it in their minds, too, was melting her where she sat.

"We've been to the Motherland," Carlos said, glancing at each face on the team, "but Africa is so huge that we need to break it into like three or four zones to get the word out, and the Sudan is crazy-hot right now. The Canadian-Greenland and Mexican teams, as well as the Central American and Caribbean Guardians know us from Morales. We just came out of the South Pacific, while we were in Tahiti, and our U.S. teams all the way up through Alaska got us on lock from all the cross-country battling over the years."

"So, where's that leave us?" Shabazz asked, rubbing his belly and leaning back in his chair. "Tokyo, Moscow, Delhi, London, Rome—just because of the Vatican, for a nice worldwide spread . . . Ireland for the standing-stones community," he added, looking at Heather, "Gambia . . . But I see nobody mentioned the obvious."

"Where, Antarctica?" Rider said with a wide grin.

"Oh, he got jokes," Mike said, laughing and unbuckling a notch on his belt.

"Yeah," Dan said, running his fingers through his hair. "You know that's why the Covenant is meeting. The Middle East is hot, we know the deal with Iraq, Afghanistan, Turkey—the region . . . so many troops from so many nations, pulling our Guardians to our signature there will be asking for a tragedy. One false move by any side of the equation and it'll pop off another whole wave of insanity. But now, with Israel and Hezbollah squaring off, trading missiles over Lebanon, Beirut, getting close to Tel Aviv . . .

one hit to the three main religions' complex in Jerusalem, and it's on."

"I know," Carlos said. "That's why, after thinking about this hard and long, I'm suggesting a more conservative approach."

Mouths dropped open at the table and didn't close.

"I'm serious," Carlos said, glancing at everyone's expression.

"We know," Mike said, leaning forward and glancing at Shabazz, then Inez. "Baby, you ain't root the man, did you?"

"Naw, that would have to be Damali," Inez said. "Carlos, you feel all right? *Conservative?*"

"You?" Marlene said, fanning her face. "Oh, now I *know* it's the end of days."

"C'mon, y'all, I'm not that bad," Carlos said, laughing, but he glanced at Damali for support. He smiled wider when she could only shrug on his behalf. "Okay, maybe conservative is the wrong word. Maybe I should have said smarter . . . hit 'em how they don't expect."

"Okay, now that's my husband," Damali said, leaning forward with her elbows on the table and making the group laugh. "Semantics. Let's go before he starts talking in *Dananu.*"

"I'm crushed, girl," Carlos said, flinging a balled-up napkin at her, that she caught. "But we did this before in Sydney, sort of."

Damali closed her eyes and laughed. "And the man said conservative."

"Can I state my case, please?"

"Go ahead," Damali said, waving her hand. "At least this time we get to hear it before you make it up as we go along."

Carlos laughed. "Yeah, well, I'm mentally designing this on the fly, so think about it. J.L., I need your technology expertise on this." He looked around and J.L. leaned forward and nodded. "Cool. I'm thinking, since you know who owns the airwaves, and we have solid Guardian signature patterns in several locations already, we simulcast the concert, live, just like they do the international New Year's Eve countdowns, into zones too hot to get our team in and out of quickly. This means teams don't have to necessarily gather."

"I'll be honest," Dan said, "I really wasn't feeling dragging the team in and out of all these airports . . . uh, right now, with things being as hot as they are."

"We feel you, man," Shabazz said. "We know the deal. But we've still gotta work—just find a way to work smarter, not harder."

"That's where I'm going," Carlos said, nodding to acknowledge Dan's concern. "We've gotta use the technology like they do. Shabazz said it—work smarter. So, we get underground units of Guardians that we already know to send clips from the concert to each other on the Internet, bounce 'em through the Covenant, who can flip 'em to teams we haven't yet met. When they make the clips, they can edit the tactical energy wave pattern for me and Damali right into the clip like a subliminal message or code encased in mental silver—white light."

"That's smooth, man," J.L. said, rubbing his chin.

"This way our own can know what to hone in on." Carlos stopped for a moment and looked out toward the beach. "Yeah, by doing it over the Net, we have a way to secure the data bursts with some type of prayer encryption code or password—so when the darkside hacks it to try to see what this special flurry of messages are that're spiking on the Internet, it fries their brains, their tubes, their sight. It oughta backward protect the sender and receiver's machines, too, if they're our people—so if the wrong side gets it, bam . . . smoking black hole. They don't even know where it came from, no trace. In and out, smooth."

"That is *nasty,* man," J.L. said, reaching around several Guardians to slap Carlos five. "Like our teams caught behind firefights in Lebanon, Tel Aviv, Beirut, Iraq, we could ask Rabbi, Imam, and Father Pat to give us some strong prayer ammo, word phrases, specific passages in the old texts that if the wrong side opens it—"

"Yeah," Carlos murmured. "Like a silver shot virus that keeps imploding throughout their network, and the only way to get at it is to shut down cells, cut it off, black out a part of their network before they can bring it back up again. We've been going about this the conventional way. High body count on our side. We saw what one backfired spell did— shut 'em down for twenty-four hours. We've got to fight nasty, like them. Send them some bugs they can't shake in their house."

Damali watched him take a slow swig of sweet tea and set the glass down with precision, and run his fingers down the glass's condensation absently as he spoke. Watching the general work, his mind on fire, was the sexiest shit . . .

"Me and 'Mali are always bait, this protects the team, second line of defense. Guardians need to be homing to us, not the team, especially in a firefight. Trapped teams in Malaysia, Indonesia, India, Pakistan, anywhere it's hot, they get Internet transmission from their nearest Covenant connection, from downloads doctored by teams in strong locations that know how to capture our patterns through their tactical units." Carlos glanced around the team. "Now, this way, when we do hit London, Rome, Tokyo, Moscow, et cetera, which we will, our teams will feel the energy signature the moment we hit their soil. Right now, the only ones that feel us like that are the wrong side—which is crazy. Our people gotta know, and not just by calls from the Covenant, when we're in their zone."

"But, Carlos, doing such a big concert, even if it's here in the U.S. and broadcasting around the world . . . won't that let them know who we are?" Marjorie glanced around the table nervously. "I'm not trying to be negative."

"You're right, and you're not being negative, Marj. Your point is valid. Here's the thing," Carlos said, talking with his hands. "People, the darkside already knows who we are, so it's not like we're blowing our cover, they just can't pinpoint us at any given time. Our Guardian teams are in places we can't reach all over the world, and they aren't all sure who we are—bad position to be in. Once we do the concert, they'll know. They'll be able to feel our exact-match energy signature in a territory the way vamps know when one of theirs has left or entered a zone, or a zone has been breached."

"So you did learn something valuable while taking a walk on the wild side," Rider said, smiling.

Carlos play-boxed him across the table. "Use every gift you've got, brother." He dropped back to his seat, smiling. "While we do the concert, just like any other firefight, we're open for a minimal time of exposure. However, the darkside will watch us . . . they'll be curious, trying to see what our angle is. They'll be baited in, wondering, and then all of a sudden all these blogs and video packages, podcasts, and e-mails will start flying. Our inside man, Yonnie, can help with the hype, tellin' them he got word from me that we'd be passing secret messages. That way I know they'll open up anything about us with an encryption seal on it."

"Or, we could tell them that he compromised me," Tara said, staring at Rider. "To make it more credible." She reached for his hand and held it under the table as he conceded with a nod. "And we should let them open one or two of the first ones to draw them in to download it deep into their network . . . and let it be something they can't figure out readily, referencing the Holy Land or Nod to keep them hungry for more." Tara glanced around the table. "I do remember how they think," she added quietly. "Carlos is dead on. Let them put their best vampire and demon minds on it, and then when they open subsequent packages, they fry."

"Girl . . ." Juanita said, as Krissy tipped her glass of sweet tea against hers. "Remind me to stay on your good side."

"Right," Heather said, clearly impressed. "Good lookin' out."

"Just like Tara said," Carlos pressed on, making his point with conviction. "We don't have to find them, they'll find us. They'll grab everything that's gift wrapped, try to decode it to see what hidden subtext in the lyrics or battle logistics we might have been communicating, and ka-boom. Meanwhile, we're back home, chillin'." He looked around. "Minimal team risk, maximum exposure. Dan can set us up to play L.A. with no stress instead of beating his head against a brick wall with uncooperative venues, and we could drive up, wouldn't even have to take a flight."

Carlos opened his arms. "Sometimes the universe is trying to put stumbling blocks in your way to make you change direction. Normally, we just grind through it, too damned stubborn to yield, back up, and punt. Gotta change that dynamic. New situations are happening, and we have to make course adjustments." He glanced at Heather. "Might have to change the way we do business all the way around—our team is young. Got a lot at stake here. I heard everybody loud and clear." He briefly glanced at Damali and held her gaze for a moment. "I'm right there with you."

"That's deep," Shabazz said quietly. "Damn, man."

"We need to evolve this operation," Carlos said, leaning forward. "We got teams trying to hold it down, so they need to be able to reach out to us and call *us* in as their Green Berets, ya know? Like, the way that thing went down in Morales, still ain't sitting right with me, man . . . they came and helped us, and we lost a lot of good men and women. From this point forward, after the concert to get a beacon on the horizon, they should be calling us to say, 'Yo, we need backup.' Then as the hard-hitting Neteru squad, we go get our people some relief. In and out. Can't lose a whole team again like we lost Brazil."

Carlos sat back in his chair hard and rubbed the tension out of his neck and then looked at Damali. "I don't know—that's my two cents. It was off the cuff, on the fly. D . . . what's your take? How you think we should play this? Concerts are your specialty; I'm just mapping it out based on old power paradigms I knew."

It took her a moment to make her vocal cords work so she could answer, and a few seconds more to keep from sliding out of her seat. He'd blown her mind with an ingenious plan, one that had the best odds of keeping the family safe, and he had yielded the floor, no macho bravado . . . and had moved furniture all day, too, and was sitting there actually waiting for her plan or endorsement, not just saying that . . . she could feel the strain in his voice when he'd said it. He wanted her opinion, her view mattered. *Talk about evolution*—her mind was singed at the edges from the straight silver charge he'd shot into it. Her throat was dry, her mouth had gone dry, but she had to sit very still and keep her knees together because all the moisture from those sources had collected at the other end of her continuum.

She couldn't believe the words that were forming in her head. Her, a Leo—a Neteru, a Queen. Her breath came out in a rush, coating her reply. It wasn't supposed to, after all, she was co-leader, co-general, partner, but . . . dang! Could dinner just be over now, and dishes wait 'til the morning?

"Everything he said works for me," she said quietly, then stood up and walked into the kitchen with both of their plates.

CHAPTER FOURTEEN

Meeting was *definitely* adjourned. Damali took *his* plate up from the table for *him*—in front of the team? He just stared at her retreating form, the way everything just sorta moved in slow-motion beneath her clothes. She'd gone along with his plan—just like that? No amendments. No drama. Just a clearly stated "What he said" . . . Whew.

Carlos thought he'd heard Big Mike mumbling something about him and 'Nez had the dishes. That meant him and 'Nez had the kitchen. True, on the surface it was an admirable volunteer move, given 'Nez had cooked, somebody else shoulda had the cleanup with Mike. But no doubt about it, Mike had made the first household claim on community space—message was simple: not here, tonight.

The table was now in the process of getting cleared faster than it had been set. Guardians had almost created what looked like a military sandbag line, passing off casseroles, stacks of silverware, and plates, getting soiled utensils into the sink, dishwasher, and refrigerator so they could move out. Then he watched Damali go MIA. The urge to track and hunt her through the mansion was almost making his hands shake, but he remembered he had to go outside and talk to Yonnie. *Yeah, handle your business, first,* he told himself, watching the sun kiss the horizon good-bye.

He set the last platter on a side counter by the door, washing the image out of his mind of Mike backing Inez up against the sink. He was out, motion, headed for the mountainside, silver barriers up—tonight was not a night he was trying to drag anything but his own ass home.

"Nice digs, man," Yonnie said over his shoulder as Carlos cleared a ridge.

"Couldn't have done it without you, brother," Carlos said, watching Yonnie stare at the house trying to approximate Tara's position inside.

"Hey, wouldn't have been able to flip the digits if you hadn't made the come up, 'Los."

"Cool," Carlos said with a smile. "So, we're even—and I guess you won't take it no type of way if I don't lift the silver block on her room or her motions within the new compound."

Yonnie put his hands behind his back and closed his eyes. "That's cold, man. You silver shielded me out . . . damn, my own boy don't even trust me."

"She's married, *holmes*. C'mon now. You're talking to me." Carlos smiled as Yonnie peeked at him with one eye. "I trust you about anything but her—and you almost got my ass kicked by my own team behind a chat on the beach."

"We was just talkin'," Yonnie said, opening his arms and trying not to laugh.

"Councilman Yolando, be real," Carlos said, opening his arms and laughing. "There was seduction signature all in that shit when she came back, man . . . and she's married to a nose."

Yonnie held up his hands in front of his chest, chuckling. "Aw'ight, aw'ight, what can I say? It was the first time I held her where . . . damn, man," he said, suddenly allowing the mirth to drain away from him as his arms slowly lowered and his gaze went back toward the house. "First time she had a pulse . . . had red blood flowing in her veins . . . was warm. No illusion, really was warm from life." He looked at Carlos. "I make no apologies, brother—I couldn't help it."

"What can I say to that?" Carlos muttered, truly

understanding. He looked at the house with Yonnie and rubbed his jaw, hoping they wouldn't have to come to blows over the situation.

"She was a master, too," Yonnie said offhandedly. "Damn . . ."

Carlos frowned and looked at him. "Now you've lost me."

"You came up, dragged me with you. I had the elevation capacity, took her where I went with a no-bullshit mate bite." Yonnie shook his head, his eyes never leaving the house. "I didn't know I'd gone up a notch, definitely didn't know she had, 'til she bulked one time out in Arizona during Cain's time when something spooked her . . . but hey."

"You gotta let it go, man . . ." Carlos let his breath out hard. "Don't make me regret leaving a back door open for you to come on the property, brother—c'mon, work with me. Damn. As it is, your ass is standing on hallowed ground, and they can't monitor open conversations here because the four corners all the way to the epicenter have been barriered. Now, if I lift the ban, you fry. So, chill."

"All right, aw'ight, damn." Yonnie turned away from the lit house below and closed his eyes. "Don't act like you haven't been here."

"It's *because* I've been here that I know that the only instinct greater than the one you're battling at the moment is the survival imperative—and *that's* why I'm not playing when I say, do *not* take me there and make me lift the ban while you're on the property."

Carlos looked at Yonnie and didn't blink.

"Aw'ight, Mr. Chairman," Yonnie grumbled.

"Don't be like that, man."

"How am I supposed to be?"

"Grateful that I'm about to drop some science on you."

"Yeah, right," Yonnie said, releasing a bored sigh of frustration. "Why you call me tonight?"

"'Cause I wanna tell you something, man . . . like, I ain't in your business, but you might wanna watch the company you keep."

Yonnie tilted his head. "Come again. I live in Hell, dude. What—"

"You know a witch named Lorelei?"

Yonnie paused for a moment, thinking. "Oh . . . yeah . . . damn . . . Straight skeezer, gives good rim."

"Yeah, well, she gave you more than good rim."

Yonnie opened his mouth then walked a hot path away from Carlos and came back. "I do not *fucking* believe—"

"Yeah, she left you burning, brother," Carlos said calmly.

Yonnie tilted his chin to the sky and closed his eyes, fury making his fangs drop. "What kind of STD was it?"

"Dissension demon," Carlos said flatly.

"Oh, shit!" Yonnie began pacing again.

"Nasty little motherfucker, too. Me and D got him before he burrowed deep into the team."

Yonnie stopped walking. "Tell me Tara ain't see that shit."

"You want me to lie to make it feel better, or you want the truth?"

"Oooooh, shit." Yonnie walked away from Carlos shaking his head. "I'ma kick that witch's ass, yank her sorry spine right out of her—"

"Before you get melodramatic," Carlos said calmly, studying his nails, "here's what's up."

He waited until Yonnie had calmed down enough to listen, and took his time laying out the pros and cons, risk factors to both Yonnie and the team, then stepped back.

"So, that's why I'm saying, you might wanna let her think me and you don't talk like that . . . not where I'd let you know we had to kill a dissension demon you carried to us. But, however you wanna play this is up to you. I'm trying to figure out ways you can pass them bogus info so that you can put your hands up and claim plausible deniability, if you get caught."

"Cool," Yonnie said, nodding. He was about to pound Carlos's fist when Carlos drew back his hands with a smile and held them up in front of his chest.

"No offense," Carlos said.

"None taken—my bad," Yonnie said, wiping his hands down the front of his Armani. "It's gonna take a lot of restraint not to just wring that bitch's neck."

"Well, at least she didn't give you nothing permanent that could cripple you, like a were black blood exchange."

Yonnie walked away from Carlos, pointing when Carlos laughed. "You ain't right, man. You know down in the realms we gotta do a lot of insane shit to survive. And, yeah, I've done some shit I ain't proud of, but—"

"Relax, man, damn, I'm just messin' with you." Carlos shook his head. "I almost got jacked by a were-jag in the Amazon, that's all I'm saying . . . just warning my brother to be more careful with your shit."

"Oh, aw'ight," Yonnie said, shaping up his Afro. "Thought you was signifying."

"No." Carlos folded his arms over his chest and kept a straight face for a second. "I ain't got shit to say about Lilith." He couldn't hold it when Yonnie cracked a smile, and they both burst out laughing.

"Maybe Lilith wants the little critter back tonight?" Yonnie said, chuckling hard. He winked at Carlos. "By now, they oughta be good ta go in my system."

Carlos cringed. "Aw . . . man . . . that is *so nasty.* You definitely don't have to go there for the team. Go get your shit cleaned—"

"Fair exchange," Yonnie said, shrugging. "She's gonna try to kill me anyway . . . so, what's a little dissension down in council? I didn't know." He opened his arms. "I got blindsided by one of her witches."

Carlos's face was still contorted with disgust. "But, Lilith? Naw, man, you don't have to go there."

"Listen to me," Yonnie said with a sly grin, and then produced a toothpick in his mouth and began manipulating it with his tongue. "She liked some Yolando, okay. And girlfriend got some throne installation moves that date back to the dawn of time—first female type shit."

Carlos held up his hands and began walking toward the

house. "I don't wanna know." He had to get all images of
that out of his head before he stepped to Damali.

"You might wanna know this, though," Yonnie said, staying Carlos's leave.

Carlos turned and simply looked at him.

"Aw'ight, yeah, when I came up here I was gonna bargain
with you, man . . . for just one more time to holla at Tara.
But, given my situation and that I've gotta go get blasted to
get this STD shook loose . . . I'm not trying to bring that
home to my baby—so . . ."

Carlos's gaze hardened as he waited.

"She installed *me* in my throne when she was weak,
when forces down there had been drained, feel me? Under
any other circumstances, it's doubtful that any of her shit
would have bled over to me, being how old she is
comparatively—but I was topside and unaffected when
contagion hit subterranean. Now fact, girlfriend got so
much game, I couldn't even begin to get all the shit she did
eons ago—way deep. But there's something real new going
down that's worrying the shit out of her . . . real close to the
surface. It's somewhere she can't see into and none of us
can, either. Maybe it's in a church, I don't know."

Nod reverberated inside Carlos's head, but he just kept
listening and rubbing his jaw as Yonnie talked.

"All I'ma say is this," Carlos warned. "Next time, Lilith
will be real strong. She'll siphon your ass dry, if you don't
watch yourself."

"Yeah, yeah, aw'ight." Yonnie grinned at Carlos, flashing
a hint of fang. "But the woman can throw down, C."

"I'm out."

"Oh, so now, no thank you, Yonnie. No exchange for the
info—"

"I gave you valuable info," Carlos said laughing. "Told
you your ass was burning so you could go to a dark coven
clinic and get your shit sandblasted."

Yonnie flipped Carlos the bird, making him laugh harder.
"Oh, so now it's like that?"

"See you tomorrow night, man," Carlos said, walking away and shaking his head.

IT WAS SO peaceful outside as he made it down a part of the ridge and through the front gardens that he almost wanted to stop and just listen to the night sounds, breathing it all in. But there was something much more pressing propelling him toward the house. Just seeing his friend's jacked-up situation reminded him of all the things he needed to be thankful for once again.

Carlos stopped before he got to the front door and said a prayer to jettison anything off him that he might be carrying as baggage from his brief meeting outside with his very wild friend. But as he crossed the threshold, he knew he couldn't judge Yonnie. They had walked similar paths, but very different circumstances prevailed. For one, during the entire time he'd been a vamp, he'd had Damali.

He crossed the great foyer with that singular concept in mind, and bounded up the right side of the dual staircase to reach the second floor. He'd been real lucky that he'd never been subjected to an installation by Lilith, or worse. Timing— whew, Carlos wiped his brow as he paced down the hall. When his moves had landed him dark promotions, Damali had always been there to passionately celebrate with. Same deal in the reverse. She'd been right there with him by his side in the Light. He hadn't ever needed to go anywhere else, where he could have picked up something nasty he couldn't shake. Anything wild and elaborate he did had been because . . . yeah, he was out of his damned mind.

When he pushed open the bedroom door he stood in the archway of it for a moment. She had put tallows of all shapes and sizes on the wrought-iron racks he'd set up for her around the bed. He could smell the fire combining with melting wax, shea butter, and something deep and musky and sensual coming from the bathroom . . . running water. He stared at the buttercream-hued sheets and satin duvet she had turned down, suddenly feeling too grimy to enter the sacred space she'd created.

"Hi," she murmured, coming out of the bathroom.

He didn't move or immediately answer. He couldn't, but just allowed his eyes to drink her in. Soft candlelight from the bathroom and bedroom framed her in a muted golden glow. Gentle light caressed the semisheer, long ivory satin sheath she wore that was held on her shoulders by the barest wisp of cord. The illusion of her nude form, just the outline of her body, was paralyzing . . . where her breasts rose, her nipples pouted against the silk, the swell of her hips, the dip of her waist, the smooth crest of her thighs, the way her mound rose slightly between the V between her legs . . . He loved watching the colors dance in the reds and golds and browns of her hair, and the way it played across her caramel skin, her eyes making it sparkle. Oh, *definitely*, thank you, Lord.

"I need to strip by the door . . . just in case," he said quietly, ashamed to be so dirty in her presence. "I had to deliver the message to my boy, start the ball rolling. Sorry I'm late."

She crossed the room with a security clothing bag, her expression serene, and handed it to him. "I know. It's cool. It gave me time to get ready for you."

He looked at her and started peeling away the offending fabrics. The way she was staring at him made it hard to breathe as he sealed the bag and dropped it by the door.

She nodded with a smile toward the deck.

"Oh, yeah, right," he said, remembering protocol, and picked up the bag, tossed it out into the bonsai garden, then locked the sliding glass door.

She chuckled. "C'mon . . . let me get you into the tub."

He didn't have to be told twice. He let her lead the way and made sure he didn't touch her. He briefly hesitated as she rounded the tub and stood at the head where the fixtures were. Low jets churned the water into a sudsy froth and humidity in the room had fog-coated the mirror and shower glass across the room, as well as halfway up the windows. She'd rimmed the foot of the tub in a half-moon of white tallow and it was difficult to stop staring at the hypnotic waterfall that cascaded down the wall fountain over rocks, picking up candlelight and her in the shimmer.

"Get in, all the way down to the shoulders . . . and lemme douse your hair."

If there was a dissension entity clinging to his spirit, it was pretty much fried away by the sudden heat Damali had caused to slingshot through his system. He was agreeable to anything she wanted to do right now. There was no resistance in him whatsoever as he slid into the fragrant, opaque water and then immediately realized with a groan what part of the sensual aroma contained. Oil of Hathor.

Carlos closed his eyes and began breathing through his mouth. She'd supercharged the malachite tiles in water . . . in a white bath, with her own special blend of whatever that had oil of Hathor as its base.

"What are you doing to me?" he murmured with his eyes closed while she sponged water into his hair. It drizzled down his face and lashes.

"Watering my warhorse . . . just like you said," she murmured and kissed his temple.

If he hadn't been holding on to the side of the tub, he would have just slipped beneath the surface and drowned. The jets were on low. That, combined with the tiles, were sending bubbling tingles of chakra stimulation down his spine. Her gentle massage of his scalp while kneeling behind him outside the tub was making him irrational.

Suddenly she nuzzled his cheek so passionately that it put fangs in his mouth. It was the way she did it while working the knots out of his neck with her thumbs underwater, then she'd rubbed her face against his damp neck when he leaned up for her. He needed her mouth on his, but she stayed positioned behind him, just out of reach, alternately hard-nuzzling the sides of his neck until he arched in the tub.

No longer able to stand the tease, he turned quickly to capture the nape of her neck with the cup of his wet hand. He needed her tongue to twine with his so badly now that when she opened her lips to accept his kiss he moaned right into her mouth. Oil of Hathor with her soft touch, the tub jets hitting lit pulse points and meridians, made him pull her closer, sloshing water on the floor. The only reason he broke the kiss was so they could stand, but he had to be careful not to trip over the fixtures as he looked at her wet gown clinging to every conceivable curve she owned.

She stood there, transfixed for a moment. This wasn't part of the plan. Tonight was his gift and yet try as she might, the look on his face was making her forget all that she'd intended to do. She couldn't help it. The oil in the water had left him with a glistening sheen over golden skin fired by candlelight. It dampened his dark lashes that now partially hid his intense, silver eyes, and highlighted the contours of his strong jaw, down his throat and over his Adam's apple, down his cinder block–defined chest, all the way down his beautiful abs to that dark silky trail of jet black hair curling just below his navel.

Compelled, she ran her thumbs over his dark, raisin-colored nipples and watched his eyes slide shut with a hard swallow. Her mouth found the scar at the center of his chest right over his heart, the brand mark where her fist holding an Isis had permanently marked him so many years ago.

With a quiet gasp he held the back of her head with trembling fingers and then slowly pressed her closer so that her cheek could rest against the scar.

"It's too sensitive right now," he whispered, his entire body shuddering from her attention to his scar while her thumbs grazed his nipples. "I feel it in my shaft . . . old wiring you did years ago."

"I know," she whispered against the scar, breathing warmth into it. "I remember every . . . single . . . one of those places."

He bent, took her mouth hard and held her jaw with his hands, then broke away to begin kissing her face frantically in hot, passionate bursts. In one lithe move he'd stepped out of the tub blindly and pressed the length of their bodies together with a deep groan. When he broke away from her mouth again to catch his breath, she watched his eyes cross beneath his lids as he flattened his palm in the dip of her spine and made her pelvis collide with his. She knew where he was at; his body demanded friction, even more urgently, penetration, but she wanted to take him to a transcendent place in his mind . . . the only problem was, he'd begun to unravel hers.

His palms slid down into the dip in her spine to capture the rise in both halves of her behind, and the heat he applied there made her want to climb up his body the way her Sankofa tattoo was climbing up her back. Soon she could see liquid, shimmering hue from her aura spilling off of her skin onto his, something only he'd been able to see on her before. As his energy essence commingled with hers, the unanticipated sensation made them both cry out.

She threw her head back, holding on to his shoulders, nearly faint as the urge to draw him inside her reached a fever-pitch just from their heated embrace. His hands were wreaking havoc with her chakras, hot sweeps delivering spontaneous tactical charge, sending hard contractions throughout her canal, quaking her womb, and releasing choked gasps just from his touch. Somehow the oil of Hathor had become her ruin, too. Carlos's hands slid up her spine and caressed her shoulder blades where her wings normally crested, but his touch created agony, his will able to forestall them from presenting and making her crazy.

It was as though she couldn't get enough of his skin to touch hers at one time. His labored bursts of warm breaths against her neck drove her hand between their bodies to stroke him, but he wouldn't let her. Instead he quickly captured her wrist, brought her palm to his mouth, and placed a deep kiss in the center of it until she practically dissolved like another puddle on the floor.

Every sensitive point on her was on fire and had made her

nearly insane with need. All she could do was rub her body against his, allow her breasts and her belly and fevered mound to graze his hard burning surface, trying to capture his mouth again while on her tiptoes. She loved this man so much she couldn't breathe.

The moment he put his hands in her hair, her locks ignited with a blue-white erotic charge that buckled her body to a near orgasm. But rather than allow it to run its normal course, he caught it in his fist, drew it from the crown of her head, down through her body in agonizing increments, and finally pulled it out of the base of her spine so slowly she wept.

"Your eyes are silver," he said in an awed, satisfied murmur. "I've *never* seen that happen before."

She grasped his biceps hard as she turned her head and looked away. She squeezed her eyes shut. Her nails had begun to score his skin. "Please . . . let it go," she whispered hoarsely, unable to move as she stood trembling, waiting, needing him to release what he'd captured inside a small, pure silver energy orb.

"I will in a minute, *tesoro*. After all you've given me, let me give you back something, beyond all twelve of the planets . . . Oh, baby, you showed me creation point with oil of Hathor as a catalyst before," he murmured quickly in her ear, sending heat chills through her as his voice hit a low decibel that clenched her stomach. "Let me show you the outer limits . . ."

She felt her legs give way and his arms were suddenly under them. There was no resistance, no argument, no dissension whatsoever. It felt like her mind was turning into liquid quicksilver and threatening to run out of her ear, he'd made her so hot. The outer limits? Damali closed her eyes and crushed her face against his chest. Her husband was insane. He'd walked her into the bedroom so swiftly with so much energy wafting off him that every candle went out the second he neared the bed.

Carlos sprawled her across the bed, just let her spill from his arms onto the butter-cream bedsheets, and the pale blue-white wash of light that came from his silver stare and the moon made her do the only thing she could—reach for him. But rather than immediately come to her, he opened his palm at the side of the bed and let the orb he'd been grasping float toward her. She didn't know what to do, had no frame of reference for where he would take her. Instinct made her open her hand to accept it and she closed her fingers around it. Yet the instant she did that, the shell of it shattered, and sparkling, confetti-like energy glitter rushed out, floated up and then slowly floated back down like an iridescent, gentle rain.

She didn't understand why he'd stepped back. Curiosity made her lift herself up on her elbows and stare at him through a heavy-lidded gaze, and then she looked up at the sparkling dust that was backlit by the moon and stars that were peering through the skylight.

"I love you, baby," he murmured, and watched with utter satisfaction as the sparkling particles began to touch her. "Experience the galaxy . . . then I'll join you."

At first, all she could do was open her mouth and clutch the sheets, so blown away that no sound exited her lungs. Every infinitesimal place a glittering speck hit her sent orgasm trauma through her skin, her hair, her breasts, over her shoulders and belly, and down to her toes. Her skin was covered with the shimmering substance that continued to pelt her gently until she fell back against the bed, spent. But as long as it coated her, it continued to send climaxes through her 'til she shrieked.

Prone, then arching, a wail so deep and filled with precious agony opened her mouth, making her taste the shimmering energy, swallow it, letting it turn her inside out as it coated her insides and pulled her up in hard jerks from inside her belly. It was all over her, everywhere, and her pleasure sobs turned into a bleating refrain of Carlos's name, reaching for him. He had to get deep inside her, touch the one place that the shimmering energy missed before she went insane. Acute need demanded it.

When he blanketed her, she lost what was left of her mind. His sudden weight was just a tease, something that had made her eagerly lift her hips in frustration to claim him. But just as quickly as he'd covered her with his hard body, his shaft pulsing against her thigh like a promise, he took back his wondrous body heat. She almost screamed as he just pulled all that phenomenal maleness down her torso by increments until he opened her with his tongue, inviting more energy flecks to sprinkle her there and join his ardent kisses.

Pleasure had sent her away from herself, out of body, out of mind, out of breath, to an outer limit where ecstasy could exist in a sliver of universal fabric between one solar system and the next—a void, when a holler was an open-mouthed, silent scream, a breath truncated to gulp nothing but tongue, to a place where it seemed like one was floating but was moving at incredible speeds yet unmeasured by mortal man. When he entered her she saw Light, a brilliant nova's edge of a place that left the sparkling flecks and the void behind.

Her voice bounced off the walls, her flat palm slapped the sheets, his back, his shoulder, turning her legs into a vise as pleasure hysteria lifted her up, wrung her out, had her speaking in tongues begging him for what, she wasn't sure. Her mind couldn't even process her own request, just burst with the hollered litany, "Please! Oh, God, please!"

The bite he delivered broke the last of her down, made her lose contact with her mothership of reason, separated her from her body, thrust her onto her own astral plane in a hot, slick, wet slide of skin against skin, perfectly fitted bodies made one for the other, his pure piston energy about to spontaneously combust with every holler, so crazy, temporarily losing orbit with one another in a hard roll that collided with wood and an unseen barrier——her blunt-edged bite making him see stars inside her head, the line between his and her body pure vapor, impossible to judge as his voice hit a crescendo, then bottomed out and became distant

thunder. *Ka-boom.* He was stardust, too—subatomic pleasure particles, a meteor shower of hot molten rock threatening to give them both heart attacks in bed.

His palm connected with an oak post—something, anything, he had to stay grounded and stop the charge. Her wet,
spasming canal felt so good he'd almost swallowed his
tongue . . . had only been a mad scientist experimenting
with raw power, didn't know the outcome, had been talking
shit, playing—*oh, damn,* it felt so good.

All his plans for the evening had gone up in flames with
reentry. He couldn't pull out, stop to taste her, or anoint the
bathroom rocks with her wails, not tonight. Not after her energy hit his energy and he'd blanketed her too soon, mistake.
Falling flecks of orgasmic release coated his back, absorbed
into his chakras and spine, her furtive sweeps down his back,
maddening, her breasts crushing the air from his lungs—a
hard roll was the only way to save her wings.

Pinned down at the shoulders, her full weight and energy
demanding recompense, with her head thrown back, silver
tears streaming, she rode him so hard he was catching
cramps in his quads. But stop, how? While snorting blue
flames? Oh, hell yeah, she'd watered her warhorse 'til he
was sweating gold lacquer, her hands rubbing silver sparkles
into it through his chest.

His heart was in arrhythmia. Every convulsion that
dredged his sac on each upthrust felt so damned good that
his rib cage seized with his breaths, her down-strokes like a
CPR hit necessary to save his life. He could barely watch
her, his sight blurred by silver-gold tears, her hair wild,
wings spread, skin slicked silver from her Neteru sweat,
beautiful eyes shut, luscious mouth open gulping air, breasts
bouncing, knees bent, thighs clenching his hips, riding him
bareback, no hands, her stomach a network of flexible muscle that made a grown man cry.

He could feel her dragging him somewhere so fast so
deep into her universe that he released the post, sat up, and
wrapped his arms around her waist and hid his face against

her breasts. Blackout. There was no sound. Blackout. There were no heartbeats. Blackout. There was no light. Blackout. The darkness gave way to blinding light. Then he felt it all. Oh . . . shit . . .

Her name fractured in two like his sanity—*'Mali!* Release convulsions kicked his ass for playing with the unknown, messing with her mind, got all inside his, curled his toes, made his pants shallow, fast, and hard, tore his voice up from the roots and twisted it around her name three times—*Da-Ma-Li!* Oh, shit, it was so good, don't stop, but make it end, dear God. He was only human, she was only human, this time maybe he'd gone too far. "Please, baby, ground the charge!"

They both reached out at the same time, each lunging toward opposite sides of the bed without breaking their physical connection. She touched the headboard, he'd grabbed a post. Neither said a word as the final orgasm crested and slowly ebbed away. She dropped like a stone against his chest. Gold-splattered feathers were everywhere, so were minor traces of blood from his bite. They lay like that for a long time, her sprawled on top of him, him spread-eagle under her, both of them gulping air.

When he could focus, he opened his eyes and stared up at the stars through the skylight and studied the moon, catching his breath—now philosophical, a respecter of gravity.

"Don't ever do that again," she said, breathing hard and laughing softly. "At least not without warning me."

He shook his head, still in discovery shock. "Trust me, baby. I won't."

"THEY KILLED IT," Lorelei wept with a shaking voice, engaging her crystal ball.

"What did the Neterus kill?" Lilith's voice hissed.

"They killed my dissension demon . . . it was conjured up with such a wonderful spell."

Lilith didn't immediately answer. If the Neterus had detected something as deeply embedded and insidious as a dissension demon, then what else had they discovered? She needed to speed up her strategy. Her nerves were wire-taut; nothing could make her plan fail. Almost half a month had passed; one full moon had come and gone. If she didn't get to her secreted-away heir in Nod before the next full moon and bring it to where it could be given a creation pulse to grow, then she would have again failed her husband—an unacceptable consequence.

"You passed it to them through Yolando, where is he now?" Lilith asked, prying for information without divulging her hidden plans to the other high-ranking vampires that surrounded her. "We must ensure his safety. They could have found out that he was a carrier, and might have also begun to question his adherence to the team—what if his infiltration strategies have not worked?"

"I lost track of him in the mountains . . . there are a lot of ancient Native American sacred grounds near where he'd been that create interference sometimes," Lorelei said, sounding unsure. "I'll find him, though."

"We will put out a call," Lilith said crisply. "We must also be sure he is still with us at all times."

SHE WAS IN no shape to meet the Covenant this morning, much less to go meet the Neteru Queens in order to check on the status of her oracle. About the best she could do was possibly hobble down to the kitchen with Carlos holding her up to eat breakfast.

Damali looked at Carlos, and he glanced at her and winced, trying to lift his leg into his jeans.

"This don't make no sense," he said, finally laughing and falling back on the bed. "You've gotta heal a brother, for real."

"Me?" she said, aghast. "You were the one just playing with—"

"I know, I know, my bad," he said, chuckling with his eyes closed, sprawled out. "But, maaan, was it good."

"My voice is still hoarse," she said. "I need some herbal

tea or I'll be sooo embarrassed when the clerics get here, Carlos—why do you *do* this kinda stuff to me all the time?"

He leaned up with effort and offered her a big grin. "If I have to tell you that, then I guess it's worse than I think . . . I'm losing my touch."

HUGS AND WARM welcomes passed through the new compound, otherwise known as *the house.* It was far from a house—part dorm, part base station, part studio; it was truly a citadel just missing visible cannons. But this morning, before the Covenant arrived, it was home.

Damali smiled and tried not to talk so much. Her body aches had been healed in a long, solo, Epsom salt bath, much to Carlos's dismay, but the team—even if the clerics didn't—would have to know there was only one reason she sounded like a bullfrog. It didn't matter that the rooms were reinforced against sound for privacy's sake. The night before she'd sounded normal at dinner, and all the pollen in the world wouldn't account for the vocal loss. Her attempts to heal herself hadn't worked, and the fact that Carlos found it to be a badge of honor simply got on her last nerve.

The vibe radiating off the kitchen was so white-hot, she had to check to see if the oven had been left on. She was not about to inquire and was just glad to see that Inez's mood was so buoyant that the chile was practically skipping—which meant the grub would be off the hook for the visit.

Dan and Heather had even braved coming into Inez's world to teach her how to separate various foods and kitchen equipment out properly to keep certain dishes kosher for Rabbi Zeitloff. To her surprise her normally prickly girlfriend was in such a good mood that she took it all in stride. Inez even let Marlene and Marjorie come in there to help, while Krissy, Jasmine, and Heather set the table, with Tara and Juanita on detail to bring fresh flowers in.

At loose ends, she saved her voice by prepping rooms, making sure guests would have linens and towels, and watching the male squad racing around trying to get the last of the boxes unpacked and furniture in place. Why everybody was so hyped about the Covenant's stay, she wasn't sure. But in the absence of parents, and regular neighbors and such, she figured it all had to do with the semblance of normalcy thing . . . and having good vibes and blessings cover one's union didn't hurt at all.

The vibe in the house from the tactical squad was so powerfully positive and uplifting that furniture kept levitating a few inches off the floor when one of them passed. Coffee table books, magazines, vases, silverware, nothing would stay put as they walked by. Finally they got sent to ground their energy in the earth outside. Murmurs of "My bad" and swallowed smiles just made Damali shake her head.

The seers were no better and were making her eyeballs hurt. Their auras were neon and when they walked across the floor humming they left multi-hued footprints for a second. The trackers were the worst. Every few minutes Jose and Rider would stop whatever they were doing, close their eyes, inhale deeply, and release it with a shudder and a sigh.

If they could just get through the meal, do the meeting, and show the clerics guest quarters, then maybe, just maybe, she could pass out for an hour or two and then summon the energy to go have a talk with her Queens.

HE WAS GLAD he'd been sent alone to go collect the clerics from the safe house to bring them home. It gave him time to think, time to keep his mellow groove shielded from chaotic house details.

Carlos gripped the wheel of the rented SUV. Home. He'd finally set up a place that, for real, felt like home . . . felt permanent. He allowed the concept to sink in and filter through him like a good clean rain. Every man in the house felt it. The evidence that every brother in the house had christened his home was seen in their relaxed swaggers and easy smiles, everybody so chill they were practically liquefied.

He also understood why there was so much frenetic activity around the visits, every brother up in the joint, including him, was hoping for a one-on one. Their wives obviously were, too, pulling out the stops like no warriors normally would. They were breaking out holiday silver, good plates, the whole nine like polishing brass for a Vatican inspection. Everyone clearly wanted a verse said over their loved one's head from the real McCoy, prayers walked across the floor while they saw it done, their bedrooms sealed against entry, hands placed on heads from old men of the cloth . . . just to be on the safe side, and keeping it very real.

As Carlos turned into the inconspicuous block and began to slow down to find the house, he had to admit that, yeah, he wanted to get whatever blessings, absolution, whatever was possible to keep his woman safe, too.

There was no faking it, no denying he wanted Father Pat to give him one of those old, gruff stares that said it would be cool. He wanted assurances, despite knowing better, knowing such things didn't exist. But if the old man had insight, a special direct SAT phone to On High, he wanted to get a message through that if his lady got pregnant again, please, God, let it be normal, make sure the kid would be his and safe . . . no matter that he'd seen all he'd seen and knew what he knew.

Last night changed everything for all of them, he was sure. But he could only speak for himself. To his mind, he'd made love to his wife for the first time in their own first home. They'd put down roots and the next steps were imminent, regardless of their job descriptions. Little ones were on the way—it was in the air, thick. The procreation imperative had put down roots, too, like a redwood. And if having clerics physically reside in the house and send good vibes through it would help the cause, superstition or not, he was down. Because last he'd heard, there was no bargaining with On High—you took your lot and lived with it in peace . . . and while not a single soldier was trying to fly in the face of such absolute power, given their job risks, it was only human to want to even the odds.

Father Patrick opened the front door as Carlos pulled into

the driveway. He smiled. True to form, the old man was reading his mind. Carlos tried to be cool and get out of the vehicle, taking his time, but still found himself rushing, despite it all. A broad smile spread across the elderly cleric's face and Carlos took the steps two at a time to greet him. Not a word passed between them as that familiar hug got exchanged. A rough slap on the back felt like a slice of heaven. When they both pulled away they nodded, chuckling, and trying not to sniff too hard.

"You look good, Father," Carlos said, relieved to see him healthy and hale.

"You look like married life is treating you *very* well," Father Patrick said with a merry twinkle in his eye.

"It's aw'ight," Carlos said, laughing and rubbing his jaw.

Father Patrick smiled and then nodded. "Yes, son, it is. It is going to be all right."

There was nothing else to say as the others began to gather at the door and warm greetings were exchanged. He'd gotten his answer, direct from the source . . . sent down through channels from the man who'd saved his life, saved his soul, brought him to a safe house when he was dead to the world. After all was said and done, it was gonna be all right.

CHAPTER FIFTEEN

Practically bowled over at the door with hospitality and swamped, the Covenant finally made their way inside the new compound, each assessing the scene in their own quiet way with a private chuckle. Those clerics who were allowed to be hugged were practically swept off their feet. Those who weren't received endless bows and verbal accolades until they blushed. Before they could get their bags to the room, they'd been swept into a whirlwind tour.

Carlos glimpsed Damali from the corner of his eye, relaxed, relieved, and oh so glad he got his petition in first. More important, he was able to update them on the plan and debrief them on the issues they'd been dealing with. He told all, left no stone unturned—especially the part about the fawn hybrid and information he'd received from a nameless source regarding Lilith's worry that had to be Nod. The only disclosure he didn't give up was Yonnie's role and contribution to the cause, but did give each cleric a mental picture of his friend, lest they be caught in a firefight and aim for the wrong entity. Father Pat knew him, and although he wasn't comfortable, gave the stay order not to shoot unless absolutely necessary.

But as they passed the huge, industrial laundry room, Carlos noticed his wife lagging behind the group. As everyone moved around, giving the clerics the lay of the land, Carlos slipped his arm around Damali's waist as they walked. It was a loose, easy, natural embrace, a warm pull of energies touching. She rested her head on his shoulder when they came to a stop outside the technology room.

"I had to let 'em know what was up . . . they'll wanna talk about the fawn hybrid and what it means after dinner," he said quietly.

"I know," she murmured, "although, right now, let's just live in the present. Everybody seems so happy."

He nodded and kissed her hair. "You happy?"

"Yeah."

WITH DAYLIGHT AS her cover, and the only member of the Vampire Council who was of Level Seven origin, Lilith made her way topside to find the shadow wall—the weakened section of universal fabric that separated Nod from the earth plane. On the other side, in the dank, forbidden alley where hybrids stole away to seek traces of earth plane sensations, she called out to old Cain loyalists—now her followers—whispering to the rubbery surface until their faces strained against it.

"The time is nigh, be ready for my call. My scientists are back at work, undoing Ausar's shields. He cannot hold the fabric between worlds together indefinitely with his resources so severely strained, like mine. Wait for me near Masada . . . near the original lands that the foolish humans deemed holy. Just like the Romans finally overran them there, my heir and your numbers shall spill out of the banishment zone in a place where the Neterus will not want to fight, will hesitate to take a stand . . . the very location itself will inspire fear. But I will have at my disposal human troops on both sides, as well as any of their allies, to manipulate as always in any human confrontation."

She chuckled as gaping mouths and contorted faces and bodies pressed against the rubbery surface. Seeking hands tried to push through to touch her and she opened her arms and leaned against the moaning, yearning forms. "Soon, there will be nothing to separate us," she promised, then was gone.

LORELEI FELL OUT of bed as she awoke with a start to see Lilith reclining next to her with a wicked smile. She immediately went down on her knees and cowered.

"I hope I have not displeased you, Your Majesty. I did find him, Yolando went to a coven in Tijuana, and they're so territorial there, that they blocked my sightline to him."

Lilith sat up with a bored sigh and stood. "Yes. We sensed him. A new councilman indulging his topside passions. I should have known." She smiled thinking of Fallon Nuit and Sebastian's jealousy that only Yonnie seemed to be able to move about in the earth gray zone that they dearly missed, unafraid of Neteru reprisal. It quietly gave her pause, but she'd never reveal her hesitation to Lorelei.

"I was able to pick up a detail he left floating in the breeze when he made contact with the seduced Guardian," Lorelei said quickly, trying to appease her ruling entity. "The Neteru Guardians are resource challenged and are going to try to host a worldwide concert. They want to call all their Guardian units to a summit, have a message for them in the last days, and may use our airwaves to broadcast simultaneous images. It was at the forefront of Yolando's mind before he sought to indulge himself across the border."

"Make it impossible for them to get a worthy venue!" Lilith railed. "*Crush* their attempt to get word out to their own kind and monitor anything they send via any form of airwave we own. I want their music crushed, their message lost, and only violent, foul, and lewd images from our realm to blot out whatever the Neterus have to communicate." She hissed. "I will tell Sebastian to invoke Rasputin for this!"

"We can block her access to all the best venues, sway the radio stations, television stations to not broadcast her event. We can even block her getting those best locations by tying up the process through haggling unfavorable terms . . . but it'll be more difficult to actually stop them from getting their call to Guardians out over the Internet," Lorelei said, bowing lower. "That's a potential leak."

"Monitor it!" Lilith screeched. "Put our best on it to ensure anything the Neteru team sends out gets virally attacked, gets deleted, garbled, and does not reach its destination . . . but I want to know who they are sending to, I want every Guardian cell found and destroyed. Rooted out."

"We'll have our best cyberterrorists on it, Your Majesty," Lorelei promised and then clamped her lips shut and cringed.

After a moment, Lilith calmed herself and swung her legs over the side of the bed. "You have done well. I have something for you."

Lorelei slowly looked up with gratitude in her eyes. "You'll finally make me one of the revered?"

Lilith rolled her eyes and scoffed. "No . . . not yet." She flung a phony passport, travel documents, plane tickets, and an itinerary across the bed toward Lorelei. "You're going on a trip. Dress like it's a pilgrimage. It is, in a way," she said, laughing in a cackle.

"Jerusalem?" Lorelei whispered with a frown, confused and put off.

"Yes. This way you will have access to travel quickly to Masada when the time is right. The deep caverns and the desertlike mountains around the Dead Sea, also give us endless fallback positions, should we need them. Go to Jerusalem, hide until I call for you—then be ready to go to Masada and await my command."

Lorelei looked at Lilith, a question forming in her mind that she couldn't hold. "But why pick a place where there's so much . . . history and energy for the three strongholds of human faith?" Lorelei's confused gaze searched Lilith's face for a moment before she ducked her head. "I only ask because I am ignorant, Your Majesty, and wouldn't want to ruin whatever plan you have conceived."

Lilith stood, her black gown trailing behind her, and her

gaze narrowed as she folded her arms before her. "Built in Herod's time, Masada was thought to be a palatial and impenetrable citadel, but wound up representing great victory for us once, Lorelei. Eight Roman legions surrounded an encampment of a thousand men, women, and children and drove them to take their own lives rather than face the inevitable torture we would foist upon them. Their own men had to slaughter their wives and their own babies, and then turn on each other to kill themselves until the last man stood. Masada, their refuge, ran with their blood—and my Roman legions were victorious." Lilith closed her eyes as her voice dipped to a satisfied hiss. *"Masada is perfect."*

FOUR CLERICS HAD been settled into the compound, given a chance to relax, and then four blessings had been said over the food. Conversation was easy, unhurried, but it was moving toward the unmentionable subject of war, nonetheless.

"That's just the thing," Dan said, picking up on a strand of Jose's explanation about the concert. "I know she's been on hiatus, but every venue I call it's like we were a neighborhood band. I've never seen it this bad." He looked at Damali and then Marlene with an apology in his eyes. "It's like I lost my touch or something . . . I can't even get 'em to negotiate."

Carlos glimpsed Damali and then Father Pat. "It ain't you, man. Sounds like the other side is shot-blocking."

"You think so?" Dan asked, his gaze riveted to Carlos.

"I know so." Carlos took a careful sip of lemonade and winced like it was Remy neat. "Yeah. My inside man dropped the word to get the sting started. Now they're hard-balling on the venues."

"That's a good thing, though," Damali said with a sly grin. "Check it out. They block me from a simulcast, from the best stadiums. Cool." She looked around at the puzzled faces and smiled wider.

"But I thought the last plan was to do a big, international extravaganza?" Bobby said, searching the faces in the group for answers.

"Yeah, true," Damali said with a shrug and flipped her locks off her shoulders. "Hey. They changed, we change. This is better." She glanced at Carlos.

"Smaller population, less risk of civilian casualties at the venue," Carlos said flatly.

"Reason numero uno," Damali said, nodding. "But check it out. Think of the *buzz*, the media capital on the underground circuit it will have if the Warriors of Light have new music that is sooo freakin' hot, so off the chain, that the mainstream venues won't play it—and the only way you can see it is if you were there, or you get a Podcast off the Net."

"Genius, baby," Carlos said, just shaking his head. "Go guerrilla, straight gully, underground combat. You know I'm lovin' it, right?"

"That's just freakin' phenomenal, D," Dan said, waving his hands. "Like, if we got a spot about the size of the House of Blues, or something similar, I could probably book it real quick on an off night, that way it's like a pop-up, surprise thing . . . and I can cyberpromote it to Listservs that will hit Guardians all over the place."

"All we need is somebody to hold the digital video— don't have to be professional, if we going bootleg, underground," Shabazz said.

"I can do the camera," Marj said. "As many Little League and cheerleading events I, as proud mother, videoed, puhlease!"

"Okay," Carlos said, laughing. "So, we got our soccer mom on video."

Berkfield laughed. "It'll come out looking like *The Blair Witch Project*."

"Don't hate," Bobby said, teasing his dad. "They made a mint, shaking camera angles and all—adds to the authenticity effect."

"Makes it really seem like we were on the run, had to do it quick and dirty, so it'll hype the message, make 'em open the package quicker," J.L. said. "This is awesome."

"And just think," Monk Lin said calmly. "Had not this

string of negative events happened, you would not have found such a superior, creative solution."

"Silver lining to the cloud theory," Father Pat said with a smile, helping himself to more of Inez's macaroni and cheese.

"Yo, Carlos—from your old club network, you think your boy, Yonnie, might be able to get one of those venues to turn over for Dan?" Jose glanced between Carlos and Dan. "I'm just saying, if we've gotta get in and out real soon."

"Naw, man." Carlos said, sitting back in his chair. "That's a problem. Yonnie can't be seen helping us do something that, clearly, his management is against. If they're blocking premo venues, then obviously they don't want us to get the message out. We have to go to a Guardian spot for this, and I don't care if it's a joint with sawdust on the floor. To do this thing like Damali is saying, we gotta be in friendly territory. Go to one of my old joints that's now loaded with vamps and whatever else . . . the second Mar poured libations, it would be on."

Father Pat looked up from his plate at the other clerics who had remained unusually quiet. He wiped his mouth and set down his napkin beside his glass of lemonade and sighed. "We can't get you into the big televangelist theaters or on their networks, due to your lyrics and some of the, uh, explicit content . . . but we do have to ask you to move as quickly as possible on this leg of the plan."

All eyes went to Father Patrick.

"My buddy, Duke—ex–Hell's Angel and a helluva Guardian brother," Rider said, glancing around the table. "Y'all remember him from the battle at la casa—big, burly blond biker."

"Oh, man," Jose said, "How could we forget? The guy has mad-crazy moves and uses a pump shotgun like it's his right arm."

"Yeah, well," Rider said, his expression somber, "he lost one of his best friends out there, Joe. The brother is still shook behind it, never got his piece of justice in a way he could see, feel, and touch it, ya know?"

Everyone around the table fell silent, remembering all the Guardians who had been lost at Morales.

"Well, this type of situation would be perfect for what's left of his squad," Rider finally said. "They have this bar . . . on the wrong side of town in Death Valley. They left Texas, resettled right in the middle of the hot zone, suicidal, after what happened. Wanted to be where there were no civilians, and the joint has sawdust on the floor, with rednecks to go with it—but if you need a spot, all I gotta do is make a call, and Duke will line up the act, have his bouncers in place, and if I know him, will be taunting vamps the night before just to stir up some action."

"Sounds like my kinda joint," Big Mike said with a smile.

"Sounds perfect to me . . . we can take a nice drive on over, do the thing, and clean out a nest or two while we're at it," Damali said with a stretch.

"Well, this needs to happen quickly, as Father Patrick suggested," Rabbi Zeitloff said, leaning forward to peer around bodies to better see Father Pat. He hoisted up his short frame in the chair and blinked quickly behind his thick, round lenses, folding his hands before his plate, resolute.

"There is no time like the present," Monk Lin said in a gentle voice, his aged eyes sad, which made his dignified face and small, sinewy frame seem older.

"There is indeed no time like the present," Imam Asula agreed quietly. He rubbed a large, rough palm across his dark, walnut-hued face as though chasing sudden fatigue. "I know it is hard to break up family togetherness . . . but . . ."

The team fell quiet again as Monk Lin averted his eyes. Father Pat nodded and let out a long, weary sigh.

"The scientists have been bombarding the atmosphere again," Father Pat said, shaking his head as he dragged his fingers through his thicket of white hair. "They'd ceased for a while and have recently begun doing things that disturb the electromagnetic integrity of the planet. The technology advancement groups you met with on the way to Tibet are not responsible, and have been aiding us, worldwide, to hunt down these rogue elements. But they move like air—you can't get your hands around them."

Damali briefly shut her eyes. "We saw what can come out of Nod."

"Yeah, well, that little fawn that went AWOL on Hubert, Sedgwick, and Sara, washed up on the beach by the hotel, half-eaten by Harpies, we thought, but who knows if anything from Cain's old troops may have stayed stateside." Carlos rubbed the tension from his neck.

"Oh . . . no . . ." Marlene whispered. "Why didn't you tell us?"

"Because you guys needed at least twenty-four to forty-eight hours to get your heads together. So did we. We all did," Damali said, glancing around and finding no disagreement in anyone's expression. She turned to Carlos. "We've gotta go block the hole. I need to get my . . ." She let her voice trail off about oracles in front of the Covenant, but it wasn't necessary for her to finish the statement. Carlos was right on it.

"I know we're not supposed to breach Nod," Carlos said. "So, we're not proposing anything radical. But we do need to know what's up with Ausar's shields, why they aren't holding. Both Damali and I could make a quick run to meet with our councils, get their take."

"If you can do that quickly, it would be advisable," Father Pat said, holding Carlos's and Damali's gazes. "Any insight from whatever source would be helpful at this time."

"We all have to be in Jerusalem in the next few days," Rabbi Zeitloff said, growing impatient.

"Jerusalem?" Rider said, first staring at the rabbi, and then sending his panicked gaze to ricochet around the table. "As in the holiest city on the planet—like the one that's considered the center of the world as we know it . . . biblical Jerusalem?" He stood up and sat back down. "And I stopped drinking."

"What happened in Jerusalem?" Damali said in a tense murmur.

"Nothing," Father Pat said, his gaze now anxious. "The three major branches of faith said that you'd all been to Tibet, had touched and been infused with the energies of that faith, and felt that you needed to be girded up in the others—at least the four to ground you." He let out an exasperated breath. "Think of it like you would the cardinal points."

Bodies relaxed.

"So, essentially, they want us to go to church over there, right?" Berkfield said with a shrug. "Ain't nothing wrong with that, I guess. Just the timing, Father, is a little bad."

"Tell them, Patrick!" Rabbi Zeitloff exclaimed, becoming emphatic. "This Neteru team must go to the city of David, the Old City section of Jerusalem. Daniel and his new wife must enter through the Dung Gate to visit the Western Wall—*Kotel* . . . The Wailing Wall . . . they must touch the stones to feel the tears, martyrs, and history. They must touch the prayers that have been fervently uttered for centuries against it, and now resonate from that stone." He looked at Shabazz. "You must go with Imam Asula to answer the *muezzin* there in the holy city at El-Aqsa Mosque—the third holiest mosque in the world, then the Dome of the Rock, where the stone that Muhammad stepped on to ascend into Heaven lies. He rode to that place with Archangel Gabrielle on a winged horse."

Carlos and Shabazz looked at each other, eyes wide.

Rabbi Zeitloff nodded. "It was called Muhammad's Night Ride. He was taken there to the Masjad El-Aqsa, the farthermost place."

Carlos wiped his palms down his face as Shabazz raked his fingers through his locks.

"Yes," the Rabbi pressed on. "Mount Moriah, Temple Mount, or Hara mesh-Sharif, same place, is where you must go." Rabbi Zeitloff glanced at Carlos. "You, in particular, because it was first built by King Solomon, and now it is administered by the Waqf. The first temple was destroyed by the Babylonians, Carlos."

"The Waqf?" Berkfield asked quietly, his attention paralyzed by the clerics. "I'm sorry, I don't know . . ."

Imam Asula nodded. The Waqf is the Muslim Supreme Religious Council, and during the twelfth century," he added, "the Templars made their headquarters there at the Dome. But also understand that the Dome of the Rock is considered by more than one faith to be the center of the world."

"Where Abraham bound his son for sacrifice," Rabbi Zeitloff said, nodding. "And David made incense offerings for his offenses . . . and subsequently where David's son, Solomon, built his temple."

"There is a staircase leading down into a small grotto," Imam Asula said, his gaze riveting the group to utter silence. "The Well of Souls . . . where the dead pray."

"It is here that we heard pieces of prayers," Father Patrick said. "Angel-hybrids being slaughtered . . . your team under siege in a way like never before. You must strengthen yourself because something horrific is about to be unleashed on the holy city." His gaze shot around the table. "You must follow Via Dolorosa—the way of suffering, the path Jesus took through the city during His crucifixion . . . you must walk on the same cobblestones, feel the incomprehensible, then observe the Stations of the Cross while there, too. Some of this is at the Church of the Holy Sepulchre, and the room of the Last Supper is something you must feel through your skin. At the great church is also the Ethiopian monastery, and next to the ninth Station of the Cross, the Egyptian Coptic monastery . . . so many variations of Christendom, too."

The four clerics became suddenly impassioned as the Neteru Guardian team looked on, silently horrified by their news and vastly overwhelmed.

"They must also go to Jericho—not far," the rabbi said, as though speaking only to his fellow clerics. "Most of this can all be done in three days. Even to the tower of David and Mount Zion."

"The Mount of Olives, the last stop before heading toward the Dead Sea, and the Garden of Gethsemane—*are a must*. There, after the Last Supper, Christ prayed and sweated blood, and *there* is where the Church of All Nations is built, and in it is the Rock of Agony . . . where Jesus endured his passion in what was previously known as the Basilica of Agony," Father Patrick said, pointing down on the table hard. "I want them fortified! Just as when they are in the Church of the Holy Sepulchre, where Christ was crucified by the Romans, we must go to the Chapel of Helena there—where Constantine's mother, Helena, found the actual cross."

"All right. We fly them in under pilgrim status," Imam Asula said, glancing at his clerical brethren. "They enter the country via Ben-Gurion International Airport, ten miles east of Tel Aviv, and only thirty-one miles northwest of Jerusalem. First day, they can either stay just outside of the Old City in West Jerusalem at the King David Hotel—one of the most luxurious in the Middle East, or stay in safe houses in the Jewish Quarter, under Rabbi Zeitloff's instructions."

Damali cast Carlos a glance, secretly mouthing the words *King David Hotel*?

Imam Asula pressed on, not even seeing Damali's question. "Under Rabbi, the team can enter the City of David through the Dung Gate, see the Western Wall, and then we lead them to El-Aqsa Mosque and the Dome of the Rock on Temple Mount. From there, they move to the Muslim Quarter, under my lead, near Herod's Gate and Damascus Gate, where I then hand them off to Father Patrick to lead them through the Church of the Holy Sepulchre, where they will enter the Christian Quarter by New Gate and Jaffa Gate."

"I'll also take them to the Pools of Bethesda—water, where healing in the New Testament John 5 occurred," Father Patrick said, now looking at Damali. "Then to St. Anne's Church, which has the most angelic acoustics . . . you must hear, child." His voice dropped to a whisper. "The

Virgin Mary was born on the grotto where this church was built, and it is named for her mother, Anne." He sighed hard. "If we have time, by the third day, perhaps we can drive out through the Armenian Quarter by way of Zion Gate, to head down to Bethlehem to see the Church of the Nativity, or even go over to Solomon's Pools and Rachel's Tomb . . . but I doubt we'll have time to drive north to stop at the Inn of the Good Samaritan. All in all, we want you to see the four communities, seven gates, and three major faiths that touch each other within one square kilometer there."

The clerics fell quiet, sat back, and closed their eyes, each seeming thoroughly spent. Even Monk Lin seemed haggard from the conversation, as though he'd been shock-absorbing the tension from the others so that they could articulate their points.

"I guess I'd better call Duke . . . and get the venue set for tomorrow night, if he can swing it," Rider said, standing.

"I'll, uh, call the dealerships to get us some wheels," Jose said. "Rentals ain't gonna make it."

Mike stood. "Yeah, gonna go check ammo for the gig."

"I'm right there with you," Shabazz muttered.

"I'll get our travel docs straight," Dan said. "Will work with Marj on the camera—Krissy and J.L. on the Internet."

Carlos and Damali stood, watching the clerics watch them.

"We'll go get whatever word we can," Carlos said in a flat tone.

"Yeah. What he said." Damali stood and wiped her palms down her face.

THEY DIDN'T SPEAK until they got to their bedroom, but as soon as they closed the door behind them, Carlos and Damali both began talking at once.

"Oh, shit," Carlos said fast, walking in a circle, rubbing the back of his neck. "You see how freaked those old hombres were, D? Like they was holding it all in, then as soon as we mentioned the fawn, they bugged."

"I know, I know, but you told them already on the way here. This was something they'd been meeting about, discussing before—you could tell. It wasn't just about the fawn." She folded her arms over her chest. "It's deeper than that."

"You tellin' me?" He walked over to the window. "It's weird, but it's like you'd think the Holy City would be the safest place in the whole world, but it's also like . . . the eye of the storm." He turned and looked at Damali. "You know what I'm saying? You hear all that stuff they were talkin' about that went down there, which you and I both know is only the tip of the iceberg."

Damali nodded and went to him just to stand near. "Carlos . . . they're preparing this team for the Armageddon." She paused as she touched his arm. "Baby . . . they know what could happen if demon hybrids that can come out by day escape the walls of Nod, and by the way the clerics are acting—even if they don't tell us, they must have heard something that freaked them out . . . maybe something they're not at liberty to tell us. But I know one thing, those old guys have been to war with us in how many battles? They started with twelve and are now down to the last four. You notice they never got replenished like they always do? No new clerics added. Don't you find that strange?"

Carlos looked away for a moment and then drew her into an embrace. "This is it, I guess. They must have gotten the word that it was going down." He let his breath out hard. "What they knew probably didn't make 'em wig, D," he said, burying his nose in her hair. "They felt the vibe in this house, with this family—and they had such bad news to deliver, it jacked 'em around . . . so they're grabbing at straws, want us to go places, know things, pick up white light power jolts from the original sources . . . anything to save our asses in a firefight."

Damali nodded and held him tighter. Her voice was a tense whisper against his chest. "It was the way their voices broke as they told us, unshed tears in their eyes. The rabbi couldn't even look at Dan and Heather . . . It was like they were having their own version of the Last Supper."

"Aw'ight, D," Carlos said, holding her back to look at her. "I'm not ready to go out like that. You?"

"Hell no," she said, wiping her face.

"Then me and you gotta pull it together." He waited for her to nod. "Call the Queens, hold my hand while I call the Kings—we go in together, assess the damage—come out, do the show, get on a plane, and rock the bells over there in Jerusalem."

THE TRANSFER WAS instant. A blinding gold and violet haze blended into one spire, sucked Damali and Carlos up and through it at a dizzying speed, and opened up to gently deposit them in full Neteru Council session. The debate was so intense that the verbal combatants didn't miss a beat. They only stopped as an afterthought and turned to look at Damali and Carlos.

"Ausar's energy is degenerating as we speak, for he was never supposed to continually support the outlying structures of Nod," Hannibal bellowed. "The time is now to break the next seal to put an end to this madness once and for all!"

"Earth's scientists that have no respect for the delicate balances of the ecosystem have created the havoc, therefore, it should be within our purview to knit the fabric of the universe back together. This is a man-made crisis, not one based upon timing of the sacred texts," Eve argued. "We must endeavor to use restraint."

"Look at our brother, though," Adam contended. "This recent assault on the veil between worlds has left him depleted trying to hold up multiple shields. How long can he maintain this without serious injury to himself?"

"It is because of the broken seal," Aset said, sweeping away from her throne and collecting her gown in a swishing rustle of golden fabric over her forearm. "Tell them, Solomon. Bring David into the accord as well. Is it not true that once any of the biblical seals are broken the veil begins to weaken on its own? Are there not to be sightings of beasts and angels during said time? That is a *thinning,* if not a complete rupture, when humans readily see what has been hidden to all but very few over centuries." Aset went to her husband and laid her hand on his shoulder and wiped his glistening brow. "It is not his fault, or due to any waning power on his part. This was foretold."

"What can we do on our end?" Carlos said loudly, trying to get the combined councils' attention. When the debate stopped and they looked at him, Carlos began talking fast. "Ausar can't be expected to hold shields alone, true, but at the same time, just letting demon hybrid squads roll on earth isn't acceptable, either. Like, we could go over there tonight, me and D, and do some damage so our brother can rest."

"One male Neteru kept them in check for eons, right?" Damali said, her hands on hips. "Can't we go in, do a cleanup battle over there with blades raised, take some of the weight off Ausar, but back 'em up off the breaches?"

"Meanwhile, if the Queens could rig something, anything . . . silver energy nets, I don't know what—Ausar could recharge his battery, so to speak, while we reduce the threat level in Nod. Then, when he's got more juice, we raise shields again." Carlos looked around, tension slowly coiling within him as the council members took their time to decide.

"It could be worth an attempt," Adam said, "an important one. Know this, young brother . . . as Ausar's energy dips, it will soon affect each of our power, hence Hannibal's outrage and readiness to go to war now, rather than later. So this has to work, or there will be no alternative."

"Can we get three to five days?" Damali asked.

"We are not supposed to sanction any transgression into Nod," Solomon said.

"Unless it is during the end of days when a seal has been broken," Adam countered. "Remember, during the last days, it was expected that armies of strange beings would flood the earth, just as strange occurrences in weather and natural disasters would increase."

"Can you hang for three to five, man?" Carlos asked Ausar with genuine concern lacing his voice.

"Yes. As long as I conserve energy and remain very, very focused," Ausar said with a labored breath, closing his eyes again.

"Okay, we're in," Carlos said, looking at Damali.

"My oracle," she said quickly, glancing at her Queens. "Has there been any change? Is there any information we can work with?"

"Bring her the pearl," Aset ordered, sending away two female Guardian spirits to quickly return with the translucent energy bowl filled with ancient Blue Nile water.

Damali quickly went over to the bowl and caressed the water's surface while two armored female Guardian warriors held it out for her. "Zehiradangra . . ." Damali called gently to her oracle and then nodded to Carlos.

"Z, baby . . . how you feeling?" He dropped his voice to a gentle, sensual murmur. "We miss you. C'mon home." Carlos looked at Damali and shrugged *what?* when she simply shook her head.

Aset also shook her head when the water's surface began to move with a steady, tiny stream of small bubbles.

Damali cut him a glare with a smile. *Figures. My damned pearl and she only comes when you call her.*

"Carlos?" the pearl murmured.

"Yeah, baby, I'm right here," he said, trying not to look at Damali. "You okay?"

"It was *terrible*," Zehiradangra said in a long, sad croon.

Carlos touched the water with his fingertips and ignored Damali's elbow to his ribs. "It's gonna be all right. I know you saw some really horrible things, but we got you now, boo."

The Kings nodded with satisfaction. Nefertiti, Eve, and Nzinga rolled their eyes and conferred with Aset.

"How the hell did he get her oracle to respond to him like that?" Nzinga fussed under her breath. "Untoward, I tell you." She sat back and folded her arms.

"Let it go, he's getting results," Aset said.

"Hi, Z," Damali said with a tight voice.

"Damali!" Zehiradangra said, perking up. "I thought I felt you, too."

"I love you, too," Damali said, sarcasm lacing her tone.

"You don't sound like it." The bubbles in the water stopped moving.

Carlos shot Damali a look. *Chill . . . c'mon now.*

Damali sighed and blew a lock up off her forehead. "I'm just stressed from all that's happening, Z. There's so much unrest over in Nod," she said, baiting the pearl back to life. "I don't know what to do. I know there's entities over there me and Carlos should go help, but who, where, we don't know where to begin."

A flurry of agitated bubbles hit the once still water's surface. "Oh, please, please, you must go help Valkyrie!"

"I don't know how to find Valkyries unless they come to collect fallen soldiers in battles, Z," Damali said, watching the expressions of the gathered Neterus.

"No, no, my best friend, after Cain—Valkyrie. She is sooo good and honorable and beautiful," Zehiradangra said with pride. "I was so upset after seeing where Cain went after he left Nod, I retraced my energy back home to visit with her. She helped me put things into perspective. Her energy is gorgeous . . . I just needed to get away from here and go home . . . but she's having trouble keeping her troops guarding all the breaches. Can you help her? She's not mean inside like Cain."

"Yeah, we can help her, Z," Carlos said quickly, looking around at the others. "She's got troops, forces over there covering breaches?"

"Yes, and she's valiant. She now leads the resistance . . . did you know she was named for the sacred race of angels that help the fallen—her father was a fallen soldier, I believe in Troy or was it during the Viking era . . . she did tell me once, but I am so forgetful. Maybe it was Beowulf's era?"

"It's all right, baby, you rest," Carlos murmured in a deep, soothing tone. "You shoot me and D an image of what Valkyrie looks like, and we'll go over there, give her some reinforcement at the breach-points, all right?"

"Oh . . . Carlos . . ." the pearl gushed. "It is so nice to have a real man around the house again."

"I love you, too, baby," he said. "I gotta go to work."

Carlos quickly put a finger to his lips when Damali's eyes flared. He mouthed, *I love you, too.* But when Damali shot it to him as a silent message, he shook his head and pointed to the pearl.

"Oh, yeah, I love you, too, Zehiradangra." She withdrew her hand from the bowl and folded her arms. "Yeah . . . I gotta go to work."

"Bye," the pearl said and yawned. "I'm still not one hundred percent. Just that little bit really wastes me." Then the water went still.

The Guardians who'd brought the bowl in quickly retreated. Senior Neterus swallowed broad smiles.

Solomon chuckled quietly. "Let's get you both to Nod to see what can be accomplished." He gave Carlos a private glance and message as he and Adam stood to begin the power transfer. *Just imagine my days with over three hundred beautiful ladies just like that . . . and you wonder why I'm chief counsel and negotiator? Brother, you just don't know.*

CHAPTER SIXTEEN

The energy that pushed them through the veil was so subtle that it felt as though an autumn breeze had kissed their backs. Both Damali and Carlos looked around. The entire aura of the environment had changed. The dual discs of one radiant solar sun and one opalescent one fueled by an unseen source still loomed high in the sky, but a thin layer of gray seemed to darken everything like impregnable soot.

"It's almost like the heavy density of the earth plane is seeping in here," Damali said quietly, drawing her Isis into her hand as she glanced around the main square.

Carlos nodded. "It's too damned quiet for me, too," he said, drawing the blade of Ausar into his grip. "The hair is standing up on the back of my neck."

"Get down!" a disembodied voice yelled from behind a monument.

Both Neterus looked up just in time to see a large, dark orb break through the sky like a mortar round, its streaking approach whistling as it hurdled toward them. They dove in opposite directions and flattened themselves on the ground at either side of the wide boulevard. The hit was instantaneous and tore through the street, dragging several buildings down into the gaping hole behind it. Unable to do much else but hang on for dear life, they watched in sheer awe, holding on to the paved stones by digging their blades in and grabbing on tight as the buildings that got sucked into the abyss seemed to melt over the edge of the hole and disappear.

As soon as there was nothing else substantial to draw into the energy bend, a hard suction force literally lifted their bodies up off the ground while they gripped their blades with eyes closed and as gale-force winds beat against them. Then as though someone had suddenly turned off a giant tap, the noise, wind, and suction abruptly stopped, dropping them hard with an umphf—and the opening in the ground resealed.

They both looked up quickly at each other, breathing hard and sweating.

"What the hell was that?" Damali said, pulling herself to stand.

"Humans, take cover! Your sweat draws them!" a voice called out. "Raid!"

Carlos immediately looked up. The sky was going black. The sound of leather wings beating against the atmosphere created a slow Doppler effect in the air. He yanked his blade out of the pavement at the same time Damali extracted hers, and began running with Damali, trying to get them behind any building that remained.

A flaming black arrow whizzed by Damali's thigh, and just as quickly as it landed, a six-foot-tall, female angel hybrid, dressed in ancient Viking armor with a startlingly beautiful contrast of long, platinum dreadlocks, amber eyes, and ebony skin, somersaulted out from behind a huge palm that lined the boulevard, dropped to one knee, took aim with a massive crossbow, and fired.

Damali and Carlos glanced at each other, the same mental thought stabbing into each other's brains—*Valkyrie.*

Whatever the warrior had shot at, she apparently hit, because the cloud stopped approaching, turned on what had begun to fall out of the sky, to rip it apart to consume it.

"Go, go, go!" the angel hybrid shouted, pointing to a cluster of monuments in the distance, then began running after Carlos and Damali, turning occasionally to fire in the air.

But the targets she hit were eaten quickly and it only gave the huge flock of beasts momentary pause.

"Go without me—seek shelter with the others in the old palace!" The angel hybrid turned to run back toward the approaching cloud to draw the fanged entities away from Damali and Carlos. "Run now, humans!"

Damali and Carlos took one look at each other.

"Aw, hell no!" Damali shouted.

"We go out swinging!" Carlos yelled.

"No!" their would-be protector shouted. "You do not understand. They'll eat you! They've been driven to frenzy. This is unlike any battle you've ever known! Most humans come through in bits, not whole like you, already mutilated flesh in the bombardment from earth plane. Go, humans!" she shouted, her voice strident as she began running again.

"No—you don't understand!" Damali shouted, running behind her and then past her. She spread her wings quickly and held up her blade. "Neteru, not straight human," she said, her breaths coming in bursts. "And a little something else called crazy."

"Damned straight!" Carlos said, jogging to Damali's side, eyes lit silver, battle-bulked, fangs fully dropped to battle length with blade raised. "Let's do this."

The entity before them slammed her forearm across her chest and swiftly bowed. "I am Valkyrie, sworn like my kind, to follow the carriers of the sacred blades." Her big, beautiful amber eyes shimmered with unshed tears. "My honor is to die beside you!"

"Ain't trying to die today, sis," Carlos said.

"But we are gonna clean out a nest. Fall back; hold the line for the refugees. Let us draw the fire as bait."

Damali glanced up at the quickly approaching darkness that covered the sky then looked at Carlos and shot him a mental image of the two Neteru battles that had taken place in the Black Forest glen. All it took was a nod to let her know he got it.

Both Neterus began running, increasing in speed as

Damali pulled her wings in close to her body, then both leapt up off the ground, locked left arms at the elbow, blades out, and spun. Like a gleaming silver tornado of fury energy they went headlong into the airborne mass of leather-winged predators creating blood-splatter carnage in a horrific aerial display. Body parts began dropping from the sky as demon-hybrid blood streamed in ribbons. The chaotic dark flock soon broke into disorganized clusters of entities diving and bobbing in screeching clouds to attack what had been maimed. Like sharks cannibalizing their own in a feeding frenzy, they began to fall. But the Ncteru whirl of white light outrage then sent strobe pulses of blue-white charge from the ends of their blades, the bursts made almost nuclear by the combined force of their locked bodies.

Demon-hybrids incinerated on impact as though na-palmed. Bits of bat wings, thick portions of spaded tails, limbs, and entrails rained down on the square in a gory del-uge. Those hybrids that made it safely to the ground ran amuck greedily gathering the spoils of war in their claws and blood-slicked arms, eyes glowing and nearly drunk off the feeding.

But the more aggressive of the airborne backed up, and dropped low to try to bring the fight to the ground.

Carlos let Damali go and both brought their blades into a vertical hold until their speed decreased. He went into an in-stant energy fold and came out on the ground behind a fifteen-entity squad of Darkness. She opened her wings and rushed against six huge predators still in the air, dodging black flaming arrows, using her dagger like a boomerang to fling as a death-blade to be called back into her hand. Isis outstretched, anything within range lost a body part until the last of the airborne retreated.

Damali headed for the firefight on the ground. Carlos had a shield in one fist, using it to bash in demon skulls and break jaws while his deadly blade sheared heads off at the neck. The disc of Heru was hardly a protector; the way Carlos was using it was like it were another weapon. Blind rage had him in a chokehold, personal safety an after-thought. She could see it from the air as she dove toward the battle. At one point he was so lost to the conquest that he'd grabbed two retreating hybrids by their tails, drove his blade into the ground, flung his disc away to shear off two more heads, just so he could round the screaming entities that were struggling to get away, and personally rip out their hearts.

By the time she'd reached him, Carlos had demon organs in his raised fists and he'd thrown back his head and released a Neteru battle roar of sure victory that echoed in the deci-mated square.

When she touched down, he spun on her for a second, slightly disoriented, then spat. They looked around. Eerie si-lence and sulfur fumes made the day overcast. Only their ragged breaths could be heard. Carlos flung the gore away from him and wiped down his arms. He was bloody to the el-bows. She smiled. Sick as it was, she'd always liked to see him that way.

Both Neterus leaned on their swords, slowly beginning to feel the battle as the adrenaline receded. The light rustle of feathers, however, made them both jump back and take fighters' stances.

"Friend, not foe!" Valkyrie called out. "Come seek shel-ter and replenish yourselves."

They looked at Valkyrie and began to jog in the direction she'd motioned toward. As Damali passed what had been their downtown area, she was mortified. No matter how odd it seemed, just remembering the gorgeous, white alabaster pavements and beautifully mosaic tiled streets and gleaming buildings that had now gone to ruin put an ache in her chest that she didn't expect.

She remembered how a then-dignified Cain had walked her down beautiful palm-lined promenades, showing off wondrous feats of architectural creativity that were now ei-ther bombed out or missing or merely a heap of rubble. Trees had been incinerated in previous battles. Evidence of blood splatter and carnage was everywhere, along with threatening graffiti taunting survivors. Gone was the serene and sparkling light. Now all was gray and a dense fog permeated the streets knee deep so that it was hard to see one's feet. The only thing she could think of as they made their way to what had been Cain's main palace and court—what a waste.

"HAVE YOU INFLUENCED human minds and thoroughly shut down their concert opportunities, as I have instructed Lorelei?" Lilith murmured, lifting her head from Sebastian's throat, her fangs dripping with his blood.

"Yes," he whispered with a thick groan and then twined his fingers deeper into her hair. He arched to bring more of himself into her, grasping her dark tendrils tighter as Fallon blanketed her with a kiss.

She leaned into his kisses along her spine as he pressed his perspiration-damped cheek to her back, suffering for entry.

"And you had the scientists send bodies with the veil bombings . . . to increase the demon-hybrids' strength and their drive to slaughter?" she cooed, not mentioning the importance of feeding one hybrid above all others. "I want any force that could come to the Neterus aid destroyed."

"*Oui,*" Fallon breathed urgently against her throat, his body shuddering and undulating with hers and Sebastian's. "I have had them send so much flesh that they should be gorged by now." He dragged a fang slowly up her jugular, testing for her acceptance.

"Excellent . . ." she murmured and slid her eyes shut as his hands captured her breasts. "Then you may join us."

His sudden vicious strike and violent bodily entry caused Lilith and Sebastian to gasp in tandem. The sensation of Nuit's member slowly sliding against his, separated only by the thin barriers of Lilith's canal and anal flesh lifted Sebastian's shoulders from the crimson silk and put tears in his eyes.

Nuit peered over Lilith's shoulder as he slowed their previously demanding pace to a crawl, then reached out to run a thumb over Sebastian's quivering jaw. *"This,"* he murmured with a bloody smile as his eyes slid shut, "is one of my specialties, *mon ami.* Ménage à trois, as only the French can do."

SHE COULDN'T BELIEVE her eyes. Damali stood at the inner entrance to the once grand palace and stared down the steep flight of white marble steps that led to the huge pool facing what had been Cain's parliamentary court. What had once been pristine dignity was a cross between a dirty triage unit and rebel hybrid headquarters. Her gaze sought Carlos's, and his was harder than she'd expected. It only took her a moment to figure out why.

"That was one stupid motherfucker," Carlos muttered and spat as they followed Valkyrie down the steps. "He had all of this, a whole kingdom in check—gorgeous options, too," he said, passing huddled female hybrids attending the wounded. "And he had to have more . . . had to step into my yard. Look at this shit!"

Damali touched Carlos's arm. "Look at all the wounded," she said, her tone shocked but gentle. It was imperative that she keep Carlos focused on the present, and not allow him to dangerously let his mind to get trapped in the past.

"There are only three hundred of us left," Valkyrie said, lifting her chin and steeling herself to the whimpers and moans. "Not all of them will make it, however. Some are badly eaten . . . it is only a matter of time."

"Eaten . . ." Damali briefly closed her eyes as a horrified shudder passed through her.

"The gray zone seepage around the edges of the shields pollutes what had already been a fragile balance," Valkyrie said bitterly. "The taste of flesh, the scent of it, and the experiments that send whole morsels for them to fight over . . . incite roving bands, and once their appetites have been whetted, they go on pillaging missions. The veiled distortions allow us to bleed and be more than energy. We are now flesh."

Valkyrie looked toward the angel hybrids, hiding behind floor vases with vacant stares, who'd wrapped broken wings around their desecrated bodies. Swallowing hard, she tearfully glanced toward several leather-winged demon hybrids by the soiled pool, who hid their faces against their forearms as they gathered their bodies into fetal positions on the floor. "It's the same with the rapes. But those are the lucky ones."

Carlos shook his head, so upset over the injustice that he was trembling. "How many of Cain's forces are left?" He glanced at Damali. "Let's clean up this sewer once and for all."

"We can never tell," Valkyrie admitted. "Their numbers are always double . . . maybe triple ours in any battle. We started off guarding the shields to keep them contained within our realm, as the Heavenly edict dictated. But as the leaks became worse, so did their aggression. We were closest to the shields, thus the toxic gray zone leaks. This is how we became flesh, came to bleed—which puts us at such risk as you can never fathom. The ones that came back from the campaign with Cain . . . the ones who'd fought by his side were the worst. They became the generals, and have taken up a position high on the ridge where Cain's cliffside lair used to be."

"I know the location well," Carlos muttered, fangs beginning to lower again.

"We can't go up there without a strategy, baby," Damali said, placing a hand on his chest. "This is about them, right now—not the past." She turned to Valkyrie. "The way they die, now, is different—the same with your injuries. Is this also because of the gray zone pollution?"

"Yes. It is the only variable, the only change to the energy here that makes sense." Valkyrie paused, gathering her words with care. "Hence the physical abuse." She looked away as she spoke. "Before this was a sensationless realm. Only human blood, which rarely crossed over into our world, could be tasted, fulfill blood hungers . . . and only human flesh could fulfill the baser hungers. But once the leaks became significant, no entity was safe. They'll even eat their own, as you saw."

"We need to go over that ridge," Carlos said through his teeth. "Right now I really don't care how many of them are over there, D."

"Will healings work here, you think? Those not mortally wounded—maybe I could relieve some of their pain?" Damali held out her hand for Valkyrie to grasp in a warrior's embrace. "Starting with your heart," she murmured.

Valkyrie nodded as she clasped Damali's forearm and slowly entered her embrace. "My Neteru Queen, it has been broken into a thousand pieces," she whispered against Damali's hair. "I can't save them . . . I fought as hard as I could, but I couldn't save them all and those left . . ."

Damali dug the Isis into the floor and rubbed Valkyrie's back. Wings wrapped around wings and Damali held her sister warrior until the quiet sobs abated. "Let me see your injured. Maybe the Caduceus could help?"

Valkyrie nodded and began to lead Damali and Carlos through what had become a makeshift ward. Every few paces they stopped, stooped down, and placed their hands on a maimed or injured hybrid until both Neterus were drenched with silver healing sweat and panting.

"Call for the Caduceus," Carlos said. "We aren't even a third of the way through, and you'll burn yourself out, D. I will, too, and we might have to fight our way home."

They joined hands and called out with a singular urgent prayer, and were rewarded by the warmth of heated metal soon entering Damali's palm. Walking the ward together with the healing staff, Carlos held agonized hybrid bodies in place as Damali administered the golden light of healing peace to all those who'd been torn and battered. However, those too far gone simply slipped away with a smile on their faces, and before long, Damali had tears streaming down her cheeks as so many called out to her, "Powers angel, hear my cry and take me home—send me beyond here. Don't let me live."

At one point, Carlos had to make her stop as sobs overcame her. Damali buried her face in Carlos's chest, heaving in shuddering breaths when she came upon one border-raid victim who had been so badly molested he had gone psychologically blind. The huge demon hybrid reminded them both of Hubert. His wings had been ripped away, leaving bloody gristle and exposed sockets. Deep claw gashes filleted his back and hips and thighs. He simply stared at Carlos with blind eyes and asked in a quiet, dignified voice that they let him die. When Damali had neared him with the Caduceus, he held up his hand.

"No, please," the unknown soldier said in a soft, broken voice, and then turned toward Carlos's energy. "Like a warrior . . . not defiled and then healed and left to remember."

Carlos nodded, lifted his blade before Damali could scream no, and removed the hybrid's head from his shoulders. "It was his choice. His right," Carlos said. "I felt what they did to him through every fiber in me." He walked away and drew in several steadying breaths. "I would have wanted the same thing—to go like that."

"I, too," Valkyrie said and swallowed hard, landing a firm grip on Damali's shoulder. "He was a good warrior. Rest his soul now in peace."

Resigned, Damali picked up both the Caduceus and the Isis, one in each grip, feeling more like an angel of death than a Powers angel hybrid of healing, or even a Neteru. Oddly, the ones that had been badly injured in battle, their wounds physical and seemingly worse, cried out for the Caduceus, whereas those who'd been violated quietly stared at her Isis and spoke in a whisper. The moment the choice flowed from their lips, Carlos ceased their misery, refusing to allow her to have their blood on her conscience.

"You heal, I'll deliver mercy," he said, holding her arm. "Because when this is done, we're gonna both need to heal our minds."

She didn't resist, as she felt hunger and pain and fear and regret enter his system. Rage, humiliation, thirst, conflict, and inner screams filled her as her hands touched broken bodies and splintered souls, tried to knit back together fractured minds until she openly wept as she touched the next hybrid. She pulled her hands back, feeling dormant life waiting within a violated cherubic-looking hybrid, and she covered her mouth with her hand and turned away.

"Oh, God . . ." Damali whispered behind her hand.

"I want to live anyway," the fragile being said, as she clung to the hem of Damali's jeans. "My father was a carrion angel and he couldn't drag my dark coven mother down into the pit, even after all she'd done. He had mercy at the end. My choice is to survive with whatever outcome the violation brings."

Damali turned back to her and touched her amber wings as she covered her half-nude, dirty body while shivering on the floor. "I pray that you survive," Damali murmured, placing her hand over the victim's forehead and then made the Caduceus glow. "And may you know peace."

The moment the hybrid opened her eyes, Damali quickly stood, suddenly feeling nauseous. She needed air, had to get away—felt like she needed to flee from this dirty place. Filth and carnage seemed to be clinging to her to the point where she was nearly ready to shriek. Carlos sensed her alarm and pulled her away from her last patient, walking her quickly to the next.

"I got this, D. We're almost done. Take some breaths. I know—c'mon, breathe."

She tossed him the Caduceus and wrapped her arms and wings around herself, panting, hyperventilating, gulping air, then turned, heaved, and vomited on the floor. In the back of her mind she saw Carlos working to restore the injured, and Valkyrie led her away to stand where a breeze blew in through the open arches.

"Physician, heal thyself," Valkyrie said in a mercifully private tone.

Damali nodded quickly, feeling acute thirst. "You all are going to need supplies, if earth plane energies are here— water, food, blankets . . . soon your bodies will start requiring those things. I just felt a hybrid rape victim with a dormant pregnancy."

Valkyrie closed her eyes. "Nooo . . . then it has started."

"What's started?" Damali said, her gaze frantic.

"The time of all times in our prophecies here, where the veil will rip open and those of us who are worthy shall be freed." Valkyrie looked at Damali without blinking. "This is why we've fought so hard. We always thought Cain would lead us out, lead us home, in the ultimate battle against evil to take our places On High . . ." Her voice faltered. "It is such a bitter disappointment." Valkyrie spun and pointed at the broken huddles being healed by Carlos on the floor. "Look at us!" she shouted. "Do we seem like the great cavalry of the sky led by our Neteru?" She covered her face with her forearm and sobbed. "I am so ashamed of who we've become!"

Damali went to her and took her by the shoulders. "Valkyrie, you are great—great that you've been general here, have held the line, even when all seemed lost. Your forces will be replenished; we'll get food and supplies in. Keep the faith, and call us back if you're attacked again— use the oracle, the conduit to me is Zehiradangra, my pearl."

Valkyrie clutched her briefly and then let her go. "At your service, until forever, my Queen. Bless you."

Both female warriors wiped their dirty faces and looked out over the small band of restored troops.

"I'll start a funeral pyre," Valkyrie said, beginning to walk away. "They shan't have them even in death."

"How are you keeping them off you here, in the central palace?" Damali asked, panic rising as insanity slowly brewed within her husband.

She glanced at all the openings, which were too many to cover and monitored Carlos's inner turbulence as he knelt beside victim after victim, absorbing their pain and humiliation until he stood abruptly with eyes gleaming silver and fangs lowered, ready to roar.

Valkyrie laughed a sad and exhausted laugh, her crossbow

dangling at her side. "His sphinxes." She nodded. "The irony is compelling. Cain slaughtered his own pets at his cliffside palace, but the main palace guard lions attack anything that sieges the entrances—and even his loyalists beware." She motioned with her chin toward the huge marble sentries that flanked each open doorway. "His pets mourn for his return . . . they don't understand. They cannot conceive that he went dark and attack anything hostile that encroaches what had been the place of peace and justice, Cain's court. If it seems that it is not of their former King, they dispense swift justice, thinking these palace swarmers might have made off with their master and harmed him, too."

"Damn, that is some crazy shit," Carlos said as he came near them. He rolled his shoulders and rubbed his neck. "We going up on the ridge, D, or what?"

"Yeah," she muttered. "We're going up on the ridge."

THE FACT THAT they both knew the way to Cain's cliffside lair was something they didn't speak on. It just stood between them like an invisible land mine of demarcation that they'd both secretly vowed never again to cross. The Caduceus went back to the Queens by Damali's hand as Carlos drew supplies into the main palace as a gift of mercy from the Kings.

You know this is what the clerics were probably worried about, but didn't tell the team, Damali said mentally.

Yeah, Carlos replied flatly as he watched thirsty hybrids guzzle water and tear off bread hunks and eagerly consume fruit. *They must have gotten word from On High that these refugees would soon be coming over the edges.* He looked at Damali dead on. *Let's just make sure nothing from up on that ridge gets out, too.*

"I'm going with you," Valkyrie announced as she reloaded her crossbow and filled her quiver with arrows, checking her blade at her bare thigh.

Both Damali and Carlos nodded. "Three is always a good number," Damali said.

* * *

WHEN THEY GOT to the edge, the threesome fanned out, peeping over the edge of the precipice. Night shadows were beginning to fall in the realm that was always supposed to experience perpetual Light. The three moons struggled to stay lit.

Carlos motioned with two fingers for Valkyrie to sneak up to a higher position on the cliffs where she could take aim and be sheltered. As soon as she was in position, Damali and Carlos glimpsed each other.

About a thousand, Carlos said.

A thousand may fall at my right hand, Damali said, quoting a section of Psalm 91 as her gaze narrowed and she readied her Isis.

Ground pulse, then over the ridge swinging.

On three.

Holding onto the edge of the cliff, the Neterus swung hard, blades coming together with a clang to suddenly penetrate the earth. Demon hybrid and fallen angel hybrid heads lifted from their gruesome meals of raw and charred flesh. They stared at the ground, momentarily confused as a rumbling pulse of white light suddenly rolled over the edge of the ravine, burning out withered grass, making them fall off rock perches. They settled and unsettled, trying to regain their footing like occupied buzzards, screeching in complaint. But the food was so tempting that they were initially unwilling to part with the human appendage they clutched. Then all of a sudden they understood the danger too late as the heat wafted from the rapidly moving white carpet to fry them where they sat.

Hybrid bodies exploded on impact, screeches echoed from inside Cain's old lair. Smoldering ashes were everywhere, and within seconds the entryway to Cain's cliffside palace filled with flying, swarming bodies trying to get out. The hole in the vaulted ceiling erupted in a plume of darkness. Valkyrie began felling fast-moving aerial attackers with dead-aim crossbow hits and flaming white light arrows. Carlos and Damali were over the ridge in seconds, too, wildly swinging, connecting with anything that moved, rage and outrage blending as one. Demon heads on pikes was not out of the question.

Expending her ammunition, Valkyrie took flight, rage making her reckless as she dove into a cluster, dagger in one hand, spent crossbow in the other. She knocked an aerial aggressor back with the bow, and stabbed him in the heart as his head tipped back, and then spun on a raven-winged female who brandished a machete. The moment her attacker swung, Valkyrie ducked, ripped down her arm with the dagger, and stripped her of her own machete to lop off her head. The cluster that surrounded her retreated, but she flew after them with a vengeance, burning wings with a flung arrow torch that she lit with the pure fury of righteous indignation.

Damali was directly under her on the ground, ready to slaughter anything that Valkyrie felled. As soon as they began an uncontrolled spiral, Damali was up, blade swinging. Carlos saw half the loyalists begin to retreat down into the ravine and the threesome gave chase, Neterus firing unrelenting power pulses, further thinning the numbers down to less than one hundred before they got away.

"The seeking wall," Valkyrie said, breathing hard through her mouth and leaning on her knees with both hands. "We have to stop them before they get to Lilith."

Damali didn't wait to hear anything else. She nosedived over the edge of the ravine, sweeping her blade with crackling light coming off it before her, claiming some hybrids in the air, and then somersaulted in front of the dank place Cain had once brought her, the place that almost made her lose her mind. She opened her wings in a challenge, taking a fighter's stance to block them entry to the rubbery surface that would allow them to whisper to Lilith for backup. Carlos landed with Valkyrie behind the trapped loyalists.

"You'll never take us alive!" one demon hybrid leader shouted as his exhausted troops turned about in circles, not sure where to attack first.

Carlos smiled. "That was never my intention, holmes."

He rushed forward and slit the leader's throat so fast that some of the remaining hybrids held up their hands.

Valkyrie rushed forward, her machete raised before Damali or Carlos could protest, and swung. The moment one of the loyalists raised a weapon, it was on—and over in thirty seconds. Valkyrie grabbed the leg of one mortally wounded survivor who still tried to crawl into the alley as a last-ditch effort. She looked up with defiant eyes. "You haven't gotten all of us," she said, just before Valkyrie took off her head.

Carlos wiped his nose with the back of his hand, breathing hard. He looked at Valkyrie and then Damali. "Feel better? 'Cause I damned sure do."

THEY SORT OF half-fell, half-landed in the living room where the team and clerics were drinking coffee and tea and beginning to enjoy some of Inez's many fantastic desserts. Bloody, ripped, dirty, but vastly satisfied, the Neterus staggered to lean on the wall, then looked at the pristine new furniture, and finally decided to just hold each other up.

"Okay, it's cool," Carlos said, barely able to lift his blade.

"Yeah," Damali said, weaving against Carlos and speaking in bursts of breath, gulping air. She lifted her necklace, which was clutched in her hand. "It's all good."

The team and the clerics just looked at them for a moment, coffee mugs and tea cups suspended midair, forks poised over plates.

"Then I guess you guys want me to call everything off for the night and call Duke back to cancel the concert?" Rider said, glancing from Carlos to Damali. "If you don't mind me saying, you look like hell."

Carlos and Damali looked at each other, closed their eyes, and groaned.

"Want me to send back the bikes and the Hummers, man?" Jose asked.

"No, it's cool," Carlos said, walking away from Damali stiff-legged. "I just need to get a shower."

"D, you gonna be able to perform?" Marlene asked, concerned.

"Yeah, I'm good," she said, waving Marlene off and walking away, stiffly rubbing her back with one hand. "Just give me some Epsom salts, tea, and about two hours to crash and burn."

SHE WAS STILL sore when the team mounted up. She didn't even half-remember the impromptu lyrics she and Carlos had spit while just playing around. She knew her old standards like the back of her hand—but dang this shit was crazy! What was crazier as she walked out the front door was seeing a gleaming silver Bugatti Veyron in the driveway. Sore as her body was, that made her run across the expanse and grab her husband's arm. She spun him around so fast that he laughed.

"Hey, watch it, baby—that's my blade arm. Gonna need it tonight."

Damali thrust her chin up, double sealed the channel around them when curious stares met them. "A word. Briefly, Mr. Rivera."

Quiet chuckles followed them as she strode over to the shining silver car, but everyone kept loading equipment and ammunition, trying to pretend to be minding their own business.

You stole a car with clerics in the house? You crazy, Carlos! She folded her arms over her chest and glimpsed over her shoulder. *We can't be rolling like that no more.*

I didn't steal it, I borrowed it—plus I had a four-hundred-thousand-dollar deposit down on it, and—

Oh, my God, I'm not hearing this—take it back.

But, baby, I paid for it in full . . . wire transfer. It's all legal.

You doctored the paperwork, tell me I'm lying. She got in his face, her eyes hard and her mouth in a tight line. *This was their only floor model in the region from the car show and you jacked it right off the showroom floor and changed all the mess on the papers, didn't you?*

He touched her face and began to stroke her cheek. *I did it for you, baby . . . after the way I saw you fight over there in Nod, and all the healings, all the—*

You did not do that for me, she said, pointing at his chest hard with every word.

"Ow . . . dang . . . well, the car is in your name." He cocked his head to the side with a chuckle and shrugged.

"My what!"

"If you don't want it . . ." His smile widened. "But that pretty, red, sassy, Saleen S7 parked behind the cleric's limo is mine."

"Take it back." Damali grabbed her locks with both fists. "Take them both back. We're going to jail."

"Now how would that seem? We ain't got time, it would raise all sorts of legal questions, and—"

"Carlos Rivera, I swear to you—"

He kissed her quickly and held her face. *I did too do it for you. You're exhausted and can't fly—now this time you tell me if I'm lying.*

When she didn't answer he nodded and kissed her eyelids until all resistance left her. *This is the closest thing to a rocket on the ground that I can give you to get you out of harm's way. I'm exhausted, too. My foldaway needs about eight hours and a daggone bowl of Wheaties, ya know? So I want my wife to put her key in the car, crank the engine, and get out of Dodge with the team, if something crazy jumps off. That's all I'm saying. Is that so wrong?*

"How come when I argue with you, I always feel like I'm the one who's crazy?" she said, finally hugging him.

Carlos smiled as Rider called out, ribbing him. "Hey, D, I *love* the new ride!"

CHAPTER SEVENTEEN

It was everything Rider told her to expect, and probably a whole lot closer to what she knew it would be—a honky-tonk dive. She would slay any vamps left topside and go after Lilith's foul ass again, too, for making her have to deal with this again in life. Two steps forward, three steps back. So the vamps wanted to play hardball and make her team start at the bottom again. Aw'ight. Cool.

Damali stared at the chicken wire that protected the stage, making a mental note to have the tacticals light it up for sure.

"Well, it's homey," Rider said with a big grin. "Has atmosphere."

Mike and Shabazz just looked at each other and shook their heads.

"The only reason I'm cool with this," Carlos muttered, "is because it's a Guardian joint, owned by your boy . . . but let one of them rowdy yahoos out there who ain't a Guardian throw a beer at my wife, and—"

"Hey, hey, hey," Rider said, laughing. "Duke'll bounce 'em, and remember, we are the world—rednecks need love, too." Rider laughed harder as Carlos bodily pushed him away.

"Rap, in here, dude?" J.L. said, glancing at Rider.

"Yeah, okay," Rider said with a grin. "Might be a little problematic, but what can ya do?"

"I know, Jack-o boy," Father Pat said, glancing around uneasily as hard glares over beer met Monk Lin, Rabbi Zeitloff, and Imam Asula. "We could have a non–vampire-related incident before the band hits the first note . . . and if Marlene starts pouring libations in here—I don't think this is the crowd that would appreciate high art."

"Ya think?" Damali said from the side of her mouth. "And you have me roll up here in a Bugatti—they don't even know what it is, while you're flossing a Saleen S7?" She cut a hard glare at Carlos. "This ain't Hollywood Boulevard or Beverly Hills."

"I think maybe our clerics might want to go upstairs and watch from the light booth where Marj is working with Bobby and Krissy," Marlene said calmly.

"Yeah, take Dan and Heather up there, too, while you're at it, before Dan unloads a clip up in this piece."

"Okay, okay, lemme get Duke on it," Rider said, leaving the group. Then he stopped and went back to Tara. "Darlin', why don't you come with me so I won't have to blow that sonofabitch sitting at nine o'clock away."

"See what I mean," Damali said without missing a beat. She kept unpacking gear, pulling out instruments with the team, just to hurry the process.

"Okay, all right, sue me," Rider fussed, pacing away. "What did you guys want on such short notice? Gimme a break. This is Death Valley, not Vegas. Geeze!"

SATED AND SPENT, Fallon Nuit lay prone within the heap of bodies in Lilith's subterranean chamber bed. Rousing himself to feed was even too much of an inconvenience at this point. However, when a familiar deep voice entered his consciousness, he drew away from the pile of nudity very slowly, thinking out each muscle pull before he extracted himself.

You remember when I asked for a bargaining chip?

Nuit nodded and stood very still, not breathing.

Bring me one from Death Valley tonight. I want a hostage.

The Dark Power released his mind and his shoulders slumped. Lilith stirred and smiled at him, crooking her finger for him to come back to bed.

"I'm afraid that Sebastian, even with his cunning sorcerer ways, is too new to our fanged existence to have built up endurance yet." She blew Fallon a kiss as she shoved Sebastian's sleeping form aside. "Maybe if you and Yolando could stop bickering . . . I could coax him to join us one evening?"

Fallon feigned a smile and began to dress. "Not likely. We are from two different classes entirely, and our sensibilities hardly mesh. Yolando prefers Tijuana . . . what would he and Rivera call them—*putas,* I believe, if memory serves. But after being with you, dear Lilith, the sudden urge to hunt something has me in its talons . . . shall I bring you back something freshly killed from topside, or would you prefer for me to bring it to you still struggling and screaming?"

"Ah . . . chivalry is not dead, no matter how many times I've tried to kill it." Lilith licked her lips. "Always the consummate gentleman, monsieur, please bring it to me screaming its head off."

Nuit presented her with a grand sweeping bow. "Be naked and wet when I return. This won't take long, madame, I assure you."

THIS WAS QUITE possibly the worst gig they'd ever done in their lives. While libations got poured, folks screwed up their faces and yelled loudly to passing semi-topless waitresses for more beer. Cigarette smoke hung so thickly in the air, every eye was watering. Damali was just glad that they got the first song off, the call to arms for all Guardians, without incident. That might have had something to do with the fact that Duke and a table of six burly Guardians sat in the front hollering and cheering like they were at a Smack Down event. That was real cool of them.

Carlos was done, though. They had run the lyrics so ice cold and so on-point that it even gave her the shivers. Her man had broken a sweat, rolled the lyrics off his tongue so fast that the band was slapping each other high fives.

But the crowd was getting restless by the third song. The band had been giving it up, playing their hearts out, bass thumping, axe walking the scales, percussion section going bananas, keyboards *stooooo*pid, cowbells ridiculous—however, the people in the audience weren't feeling it at all. It was a team decision not to let the ladies dance—uh-uh, not in here, they'd have to shoot somebody.

Half of her knew it was to be expected given the vibe people walked in there with; wrong place, wrong audience. Then again, another part of her wondered if foul play was involved. One could never tell. One thing was for sure though, these were humans, and if they were gonna get stupid, the best option for all parties would be for her and the band to leave.

"All right, Death Valley—give it up!" Damali shouted into the mic, getting one lone clapper in the back, and Duke's poor table trying to ignite an audience fire that refused to be lit. "We're gonna take a little break and uh, we'll be back."

She ignored the boos, but her peripheral vision caught a bottle leaving a guy's hand at the same time Carlos saw it, at the same time Shabazz saw it, at the same time J.L. saw it, at the same time Dan saw it, and at the same time the collective group vibe felt it.

Twenty-nine guns of various calibers got drawn in one hard pull. Shabazz had zapped the bottle out of the air and hot shot the offender with a tactical charge so hard that he seized and pissed his pants.

"Sit your stupid ass down," Shabazz said, Black Beauty cocked. "As long as you be cool, she'll sleep. But we don't play that shit."

Duke lowered his weapon slowly. "All right. Show's over, folks. Why don't we give these fine people a round of applause for a most excellent show, and let 'em pack up nice and easy, and leave with my bar still standing."

"Warriors of Light!" one of his crazy Guardian brothers said, clapping hard with a nine millimeter in his hand and then whistling through his teeth. His wild red hair was all over his bare shoulders, and he had so much ammo in his vest that a stray cigarette ash could have taken out half the building. "Aw, yeah, Duke, this is what I call me a concert! All that's missing is the bar fight, man."

Duke jumped up onstage and went around the chicken wire. Disgruntled audience murmurs pelted his back, but apparently no one was drunk enough or crazy enough to challenge the huge blond bar owner carrying a Glock nine. He gave Rider a bear hug with massive, meaty biceps almost crushing the wind out of Rider, and then stepped back and shook his head.

"You see what I'm dealing with, dude? But this is my corner of the world, love it or leave it." Duke glanced at Big Mike. "You mind telling your big guy to, uh, put down the RPG? He's making patrons nervous."

"I'm just helping drive up liquor sales at your bar," Mike said with a tense smile and lowered the weapon. "See? Now everybody is ordering extra shots to go wit dey beer. Bad nerves is good for the bar."

"We're out," Rider said, raking his hair with his fingers. "But thanks, dude."

"I just hope Marj got that video, because I definitely can't see doing this again," Berkfield muttered as he helped the band pack up.

"Can you say career killer," J.L. grumbled, dragging a duffle bag. "There wasn't even anywhere to set up half our equipment."

"Be thankful," Damali said, glancing around as they collected the last of their gear. "It was less crap to pack up this way. In and out. Like we said." She gave her guys a hard look with Marlene. "Don't make Duke feel bad. It's not his fault. Rider, either."

Carlos chuckled as he hoisted up an equipment case. "I ain't saying nothing—I'm gonna save this, tuck it away, and use it for when Rider starts some shit with me. Then I'll whip it out on him, like an ace up my sleeve. You know me."

"Yeah, yeah, I know you," Damali said.

She was just glad that they were all finally filing out the back door to the big open parking lot. She needed air. It was stifling inside. If Marjorie got at least one decent song recorded, they could also record an interview in the studio to wrap around it and J.L. and Krissy could drop it like it's hot on the Net tonight. Damali stopped walking, lowered an equipment bag, and slapped herself in the forehead.

Everybody stopped walking.

"What?" Carlos said.

"We could have just done it all in our own studio, guys. It didn't have to be all of this—but we're so used to being on the road, needing that live audience feedback . . . oh . . . man . . ."

The entire squad groaned, even the clerics.

"Hey," Marlene said. "Let's not go there. This was an unusual circumstance. Under normal conditions we do need that live vibe, that's what makes you jam harder, gives you energy when you're out there giving it up." She looked around as heads slowly began to nod in agreement.

"It all just felt so weird, Mar," Damali admitted, her voice defeated. "Never had 'em respond to me like that anywhere in the world . . . to feel it in your own backyard is . . . I don't know. Pretty weird." She let out a hard sigh and hoisted the case. "Probably how it feels when it's time to stop gigging."

"D, I'll only accept that tone in your voice if you try to do New York or L.A. or the ATL and they treat you like that— then, yeah, it's time to stop gigging before you wind up being a lounge lizard. But until then, boo, fuck their backward asses out here." Carlos looked around at the four clerics and then rubbed his jaw. "My bad . . . I mean, forget them, baby."

"Hey, at least Duke put some of his boys out here to

watch the cars so they didn't get keyed or have the tires slit while we were in there. Now that was mighty hospitable," Rider said, trying to make jokes. "Still got all our headlights. That's a good sign."

Damali looked around, counting heads in the lot. She jumped down out of the Hummer she'd been loading and began running. "Where's Dan? Where's Heather! Ohmigod, where's J.L. and Krissy?"

Carlos and Berkfield began running back toward the building. Marjorie gasped and flung the camera into the car, then rounded the cars, but Bobby caught her arm.

"Mom, it's all right. Dan and J.L. walked Heather and Krissy to the ladies' room, plus Duke's boys got their backs," Bobby said.

"No, it's not all right!" Marjorie shrieked. "It's never all right in a place like this—we move as a group! You never leave your sister, not even if she's married!"

Rider sniffed the air, hocked, and spit. His eyes met Jose's as he did the same thing, then both Guardians drew weapons at the same time. Every Guardian went on vamp alert.

"Incoming!" Duke hollered, stumbling out of the back of the building shooting.

Patrons screamed and flooded through the back doors into the lot, causing a potential civilian nightmare. Dan and J.L. got blown through the door Duke had just exited, but even flat on their backs on the ground and being dragged by something powerful and invisible, they held whatever they'd caught in their combined charges, refusing to let it go.

Feet pressed against the dirt, wildly kicking up dust. J.L. and Dan struggled to hold on as Shabazz joined the tactical battle with Marjorie, Bobby, and Marlene, sending kinetic surges over the blue-white static that held the unseen. Rider and Tara took positions behind Hummers adjacent to Mike and Inez, Jose, Juanita, and Duke to be ready to shoot whatever came out of the tactical energy hold.

Carlos and Damali had rounded the building with Berkfield, swimming upstream against a flow of panicked bodies stampeding out the front doors. Using sheer force, guns raised above their heads, they jostled their way inside trying to get behind whatever Dan and J.L. were holding.

"Hold your fire!" Duke shouted as Guardians leveled weapons at the back door over Dan and J.L. "It's got one of the ladies; the other one got pushed down and might be nicked."

"Cover it with prayer," Father Pat said. "Burn the bastard out!"

Four clerics ran low and each took a side of the building and began shouting prayers at the tops of their lungs. Before they'd each gotten to the third stanza, a part of the back wall blew out, a high-turbine vampire funnel whirred out, and Damali and Carlos hit it with a combined pulse from behind. Fallon Nuit fell forward, his whirl temporarily interrupted. Heather hit the ground screaming, and Dan's dragnet immediately pulled her to him. J.L. was on his feet, had barreled into the back door, frantic, searching for Krissy. Dan was on his feet, Heather in his grasp, and he jumped back, narrowly avoiding a black charge as Guardians opened fire.

Nuit was on the roof, unable to go inside the prayer-stained building for cover. As Carlos and Damali drew blades into their hands and Carlos battle bulked, Nuit reached out and pulled at Heather's back. Dan whirled, feeling her slip away again, and reinforced his hold, sending a charge so furious and so direct that it blew Nuit back long enough for Carlos to scale the roof.

But Nuit's attention remained focused on Heather, and Dan saw it. Panicked, he jumped on Duke's Harley, pulling Heather with him, and took off. Nuit was gone in a flash of vapor. Berkfield came out of the building behind J.L. who had an unconscious Krissy in his arms. Carlos jumped down off the roof but not in time to catch Damali.

"He'll kill them both! Dan can't ride a bike!" Damali yelled, sliding into the Bugatti.

The bike was a mile in front of her; a vampire cloud was

downwind in the distance. Dan was eating up road at a speed where a wipeout for a novice was imminent. One false move, one pebble or road divot caught wrong and her Guardian brother and sister were dead. No helmets. A thousand and one horses were running for her under the hood. She had to get past Dan and Heather and get to Nuit. *Slow down, Dan,* she prayed. *Hold the bike steady, don't drop that girl. Jesus.* But as the funnel cloud thundered in Dan's direction, she knew they'd die, Dan couldn't turn off. It had to chase her.

Damali's foot stomped the accelerator at the same time she turned on the launch mode. The centrifugal force thrust her back into her seat so hard that it felt like someone had body slammed her chest. She vaguely felt the car drop down low to the ground. Whatever was outside whirled by in shadowed blurs. On the opposite side of the road from Dan, she realized that if she rocketed past him just the wind-drag coefficient would be enough to wreck him—but she couldn't see.

Opening her third eye, the huge roadside concrete drain-pipe and construction site became a target. Thread the needle, see it in slow motion . . . she turned the wheel slightly as the vehicle left the road just before she would have buzzed Dan and Heather, but the car kept rolling, over and over and over in a spiral, driving upside down inside the concrete tunnel to fly out the other end, hit the ground with sparks right side up, and still moving at two hundred and fifty miles an hour.

Her body was instantly covered with sweat. She plowed through Nuit's funnel and came out the other side with his face pressed to the windshield. Immediately Damali charged it with white light, making him lift his face, yelling. Furious, he raised a fist to smash the crystal windshield, but the open motor hood sucked his body down and burned him, making him roll off the hood of her car, hissing. In the rearview she saw a red Saleen S7 skid in what seemed like slow motion, becoming a red diagonal blur in the road as the driver's-side scissor door flew up and white light pulses fired, torching the ground, and burning out Nuit's black shield. She slammed on her brakes, taking almost a half-mile to slow down enough to turn the wheel without flipping over. Screeching, she burned rubber and skidded to a stop where Carlos was standing and cussing in a rage.

"I almost had that motherfucker!"

She knew exactly where Carlos was at. She wanted Nuit's neck so bad her hands were trembling.

"NO, SHE DIDN'T get nicked, either," Marlene said, holding Krissy's hand. "But she hit her head good when she went down in the ladies' room—corner of a sink got her."

Marjorie stroked her daughter's hair and after a moment, at Berkfield's gentle insistence, let J.L. get in next to his wife.

"She was trying to grab my hand when he pushed her," Heather said, tears streaming. "He knew we were trying to join hands to combine our energy against him."

"But why come feeding in a place like that—a councilman?" Dan shouted, pacing in the living room as the team tried to steady their nerves. "It doesn't make sense!"

"He wanted a hostage," Carlos said. "Plain and simple. But he came away empty-handed."

"A hostage for what?" Dan snapped, his nerves raw.

"I don't know," Carlos muttered and leaned back in his chair then wiped his palms down his face. "Maybe as payback since we kicked their asses so hard in Nod."

Silence strangled the group.

"You rode like a pro, Danny boy," Rider said, glancing at Jose and trying to diffuse the new layer of tension that had just been added to the group.

"Yeah, man, but if you're gonna snatch a bike as your getaway transpo, me and Rider gotta show you how to lay it down so you don't kill yourself." Jose smiled and kept a steady gaze of support on Dan.

"Yeah, man," Dan finally said, chuckling nervously. "All that was holding my bike to the road was tactical charge, then D blew past me and I started slowing down." He looked at Heather. "Precious cargo . . . it wasn't just me on the bike."

"Been there, and can appreciate where you were at," Carlos said calmly, glancing at Jose with silent thanks in his eyes. "Look, why don't we all just chill for a minute. Everybody in here is left of center. Then J.L.—so that this bull we just went through wasn't for nothing—we need you and the clerics, with the other tacticals to package up an Internet bomb for the darkside. You up for it, brother?"

"Like never before, man," J.L. said. "I will blow their . . . yeah," he said, curtailing his language. "I got it."

"Cool," Carlos said, stretching. "Then, healers on your marks. I'll debrief senior staff on what happened in Nod while Damali works on the ladies with Berkfield." He let out a weary breath. "Everybody else just pack for Jerusalem— the clerics will tell you what to wear, but I suspect everything is covered up and conservative, especially for the ladies."

Rabbi Zeitloff nodded. "It is."

IT HAD BEEN a very long time since she'd seen her husband so thoroughly fatigued. Physical exhaustion was one thing, but the mental toll of this last attack that Nuit had launched unexpectedly was something entirely new. But she had to admit that she was able to relate, because just healing a minor concussion had almost put her flat on her back. She knew for a fact it had everything to do with what they'd seen in Nod. How did one ever get used to, or harden themselves to seeing the bitter devastation of war? On television from far away it looked like shock and awe, but up close and personal, right there on the ground, it was horrific—topside's version of Hell.

Heather's light knock on the bedroom door gave Damali a start. She abandoned her packing job and called out for whomever it was to come in, already knowing which Guardian sister had come calling. But as Heather opened the door, Damali ran across the suite. All the color had drained from Heather's beautiful face, her eyes were wild, and her lips almost bloodied from biting them. Her chest held a hiccup wail so close to the surface of her skin that Damali felt her own lungs constrict. She collected Heather into her arms, pulling her toward the sofa.

Damali knew that look. She'd owned it once herself. Sympathy pains for her Guardian sister made her heart beat fast. Heather spoke in halts and jags in such a tiny voice that all Damali could do was make her lie down and kneel beside her, petting her hair.

"I'm bleeding," Heather whispered, her Scottish brogue becoming more pronounced as her voice became quieter and the hysteria blossomed. "I d'not know what to tell Daniel, I cannot tell him yet. I never really knew if I was . . . I never got a test from the drugstore—with this crazy life, when was there time? I never saw a doctor, so I know God wouldn't do this to us, so I cannot believe that this bleeding is our baby, tell me it's not, angel, please. My husband will never be the same, he'll swear it was his fault . . . his pulling me to safety, or the bike ride, or whatnot, I d'not know—but, oh God, me Daniel cannot suffer such thoughts." Heather's hand became a fist clutching Damali's as she turned her face into the sofa and let out a soft, piteous sob, just shaking her head.

"It's not, it's not, listen to me," Damali said as she lay her cheek against Heather's back and covered her shaking body with her wings. She let the pain come to her and only left Heather with cramps. "Honey, you were just late because of all the stress, just getting married, then we were on the road, on the run, and finally, once you felt safe . . . your body melted down. Shsssh . . . that's all."

She rocked Heather until her sobs abated, and held in a feral scream that came from heart anguish so deep she could barely breathe. Finally Heather lifted her head and turned to Damali and kissed their joined hands.

"Forever sisters for letting me be silly, when you have all the world on your shoulders."

Damali closed her eyes, tears spilling as she kissed their clasped hands hard. "Forever sisters," Damali said, wiping

Heather's face and then her own. "This kinda stuff is never silly." She gently brushed Heather's spirals of auburn curls away from her face and looked into her luminous gray eyes. "Married or single, the creation of life is sacred. To feel it inside you, divine. Only another woman would understand that . . . but there'll be your time, and when that time comes, I'll be the best auntie for you."

They both smiled sadly as Heather kissed both of Damali's cheeks. "Guess I'd better go pack for Jerusalem, then, and take some Motrin."

"Yeah, and get some rest. It'll be a long flight and a long security-clearance process."

Heather nodded then left. Damali pulled herself up using the sofa and staggered to the bedroom, closing the inner suite door, then went to the bathroom and closed that door, too. She turned on the tub water to drown out the sound bubbling within her. Numb, she found the farthest corner away from the doors and pressed her body into it, her hands covering her face, wings shielding her head and arms, as she let out a moaning wail washed by bitter, bitter tears.

"I THOUGHT MY request was clear," the beast said, his voice a deep rumble within the Level Seven caverns.

"I was ambushed, and—"

"So, then, let us dispense with quibbling and splitting hairs, Nuit. You failed."

"*Non*," Nuit said, trying to hold his own against the complete Darkness, unable to fathom another round of torture. "I brought you a hostage. You were not specific in what that might be."

A deep chuckle filled the cavern. "Ohhh. . . . And you now bargain with the bargain master. How droll. Amuse me."

"Bringing you a body is passé. Soon people write the victim off as a lost cause and resume their lives, even if shadowed by the loss. But a person's sanity is something that you can play with forever."

Silence greeted Nuit for a long pause.

"Whose sanity did you bring me?"

Nuit sighed, satisfied. "I'm sure by now Damali Richards's . . . if she tried to heal that poor Guardian sister of hers."

"MY, MY, YOU'RE in quite the chipper mood," Lilith said, looking Nuit up and down. "Topside seems to do you well, I see."

He smiled. "Yes, Lilith, I always loved the unfettered night . . . the way she smells, her perfume of blood in the air. But when you sent me on your food errand, *cheri*, you did not say if you wanted it to be male or female . . . you know how temperamental you are. Unable to decide," Fallon added with an aristocratic wave of his hand, "I picked them up at a quaint beef-and-beer establishment in Death Valley. I think the male might even be a genuine cowboy."

He snapped his fingers and her Harpies dragged in two struggling, muted victims. Leaning down, Nuit stroked the young barmaid's blond hair and then slit her tight T-shirt off her with a fingernail to allow her breasts to bounce free. He yanked a handful of brown hair and made the strapping young man the Harpies held almost fall. Sebastian sat up, and Nuit sighed. "Must I feed him, too?"

"Be nice, Fallon," Lilith cooed, staring into the terrified eyes of the dinner Nuit had brought. She glanced up at Nuit. "I like your choices. You can let them scream now. It makes the food taste so much better, *n'est-ce pas?*"

CARLOS STOOD OUT on the mountainside overlooking the house. He'd put a call out to Yonnie, and he waited as fatigue threatened to make him collapse. Soon the familiar signature flowed through his sinuses, and Carlos didn't even turn.

"Hey, man," Carlos said, relief settling in his shoulders. "You cool?"

"Yeah, brother. I'm all good. Few nights over in Tijuana, ya mean. If you wasn't a married man—"

"But I *am* a married man," Carlos said, putting up a hand. "So don't even tell me."

"Aw'ight, but you know the honeys over there ain't no joke—"

"Yonnie, man, I'm real tired." Carlos wiped fatigue from his face with both palms. "We gotta go on a pilgrimage . . . Jerusalem. I wanted to let you know we might be gone for a few, so not to panic."

"You know me," Yonnie said calmly, but there was strain in his voice. "I don't never panic, bro."

"Here's the thing," Carlos said, turning to look at him. "If they're sending our team to the original holy land . . . then it's gonna get hectic—everywhere."

The two fell silent, holding each other's line of vision.

"I feel you," Yonnie finally said. "But, you know, since all the masters are gone and topside zones are all fucked up right now—since y'all did your thing, there ain't no international pass required, or embargoes on subterranean travel, and shit. As council, until the empire is reestablished, I can go where I want . . . so, if a brother needs backup, you know, I can make that happen."

For a long while Carlos didn't answer as he turned away and gave Yonnie his back to consider again. They both knew that Yonnie was talking fast because he didn't want to hear what Carlos had to say. Neither of them did.

"Appreciate it, man," Carlos finally said. He let his breath out hard. "As my boy . . . my blood brother, I'm gonna ask you to stay outta the hot zone." Carlos shook his head and kept his voice to a dull rumble. "It's 'cause I love you, man. It's gonna get crazy, I can feel it. White light everywhere and my side will smoke anything with fangs . . . shit, I might get hit with friendly fire, when it's all said and done. Your people don't need to see you helping us, either . . . because something tells me this battle might kick up enough dust for Level Seven to get in the mix directly." He turned and looked at Yonnie. "Bad enough Nuit and them is on your ass.

You don't want the granddaddy of Darkness to catch you messing with his game over there. Believe it."

Begrudgingly, Yonnie nodded. "Since you put it that way . . . I hear you. But remember what I said before, too. If you do see me, and it's too late, make sure you do the honors."

Carlos simply closed his eyes and nodded. "All right, man. I hear you, too."

DAMALI STEELED HER nervous system for the most intense security checks they'd probably experienced to date, followed by a twenty-three-hour flight from LAX to Tel Aviv. It didn't matter that the drive up to LAX was only a few hours, or that the airport would be thirty-one miles west of Jerusalem when they got there. It was déjà vu. They'd be flying out at 6:40 P.M. to arrive the next day at 3:40 A.M., crossing however many time zones, night into day this time, and she told herself to simply hunker down and sleep on the plane.

She didn't think that was possible, until Carlos kissed her temple and told her he knew . . . and that it would be all right. He'd felt it, too, that's why he'd lost his mind trying to kill Nuit . . . and he held her next to him just rocking that pain away, no words, just knowing right beside her the same way he knew what was inside those they'd healed together in Nod.

Knowing that he knew, that he'd not just heard her but also felt it in his bones down to the marrow with her was more than enough. She wrapped that silent comfort around her like a blanket as his heartbeat and body heat lulled her to sleep. A caress at the crown of her head and a gentle, deep voice inside her mind finally made her let go. She had no choice, because what her husband told her was filled with the sweetest, most profound truth he'd ever uttered.

Don't let them take your sanity, baby. That's what they want. As long as you have your mind, that means you can access your spirit . . . so even if your body is gone, they

haven't won. Don't let them take my wife from me, boo, be-
cause they're twisting the knife in an old wound . . . together,
me and you, let's let it go.

DUE TO THE insanely early time of arrival in the morning,
the Covenant set it up so the team could lodge at the King
David—and even sleepy, jostled, hot, and cranky, she wasn't
mad at them at all for the choice.

True, it was set in the New City part of town, west of the
Old City. But as the team filed into the grand lobby with its
gracefully arched ceilings and columns covered with ancient
geometric designs, and into rooms in warm cream and
brown hues set off with Old World elegance and writing
desks, there was no complaint whatsoever. Not even Rider
said a word. Mostly, they were just grateful that they got
there alive with no midair plane attacks, bomb threats, or a
million other things that could have gone wrong. Even their
luggage came, and everyone in the group credited the clerics' solemn prayers.

When she came out of the shower she watched Carlos at
the window. He was watching the sun rise over the Old City
and for a moment she hesitated, not wanting to encroach
upon his private rapture. But the draw to be near him as he
witnessed the past, present, and future was too much of a
lure. She sidled up beside him as he stood in the open window, her breath momentarily trapped in her throat as she
watched the Middle Eastern sun paint Jerusalem stones
bathed in rose-gold.

The Muslim call to prayer rang out as a distant herald,
blending in a symphony of church bells to create a cultural
fusion rarely found anywhere else. Certainly this was the
center of the world in so many respects. The golden hues
that spilled down from the heaven lit the path of stones that
had been on the planet as silent witnesses to the greatest stories ever told. She reached out her hand through the open
window just to let that part of the sun touch her, too. They
had made it this far by faith. Carlos's grip pulled her in

tighter as he swallowed hard, feeling it too, so overwhelmed it was impossible to articulate.

How could one properly express awe as one looked at domes and spires and ancient walls that commingled with modern office towers beyond them? How was it possible for Judaism, Christianity, and Islam to all share Torah traditions, biblical echoes, and Koran refrains among hills after rolling hills of lands that ranged from bleak desert vistas to brilliant green oases in mountain isolation that gave rise to Dead Sea scrolls? How?

There was no way to wrap words around the palpable spirituality or the fracturing experience of being in the midst of the archaic, as though time stood still, while vibrant, modern markets would soon unfold, as though caravan camps in the desert along the Silk Road. Pricey souvenir shops, and bearded men in Orthodox garb, street performers, and hagglers at the Muslim Quarter market—the *souk*—a babble of languages, smells of turmeric and fenugreek, modern museums, universities, and coffee shops, and wheelbarrels bringing spices to the outdoor market. A finely woven tapestry, not so much a collision of cultures. It all left her with a sense of profound vertigo to experience the past, present, and future so compactly and beautifully arranged all in one place—at the center of the world.

A soft kiss broke their trance. Her husband's sad eyes and caress along her jaw with the pad of his thumb brought her back to the present.

"It's all so magnificent," he said in a gravelly voice. "Humanity, and the passion to live, you know? I can't bear the thought, D, that it could all be over in a flash from the sky. They said the fire this time."

CHAPTER EIGHTEEN

Whatever the clerics lacked in youth and vigor, they made up for in zeal. Despite their age, they'd set up an aggressive schedule. Everyone was to be downstairs by 8:00 A.M. to meet in the lobby, and have already eaten whatever they wanted. The Covenant was in full effect. It was time.

No excuses or arguments were accepted. They loaded sleepy Guardians into a minibus after much clerical debate about the safety of such an endeavor during the current climate of regions trading missile fire, and headed east to begin at the Mount of Olives. Once they'd reached the Seven Arches Hotel, all the commotion ceased as Guardians disembarked to view the Old City looking back west across the Kidron Valley. Again, a remarkable fusion stayed words as a huge, ancient Jewish cemetery spread out below them and Christian domes and spires surrounded them.

Only one hundred and fifty yards back they found the approach road to the hotel that allowed them to meander through a stone gateway that yielded to a ten-foot round-diameter stone structure.

Father Pat crossed himself and brought the group to a halt. "The Dome of the Ascension," he whispered. "The rock that bears our Savior's footprint."

He let each person absorb what they would and the group stood, quietly steeped in each private communion for what felt like a long time, until the elderly cleric pushed onward, making an abrupt right in their walk to take them into Pater Noster Convent.

"Whoa . . ." Bobby murmured, looking at the dozens of ceramic tiles in every conceivable language.

Father Patrick nodded. "Here is where He taught the disciples the Lord's Prayer," he said with a wave of his hand. "Every language, so many nations passed through here, but I wanted you to see this, and the path down the steep hill outside to the Garden of Gethsemane where He was arrested after the Last Supper. The Church of All Nations is there, too, but I want you to feel the sacredness of the very ground you stand on. At the foot of the Mount of Olives is a staircase, and once we descend there into the underground Church of the Assumption . . . we will find the Tomb of the Virgin."

Damali squeezed Carlos's hand, and he silently returned the pulse. No one in the group said more as they left and continued downhill witnessing the breathtaking gold, onion-shaped domes and sculpted white turrets of the Russian Orthodox Church of Mary Magdalene that sat along the traditional Palm Sunday Road.

In a grove of ancient olive trees in the Garden of Gethsemane stood the Church of All Nations, and Father Patrick took them inside the dimly lit cathedral whose interior domes housed mosaic symbols from nations around the world, and where the windows were awash with translucent alabaster over amber and purples. The somber hues and echoes added to the mystical atmosphere as he finally brought them to the altar to each touch the Rock of Agony.

Once outside again in the bright light, Guardians squinted and huddled closer together, each seeming caught up in their own private life review. But once they'd gone down into the subterranean church to view Mary's tomb, every man and woman returned to the street level so solemn that even the sound of a cleric's voice seemed like an intrusion.

"Rabbi Zeitloff will take over here," Father Patrick said quietly. He looked up at the hill they'd just left. "One of our members will bring the minibus down to meet us. But there's only one way to truly experience the Old City, and that's on foot."

"When we enter through the Dung Gate, one of the Old City of David's seven gates, our first stop will be the *Kotel* . . . the Wailing Wall, or Western Wall." He looked at Dan and Heather. "Leave your petitions there."

Again, Damali felt her heart spent to overflowing as they entered the city walking the cobbled paths of centuries of history. She could feel it seep up into her sandals and the heat of the day, combined with the spiritual awakening, made the long-sleeved, embroidered ivory muslin fabric cling to her, yet a slight shiver also made her gather her arms about her waist as they pressed forward. Her wrapped hair made it feel like her scalp was tingling, as though information from a supreme source was sending blessings down upon her head. She could tell every Guardian also felt it. All heads in their group were covered, male and female alike, as they pressed through the throngs of the devoted.

They came to a stop along a section of the wall and in Orthodox style, the men and women were separated—men on the left, as Rabbi Zeitloff officiated a group blessing, and then allowed each person to privately make their own prayers.

Damali simply hung her head and closed her eyes, touching the wall gently and reverently as Heather slipped a small piece of paper between the cracks to join the thousands and thousands of other notes sent Heavenward, tears wetting her lashes. She could feel through the wall's agony the exact moment Dan's forehead touched it, and could feel his deep, pain-filled sigh exit his body, even though her eyes couldn't see him. It was then that she added her tears to the millions of others that had spilled against the ancient stone.

When they came out of the square, Imam Asula took over to escort them to the El-Aqsa Mosque, and Dome of the

Rock. Again they were separated by gender to enter by separate archways as they approached the landmark copper dome and passed through rows of square columns to enter a space richly carpeted with Persian rugs and modern runners with stunning stained-glass windows. Being with Rabbi Zeitloff, the male Guardians were guided by the Imam, and the female Guardians escorted by a demurely covered woman who'd been sent to lead them.

Shabazz and the Imam found the *mihrab,* the niche indicating the direction toward Mecca, and the group followed the devotional prayers offered on behalf of the world in Arabic.

However, nothing could have prepared her to behold the Dome of the Rock on Temple Mount. The group went slack-jawed as Imam Asula brought them to the structure, whose exterior was a mosaic masterpiece of blue ceramic tiles topped with a dome consisting of one hundred and seventy-six pounds of twenty-four-carat gold leaf electroplated on copper.

Entering in the traditional way through different entrances by gender, they were met with huge granite columns and support arches richly adorned in the original mosaics that observed Islamic tradition in the artwork, of showing no animals or human forms, simply Arabic inscriptions for the holy texts. Then in his very quiet and unassuming way, their clerical guide brought them to the reliquary where they were, under special conditions, allowed to touch a section of the sacred rock that only was available to the public once a year during Ramadan.

"The Well of Souls is here," Imam told the group in a reverent voice, leading them down a staircase to a small grotto.

They stood within the space, and the prayers of the dead besieged Damali so powerfully that she had to get out and get air. Sensing her distress from her labored breathing, and then watching it ricochet to every other seer in the group, they hurried outside yet kept a diplomatic and respectful pace in so doing. But the moment they reached the sunshine, it was imperative to find water and stop to rest.

"We should stop and eat," Father Patrick warned, looking at the already spent group. "We can have lunch at the Israel Museum, where you can see the Dead Sea scrolls. After that we'll be walking the Via Dolorosa, the path Christ took as He bore the cross . . . we'll pick up the path near the court-yard of St. Anne's and the Pools of Bethesda, where the healing of the lame took place—and we'll follow the Stations of the Cross all the way to the Church of the Holy Sepulchre." He glanced around the team. "From there, we'll push on to the room of the Last Supper on Mount Zion, and reconvene with our minibus to bring us to Bethlehem—which is only fifteen minutes away—so that we can see the Church of the Nativity."

The team simply stared in awe at the old men on a mission, privately wondering if their stamina came from On High.

SHE AND CARLOS exited the Church of the Holy Sepulchre like Shabazz had come out of the mosque—practically shaking from the overwhelming emotions brewing up to overflow inside. The walk of Via Dolorosa made even the most leathery Guardians simply shake their heads with tears in their eyes. But she lost her composure at the final Stations of the Cross inside the magnificent central chapel that was lit with all golden candlelight and oil lamps, re-splendent with icons in Greek Orthodox tradition.

Her hand went to her mouth to hold back the sob as she looked at the bronze disc beneath the altar where the cross actually stood at Station XII, hence where Jesus died. She thought they might have to carry her out by the time the tour was done.

Father Patrick, not to be dissuaded, still insisted that they also see the Ethiopian Monastery on the grounds there, where artwork depicts the Ethiopian tradition that holds that the Queen of Sheba and Solomon's relationship produced an heir to the Ethiopian royal house. He said that was some-thing Carlos needed to know, but no one questioned why as the clerics led them to Mount Zion to visit the Tomb of David. Stepping into that tomb represented another nexus of cultures, where a massive stone was draped with a Star of David and beautifully engraved silver Torah scroll canisters sat just outside what was considered the oldest synagogue. Yet in an antechamber opposite the tomb was a *mihrab* surrounded by green ceramic tiles, so that faithful Muslims could be oriented toward Mecca to honor Nebi Daoud—the Prophet David.

Reeling as they entered the large, bare, medieval chamber with flagstones and gothic arches, they all stopped to wonder at what could have entered the hearts, minds, and spirits of men knowing this was the last of days as they knew it. Here, even in this sparse space, there was human glue that crossed barriers. An ornate *mihrab* blocked one window, with other windows elaborately restored with stained glass bearing Arabic inscriptions in Gothic windows, with a Levantine dome.

When they left the twenty-one-hundred-year-old walls of the Old City, a vast sense of connectedness linked them even closer as a team, but closer to the human family. Descending into the Tomb of the Kings, she could feel Carlos leaning on her more than he had been all day, as though this place of wide, rock-hewn steps in a cavern below, with rain-catchment pools that opened out into wide courtyards excavated from solid rock was just too reminiscent . . . so close to what he'd seen and known, but under such different circumstances.

She could feel the tension within him, but also the reverence as he stared at the huge stone slabs that were used to block tombs from biblical days gone by. Tears filled his eyes as they passed the weeping chamber inside the low doorway of the catacombs where mourners could light oil lamps in small triangle niches and sit on rock benches. He didn't want to see the alcoves and ledges where the dead were wrapped in shrouds. Sensing he was ready to bolt, she left with him, and his exit brought the group to the minibus where they found Carlos leaning against it, hands spread, and gulping air.

"It is intense," Monk Lin said, looking around the group. "You have experienced these same feelings in Tibet. This is the link, we are all one."

"There is no separation," Imam Asula told them, glancing around the group. "The human family is that—the human family. You had to know this without flinching, without any shadow of doubt as we come toward the final hour."

"In one very long day," Rabbi Zeitloff said with genuine pride shining in his eyes behind his glasses, "you have taken in years of scholarship—just through your skins, through your spirits, and hearts. You have been fortified as much as we can do on short notice. But you had to come here and see the connection to something so much greater than yourselves."

"On the road to Bethlehem, you'll also feel it . . . the hope of a beginning," Father Patrick said.

ON THE MINIBUS heading south, the clerics prayed over and passed out *bourma,* honey-filled pastries stuffed with whole pistachio nuts, to keep the group going, along with bottled water. And then the old men promptly scared everyone half to death by reminding them that in the northeast area of Tel Jericho, to the west of that city, was the Mount of Temptation where Satan tempted Jesus with dominion over all the kingdoms of the world during his fast of forty days and forty nights.

Damali looked at Carlos.

"I know," he said, under his breath. "Why'd they have to go there?"

She shrugged and shook off the shivers as Rabbi Zeitloff belabored the point about the vast cave network throughout that area. She felt better to at least know that a monastery was also tucked away in the cliffs there.

But as Rabbi Zeitloff began to describe the horrors of

Masada, a place only a little more than an hour's drive from Jerusalem sixty-four miles away, the hairs on everyone's necks, including hers, literally stood up.

"The palace there was gorgeous. Opulent. Gold and friezes such as you've never seen. State of the art for that time, with the entire mountaintop—twenty acres, that had a double wall around the whole thing, and inside that were buildings, granaries, you name it, and where people could live . . . the palace itself at the northernmost point had a bathhouse with hot, cold, and lukewarm taps, even saunas. They were *smart* and didn't have to haul their water from the Ein Gedi oasis ten miles away. No. They used their noodle and captured floodwaters in the streambeds west of the mountains," the rabbi said as the minibus lumbered along.

Excited by the epic nature of the story, Rabbi Zeitloff talked with his hands as he enjoyed a *bourma,* occasionally flinging crumbs. "Herod outdid himself, went all out. It had to be able to stand against Cleopatra's armies or his own populace—which would sometimes have civil unrest like you would not believe. He built it way up high on a flattop of solid rock. No one could get to it, and when the Romans came, the people thumbed their noses at the invaders. We took a stand! That is what's important about Masada. We had had enough. The Romans never took them alive."

The elderly rabbi looked around the group. "They even have cable cars—we should take a tour up, if there's time."

Carlos rubbed his jaw and sent his gaze out of the window. Damali gently probed his brain as his complexion went gray.

Baby, what is it? She squeezed his hand. Her husband was barely breathing.

They got trapped up there by eight Roman legions of death, he said quietly in his mind, so horrified it came out as a mental whisper. *Throne knowledge. It's the big history lesson in all of them around the Vamp Council table.*

Whatever prattle was going on in the van she became

deaf to it instantly. Her focus was singular, a soul chant—*please, God, no.*

How bad . . . how many casualties? she finally managed to ask. *They won, right—like Rabbi said, though?*

Carlos shook his head. *Winning is a matter of perspective. They won because they were never taken alive and desecrated by the enemy. It was a total camp wipeout, but by their own hand. That's why Rabbi said they won.*

An entire team? A silent gasp had passed through her skeleton, and she couldn't go back to looking out the window. She never blinked as she stared at Carlos.

A tortured expression entered his eyes. *A thousand men killed their wives and children and then drew lots to make sure they'd all assassinate themselves rather than be dishonored—you saw it in Nod.* Carlos glanced away.

She could feel him beginning to slowly wig as the information imploded within her and the horror within her soul must have mirrored itself in her eyes. *Oh, dear . . . God . . .*

I never want to visit there, D. I can't! Carlos mentally shouted, beginning to breathe through his mouth. *The ghosts that cry from that isolated palace have to be maddening . . . I don't know what I'd do if you were up there with a child in your arms while Romans walked eight legions around a band of a thousand Guardians, building a ramp . . . penned in by forty thousand sick bastards looking for blood—so-called soldiers, punk bastards, going against men of honor with their wives and babies trying to hold on. No reinforcements, no cavalry coming.*

Stunned silent, her vision blurred with pain as she tried to imagine it but fell woefully short. Her husband drew a shuddering breath and stared out the window, the muscles in his jaw pulsing.

A Roman legion is five thousand men strong, D! he said, quickly looking at her as the reality finally turned the blade in his soul. *The encampment at Masada only had a thousand men, women, and children, so that meant it wasn't even a thousand-to-forty odds. It's classic vampire history, from the Romans' point of view. This was during Lilith and Dante's heyday. Imagine the agony of that no-win decision beyond a rock and a hard place—a man having to walk into the room, draw a blade, and execute his own wife and child? Or the other option would be to watch them passed around to forty thousand deranged motherfuckers, tortured, crucified, and whatever else I don't wanna consider.* Carlos shook his head. "No," he said, not being able to hold it in his mind any longer. "Never like Masada."

The general conversation in the minibus ceased. Everyone looked at Carlos as Damali's hand rubbed his back. She looked up and her eyes searched the clerics for answers they didn't have.

"Tell the team the full story, Rabbi . . . please," Daniel said in a near whisper, swallowing hard and looking out the window. He gathered Heather's hands within his and kissed them hard, then closed his eyes. "And then tell me that's not what we're facing. *Please.*"

LORELEI TOOK THE cable car up as a part of the tour and slipped away from the group. She secreted herself among the ruins' shadows, hiding with her backpack of supplies that included food and water. Nightfall couldn't come soon enough.

DAMALI WALKED THROUGH the Church of the Nativity in a prayer stupor, her fingers absently playing with the stones in her necklace from pure nervous energy. Everything that Carlos had told her, Rabbi repeated for Dan out loud in graphic detail in a way that gave her the dry heaves. She knew firsthand that evil existed, but even with all of that, there were things she'd heard today that she couldn't fathom. Zero mercy. No single drop of compassion . . . no wonder it had to be sent to the planet embodied in a swaddled baby born in a lowly manger.

The irony that Bethlehem was closed off due to riots and unrest made it all the more poignant that she'd been able to slip into this small space between war and peace, and bow her head in hope for the salvation of the world.

IT TOOK EVERYTHING within her not to be rude and to agree with a bright smile to break bread together with Rabbi Zeitloff and his wonderful safe-house brethren. Women from the synagogue had cooked up a veritable feast. But she, like the entire team, was so exhausted that she was weaving where she stood, stifling inopportune yawns, and trying to stay religiously coherent.

Backing out of tonight's dinner to pass out beside her husband was out of the question. It had already been decided. Tonight the team would sup with the host country's official in the Jewish Quarter, then the next night, Imam would take them to the Muslim Quarter, and then on the third night, Father Patrick would do the honors to host them in the Christian Quarter, and Monk Lin would be guest cleric of honor on each evening.

She needed more than an hour to bathe, change clothes, and be ready for dinner. Eight to ten hours was more like what she really required—eight to sleep, an hour to meditate and pray and contemplate all that she'd just absorbed, then an hour to get dressed. Carlos could barely hold his head up, and he was yawning so badly they both chuckled.

"You have to stop so I can stop," she said, covering her mouth when he flopped back on the bed, yawning.

"I can't," he said through another long yawn. "You hit the showers first. I just need five minutes to rest my eyes."

"If you lie down, you know it's all over—keep moving, soldier."

"If I get in there with you is the only way." He leaned forward and rubbed his palms down his face. "And I guarantee you, right now, you don't even have to worry about me messing with you, boo."

DAMALI HAD PUT a good face on things, and he supposed that had everything to do with her years of stage performances. He felt like shit, hadn't really gotten his balance back since all the energy they'd expended in Nod, then they'd had a bunch of drama at Duke's joint to contend with—but hey, he wasn't complaining. At least he was able to jettison word to Ausar that they'd been able to back predators up off the weak shield areas to cut his King brother some slack.

Even after he'd shaved twice, he could still feel five o'clock shadow along his jaw as they got back on the minibus and headed to Zeitloff's safe house. But as usual, Damali looked like a million bucks. He glimpsed his wife from a sideline glance. Her gaze was fixed out the window watching the sun go down over the Old City. It was as though she was being hypnotized by the sunset colors washing against the ancient, golden Jerusalem stones, with the evening *muezzin* call from distant mosques adding to her trance.

Hues from the receding light filtered through the azure blue sky only to seem to get caught in her starched white Egyptian head wrap and long bell sleeves of her dress as they played across her beautiful skin. Despite her fatigue, she showed no evidence of it. Damali's shoulders were back, her head held high, giving her a regal presence that every Queen in the long line of her Neteru dynasty owned.

Waning sunlight also caught in her silver collar that was studded with priceless stones, and it shimmered against her left hand that was weighted down by the rock he'd given her. He twined his fingers through hers, feeling the softness of her graceful hands, and suddenly wishing he hadn't been so exhausted when they'd showered together. Moments like that with her were a travesty to waste. But he knew he had to be burnt out when he hadn't even had a chance to tease her about the mad-crazy way she'd driven the Bugatti like an Indy 500 pro.

She turned to him, and for no reason, just a spontaneous thing, kissed his cheek and smiled so radiantly that for a moment he couldn't move, he was sun-blinded.

Your eyes are flickering, she teased, mentally taunting him into a game to stave off giving way to fatigue.

He smiled a half-smile and looked out the window. *Yeah, well, you're lucky I was tired earlier . . . or else your pulse points would be lit up like your necklace is now.*

Her smile instantly faded as her hand went to her throat. *My necklace is lit, Carlos? Stop playing.*

His smile was gone. *I thought it was the sunset in it—you can't feel that?*

No. Maybe because I'm so wiped out, I don't know. She reached up frantically and began removing the jewelry, but also trying to remain discreet not to alarm the others.

Carlos watched her as she took off the collar and made it appear to the others as though she'd only done it because it was making her sweat. But she held it in her palms, right hand over the left, as he'd seen on too many private divinations to dismiss. She closed her eyes, opened her mind to his so he could share in whatever she pulled from the stones. Clear as day, a battle was raging. Valkyrie's bleating call for reinforcements could be heard over the din. And then he saw it—legion upon legion of demon Roman soldiers rose from the pit fanning out underground at the base of Masada simply waiting for full darkness.

"I DON'T UNDERSTAND what is happening!" Lilith shrieked, rounding the pentagram-shaped table. She yanked open the fanged crest to peer deeply into the vast misty space beneath it, trying to see why her eyes and ears over the worldwide airwaves were suddenly going blind.

Frantic, she spun on her three councilmen. "If I can't see into these places, then that means the Dark Lord's world globe is experiencing blind spots, blackout points—how can this be? Fix it!"

"We have our best minds on this, Lilith," Sebastian said nervously.

"Our best minds are frying! The airwaves are compromised!" she yelled.

"It's the package," Fallon Nuit said in a horrified murmur, leaving his throne to peer into the table better. "Lilith—tell them to stop trying to decode the Guardian concert message! Do it now!"

"It's moving so fast, their minds are engaged with white light!" she screamed, holding her temples and squeezing her eyes shut. "I can only get to the outer regions that haven't yet tried to open the infected data!"

"You, treasonous bastard," Nuit yelled, crossing the room toward Yonnie and pointing at him. "You brought this into our networks, set us up to go after the bait, when you knew what it would do!" He looked over his shoulder at Lilith. "This is Rivera's spawn. Something that should have never been allowed a throne."

"Fuck you, you two-faced bitch," Yonnie hollered and jumped up. "I got set up, no different than you did. Least I ain't bring no spell right to the chairwoman's door." He nodded. "Oh—you thought I ain't know about that shit, huh? Yeah, well, the snakes in the caverns are still talking about let the good times roll."

Fallon dropped fang. Sebastian discreetly left his throne to stand by Lilith to watch how the challenge would be addressed. Yonnie threw a roundhouse black power ball without warning, without fang drop, that caught Fallon in the jaw and sprawled him out. The second he was down, Yonnie dropped battle-length fangs, and had ripped open Nuit's white shirt and jacket from across the room, black-arc positioned to yank his heart out of his chest if he breathed wrong.

Sebastian slid around another throne and Yonnie spoke to him without taking his eyes off Nuit.

"You know like they say, 'If you got a problem, say it to my face, 'cause we can knuckle-up, any time, any place.'" Yonnie glanced at Lilith. "Permission to kill his ass?"

"Sebastian, sit down," Lilith said, her tone annoyed. "Yolando, let that man up off the floor. We don't have time for this."

Yonnie reluctantly pulled back the black charge. The odds were against him. Nuit would get his heart ripped out, but he might, too, or worse. Nuit stood slowly with a furious sneer and brushed off his suit and then repaired the front of it.

"I believe the time has come," Nuit said through his teeth, looking at Lilith, "for you to relinquish your escrow of my property."

"Only if your property accepts your bargain challenge. Have you thought of it, Fallon?" she said in a playful voice, raking Yonnie up and down with a hot gaze. "I hope not, because I've yet to see just how truly talented this gentleman is."

Cornered, Yonnie's line of vision quickly shot between Nuit's and Lilith's. But a squealing commotion of Harpies vomiting up from the marble floor suddenly stole Lilith's attention.

"We will have to take this up at another time," she said, dismissing her Vampire Council. "Other pressing matters of the empire take precedence."

SHE'D DONE JUST what the Dark Mistress had instructed, had cast a lure spell to draw the Neteru Guardian team to Masada the moment their energies had been sensed on the land. Her network of dark coven whisperers had done well. They'd seen the Neterus in airports and on conveyances. Yes. Lilith would be pleased and reward her well.

Lorelei stayed in her deep hiding place amid the shadows of the palace walls. Security guards—blinded by her black magic—never suspected.

ONE OF THE biggest arguments the team ever had took place within the space that felt like a tin can. The minibus erupted with opinions and options, none of which were acceptable to her or Carlos. She also knew it had taken everything within him to finally admit that he simply didn't have the energy to whirl the whole bus, plus ammunition and supplies down to Masada—exhaustion and now humiliation

was kicking his ass. But the option of him going alone with
no backup was entirely unacceptable to her.

"So, what, D—we just drive this minibus down to
Masada in the dark, during tense conditions in the area as it
is, politely get off after tourist hours like it is now—no
ammo, no weapons, and take on eight Roman demon legions? Is that the proposal?"

"No, Carlos, I'm saying we have to wait. We can't go
down there as a team like that, you're right—but you can't
go alone. You're exhausted!" Damali said, panic raising the
volume of her voice. "If you go, I go, but we're going together!"

"It'll be Masada all over again, D. I'm not going out like
that with you—no!"

"Stop driving this van!" she shouted to Monk Lin. "Turn
it back to Jerusalem; I'm not becoming a widow tonight!"

It happened so fast that she tried to go through the window
to catch him. Carlos had touched her face; then he was gone.

Pure chaos broke out on the minibus as Damali struggled
to get to a door while the vehicle was still moving. Guardians
and clerics were shouting for her to sit back down. Her mind
was on fire as she propelled herself forward.

"He left me!" she shrieked with tears running down her
cheeks. "It's suicide!"

Too many loving hands held her to fight against them
without hurting anyone. The frustration as they clung to her
body made her sob. Valkyrie's screams sliced into her conscience at the same time. Her breaths came so quickly she
became dizzy from the adrenaline spikes. She could vaguely
hear Marlene and Shabazz begging her not to do something
crazy. She heard Father Patrick in a distant place in her
mind. Rider and Tara, Dan and Heather, all the voices in the
van repeating the same furtive words, making her reel.

"I thought you said we had to come here to get stronger!"
she shouted, feeling betrayed. "I thought we had to touch the
stones and walk the paths so our spirits would burn brighter!

You said it! A beacon on the horizon! Where are my Queens? Where are the Kings? My team needs weapons, my man is by himself! We need safe passage to Masada—any cleric in here answer me that!"

A nova burst hit the van, exploding the metal away from the interior, sucking all occupants out into a blue-white miasma that moved so quickly there was no sound, yet the vast speed gave one the sensation of moving at incredibly slow speeds. She saw them all thrust out into the shimmering nothingness, tumbling head over heels, trying to grasp onto each other, onto seats and steering columns, anything solid to no avail. Then as if a giant rubber band had snapped, they were shot across a rock-hewn palace floor in a hard thud that would leave bruises in the morning.

Carlos jumped back as Damali jumped up.

"How'd you do that? How'd you get here like a slow-mo foldaway?" His tone and expression were incredulous.

She rushed him, and pushed him in the chest with both hands, crying. "Don't you ever do that shit to me again, Carlos!" she shouted. "I'm your wife! I'm part of you now! We're one," she said, slapping her chest. "You understand? *Comprende?* If you die, a part of me dies; if you get hurt, I'm hurt—and that's how I got here—because I'm part of you and can tap what my partner gave me. But you have no right to stop my heart like you just did back there—no right!" Tears of frustration and fear glittered in her eyes as she looked away and hugged herself. "Don't do that to me again," she whispered. "Just don't."

"I was just . . ." He looked away. "I'm sorry. Okay. You're right. But I don't want my heart stopped, either. You dying up here at Masada is a guarantee that'll happen." He waited until she looked at him. The tone of his voice, the gentle but firm quality of it made her look up. *"Comprende?"*

She nodded and drew in a shuddering breath. "To the end as one, is all I'm saying, Carlos," she murmured with a thick swallow.

He nodded and looked away. "All right."

The disoriented team slowly got to their feet and one by one helped each other up. Olive-green metal military cases were stacked along the walls everywhere. Rabbi Zeitloff got to his feet with Dan's and Rider's aid and peered out at the vista. The old man wiped his eyes beneath his askew glasses, and then lifted his chin.

"Welcome to Masada."

CHAPTER NINETEEN

"This is the part that I'm not gettin'," Shabazz said, looking around the group. "Why are we here, why are demon legions forming underground—here? Why here, why now, when you thinned out their numbers in Nod? It doesn't make sense."

"Makes sense if we're being set up for a total wipeout," Mike said, packing shells into his weapon.

"But you bring everyone to the holy land to do that? Nah," Rider said, shaking his head. "Why come to sacred ground where you don't have the spiritual advantage?"

"That's the part that's bothering me," Carlos said, walking back and forth along the wall, studying the ramparts. "They also know that, out of respect, we won't wanna blow up anything, like those ramps. They've gotta come down. That's what trapped the people up here."

"Sacrilege," Rabbi Zeitloff said quickly. "I forbid it. The destruction of a shrine such as this."

"You see what I mean." Carlos looked at Mike. "You might as well put the heavy ammo down, bro, unless you got dead-aim to knock a demon funnel outta the air. Otherwise, you blow a piece of this monument, and we've got problems."

"My aim's dead-on, C-los, you know me. But if a funnel comes, I'm worrying about the living, not the dead."

"Aw'ight . . . tacticals. See if you can juice the ramp real good, and you ladies that do stonework . . . maybe see if you can get a perimeter set using the original walls here. If we use as many natural barriers as we can, then it might reduce breaking out the heavy artillery." Carlos looked down. "I can't see 'em yet, but I can feel 'em crawling under the surface like termites ready to come up. I just wish I knew why."

Heather and Jasmine screamed at the same time and yanked their hands away from the wall. The whole group went on alert as Heather grabbed a gun, pushed past Dan, and began running. The team was on her heels as she kicked in a door and held a weapon with both hands.

"Out now, bitch!" Heather shouted. "Hands on your head, blink and you're gone."

A very smug, petite woman with black and purple hair slowly moved out of the shadows.

"Who in the hell . . ." Rider said, gaping, his weapon trained on the woman like the others. "No vamp tracer. Be cool, Heather. Could be civilian."

"Yes, Heather. Be cool," Lorelei taunted.

"She's no civilian. She's dark coven all the way—second in command to Gabrielle, and probably set Gabby up, if I know her shady ways. Get up, Lorelei."

"Gladly," she said, glancing around the team.

"Tie her up—duct tape is with the ammo," Carlos said, looking at Damali. "We're not exactly in a position to deal with POWs. Damn!"

"Throw her ass over the wall," Damali said, drawing very concerned stares from the group. "You're right. We're in a take-no-prisoners frame of mind. A dark coven witch is up here obviously conjuring behind our backs," she added, white light charging the small pentagram and charms Lorelei had left, using her Isis. Damali then looked at Father Patrick for theatrical effect. "We even have a member here from the Catholic sect. What were the witch tests, Father?"

"Damali, no," he said, ashamed.

"Oh, yes," Damali said, grabbing Lorelei as she began to scream. "You mess with my family, I ain't got no love for you." Quickly she rammed the blade into the ground and yanked Lorelei's hands behind her back, kicking her legs out from under her so her cheek hit the wall. "Who sent you and why?"

Damali looked up at the stricken faces. "See? Uncooperative. Gotta go." She hoisted her up as Guardians shouted no. Even Carlos was unsure.

"I know you're stressed, but she's still human, baby," Carlos said, trying to get a sightline to Damali to negotiate.

Damali looked over the edge of the cliffside wall and laughed. "Oh, she wants to die—she won't be human for long. Don't worry." The moment Lorelei screamed, Damali heaved her over the wall and flung her as far away from her as she could.

Clerics yelled, hands reaching over trying to catch the falling girl. Eyes held terror and total disbelief.

"What have you done?" Marlene whispered.

"Found out who's gonna catch that bitch," Damali said, taking a running leap and going over the edge, wings extended.

With no small measure of satisfaction she watched Lorelei hurdle toward the ground, hands extended, face contorted, vomit choking her, body voiding—yeah, she had it coming. And just as she suspected, Lilith opened the earth and stood with arms outstretched, screaming no. An unexpected variable was that Lilith's wings had been scorched off by Eve's white light net—oops.

Harpies swirled up to try to catch the tumbling woman, but their greedy, eager little hands would fillet her, falling from that altitude as they grasped with claws. Damali brought her wings in close to her body, along with her hands and dive-bombed toward her, grabbing Lorelei's outstretched arms, dislocating both of the witch's shoulders, but keeping her from a ground collision.

As soon as they connected, Damali opened her wings and headed back to the top of the mountain. She'd been able to siphon enough from the traumatized witch to know that whatever it was, was coming out of Nod. *Amazing how fear just breaks down all communication and black spell barriers,* she thought as she dropped Lorelei hard on the palace floor.

Lorelei lay on the floor weeping and breathing hard. Damali walked over her body and looked at the team.

"Found out a coupla things," Damali said, panting. "One. Lilith can't fly. Eve permanently maimed her wings. Very cool. Two. Whatever they're waiting for is coming out of Nod—so I say, me and Carlos go back, the team hunkers down here. If we can slaughter it over there, all the better." She wiped the sweat from her brow with the back of her forearm. "I learned something else, too. Three. How badly I wanted to just drop this ho'."

"She's injured," Dan said with disdain, holding the duct tape. "What do I do?"

"She didn't want us to have any special powers from the Light working to help her foul ass," Carlos said. "Pop her shoulder blades back in the old-fashioned way, then tape her up. We can drop her at the hospital later, assuming we make it off this mountain."

Juanita, Inez, Marlene, and Heather stepped up.

"I ain't got no problem with it, Dan, if you're squeamish about doing a female," Juanita said.

Inez and Marlene slapped her five.

"Oh, no," Heather said. "Let me do the honors. I picked up something else she was party to . . . something personal." She glanced at Damali and mouthed a quiet thank you.

"Don't let Heather kill her, Dan," Damali said, walking away. "And tape her mouth up before you pop her shoulders into place. She deserves so much more . . . but, you know, we're Guardians . . . blah, blah, blah."

Mike squinted and went to go check more ammo with

Shabazz. "Damn, the ladies is cold, man. And they say men are bad."

COMPLETE DESOLATION IS all they saw when they entered Nod. Just as the Neteru Kings had communicated, the shields were still in place, but the weak spot was over the holy land. The Middle East had been the target of constant bombardment. The square downtown was so quiet their footsteps along the pavement sounded like thunder. When they got to the palace, the huddled masses were still there, but the numbers were vastly reduced. Even the lions were gone.

"What happened?" Damali called out, hoping those she'd healed would remember her. She looked at Carlos.

"Yeah. I know. Something is way wrong."

"You seek Valkyrie to assist her in battle?" the angel hybrid with amber wings called out from a bench down on the court floor.

"Yeah. Where is everybody?" Damali looked around. "Where's your sphinxes?"

"Those who could still fight went to Cain's old cliffside lair. The ravine there is where the barrier is the weakest," another hybrid called out, and then gathered a blanket tighter around him. "They are afraid to go to the seeking alleys now, because they would have to come past the central palace here. But Valkyrie takes the lions to help protect the shields that are weakening over the holy land."

Carlos nodded. "We're out. We know the way."

"VERY GOOD," LILITH whispered to her Harpies. "They're here and in position. Lorelei will crack under pressure, and they'll go into Nod, blades swinging." She petted the most aggressive little beast that snuggled against her legs. "Go tell my scientists to hit the veil between worlds one more time in the same spot they've been hammering. It's weakening so much that I can feel the pulse of my heir through it." She kissed the top of its bald, scaly head as she caressed it. "You must fly quickly. Our internal network has been temporarily shut down. I need you to do this before my husband completely repairs it and seeks me."

FULL BATTLE WAS underway as the Netcrus approached the ravine. Huge marble sphinxes made aerial lunges at loyalist forces battling Valkyrie's small but courageous band of warriors. Damali and Carlos immediately joined the fray, decimating whatever entity that dropped to the ground, blades swinging, Madame Isis chiming through the air.

Every indignity that she'd ever witnessed that had been committed against the innocent, the weak, the outnumbered, or the unprotected felt like it entered her nervous system one disk in her back at a time until the power of righteous indignation sent laserlike white light into her blade arm. When she swung, heads came off so fast and clean that it wasn't until the entity moved that the look of surprise captured its face as its head fell to the ground. The light that burst from the end of the blade was a torch. While the razor edge cut through flesh, gristle, and bone, the tip of the blade took out predators behind the one she was beheading, just because they'd passed through the swath of light.

Insane with the images in his mind, the need to ensure that not one beast crossed the shields erupted old hellfire in his DNA. His left fist became an anvil; his right hand clutched a blade of destruction. Throwing roundhouse punches that broke jaws, sent fangs in the opposite direction of their owners, Carlos cut his way to Valkyrie's side. To the point of primal fury, Carlos spotted Damali and threw her his blade. Satisfied that his wife had a double blade advantage, he spun on attackers, loving the carnage of getting his hands dirty.

Throats came out in his grasp, dangling esophagi just like the old nights. Demon hybrids backed up, now truly sensing one of their own in their midst, one insane like they knew Cain could become. One with fangs dripping saliva, silver sightline that burned with a look of near-ecstasy in the killing of them . . . they could understand that look, that passion, and it demoralized their troops. The psychological toll of seeing what to them was a chairman-level vampire in their realm, impervious to the Light, with ten inches of battle fangs, two hearts in his fists that had been snatched out so fast they were still beating when their owners dropped, gave the loyalists serious pause.

A call to retreat rang out. Damali blocked the path to escape. Her Isis in one hand, Carlos's blade of Ausar in the other, she became an angel of death, Hell, and destruction. Wings dirty and splattered with blood, she flew at the demon hybrids that were trying to get back to the shelter of Cain's half destroyed cliffside lair. There were only fifty left. Take no prisoners was her inner war cry as she saw them slow down in the air, her blades crossed before her chest as she sped toward them. Midturn to get away, her blades opened, slicing through two at a time, screams of the falling echoing in the ravine as they burned.

Think of the abuses—slash. Think of the rapes—direct jab. Think of the tears—double cut, heads roll. Think of the children—aerial fly kick, blade through a rib cage claims a heart, slice through the midsection makes one demon hybrid two. She was on fire, white light flame. An avenging angel; a deliverer. Carlos had become a destroyer on the ground with Valkyrie, rooting out hiding loyalists and sending them to Hell by hand.

At the edge of the ravine, piles of ash and bodies littered the ground. Breathing hard, Valkyrie and her meager forces of twenty-five rebel hybrids looked around as Carlos and Damali joined her. The sphinxes roared, paced a bit, and then quieted.

"Feel the vibrations in the air," she said, looking around astounded. "They're all gone. I only feel one very far away and hiding."

Damali and Carlos nodded.

"If one small one gets out, we'll get it on the other side," Carlos said, gulping air and normalizing.

"Yeah," Damali said between bursts of breath, wiping

sweat off her brow with her forearm. "The main thing is that
you guys can stay over here without fear of being attacked.
Once we can figure out a way to seal the rips, you should
need supplies like you did before, but we'll keep your people stocked until we can clean up the environmental damage."

Carlos was still sucking in huge breaths, but nodded.
"We'll get you plenty of stuff over here, maybe once we get
things secure on our end, we can help you rebuild a little . . .
but our shit is raggedy back home. We gotta go handle our
business there, too, sis."

"I understand, and we are eternally grateful for what
you've done." Valkyrie grasped first Damali's arm and then
Carlos's in a warrior's handshake, then dropped to one knee.
"My mother came from a long line of Valkyrie angels . . .
my father was a Viking, who had a near-death experience,
but was spared, and didn't die. I shall make petitions and
burn incense in your honor here, that when your times come,
a full flight escort of twenty-one Valkyries may guard your
spirits to Valhalla."

"Bless you," Damali said quietly, knowing that Valkyrie's
prayer, like all those people and beings of Light that had
prayed for her and Carlos and their team, weighed so heavily
on the thin margin and balance between life and death that
she was at a loss to say more.

All the wild, risky, edge of the razor experiences they
had, Damali knew the only thing that stood between them
and the eleventh-hour-and-fifty-ninth-minute save was somebody's prayer, somewhere, weighing in to tip the scales in
their favor.

"And, I you," Damali told Valkyrie after a moment, so sad
to say good-bye to what had become like a member of her
team . . . family. "I pray that you rebuild this place to its former beauty and dignity, and that all those who remain live in
peace, and that Nod's Valkyrie be known as one of the most
dedicated and courageous of warriors . . . like Sara, and Hubert, and Sedgwick. We must remember each one that died, so

it was not in vain. May a twenty-one-flight squadron also guide you home—with full Neteru Guardian spirit escort—when it is your time."

"You fought hard, almost to the last soldier, to defend what was yours to the end," Carlos said, lifting his chin. "Much respect, Val—because it wasn't just about the land, it was about a way of life . . . being free to live without somebody trying to jack you or your shit." He pointed up toward the white marble rubble that had once been Cain's lair and stared at it until the archway began to smolder. "Make that a museum, so y'all remember where the battle between worlds was fought and won.

"Valkyrie," Carlos said, sending her name into it above the pillars in a gleaming, silver Kemetian font. "Sara. Hubert. Sedgwick. Those are the ones we knew, who directly helped our team and came to the other side—or defended it on this side of the line. Silver. Your names stay in silver." He nodded and looked at the thinning seal. "The others you can inscribe the old-fashioned way by chisel, but y'all . . . damn . . . if you hadn't been with us, ride or die, the outcome mighta been real different."

Valkyrie stayed down on one knee and crossed her chest with both forearms in the ancient Kemetian pose of pharaohs. "To be recognized in perpetuity by Neterus and to have my name on your lips in a prayer means my destiny has been fulfilled. Forever grateful," she said in a hoarse whisper laced with emotion. "I will guard this place until my end of time."

The others who had valiantly fought to protect the veil to the earth plane from being breached surrounded Valkyrie in a semicircle and went down on one knee, facing both Neterus in a similar pose of respect. "Until our end of time."

"Until our end of time," a lame angel hybrid said, staring at the group and limping toward Carlos and Damali. Her gentle eyes looked longingly at the warriors before her and she wrapped her torn clothes in tattered, amber wings. "I wanted to fight, too. But I have missed the battle." Huge tears welled in her eyes as Valkyrie and her forces stood.

"No, dear one. You were never to be a warrior with your gentle spirit. You should help us bring peace and order and healing now that it is all done," Valkyrie said, hugging her as she came to the group.

"Thank you for healing me," the amber-winged beauty said to Damali, and then went to hug her as Valkyrie stepped back.

A sudden, shattering blast rocked the ravine making Damali lose her footing with the angel hybrid in her embrace. Something chilling attacked her mind, threw off her sense of orientation, and seized her heart as she clung to the wounded angel hybrid—trying to save her from reentry burnup as the pair slammed a frayed edge of the shielded veil rip. In the distance she could hear Carlos shouting, heard him call her name and tell Valkyrie to stay back—the area was unstable.

Pain seemed to knife her from the inside out as she came to a burning, skidding halt on the palace floor. Her team gathered around. She was semiconscious but not so dazed that she didn't know faces. Voices sounded like mud. The sky looked like it was smeared with blood from her meteoric entry. Something warm and shivering and possibly dying was in her arms. An amber-winged angel sobbed against her chest.

"Incoming," Damali said flatly. "Hold your fire, I think it's Carlos."

He hit the ground so hard he bounced twice, skidded across the floor, and came to a crashing halt against the far wall. Dazed, he lay there for a moment, not exactly sure where he was. Guardians were all around him, asking him to count fingers. He thought he saw Damali in his peripheral vision holding an angel hybrid, half-sitting up. Okay, that was a good thing. He looked up into Big Mike's face and blinked twice. But there were white things seeping from the walls, up from the floor, oozing down from the crevices. The voices of the team sounded so far away that he told them to shut up. White protoplasm was seeping from the fucking walls!

He rolled over, pushed up, wobbly, staggering, disoriented, trying to call a blade in his hand, only getting sparks of energy for a moment, the words "watch your backs," stuck in his throat. Then he was on his knees, unable to breathe, feeling like he was gonna pass out. Hell no, Berkfield was wrong, he didn't have a concussion, even though he'd hit the wall like a bullet. Naw . . . it was the stuff coming out of the walls. He needed to vomit but nothing would come up. Pain was making tears run, but it wasn't pain from the ground hit, it came from the inside out and leaked through his pores, making him holler. It was pain so intense that it threatened to explode his heart. Guardians were trying to make him lie down, but the floor was running blood.

"Get me off the fucking floor! It's everywhere! The walls are bleeding! Get off me!" He was up, a blade in hand, eyes wild. "Where's my wife? Where is my damned wife! Get her out of here, now!"

"I'm right here," Damali shouted, making him whirl.

He watched her hand off an injured hybrid to Marlene and come to him. "Look. Don't you see it?"

A cold sweat had replaced silver battle sweat. He was panting, frantic. Adrenaline was spiking flight-not-fight messages to every cell in him. Damali placed both of her hands to his temples, stared at him for a second, and then dropped them away screaming. She bent over holding her arms around her waist. Clerics and Guardians rushed to their Neterus and then all of a sudden, one by one, each cleric began to sob.

Rabbi Zeitloff went down on his knees first, pulling at his clothing and beating his chest, wailing. Father Patrick leaned over and retched, as Imam Asula dropped, shell-shocked, and closed his eyes, tears running down his dark, weathered cheeks. Monk Lin stood staring at nothing, and then walked away to a far corner to slowly sit, then lay on his side and curled up into a small ball.

Thoroughly panicked Guardians looked at their group seers for help, and within seconds the same reaction that had decimated the clerics began to run through the seers . . . then the tacticals felt it, and the stoneworkers cried out and moaned as they felt it through the stones, and Mike began rocking, covering his ears as he heard it, and finally Jose and Rider walked away, and vomited as the smell overcame them.

"Masada!" Rabbi Zeitloff yelled, crying hard. "Never again."

He began reciting rabbinical prayers in Hebrew, and then the other clerics quickly began to pull themselves together and add theirs of their own faith. The tidal wave of white light sent Heavenward helped each Neteru begin their litany, which in turn helped Guardians to find their path back to sanity as they slowly began to join in, too.

As their prayers reached fever pitch, they could all see with their naked eyes, one thousand moaning, wailing, ancient rebel spirits that had been trapped in the palace. Women grasped children to their breasts. Babies cried and older children hid against their mothers' bodies. Husbands tried to drag children away from women's arms, their own flesh and blood, while they themselves screamed in a pain so feral that thunder and lightning flashed in the sky.

Demon sulfur wafted up from beyond the wall and the wailing ghosts shrieked as they drew blades and became skeletons. Guardians broke formation and ran to look over the wall. Clerics increased their prayer chants.

"Legions are on the move, yo!" Jose shouted.

"The ground's opening up, people," Rider said. Locking a Gatling gun onto the wall.

"Decision time, D." Shabazz looked around. "The phantoms in here or the demons outside?"

Mike grabbed a bazooka. "Lemme know what to do, C! Start the party, or what?"

"Fight with us this time!" Damali shouted. She looked at Carlos and sent pure silver thought into his mind like a razor. *They're trapped. They think it's happening again. They don't know if we're Romans that made it over the wall or what, because we're foreign. Tell them you have the Ark and let them see it—you saw it in Ethiopia. Tell them we have something to fight eight demon Roman legions this time and win, baby! Together we call our families.*

The moment the thought of calling their families blazed across Damali's mind, every ancestor who was ever connected to the Guardian team stepped out of the folds of ether behind the disoriented ghosts of Masada. She could feel her team members' hearts breaking and taste their tears on the wind as the spirits of their loved ones appeared. The vibrations of love that oozed from the living to the dead and back again coated the very air with a shimmering, protective haze. Gently, reverently, ancestral spirits calmed and hugged terror-stricken phantoms. Damali's father stepped forward with Father Lopez, flanked by the Brazilian team with a readiness for war in their eyes. Kamal slowly nodded to Shabazz and then Marlene and he closed his eyes briefly as they returned his nod, acknowledging him as one.

Damali and Carlos watched mute and transfixed as their parents, grandparents, Father Lopez, Christine, so many spirits, some of whom they didn't know, whispered into ears, took up hands, wiped tears, and brought peace.

Soon the gathering of spirits parted like a fine mist and Damali's mother walked forward, spreading her set of beautiful, luminous wings. "We all stand with you as we have always, my daughter." She looked at Carlos and pure peace radiated from her expression. "You contain more than you know—use it all, son. Open that which is within."

Instantly the ghosts sent up a huge cry. Complete chaos surrounded Damali and Carlos, making them seek each other's gazes for a clue about what had just happened.

The Ark, Damali's mind shot into his. *This is the end of days. That's the only thing my mother could have meant, because surely she wouldn't want us to open a biblical seal!*

The angel hybrid huddled on the ground and slowly crawled her way over to Lorelei.

Carlos closed his eyes for a moment, remembering what he'd seen when he was in Ethiopia. The old men in the boat, the blind monks had shown him the Ark of the Covenant, and it had turned his eyes silver. He sent the image into the wall, against the floor, and into the very rock of Masada. The ghosts of Masada stopped moving and shrieking and began to silently weep. They dropped down on their knees and then turned to whomever they were next to and hugged and rocked and wept. Whole families became reunited, and then slowly men stood. Three hundred men stepped forward along with the ancestors and every felled Guardian of the past, turned in unison and faced Carlos, ready for war.

The team and clerics stared in awe and fell silent, not sure what it was that Carlos had shown the dead that made them quiet, or what it was that had made their eyes burn with resolve.

"It was the dark coven energy they were sensing," Damali said to the group, opening her arms. "The ghosts of Masada were confused—they couldn't tell who we are. Even with the prayers, something really dark was blocking their read of our vibrations. It might be her," she said, pointing at Lorelei. "Just her foul presence here is probably arcing a dark current down to Lilith's ground troops." Damali raked her fingers through her locks in bitter frustration. "I swear I'll throw her skank ass over the wall this time and not catch her!"

"No, let me," the angel hybrid said, looking at Lorelei. "I missed the battle in Nod, but I want to be in this one. Let me guard her."

"Done," Carlos said. "You keep an eye on that bitch, and if she tries something stupid, do her."

Damali turned away from Lorelei and the hybrid rebel

from Nod as Carlos's next command quickly positioned the team.

"Tacticals on the walls, supercharging all surfaces, especially the winding snake path up here, any cables overhead, and the earth around our perimeter—me and D will send cold body seeking white light pulses behind that. On D's call, Mike, you start the party and fire up those demon formations on the ground. No hits to the palace; send it south."

"I'm on it, boss," Mike said, leveling the bazooka.

"Clerics, four corners, to keep this mess at bay and to put up a prayer dome against an overhead attack—'cause once Mike fires, it's on. Everybody, automatics up. If it gets stupid, Carlos can throw up a shield, but he needs to leave you open to fire as long as humanly possible." Damali looked around. "Minimum to zero damage up here and to the cable cars. This is a shrine. The Roman ramparts they can rebuild later, but this, where we are, can't be."

Carlos nodded. "All right. Dan, you fall back, even though you're a tactical—I want you lobbing hallowed earth and silver shrapnel explosives. You got dead-aim, brother. I want an acid line of holy water . . . clerics on the four walls, that's all you. Bobby, 'Nez, Juanita, Jasmine, you're water runners and our radar from all sides—Bobby, you got da wizard moves to lift that water, steady stream from the pipe system like a fire hose, passing by clerical prayers—you're my flame-thrower, man—not a water boy, so don't get it twisted. I need your head right, and you work with Krissy on that, got it? Keep the Covenant in water, anything liquid, that they can bless and hurl over the walls."

"Got it," Bobby said, standing up taller.

"Got it," Krissy said, slapping her brother five.

"Berkfield, you're a gunner, with Rider, Jose, and Tara. One of y'all on each of the cardinal points with a cleric, a seer for radar, and a flame-thrower. Mike and Dan will move around at your holler. Marj, you lead the wall jolts, you and Heather, with Marlene, power of three," Damali said, nodding.

"Then Shabazz, J.L., and Dan can keep sending shock-waves down the walls between clicking off rounds to keep 'em back," Carlos said, his gaze going around the team. "Everybody got it?"

"Yeah," rang out in a variety of timbres.

"Move out." Damali waited a beat until everyone took their places. "Mike, fire it up."

"As the lady asks," Mike said, releasing a bazooka blast that made him take two steps back.

The hit rocked the dirt, sending a plume of dust up with sulfuric smoke. Eight demon legions immediately erupted from the ground like lava, splitting the earth in angry gashes and fissures as hellfire flared up behind them. Spaded-tailed, black Roman armor-clad nightmares with black blades, red, gleaming eyes, mangled fangs, and huge bat wings positioned for an aerial attack.

"Automatics up! They're sending in their fliers, first!" Carlos shouted.

"Wait," Damali said, looking at Carlos. "Shields up, white light it, they'll have bullets raining back down on our own team."

Carlos shook his head hard. "Damn . . . that's fundamental." He looked at Damali. "Maybe I did hit my head harder than I thought."

"No," the amber-winged hybrid said. "It's her! You can't have a dark coven witch behind your lines like a sleeper cell!"

The entity from Nod jumped up so quickly and grabbed Lorelei that the word "No!" rang out on the team in a Doppler effect. Carlos couldn't hit them with a knock-down pulse without injuring the pregnant angel hybrid that Damali had just healed and saved. She moved too quickly. Lorelei's skinny, petite frame was no match for the more muscular, winged creature. The hybrid rebel went over the wall in a suicide plummet clutching a screaming Lorelei. Everyone, including phantom warriors, rushed to the wall to watch in horror as the angel hybrid tumbled in a struggling spiral.

Demon Roman legion fliers took flight and surrounded

the spiraling pair, snatching them out of the sky. But to the team's surprise, they gently set the amber-winged hybrid down, and settled Lorelei beside her—holding her.

"Something's seriously wrong," Damali said quietly as they all stared over the wall.

"Maybe they think they've got a Nod hostage and can negotiate," Carlos said, pacing like a trapped panther as he continued to stare over the wall. "They know we won't allow an angel to be eaten. Everybody be cool, hold your fire, until they set terms."

A swarm of Harpies flew over the ground and surrounded the hybrid and frightened witch as demon legionnaires stepped back to form a menacing, threatening ring around the Harpies.

"Oh, they are definitely reinforcing troops around them so we can't do a snatch," Damali said, raking her locks. "Shit! Why would that crazy, zealot hybrid break ranks on a suicide mission like that? We might not be able to get to her."

Lilith's sulfuric plume made veins of rage stand up in Carlos's temple. He spat and then glanced at Damali. "What did I tell you? Let the games begin."

"In *Dananu* like old times," Damali said through her teeth.

"What do you want, Lilith!" Carlos hollered over the wall in *Dananu*. "A body for a body? State your terms!"

"I don't want anything," Lilith cooed in a loud echo. "I've already got what I want . . . a body for a body, and then some." She stroked the angel hybrid's hair and then tongue-kissed her.

Clerics closed their eyes and cringed.

"Desecration . . . complete sacrilege—get thee away from thy angelic host, demon!" Father Patrick shouted over the wall with his eyes squeezed shut.

"No, no, no," Lilith clucked with her tongue, leaning the hybrid back. "This is of her own free will, isn't it, my dear?"

"Away from an angel, you unholy beast! May the wrath

of Heaven scorch your vile body and exterminate your ravenous spirit from existence!" Father Patrick yelled, thoroughly undone by the cruelty he was witnessing.

"Of all people, Father," Lilith said with a snide chuckle. "I know *you* aren't the one calling for Heaven's help or casting stones. Chastising me, are you?" She narrowed a withering gaze on the elderly priest. "Why, not too long ago, I believe, you lost your faith." She glanced around at the laughing demons at her flank. "Isn't that right? Didn't he renounce the church?" Her gaze widened as she studied him and clucked her tongue. "Such a dangerous position to be in as a priest out here with all of us . . . my . . . my . . . my. Well, you all do keep it interesting, that I will give you." With a lightning quick motion, she sent a black charge toward the elderly man, but was surprised when a white-light bolt from the sky deflected it.

"I *never* lost faith in the Almighty, Lilith!" Father Patrick raged. "I lost faith in men—*men,* not God! And as we know, in the last days, the devil will even take up residence in the churches. My love of the Almighty never wavered! So I call on every prayer, every righteous cleric that ever died to protect this team! We will have your head! I still believe, and will to my gasping last breath!"

"Guess the thunder and lightning from above served as your answer, bitch," Juanita shouted over the wall, training a machine gun on Lilith. "You ain't fronting on no priest up in here!"

Mike fingered the bazooka trigger. "D, just say it, baby . . . just tell me I can blow that bitch up."

Lilith glared at the sky for a moment, ignoring the Guardians, before returning her attention to the hybrid. "No matter. I have what I want and she wants this, right, my dear? It's your choice."

"Tricks of the unholy," Rabbi Zeitloff yelled. "Fight her with your mind and your spirit, angel!"

"Link to us in prayer to keep the unclean from your soul, even if they defile your body until we reach you, do not give in to her foul words and lascivious intent!" Imam Asula shouted.

"Go to a quiet space of pure white light and find us there," Monk Lin shouted. "Now, for your safety of spirit!"

Rider slowly positioned a weapon and squeezed. "Or let us blow these fuckers away."

The bullet whizzed past Lilith who jumped back and took out a lead demon that had flanked her, splattering the site with ash. Two quick sharpshooter squeezes and Harpies that had been touching the hybrid were green gook. Lilith laughed and covered the hybrid and Lorelei with a black energy shield.

"Our negotiation was over before it started, Rivera. Tell that bitch, Damali, to watch and weep—this is her healing handiwork." Lilith took cover and ordered her less expendable guards to fall back out of Guardian weapon range. "Splatter the Harpies; they breed fast enough to replenish any you kill. But I want you to see this . . . see what a Caduceus life-saving jolt will do once it hits earth's atmosphere."

Damali looked at Carlos. "What's she talking about?" Her voice was strained as she clutched Carlos's arm.

"I don't know," he said, his gaze riveted to the two beings under Lilith's shield. "She's fucking with us, trying to mess with our heads. Block out the bullshit she's talking about and let's focus on how to get the angel up and outta there."

But before they could even take another breath, the hybrid laughed and waved at Damali. "You should have bedded Cain and been his co-ruler. We were all waiting for you to give him an heir, and you were such a stupid bitch that you didn't."

"It's the influence, Lilith bending her mind," Damali said. "Ignore it, people. Lilith wants us to fire on her, kill our own."

"You Neterus think you know so much," Lilith said, cackling. She sighed and then slid under the shield like vapor.

"Oh, man," Carlos said, wiping his palms down his face.

"Head-screw tactic, one-oh-one . . . make you watch the torture."

"See, Carlos still remembers a lot of things from his old throne. He could have been chairman and had my job and run it all, too—but just like his silly little goody-goody wife, he chose the Light. How foolish." Lilith kissed down the angel hybrid's breastbone and caressed her abdomen. "Come to me," she said in a whisper that reverberated up and over the wall.

The angel hybrid opened her legs and arched with a moan. Guardians and clerics turned away, making sounds of raw disgust.

"Everything isn't always what it seems," Lilith said, her hands gliding along the hybrid's inner thighs. She turned to the anxious witch who had been released from her duct-tape bondage. "Is it Lorelei?" she hissed, kissing her deeply and then turning her focus back to the hybrid.

"I'm gonna be ill," Damali whispered, wiping her palms down her face.

"Yes, you are," Lilith said, laughing.

"I can get off a mercy shot," Mike said, positioning the bazooka. "This don't make no sense . . . I think it'll go through the shield if y'all Neterus white light it."

"It just might," Lilith said with a smug cackle. "But I don't think even your big dumb ass wants angel blood on his conscience . . . do you, Mike?"

Mike hesitated and Lilith threw her head back and laughed.

"I guess we're at an impasse, then," Lilith yelled up the mountainside.

Stalemated, the Guardian squad peered over the wall, keeping seers sweeping the other sides of the mountain for a possible rear sneak-attack. But their senses came away wanting, and all eyes remained riveted to Lilith's theatrical display below. The she-demon had gone back to stroking the angel-hybrid's hair and caressing her lower abdomen, making the hybrid begin to sweat and strain against the touch.

"All right, Lilith! A body for a body," Carlos hollered.

"No, thank you—you waited too long." Lilith laughed as the hybrid's distress increased.

"Fine, then take me—you always wanted me!" Damali shouted, her eyes telling Carlos not to countermand her.

"Thank you, but no. I must decline. You're no longer a virgin, tsk tsk. You're soiled, used, unclean, and of no use to my empire now."

Raucous demon laughter from forty thousand troops filled the valley, making the Guardians and clerics briefly cover their ears.

"Then we will trade!" Imam Asula said. "Any man of faith here of the Covenant."

"Touching . . . and probably the most tempting offer thus far, but no." Lilith looked up as Berkfield leaned over the wall. "Don't even think about it—you are so unclean to my kind you make me retch just at the thought of what runs through your veins. The rest of you can save your offers, too."

"Then what do you want?" Damali hollered in *Dananu* as Lilith dropped fang.

"I was just waiting for you to ask me again nicely," Lilith replied as she touched the hybrid's belly and stepped back. *"This."*

To the team's horror the hybrid arched and dug the crown of her head into the dirt, writhing in pain as she let out a piteous wail. But what she said made them glance at each other, even while partially mesmerized by the way her body was contorting and expanding, as her belly grew to the proportions of a beach ball.

"Do not forget our bargain, Lilith," the angel hybrid gasped. "I have served you well—I deserve my place at your council table!"

Lilith nodded. "Once you are done, so be it."

"What will my reward be?" Lorelei asked expectantly.

"Yours will come as hers comes," Lilith murmured, and sent the echo up so the team missed none of the transaction.

Carlos had to physically restrain Damali, holding the

back of her torn white dress between where wings had ripped through the fabric.

"You ought to know by now, Damali, that a blow delivered by your own kind is the worst—and that looks can be deceiving—because you just don't know."

Lilith laughed again and shook her head as the hybrid began panting harder, tears running down her face and her nails digging into the dirt. "I am older than you can fathom, Neterus." Lilith's tone became lethal, quiet, controlled as she kept her hand on the hybrid's rising abdomen. "I was here at the beginning, at the crest of time, just as my husband was there at its dawn. You two against us? Ludicrous, if not arrogant. How many Kings and Queens have we lived beyond! How many empires have we seen rise, and then we—us—our combined evil felled? How many cultures have we ruined, and wars begun while you weren't even a shadow of passion on the horizon . . . and you *dare* challenge me as Neteru children? Fools—the lot of you!"

Just as soon as Lilith's last words were spoken, the hybrid seized and hiccupped blood. Her wings went black feather by feather, and her eyes melted from her skull only to be replaced by shining red, glowing orbs. Her humanlike screams became screeches as twisted fangs filled her mouth, and the standing legions moaned and hissed in abject awe. Then, just as quickly, she convulsed hard, her stomach ripping and her bewildered gaze held Lilith's as she shrieked. Something large and angry was clawing its way from the inside out and began to shred flesh, a spaded tail slashing its way out of her vaginal canal as an elbow presented in a gaping, blooded section of ripped belly flesh.

A small screeching demon head popped out of the hybrid's stomach, eating away organs and flesh as it fought its host enclosure. The hybrid held the sides of her stomach, convulsing with an open-mouthed silent scream, and then the feral little creature snapped and bit at her fingers, severing one. She dropped. Her hands slowly sliding down her sides to hit the ground, eyes no longer glowing but black and glassy. Whatever was inside her sucked in a deep breath and pushed, splitting open her body vertically to come out with new, wet wings trembling.

"Eat, my baby," Lilith crooned. "She took my womb but never my love of producing you."

Transfixed for seconds that felt like minutes, the team and clerics couldn't move as forty thousand demon soldiers went prostrate at the same moment the newly born creature turned to Lorelei and ripped out her throat, greedily sucking as she struggled for life and expired. Lilith dug into her rib cage and gave the bloodied thing covered with innards Lorelei's heart. "Her reward was simply to feed you, and she should have been honored."

Mike released the bazooka with Carlos's white light pulse on it. Ghosts of Masada were over the walls like teeming white foam. Every Guardian went to battle stations firing at anything that moved. Lilith covered her newborn and then had to send it in flight as a blue-white pulse charge from Damali made the ground temporarily impenetrable.

Damali was airborne, Carlos hurled discs of Heru one after the other like razor-edged, gold energy Frisbees at the thing that took flight with shaky wings and a wobbly pattern. Demons went to the air, body-shielding the creature that was no larger than a huge Harpie, giving themselves in to the blade, burning on contact with Heru discs, and fighting their way up the side of the mountain.

Flame throwers sent water over the edge to incinerate everything in their path, but the demons kept coming as though they were multiplying on the hill, heeding Lilith's battle cry to wipe out the team, clerics and all. Gun reports created a deafening echo, semiautomatic bursts lit the night with Mike's bazooka blasts. The stench of sulfur was everywhere, each hallowed earth shell hit, holy water scorch created blinding plumes.

"Open the Ark," Rabbi Zeitloff shouted to Carlos, hurling blessed plastic liter bottles of holy water like Molotov cocktails.

"It's within you, son!" Father Patrick yelled, spraying holy water over the side of the wall from a bent pipe Bobby had commandeered.

"You could not see it, unless it was within," Monk Lin called out, training a water pipe on demon incursion.

"From Ethiopia—the time is now! Do not let them take Masada again!" Imam Asula urged, firing a hallowed earth mortar the moment his holy water supply ran out.

Carlos ran to the side of the wall, not sure how to access this thing they said. He looked at Damali—nearly surrounded in the air—folded away, and did a midair grab to tumble with her toward another swarm that was amassing beneath them.

From the spiral he could see the top of the mountain in spinning flashes: the front line of Masada ghosts were ringing the mountain as a palace barrier; the entire perimeter was lit in blue-white light; the ground was white hot from prayers; an arch of opaque light created an opalescent prayer dome over the team and clerics. Bursts of golden-hued gunfire and brilliant explosions lit the mountainside. Seconds elongated. Pure Hell was beneath them. He remembered it so clearly. Damali's fist was against his chest in the exact position when she'd first branded him. She looked up at him as they plummeted like a boulder tossed from a high cliff. Demon claws reached out to rip at them, but burned away the moment they entered their combined white hot aura. Damali's mouth moved, and he read it in his mind. *Do it.*

He envisioned the Ark, but this time he saw it opened. Her mind latched onto the vision, too, and the moment Damali's mind touched his, a sonic boom and a blast hit them so powerfully that their downward spiral stopped in midair and they were thrust horizontally in a blue-white, slow-motion miasma. Suspended in midair, they watched from afar as the white lightning sent nova light upward and downward to incinerate whatever had been airborne.

Guardians and clerics had fallen behind the wall, but the

numbers of furious ghost soldiers from Masada multiplied like a thick carpet of souls that popped up, stepped out from the forms already there bearing arms. They threw their heads back and released a cry.

All the fallen martyrs, Carlos whispered in his mind, full of awe. *Every warrior felled by injustice.*

Both he and Damali jerked their attention skyward as the unforgettable Neteru war cry echoed above, the night parted, a splinter of golden-white light cut through the darkness, and winged steeds filled the air. Neteru Kings riding hard began the aerial assault, battle-axes and blades swinging. Phantoms on the ground outnumbered demons two to one. Neteru Queens came out of golden-caped folds right next to demons to stab out their hearts, incinerate them in a blink of an eye, and then fold away again to reappear as cloaked assassins. Guardians and clerics stood, weapons lowered, watching with tears in their eyes, and yells and cheers filling their lungs. A Valkyrie core flew into the distance, blades at the ready, swiftly hunting the sky for Lilith's offspring.

Damali and Carlos slowly dropped to the ground, her wings lowering them as the energy miasma around them receded. Blades filled their grips. Carlos's eyes cut a silver swath in the darkness beyond the immediate battle. Damali's third eye was keened. They both turned at the same time and headed toward the Judean Desert in his foldaway. Their minds ricocheted commands back and forth as he stopped to get his bearings so that he didn't overshoot the target.

She's moving toward Sorek Cave, east of Bet Shemesh, Carlos mentally shot. *I can feel her vibe pulling west.*

The thing she gave birth to is headed to Mount of Temptation, baby. Northeast. To get them both, we have to split up. I'll go—

No! Together! Lilith we can get to later. This other thing I don't wanna name—we do it as one. Even if it's still a baby, you know what it is. Northeast—as one.

Just as suddenly as they thought it, a large, red-winged

stallion ripped through the air snorting fire. Its translucent red hooves gleamed like its ruby coat and mane, and it moved like a missile, almost so fast that they'd nearly missed Hannibal's battle-hardened glare on the horizon.

White blurs shot out of the clouds with him like tracers, and the only way Carlos and Damali could truly see what they were witnessing was by slowing down the visual inside their minds' eyes. Huge warrior angels at the archangel level had hurtled by, the gleam from their golden blades and armor, and glowing white light auras, was blinding. Hannibal led the charge with Ausar and Adam at his flank. Hannibal spurred the great steed on with a war cry, blade raised, rocketing toward the northeast. His mental command was clear, blending in with the trinity force of Ausar's and Adam's intents.

Turn back. Lilith is not even reachable now—her husband opened the ground at Sorek. Water your horses and live to fight another day.

Carlos and Damali both stood in the middle of the desert with battle lust running through them so hard that their blade arms shook and tears of frustration were in their eyes. The need to head in either direction to finish it once and for all made Carlos ram his blade into the gravelly sand, Damali's right behind his.

"Damn!" He paced away and wiped his face.

She closed her eyes and leaned back and screamed.

They stood out there in the night for what felt like an eternity and then finally sat down hard on the ground.

"We were so close," she said.

"Right there, girl. Right there."

"That thing that got away . . ."

"Don't name it, Damali. I know our brother, Hannibal, and the rest of the brothers, they *had to* get it."

"They broke another seal," she said in a horrified whisper.

"I know, that's why I'm saying, they had to get it . . . they just had to . . . probably why they sent us back."

"Probably why," Damali said, accepting Carlos's hand as she stood. "That's gotta be why."

"Yeah . . . that's gotta be," Carlos said. "So . . . when the team asks . . . for the sake of everyone's sanity and morale . . ."

"Hannibal rode a red steed to the Mount of Temptation and got it. Hannibal, Ausar, and Adam were on its ass. Lilith—we were given orders to deal with that grimy bitch another night, but not tonight."

Carlos nodded and slung an arm over Damali's shoulder. "Right."

They both released a weary sigh and pulled their blades out of the sand.

"You wanna fly, or me?" he asked, using his sword like a walking stick.

She let out another hard breath. "Guess this ain't like New York . . . no cabs in the Judean desert, huh?"

THEY'D HALF-FLOWN, HALF-WALKED, too tired to do either for very long. But as they watched the heavens part to usher in the rose-orange dawn, sunlight painting the mountainside and sending rays of vibrant renewal to Masada, they stopped and watched in reverent awe as angels scurried to clear away demon ash from the sacred site. Bullet holes and bazooka blasts were buffed out of antiquity; the mountainside was filled with cheering spirits for as far as the eye could see. Guardians leaned over the walls yelling in victory and clerics went down on their knees, one facing Mecca, and gave thanks for the battle that was won.

It was then that they realized why they'd come to this holy land and why the tours and lessons were in such a truncated time frame. Carlos drew her near.

"We needed the renewal of faith. Last night gave them hope."

"And because we love them, we can't take that away . . . the trinity. It always comes back to that." She sighed. "What happened out there in the desert is on a top-security, need-to-know basis. They just kicked ass—beat forty thousand demons, eight Roman legions. For once, the cavalry came for our side in a dazzling display that wasn't subtle." She smiled a tense, fatigued grin. "Let them mentally have this win."

Carlos kissed her temple and nodded up to the top of the mountain where their entire team hollered and waved at them. "We were blessed . . . didn't lose anybody this time. That was victory enough for me. Living in the present, from now on, baby. That's all a brother can do."

EPILOGUE

Three months later ... New York City

Over a hundred thousand screaming humans had lost their minds in the Garden. The Internet package that the Neteru Guardian team had sent months ago actually circled the globe at least three times, with bootleg copy after bootleg copy getting posted on the underground everywhere. MySpace, your space, every space had it, the buzz in full effect—the Warriors of Light were coming out with new music so controversial that the system had tried to shut it down, but failed.

Conspiracy theory Web-talk radio had it on lock. Somehow the mainstream outlets were having difficulty getting their arms around the issue and still experiencing strange, intermittent blackouts.

Money, the so-called real root of all evil, won out over dark coven spells and deep cavern edicts—human nature being what it was and having a choice to prosper. The new sound of WOL was cash on the barrelhead that sent promoters into a feeding frenzy. Simulcast? No problem—Dan had been in a haggler's heaven. Duke even got the word out that the original transmission came from his joint and it caused a bar fight unreal. He had posted digital Web pics of a silver glowing Bugatti Veyron and metallic candy-red Saleen S7 abandoned on the road by his joint with skid marks, and used the new chichi crowds flocking to his dive from Scottsdale, Arizona, to rebuild . . . but not too much—he kept the chicken wire with a mild current running through it, just for authenticity's sake. He still had to cater to the locals, even if he did now stock microbrewery selections.

Madison Square Garden in New York was on fire from the new beats and lyrics being spit so hard at the first Warriors of Light concert in nearly two years. It was crazy. Damali leaned into the mike and spun in time to get up in Carlos's face, and he backed her up, making her laugh.

The crowd went wild when Shabazz dropped the bass hook to fuse with Jose's insane percussion. Juanita and Inez and Marlene brought the harmony to its knees, killing it, wringing its neck as folks jumped up and down when Damali layered her glass-shattering soprano opposite Mike's bottomed-out baritone, and then Carlos finished them off, talking rapid-fire cash-trash over the vocals.

Dan and Bobby stepped out on the stage with movie-set prop bazookas and street sweepers that made people holler for more. They did exactly what Shabazz told them to do for maximum effect—just stood there in dark sunglasses, long black leather trenches blowing from the hidden floor fans for theatrical composition. Then Berkfield walked across the stage as Marjorie came out from the opposite direction. They slapped each other a high-five as they passed to flank the younger Guardians already out there, and opened their long coats to show gleaming, set prop Glock nines in their waistbands. The New York audience went wild.

On the driving beat, a military-tight dance choreography squad led by Inez and Juanita, backed up by Krissy, Tara, Jasmine, and Heather, rocked the house so hard that Mike had no choice but to blow up the stage. Smoke bombs and pyro FX took the crowd to the next level.

Yonnie was jamming in the wings with a bottle of private label in each hand and a lovely lady he'd picked up in the audience under each arm. He'd told them all, for now, his job was the easiest job in the world—stay topside, keep a close eye on the Neteru Guardian team, and report back anything suspicious.

Cowbells and congas, Rider's screaming guitar, the call to Guardian arms went out like a beacon—power UV lights were set by FX to blow and allow the whole team to fold out of the white smoke cloud wearing fatigues . . . Carlos and Damali, blades in their grips. Yonnie took his party to the green room just in time, but it was still one helluva show.

"We love you, New York! Stay in the Light!" Damali hollered, and the stage went black.

"Damn, y'all," Yonnie laughed in the dark. "You make a comeback in the Big Apple, you can make it anywhere."

The team ran down the wings laughing toward semi-appalled clerics who tried to smile and who made no mention of Carlos's on-the-fly lyrical adaptations that caused them to squint. What could they say, the word got out and reached the masses, unorthodox or not. The call for an encore was so thunderous that it sounded like the roof was about to blow off.

Carlos smiled at Damali and kissed her quickly, loving the energy that zinged through her body into his. Adrenaline and joy and music were in her sweat. She smelled so good and seemed so happy, he was cresting a little fang.

"They're calling for you, boo. Go on out there and give it up. What'chu gonna do for an encore?"

"You." She offered him a big grin when his eyes flickered.

"Stop playing with my mind, girl," he said, laughing. "Seriously—you hear that crowd?"

"I'll tell you what I decide on later tonight," she said, laughing harder and teasing him unmercifully. "But they're calling for *us* . . . *all* of us. So, what are *you* gonna do for an encore?"

Carlos laughed. "I don't know—girl. I'm done. I'm not going back out there. Plus, I already showed you the galaxy, shit."

Curious glances passed between Guardians. Yonnie cocked an eyebrow, clearly wanting to hear more.

"C'mon, y'all, pick a number we used to do before they tear the roof off the mutha," Mike said with a big grin.

"Y'all go 'head," Carlos said, moving to stand in the wings with Yonnie.

"I know after you did Masada, you don't have stage fright, man," Shabazz said, laughing. "C'mon!"

Carlos smiled and looked at Damali. "Nah . . . lemme watch it from the wings, man . . . like old times. Loving how she raised that blade back in the day, strutting under the lights—her solo."

Yonnie gave Carlos a sly wink. "Aw'ight, I'm out. Got some lovelies in the green room who wanna take a ride in a brother's limo, feel me? Coupla tours around the park . . . heeey."

"Yonnie, don't make nothin' out there we're gonna have to ID on a slab or come after, man . . . and get your ass in a lair before sunrise," Damali fussed. "Love you."

"Yeah, all right, ma." Yonnie shook his head and pounded Carlos's fist as he began to disintegrate into vapor. "All I'ma say is, you are *so* lucky you're my boy . . . damn."

"All right, people, bust 'em one more time," Shabazz said, rounding up the original band members. "OG's do the encores—nobody else knows the old standards."

"L.A. finale," Mike said. "Move out."

Shabazz nodded and ran the team back out to a screaming crowd that went nuts when they realized the Warriors of Light were returning for a few more songs. The Covenant went back to their positions covering the team from hidden spaces deep within the wings.

But Damali hung back for just a moment to place her hand against Carlos's chest. Her fingertips tingled and he swallowed hard. She didn't have to say it, her eyes said it all . . . then she allowed her mouth to confirm it with a slow kiss that he answered in kind.

You're my star, Damali . . . this is you. The behind the scenes is me. Go knock 'em dead, baby.

I love you right on back . . . how about after the encore I show you how much you're my star . . . one galaxy at a time? I think I remember how you did it. She laughed when he backed up and held up his hands, laughing and shaking his head. *Yep, uh-huh, I'm pretty sure I do.*

TURN THE PAGE FOR AN ORIGINAL "BETWEEN
THE BOOKS" EPISODE.

Between Man
and Wife

TAKES PLACE BETWEEN THE END OF *THE
CURSED* AND THE BEGINNING
OF *THE DARKNESS*.

Between Man and Wife

The Helmsley Hotel, Midtown Manhattan

"Daniel," Heather murmured, making the spot where her breath caressed his chest warm, "you were absolutely *masterful*."

"Setting up that concert was a lot of work, definitely," he said with his eyes closed, stroking her lush thicket of auburn curls. "Felt good. It's been a long time since—"

Her swift kiss stopped his words. "Not the concert, although that was awesome. I'm talking about you . . . us . . . just now."

She had punctuated each part of her sentence with a long kiss and then pulled back to look at him in the dim light with a sexy smile. Her compliment made him smile and filled him with the kind of confidence that he'd never experienced until being with her, but it was also a bit embarrassing, too. He'd never thought of himself as truly masterful, as she'd put it. Passionate, with her, absolutely. But that she'd told him this made him love her even more.

"You are *so* beautiful," he said, allowing her silken curls to flow through his fingers as he stared at her large smoky gray eyes. He loved how her creamy skin soaked up the amber hue of the room's low light, making her softness nearly glow golden.

"I love you, Daniel Weinstein," she murmured, kissing

his chest and then hugging him. "I don't care how you deflect my comment, you are too masterful."

He chuckled, deeply pleased, and closed his eyes, his body drinking in the warmth of hers beside him. "If you say so . . . and I definitely love you."

"I say so," she murmured, her breath teasing his right nipple as she began to stroke his chest.

"How can you say that when, by the time we finally get together, I'm practically slobbering on myself?" He laughed, even though a part of him had to admit he was fishing for any compliment that remained within her. Something just seemed a little off when he'd made love to her, even though her body seemed to respond and her demeanor was now pleasant and appeared sated . . . still.

She laughed with him, and it was a deep, rich timbre that exited her throat and soaked into his chest, causing his libido to stir.

"You are not," she said, giggling. "You *are* terrible, Dan!"

"See—"

"No, that's not what I meant," she squealed, rolling on top of him to fuss with a huge smile.

"Oh, I get it, first the compliments, and then the real truth," he said with a grin, baiting her as he quickly kissed the tip of her button nose. With an exaggerated sigh he put his hands behind his head and looked up at the ceiling. "But that's okay. I love her anyway."

"You come back here, Daniel Weinstein," she said, laughing and climbing up his body.

Her Scottish brogue made him crazy—he loved to hear that come out when she was piqued. But it was nothing in comparison to the texture of her satin-smooth skin grazing him, or the view he had now as she straddled him. No doubt about it, with Heather, there was no such thing as being masterful. He stared at his wife's large pendulous breasts and the way her tiny nipples had puckered to small, pink, strawberry pouts. Reflex brought his hands down her arms, over the soft swell of her hips, and up her shapely thighs, saving her breasts for last. As his hands cupped the creamy lobes, she released a short gasp and briefly closed her eyes.

"Masterful," she murmured with a smile and then opened her eyes.

"Practically slobbering on myself," he said, smiling back, but finding it harder to keep a smile on his face.

"You always take your time with me, Daniel," she said in a quiet voice, her smile fading. "Even when I can tell it's the most difficult thing for you to do."

They stared at each other for what felt like a long time, and soon a blue-white flicker of static charge began to cover her skin.

"I can't even control a tactical charge around you, Heather," he admitted softly, allowing his fingertips to play over the surface of her buttery skin. "And each time I tell myself I have to make up for that really rough first time with you. . . . I should have been more patient."

"If you had been more patient, we both would have been crazed," she said, leaning into his touch. Taking his mouth slowly, she allowed her tongue to dance with his as her graceful palms cupped his face. "Daniel, the way you love me from inside your heart is masterful. The way you triumph my body is indescribable. And the way you fought at Masada was the stuff of legends." She took his mouth harder, making him respond more aggressively, his hands sweeping her back to catch her by the globes of her backside. "I never understood what it meant to be proud to be a man's wife . . . but I'm proud to be yours."

In that moment, her words, her touch, her shallow breaths pelting his neck as she delivered kisses along his jaw made him know she'd meant everything she said. And just knowing that she felt that way, even with the deeply personal loss they'd just suffered, he knew he was still blessed to have her.

"If I had lost you there, Heather, I wouldn't have been able to continue. I don't know how they did it—how they watched their wives and children perish. All I could see was you, and no matter what was flying at me, I didn't care." He gathered her in his arms and rolled her over, needing to blanket her. "As long as I have you, I can go on."

Her slender fingers parted his hair; her smoky gaze held his as her legs slowly trapped his waist. "Don't you realize that I feel the same way? Haven't you figured it out, Daniel, that if anything happened to you, I'd die?" She closed her eyes and arched beneath him, angling her body so that he slid within her on a groan. "That's why the concert meant so much to me, because it wasn't a battle . . . it was high-energy and normal. Oh, God, Dan, I want us to do more of that . . . more concerts, more normal, less demon-hunting."

All he could give her was an impassioned kiss as an answer, allowing his body to move slowly within her, allowing his tactical charge to send pleasure into her every pore. On his wife's behalf, yeah, he'd beg the team to let him book more shows, do more normal . . . but in his heart he knew that none of it was under their control.

She knew it was an unfair request even as it had left her mouth. Heather stared up into Dan's crystal blue eyes, her hands making fists in his blond hair, damp from the pleasure he'd coated her body with. The team leaders wanted more normalcy; so did everyone else. Women on the team had lost babies; they couldn't carry under the constant stress. Heather hadn't been the only one. Damali had, too. They'd all whispered about it. The music and crowd had been a release for them all. Tears stung her eyes as a wave of pleasure claimed her husband and he shut his.

"I wasn't being fair," she said, her voice strangled with passion. "Forget that—"

"Baby, I'll do what I can," he said through his teeth, thrusting harder, dropping down to his elbows to be closer, then finally clutching her to himself so tightly she could barely breathe. "I want what you want."

"I have what I want. Just love me."

Blue static climbed through their hair, making it crackle

and begin to lift. He was so close, she could feel it, feel him driving hard, trying to hold back for her, could hear impulses within his embattled mind, wishes stuttering, thoughts tumbling, angry at himself for not tasting her, not getting her more ready, damning his lack of control as pressure built in his shaft. But he didn't understand, she'd drawn him into herself at that moment because what she'd wanted was this—the connection. Feeling him fill her, feeling him joined to her, being as one.

"It's all right," she said, flat-palming his spine.

He shook his head, eyes shut tight. "Together."

She shut her eyes. "Oh, Daniel . . . this time, it's all right."

A hard shudder quaked through him, and she knew he couldn't answer. He didn't understand the vagaries of a woman's needs. She wasn't just saying that; she'd meant it. This time he was exempt, she was all right; just having him inside her had been the goal. Her mind and heart were sutured to a vision that had given her pause—there was no way he was going to take her where he so desperately thought she wanted to go. Yet his frantic attempt was so sweet that tears slipped from the corners of her eyes.

"I love you so much," she whispered, hoping that truth would make him let go, but it didn't. It had the opposite effect—making him hold out for her longer, trying to please her.

She held his shoulders, her hands caressing the thick ropes of muscles that worked in a network, her heels caressing his hard, contracting buttocks and the backs of his sinewy thighs. He didn't understand that what she'd seen in her stone-worker's vision made her cherish every moment they had to be together; this was bliss. Love poured against his skin with her touch. But for him, it stoked passion, the male version of love, force against tenderness, her yin to his yang, until his hair was standing on end.

Heat radiated off of his perspiration-damp face as it pressed to her cheek. The bed was now awash in blue static, his body shuddering with the need to release, but his stubbornness to wait for her making him suffer. Then suddenly he fisted the sheets and slowed down, taking her mouth in an agonizingly tender way.

"Heather, from the first moment," he said in a rasp, staring at her, "I knew." Gathering her slowly, he rolled over, keeping her connected to him, a fleeting grimace of sheer pain in his expression as he lay on his back, breathing hard. "I won't leave you, *ever*."

The intensity of his words matched the intensity of his stare, and it contracted her sheath around him, making him arch with a moan.

"Under no circumstances will I do that," he said, hands trembling as they swept enough current up her torso to make her entire body buckle with a moan.

She was suddenly winded, panting as she gripped his shoulders and he kissed her neck gently.

"I can feel something inside you, holding you back . . . worry," he murmured, nuzzling her breasts and then slowly taking a taut nipple into his mouth to suckle gently. "I want that gone."

He'd sent a wash of energy against her skin as he'd breathed out his intention, and the pleasure was so severe that it made her cup the other breast with her hand and begin to move against his shaft. Slowly, she would feel the vision dissipating as his hands roved over her spread thighs and his thumb found her bud. He didn't even touch it; just the warmth emanating from it sent a pleasure shiver deep into her canal on his next thrust and she felt the stone inside her shatter with her voice.

"Not till you do," he said, his voice raw, his breaths harsh as he stared at her.

Within the blue depths of his irises, total commitment resided, a love sublime. As though he'd summoned that up into his touch, his hands swept her body and washed her in it, spilling liquid want down his shaft as hot tremors contracted her womb.

Bucking wildly, she bore down hard, tears streaming, his arms now a vise around her waist. Static flowed over them and the bed, traveled across the floor, and was climbing up the walls.

Dan's body arched as though he'd been struck by lightning. Teeth clenched, the sheets in her fists, she felt it building, rising, pleasure pressure inside her canal like a hidden tsunami that stole her breath. When it hit, all she could do was hold him and wail. Then suddenly he released inside her in splinters and jags of pleasure-energy shards with such intensity that she feared for his heart. But there was no way to assist him; the violent seizure was a shared, tandem experience. The orgasm was so severe it felt like it was exiting her body through her fingernails.

Ebbing slowly, the rush against her senses finally abated. She could barely lift her head, couldn't move. Dan was gasping as if he were having an asthma attack, as was she, and then the real sobs came. Dazed, trembling, she burst out into tears. A warm hand petted her back, but that only seemed to make her cry harder. Soon she became aware that he was rocking her and kissing her temple, still winded, but in much more control than she.

"Oh . . . baby . . ." he said softly. "I know."

She was rendered mute. She could only shake her head.

"After we got back," he said haltingly, "I knew it would take time . . . you know . . . for us to sync back up, after all you'd been through."

This time she nodded avidly, hiding her face in the crook of his neck, ashamed. He did understand. After what they'd seen, after the loss they'd endured—she never thought she'd be able to experience a full climax again. It was a horrible secret. Her body had betrayed her as terrible images took up residence in her seer's mind.

Not knowing what to do and too humiliated to say a word to any of her team sisters, she'd just been glad they could be intimate, that she had accepted his warmth as enough, his touch as the gift. But that he waited her out just made her sob harder.

"Shush . . ." his tender voice soothed while his fingers traced along her spine ever so gently. "How could I leave my wife, huh?"

Her sobs had become so forlorn and hysterical that her entire body shook as he stroked her back. That a man would care . . . if she was willing and open, and partially ready?

"Oh, God, where did you come from, Daniel?"

"Ohio, by way of Anaheim, then L.A.," he said, with a smile in his voice as he kissed her forehead. He brushed her damp, tousled hair away from her face. "But an angel sent you to me, so I know where you're from." His smile faded as his hand slid down to cup her cheek and she pressed a kiss into the heart of his palm. "God, Heather, don't you understand that allowing me to give you pleasure to the fullest is the greatest gift you can give me? Loving me like that, and letting me love you back the same way, you know?" His serious blue eyes searched hers. "If ever I don't, you've gotta let me know. But I'll always wait for you."

Her kiss was a slow, reverent taking of his mouth, and she filled his with her tongue, hoping that every ounce of love within her could spill from her body into his. Images of vampires that walked by day fled from her scarred mind. Images of something withered in a shell crawling into the safety of a cave dissolved under the scrutiny of logic. Images of something large, its heartbeat slow and dark, tucked deeply in caverns escaped her thoughts as her husband kissed her deeply. Suddenly she felt so silly, so green to her gifts, so inexperienced as a wife and lover.

She just prayed that it had all been postbattle anxiety. Perhaps also something left over from the deep scars of her twisted past at Gabby's that was sparked to life from the last traumatic event the team had been through. Heather let her eyes flutter shut and hoped that after each battle her body wouldn't close off to pleasure in some self-preservation mode. That would be so unfair to Dan. Yes, she would tell him if it ever happened again.

Maybe one day, if she screwed up enough courage, she

might privately ask Damali if she'd ever experienced anything like this. But then again, that was doubtful. The Neteru going through feelings of inadequacy and quelled desire from stupid postbattle visions? Not a chance.

Heather hugged Dan tighter, basking in the afterglow, simply glad the man loved her as he did.

Turn the page for a sneak peek at L. A. Banks's
next book in the Crimson Moon series

ITE THE BULLET

Coming soon from St. Martin's Paperbacks

AS SOON AS she was sure that Hunter was out of range, Sasha ransacked the backpacks until she found their amulets. He'd shoved them to the bottom, rolled in layers of clothes. The clasps had been broken. She took shallow sips of air, gently trailing her fingers over the tender spot at the nape of her neck and then up the back of her scalp to where a small knot had formed, trying to focus, trying to remember.

They had transformed on a shadow run. He'd picked up the trail of large game—a bull moose. It was too big; she'd tried to signal him. Hunter was larger than she'd remembered when he'd transformed again; two hands higher at the shoulders, larger jaw, barrel chest. His eyes held something in them that frightened her.

Sasha shoved the amulets back where she'd found them and began to pace inside the tent with her eyes squeezed shut. "Oh . . . God . . ." It was coming back in fits and starts, jags of horror that she wanted to forget.

He'd outstripped her on the run. The animal they hunted turned and lowered its mantle. Hunter went up on his hind legs. Sasha opened her eyes and hugged herself with a start, breathing hard. He hadn't brought it down like a wolf. One powerful swipe from a forepaw had snapped a damned bull moose's neck!

How could she not remember? How could she not remember! *How could she not remember?* She tore around the tent looking for weapons, blood pressure spiking when she couldn't immediately find them.

Cupping the back of her head, she bolted out of the tent. Panic perspiration made everything she wore stick to her skin. Images of Hunter crouched over the carcass snarling as he devoured the animal's heart and liver brought her other hand over her mouth to keep from hurling. She could see it all clearly now—blue-black night, steam rising from fresh kill that had been opened and gutted. Oh, God, oh, God, when did she fall and hit her head?

Backing away . . .

She'd come to a skidding halt. Their eyes had met. She was so stunned that she'd changed back into her human form and stood. He did too, then cried out and yanked the chain from his neck . . . she'd spun to run, caught a low-hanging branch, and went down. Then she was inside the tent. His arm was anchored around her waist. She squeezed her eyes shut again, remembering his impassioned voice choking out a ragged apology behind her.

Hunter had purposely knocked her unconscious, and the reason why broke over her in horrifying clarity.

Hunter was infected.

She felt a scream of rage and grief build in her throat over the thought that something like this was happening. But she swallowed it. There would be time to grieve later.

Right now survival was imperative and she needed to find her gun.

Turn the page for a sneak peek at the next
Vampire Huntress Legend

The Shadows

BY L.A. BANKS

Coming July 2008
from St. Martin's Griffin

SURREAL CALM OVERTOOK her as she listened to Carlos. Rather than the sensation entering her, it oddly emanated from within her. She'd promised him that she would eat. Damali moved her hands by rote to appease him . . . stalling for time by picking up the paper bag, slowly opening it, taking out the plastic container, opening that with care and then allowing her meal to sit before her untouched as she listened intently to what her husband was saying. Something about the smell of the food now turned her stomach.

It was only when she saw him blink that she became aware that time had actually slowed down all around her. His lids slid closed as through a heavy curtain of onyx lashes had been dropped to thud one against the other. His voice was now like distant thunder—a rumble of unintelligible words, they were being spoken so slowly.

Background sounds thrust their way to the forefront of her senses. Her breaths and heartbeat, his breaths and heartbeat, were each so slow and so loud they created a collision inside her head. Even though she couldn't quite make out what he was saying, she gathered what she could from his private, urgent tone and then watched how he slowly leaned in close to her to speak.

Carlos's physical warmth suddenly felt as though she'd

been wrapped in a blanket and then soon became a searing barrier like one would expect if one stood before an opened oven that had been left on broil for hours. She settled back from the uncomfortable body heat radiating off him, and as she did, the sound of her clothes rustling against the chair was jarring.

He swallowed hard, pausing mid-sentence, and she almost cringed from the change in decibel that had transitioned the low rumble of his voice to the mucous-thick sound of saliva coating his throat. Yet through all of it, she oddly knew what he was saying, not from the words, but the impressions that began to form behind her wide-opened eyes.

In a vision, Damali saw it. The poisonous vapor. The way it slid out of technology orifices and opened dark portals within houses, buildings, and within human minds. The airwaves were polluted. The gray-zone, the earth plane, was becoming denser, darker, more twisted and violent.

Shadow entities spilled over the very edges of Hell and into the psyches and spirits of the unaware, diving into the pools of light that are normally within each human being.

Damali sat transfixed as she watched how the demonic forces entered a living body and then swallowed up all the clean light within it, slowly corroding it until there was simply no living aura left. At the point of total eclipse, the person was no more. Gone was their will, along with every shred of humanity that had once defined them.

"Tell me your names," she whispered, horrified. This was so much worse than the plague of The Damned. It was such a quick transition, no incubation period. No abstinence of touch could keep a person safe. The airwaves were being infected exponentially, and even people in the most remote villages had radios and televisions in small general stores!

Carlos cocked his head to the side and asked her a question. She could tell by his worried expression that he was asking something important of her. But the reply that should have been hers was instead a shadow turning to her before it entered the body of a man on the streets. It smiled a sinister smile, bearing mangled, yellow teeth in a hollow black pit devoid of a face.

Her husband's voice drifted farther and farther away until she was spinning in a panicked daze within a crowded market, then she was on a crowded street. All around her people were being taken over. All around her chaos was simmering beneath the surface of human potential. An army was being raised right on the streets and right before her eyes. Vertigo claimed her as her vision jettisoned her from New York to Copenhagen, from Kenya to Milan. Remote islands, metropolises, it didn't matter, the invasions were unrelenting.

Arms outstretched, she ran toward a schoolyard and then skidded to a halt as high school students fell into darkness. She couldn't breathe. *Not the children.* Her gaze fell upon a middle school and she watched as dark entities swarmed the windows like locusts.

Damali covered her face and turned away. *Tell me this plague's name so we can send it back into the pit!* Within seconds she was in a hospital, her hands pressed flat against nursery glass, and she saw the shadows eerily slide into the nurses' bodies, but none touched the babies. Yet that provided no relief. One nurse simply smiled and turned off an incubator's oxygen.

"No!" Damali's voice escalated with her panic. She had to know what this entity was in order to fight it. Not vampire, not succubus, the team had never seen a manifestation like this. "Tell me its name!"

Suddenly every person on the streets everywhere she looked had a sinister companion, and they all smiled at her simultaneously and whispered back, "My name is legions."

"Damali. Damali!"

A tight grasp held her upper arms and she was mildly aware of being shaken. Time snapped back. She caught Carlos by his elbows, panting and covered with sweat.

"You all right? Damali, talk to me!"

"I saw it," she gasped. "It's already starting."

As soon as she'd made the statement, she shrugged out of Carlos's hold and covered her mouth and nose.

"Get that out of the house!" she demanded, jumping down from the stool and backing away from the counter, pointing at her untouched food.

"Oh, shit!" Carlos toppled his stool as he backed up quickly and stared at the larva teeming over the edge of the container.

The moment his silvery line of vision hit it, the entire platter exploded, sending disgusting, maggoty gore everywhere. Instantly shielded by a golden disc, the couple took refuge as they watched the wriggling mass rain down on the translucent surface to sizzle and disappear with a sulfuric stench. Everything the larva plopped down on made them fry and evaporate. Marlene's kitchen was well anointed, and Inez had undoubtedly backtracked through it and given it a second blessing.

No less than they'd expected, they immediately heard heavy footfalls and knew the team was headed into the kitchen in a call to arms. Carlos and Damali shared a glance.

"Inez is gonna have a cow," Damali said, dry-heaving from the residual sulfur smell.

"After Marlene has a heart attack," Carlos muttered, checking twice before lowering the shield to be sure it had stopped raining maggots. "This happened in her kitchen." He looked at Damali. "You okay?"

"Yeah," she said, swallowing down the feeling of nausea and then stepping around his shield to assess the damage. "So I guess it's officially on now. Vacation is over."

Carlos nodded and set his jaw hard as fellow Guardians came to a halt at the kitchen's threshold.

"What the f—" Rider stopped mid-expletive as he spied Inez's mom and toddler, and he held out his arm to bar them from fully entering the kitchen. "Sulfur's so thick in here you'd think we'd entered a Hell hole."

"Jesus H. Christ," Berkfield muttered as his gaze scanned

the black pock-marked kitchen cabinets, floor, counter, and appliances.

"I'll just be damned," Marlene's words seethed between her teeth as she entered the kitchen with Inez, both women placing their hands on their hips. Marlene's gaze narrowed as she surveyed the damage. "Up in *my* laboratory . . . where I do my sacred work?"

"Aw, hell to the no," Inez said, unable to curtail her rage as she walked across the smoldering floor and folded her arms over her ample breasts. "A breach in here, *my kitchen*, where I feed my family?"

"What happened?" Shabazz said, putting the safety on his Glock nine-millimeter. His long dreadlocks were static-charged with fury and the muscles in his toned arms, shoulders, and back kneaded like that of a stalking panther's as he walked deeper into the abused room.

Yonnie's and Carlos's eyes met.

"Were they looking for me?" Yonnie asked, making the group turn and stare at him. "'Cause if it's my time, I'll go out there and let them take me rather than bring this bull on the family, yo." He glanced at Valkyrie and lifted his chin. "Bound to happen sooner or later, so, if they're—"

"They'll always be looking for you, man," Carlos said in an angry rumble. "Just like they'll always be looking for me and everybody else on this team. We ain't sacrificing no family to appease the beast—got that, man?"

"Cool. Then, I'll take that as a no, this wasn't personal then," Yonnie said, sniffing the air and retracting his fangs.

"Oh, it was personal," Carlos assured him. "They personally want me, you, and everybody else on this team dead."

1. What do you think about Damali and Carlos's new role as husband and wife even as they lead the team?

2. How do you think members of each couple are adapting to their new roles and situation, especially now that they have a stable compound again?

3. Would you like to see the team get back into music and performing?

4. What about children? Who do you think will be the first couple to conceive? Will having children be a positive or negative addition? Why?

5. What do you think is going to happen with Yonnie? Will he stay on the side of the team or go dark?

6. Do you think Yonnie will ultimately leave Tara alone? Why? Do you think she still has feelings for him? Wh

7. What did you think about the STD (sexually transmitted demon)? The harmony of the group was greatly affected by the STD. Explain how this may or may not occur in society in general with STDs.

8. What new insights do you think the team gathered from its journey to the Holy Land? How will this change them?

9. Did you like the joint Neteru Council of Kings and Queens? Would you like to see more of them? Why?

10. What do you think about Lilith's latest plan?

11. Do you feel that the action in this story is the official beginning of the Armageddon?

12. What loose ends would you like to see tied up in the upcoming adventures of the last three books in the series? Is there anything you think can be left unresolved?

For more reading group suggestions, visit
www.readinggroupgold.com.